Vitruvian Boy

by

Andrew Bone

Switzerland

Vitruvian Boy
www.vitruvianboy.com

Edition 1

ISBN **978-88-97034-00-1**

Published by
ZumGuy Publications
Via Stella 12, CH-6850 Mendrisio, Switzerland
www.zumguy.com
info@zumguy.com

Graphics by Sean Bone
seanbone@zumguy.com

Printed in Switzerland by
Veladini SA, 6903 Lugano Switzerland

The book was made in accordance with the sustainable forestry
standards of the Forestry Stewardship Council, FSC, and employing
the Heidelberg system which eliminates the use of environmentally
damaging chemicals.

No animals were injured, or even inconvenienced, in the making of
this book.

Acknowledgements:
Cavalry figure courtesy of Anne S. K. Brown Military Collection,
Brown University Library.
The fun typefaces used in this book were supplied under licence by
Ray Larabie

This book is dedicated
to the memory of
my grandfather
Henry Maurice Beach

About the author
Andrew Bone is a qualified scientist, a teacher and a translator, and has lived in Switzerland for 20+ years since leaving his native Australia.
He has one son, who shares his passions for history and science.

About ZumGuy Publications:
This is a new publishing house, located at the crossroads of Europe.
Its mission is:

To promote, through literature and other art forms, the humanitarian ideals of Professor Albert Einstein for a cooperative and non-militaristic approach to resolving the crisis besetting the world's most remarkable species, busy shooting itself in the foot.
The hope of the founders of ZumGuy Publications is to support and encourage those who share the above vision, and who would otherwise find it difficult to give voice to their culturally valuable expression.

Die Schönste und Tiefste, was der Mensch erleben kann, ist das Gefühl des Geheimnisvollen. Es liegt der Religion sowie allem tieferen Streben in Kunst und Wissenschaft zugründe.

Our most beautiful and profound experiences derive from a sense of the mysterious. It lies at the heart of religion and all deeper pursuits in arts and sciences.

- A. Einstein, Berlin 10 Nov 1930

CONTENTS

Chapter One

The House that Ate Time

EVERYBODY knew it was haunted. But just like with UFOs and economic miracles, just as many everybodies were afraid to admit they believed it. So, the town of Lugano simply decided to ignore the house at number 12, Delponte Street. But that is not really an option for a twelve-year-old boy, especially when he lives at number 14, the same Delponte Street. Something prime-evil told Sean Seulpierre that between those two numbers a cow patty of unluck lay lurking, just waiting for some flagbearer of misopportunity to make his or her shodless way to it.

Whatwhether, it was an entirely unusual house. Obviously nobody (living) lived (was not yet dead) there. Never had done. So it never had visitors. Of any type. This was hardly surprising, since the gates were rusted shut. On closer inspection also welded shut, bolted, locked seven times in seven entirely different and creative ways, and finally sewed up with some discouraging species of ivy. And for good measure an ancient condemned notice swung by one surviving pure-rust bolt, only staying intact by virtue of the mysterious forces inherent in chemical lethargy.

Not that the building was ugly or anything like that. It was well-kept, though nobody kept it, and beautiful, since its age meant no architect had applied theories to it. All around the large ornate property was a metal, nasty-spikey fence, where it could be said the strangeness of the whole edifice began. On the streetside, the metal railings of this fence were bloated with rust, which fell like cappuccino topping to the pavement. But on the inside the railings were as if new - shiny and strong, and, you would swear, renewing themselves. The metal succeeded in convincing you it was alive.

Unlike most people, Sean was not afraid of the haunted house. He had spent all his twelve years living in the large villa next door, so to him it was just part of the backdrop to larger life he encountered whenever he drew back his curtains. It is hard to get excited about anything that is a constant factor, no matter how weird it may be. He therefore hardly notched above curious when one day a group of 'experts' from some university or other had come to test this miracle ghost metal of the fence railings. Without daring to enter the property, they probed through the rust from the outside, trying to reach the shiny metal on the inside. After a middling long while, they swore, first individually, then after another last hard probe, in unison, as they suddenly dropped their tools and ran away in a terrible kerfuffle. No technical paper, no report, no research grant were forthcoming - and, as Sean noted, no more experts ever came.

The local town council decided one day to demolish the building, so they could build an empty lot. And even though it was one of the oldest buildings in

Lugano, Renaissance era, and in perfect condition, nobody organised demonstrations or 'save our heritage' protests.

They didn't have to.

On the ordained day, the now famous bulldozer raced at the speed of cynicism towards the fence. It managed to make a hole, and had even begun to pass through the gap. But as soon as its engine and driver's cabin entered the grounds, the machine stopped. Now, I ask you: what does it take to kill a fifteen-ton bulldozer dead in its tracks? The evolving legend has it that the driver had been 'stolen' by the demons that infest the house. Cooler heads admitted that he must have been truly spooked, for when all the dust and panic had subsided, he had to be taken to hospital, and the poor man has been 'absent without leave' ever since.

What they were forced to agree on was that the bulldozer stopped because its front half had, well, *aged* suddenly. By the look of the corrosion, by some hundreds of years. The beast still stands there today, its bright yellow rear projecting back into the street, like some sort of giant ferreting rubber duck, while its front half inside the property has rusted to pieces, with guillotine-like precision up to the fence line, its tyres ugly splotches of fatigue. In terms of rights by poetic assertion, it formed a far more potent deterrent to illegal entry than any number of signs and locks.

Birds (ravens make the best telling) were once known to be seen alighting on the roof of the haunted house, but were supposedly never seen to leave. Sooner or later they got the message too. There was one baby raven which Sean had found as a chick fallen from the tree that had had the effrontery to almost overhang the garden of the haunted house. Its parents had vanished. Sean raised the fledgling, feeding it worms he caught himself, and named it Baldrick. One sad day, Baldrick disappeared too. The house had an omnivorous appetite.

And Baldrick was not the only pet to be affected by the house. One day, our 12-year-old Sean Seulpierre remembers seeing the cook's cat, whose name is Shrodie, fleeing from a dog by the route of the haunted house. When she jumped through the fence, Sean swears he saw her disappear in mid flight. So does the dog, who has been a nervous wreck and has lived on a feline-free diet ever since. Don't worry, Shrodie is still with us. Sort of, anyway. As much as a half-dead cat can be.

Sometimes, when Sean comes home from school, he finds the cat dead under the stairs, or in the bathroom, or in the pantry. Other days, he would find her refreshingly alive, purring and rubbing against his legs, and asking for some of her favourite nibblets. When she was found dead, she would be put inside her box, where she usually slept. After a while, Sean calculated the cat was alive as often as dead, but he could never tell which she would be till he looked inside her box. Sometimes he had the strangest sensation that just by looking, he could cause her to come back to life, or the opposite. But he remained uncertain on the issue.

He once heard the cook, Mrs Erwin, the owner of the cat, talking to an acquaintance of hers, who said to her: 'Sorry about your cat. Funny, it is identical to the one you lost last week'. And the cook would say perfectly nonchalantly: 'Oh, she'll be right as rain by dinner time.' Mrs Erwin would then be categorised as plain eccentric, meaning people had chalked up yet another excuse for staying away from this end of Delponte Street.

Sean suspected that tendrils of eccentricity were somehow escaping from the haunted house, that the house was getting stronger, and was venturing its weirdness abroad.

As mentioned, the Seulpierres live in the house right next to the haunted house. And the Seulpierres are an ancient family.

Oh, come on, what a silly thing to say! Nobody's family is older than anybody's else's - otherwise we wouldn't be here, would we? But, if the name is in any way an indication - which it isn't, right girls? - there has been a Seulpierre family in Lugano since the town has been in the far south of Switzerland. The very last little bit of Switzerland that on the map is suggestive of a nasally supra-adequated person sticking his mountainous nose into the flat plain that gives Italy a snorting good start on its journey south.

Now Sean Seulpierre, the twelve-year-old just about to be hero of our saga, had read in one of his grandfather's even dustier books that Lugano has not always been in Switzerland. In fact, it seems that once upon an almost ridiculously long time ago it used to be in Italy. He had always wondered how they had managed to move a whole town from one country to another - if you're interested this story will eventually, and I do mean rather very eventually, reveal the secret of this little act of municipal grand larceny, and how Sean is not entirely undisconnected to it.

Ancient or not, the Seulpierre family as you will find it today is not really that different to any other family, here or there. Which means it is in every way unique.

The father of Sean Seulpierre is a banker. Now, a good image but poor definition of banker is someone who sits like a fisherman, watching the flow of life pass in front of him, ready to snatch with hooks the bits that appeal to him, not caring particularly where they come from or where otherwise they may be heading. Put more than simply, he knows very little about how the universe works, and so is in the perfect position to proclaim (to great acclaim in certain circles) that he knows everything there is to know. At least as far as he knows.

Sean had gathered some time ago that his father, whom he assumes he had christened Papi, was involved in the laundry business. Mysterious persons came to him every day with lots of small-denomination secrets in mysterious 'undeclared laundry bags'. Sean wasn't sure what they were, but deduced there must therefore be *declared* and *undeclared* laundry bags - with contents that were respectively *speakable* and *unspeakable*. Being an avid football player, he knew what such things meant, most particularly in reference to laundry bags.

The father of the father of Sean had his name abbreviated to 'Nonno', which is Italian for 'grandfather', somewhere back in a historical era called *The Mists of Time*. Inspired by his handy Jurassic timeline foldout, Sean guessed that 'Mists', being plural, must be an era divided into 'periods', which should, by convention, be called *proto* Mist, *meso* Mist and *paleo* Mist of Time.

Even Nonno's own son, the banker, had called him 'Nonno' for as long as Sean could remember. This, like many things for children, had probably been intended to clarify things for him, but had instead grown to be a nagging source of confusion.

When he had *finally* turned twelve, Sean received a card attesting that he was now officially 'of age' - it says so clearly: 'You are now twelve years of age' - which seemed to him to be a declaration of manhood of sorts. He decided that his first and foremost duty as a new adult would be to cease to ask 'irritating questions' about why we say things that don't make any sense - this being, by overwhelming evidence, the baseline attitude that distinguishes an adult from a child.

Mind you, by this definition, this would make Nonno Seulpierre the oldest living child, because he had never criticised Sean for the way he spoke, as Papi always did. This and a corroborative line of reasoning eventually led Sean to deduce that one of the two must be an impostor Seulpierre - the same family could not possibly contain two members who were so determinedly not undisalike as Papi and Nonno. He decided that the only fair thing to do, genetically speaking, was wait till he knew which of the two he himself was growing into, before deciding which of them was the impostor Seulpierre, and call the newspapers, and the police for dramatic emphasis, and make a *denouement*. He gathered he would then be required to give TV interviews, and something he had heard called *retaining book and film rights*, which is apparently what you do after making headline-grabbing denouements to the police.

One of the *Mists of Time* periods was referred to by Nonno as *In His Day*, when he had been some sort of university professor, in Geneva. By contrast, Lugano didn't really have much of a university, just some sort of perpetual building site that one summer spontaneously turned into an underground carpark, with an after-thought hairpiece of exhaust-smelly grass that dogs did their dooeys on. On a technical note, this added enticing skill and danger to illegal football games, using empty parking spaces as goals. If you missed you didn't so much make a 'post' as a 'dent', which did little to endear the sport to the university patrons.

Nonno had only one defining characteristic: he loved knowledge above all else. What made the old professor eccentric, according to Papi, was that Nonno was constantly proclaiming that he 'knew nothing' and 'how delightful that was'.

Whenever Sean came home from school, he would go straight to his grandfather, who was always 'a-fiddling and a-rummaging, yo-ho-ho' in his *doing science* room at the top of the house. It was full of books which told you what Nonno always said about how we know nothing and how delightful that was. Papi called them 'those mouldy science books' and wanted to bring in useful books on economy and 'How to make a fortune' manuals. But when Nonno said to Papi that you couldn't 'make' a fortune, only 'take' it from someone else, Papi answered that it didn't matter - a fortune wouldn't have been 'put there' if it wasn't meant for someone to 'make it', and that is all you need to know.

For the same twelfth birthday, Sean had received a digital watch. Nonno never asked questions like 'How much did it cost?', or 'Does it have insurance?', or 'Don't you want me to keep it safe in my safe?' like Papi always did. Nonno always said things like he did that day in his *doing science* room:

"Want to know how it works?"

"Sure thing!" enthused Sean, and he pulled his usual stool up to the workbench.

"It'll only take a jiffy," said Nonno, as he prepared

his instruments and a large magnifying lens for the surgical procedure on the device.

Sean had worked out, through a hundred experiences, that a 'Nonno jiffy' was not the same unit as a 'Papi jiffy'. Papi's jiffy worked by some sort of mental meter, calculated on the basis of an exchange rate between time and money. So it was definitely some sort of unit less than ten seconds, at least when it was for something that involved Sean - that is, something that couldn't be 'invoiced'. Sean gathered this meant he was 'outvoiced' by something, but by what he had never understood. Perhaps it was out of fear of being outvoiced that he always found himself speaking loudly to Papi, like you would to anyone who is habitually deaf. By contrast, a 'Nonno jiffy' was a time elastic unit, which could be anything from ten minutes to several weeks - it all depended on how interesting the matter that would 'only take a jiffy' was.

Sean laid his digital watch with its cheap plastic strap on Nonno's workbench.

"Ah, what a beauty it is." The old man picked it up reverently and read the inscription on the backplate through the magnifying lens, which made his nose even bigger, if that were possible. "Made in China - by the SANG company. Something musical in that... ho ho."

"What do those other letters mean?" asked Sean.

"Let me see... 'Re.' and 'al'. That would mean that SANG is a trademark *registered* in *all* the world."

"It has lots of functions," boasted Sean. "A calculator, a planetarium, showing the orbits of the planets around the sun, a solar panel to recharge its batteries..."

"Yes," equally enthused Nonno. He lifted off the backplate. "Here we are. Add to them this piezo-electric crystal timer, the silicon chip, not to forget the synthetic material of the strap, and I would say you have here a fine collection of technologies."

"It's not a *good* watch. Papi says there are lots more in the shops that are much more expensive," shrugged Sean modestly, but nevertheless pleased with the accolades.

Nonno tut-tutted through his few natural teeth. "It is exactly that that makes this so wonderful. We have only just started, and yet we have already found no less than six miracles of science in this little beauty. Opening this is like a journey through time. In both senses, ho-ho." Nonno's explanations always did a round-robin circuit of science - history - philosophy, then back to science. Always back to science. As if it were that that drove the mechanism of time, and not the other way round. And philosophy? Well, that just went along for the ride.

"Now, any one of these would have caused a revolution should they have appeared in any other period of history, just as any future technology would change our world suddenly and dramatically if it appeared here."

"Technology jumping back in time? That isn't possible, Nonno. You've been watching too many of my sci-fi downloads."

Nonno glanced at Sean over the rims of his spectacles. "That's your father speaking. When we don't know something, those who need to think they know everything invent an explanation, and then try to force the universe to fit it. They abbreviate 'imprecise possibility' to 'im-possibility'. The correct answer is 'We just don't know, and…' "

"Isn't that fun!" finished Sean for him, clapping his

hands happily.

"Precisely! Something I have observed is that knowledge packets are skitty things. As far as we know, any number of them may have jumped any number of times through history. We would never know because when it happened everybody would immediately start living with the new technology that comes from it, and assume it is all part of some natural state of affairs. So who knows?"

"I sure don't!" said Sean proudly.

"Always remember, those who think they know the least actually know the most. There is no greater fear than the unknown - and no greater unknown than the nature of the forces that keep the universe ticking. If nobody knows what rotates it, the high priest of know-it-all can put any spin he likes on it. And the greatest mystery of them all is …," he waved the watch, and a piece fell out, "er… Time."

Sean picked up the piece and passed it to his grandfather. "What is this?"

"A diaphragm for the depth meter."

"What's it for?"

"It tells business people exactly how far they are out of their depth."

Sean giggled. He loved having the world's most eccentric grandfather. "But, Nonno, why would a watch change history?"

"Well, … what can you *do* with a watch?"

"Only tell the time."

"There is nothing *only* about it. To most people for most of history that ability would have been a source of great wonder - and because people's minds work in a most peculiar way, wonder usually converts readily to power and wealth. Just ask your father. Now, if you are the *only one* who can, simply the ability to measure time, precisely and consistently, in the dark, in any season and any weather, on the left or right-hand side of the street - to be the only one who knows he is late for a meeting - would have been a source of great power in the past."

"I don't see why," Sean crinkled up his brow like he had seen smart people do on television. "What advantage was there in *knowing* you were late for a meeting?"

Nonno clipped the backplate back on. "Did you know that Napoleon won the Battle of Austerlitz in 1805 because Austria's allies, the Russians, were 12 days late? And you know why? Because they were using the wrong calendar."

"You're saying they were late for the battle and didn't know it?"

"That's why they were called the 'rushin's'. Like any good comedian, Napoleon was a master of timing. I wonder what his secret was?" Nonno cleaned the watch on a soft cloth, saying in his quiet, 'mystery-coming-up' voice: "But most importantly of all, with this," he waved the watch, "you can extend mathematics, the language of the gods, into the *fifth realm of the ordinary.*"

"What is that?"

Nonno put the watch back on Sean's wrist and patted it gently. "That is where the secret of Time lies hidden."

Sean looked with a new awe at the instrument which had been elevated in ranking so quickly from Papi's 'nasty, cheap foreign import' to Nonno's 'marvel of our age'. "So, how do we get to this… 'fifth realm'?"

"Trying to answer that very question, young Sean, is what cost me my job at the university."

"Oh, Nonno…!"

"I am not at all sorry. Something in the meantime has made me very glad it happened."

"What?"

"Hmmm…? Let us just say it has given me the opportunity to find out how to understand the strangest truth of all."

"And what is that, Nonno?"

"That there *is no Time*."

Sean let this one ride over him for a few (apparently non-existent) moments, before coming out with: "Cool by me."

And so that is how it was at the Seulpierre home. And much the same every day. Until, that is, Sean's mother disappeared.

Yes, you read correctly: one day Sean's mother simply vanished.

And then … nothing.

No ransom demand arrived for Papi to haggle over, so his strategy ran out of ideas pretty early on in the piece.

Nonno made no comment except to ask the TV and newspaper reporters, who ambushed them as they came to or left the house, to kindly go somewhere hot and deep.

When I say nothing happened, that is obviously a literary device, more generally known as a lie. Nonno had become totally obsessed with the haunted house from that day on, and Papi told Sean not to disturb Nonno's own, if peculiar, 'way of mourning', and unimaginatively attributed it to any one of several old-age ailments that are thrown out at random to explain eccentricities.

Sean, for his part, experienced the trauma as any child would - the effect was similar to that on a sheep of an approaching Robbie Burns night - something deep inside gets ripped out from where it is badly needed.

He spent his days longing for her to walk in, as she had always done, trailing behind her the shopping trolley that he had repaired himself with brightly coloured string, and say 'So many people in the shops today, I don't know what the world is coming to, honestly I don't!'

He missed everything about her - from Sunday morning chocolate cookies to the orders to go to bed and stop being 'the naughtiest boy under this very sky'. Without that acclaim, nothing he did seemed to have any promise of joy, because his naughtiness was now universally 'understood' and 'tolerated under the circumstances', which is the worst of all conditions for a boy who had once referred to himself as the prince of all naughties. Now, he sat long hours at the window, looking for her, hoping that each day would bring some news that would re-ignite even the faintest of candles at the end of this terrible, lonely tunnel that had become his life.

Lonely, that is, if it weren't for Nonno and his totally whacky ideas.

Sean once asked Papi that if that were the case what could he do to become 'senile' too?

Papi had recently gone from being a reasonably successful financier, to achieving what the newspapers called an 'oracle' status. As a result, the cloak of respectability was contemptuously cast aside as he was promoted to the far superior media rank of 'phenomenally rich', whose bright sun of wealth blotted out all debate and moral dissent.

What, I hear you being prompted to ask, had brought about this sudden transformation? Sean suspected it had something to do with the haunted house. For the record, Nonno knew it had.

Papi Seulpierre had gone 'all secret' about three months before Mami disappeared, which, added to the intervening period, and subtracting the number you first thought of, makes this the year 2010 and seven-eighths.

'All secret' involved Papi 'doing stuff', 'online', 'down there'. Now, 'down there' is the basement to the Seulpierre house, and 'online' means he was a blogger. He would spend all day and night transmitting his special bulletin service called the 'Oracle Line'.

Papi had subsequently become the lead henchman of a group of stock market players, whose influence reached into the most far-flung crannies of greed through their own weekly financial magazine and web gunsites. Perhaps it was Papi's lack of affinity for the ambiguities in the English language that led him to the conclusion that the name 'Piles' would be a suitable name for his online magazine. As for the group Papi led, Nonno's sarcastic suggestions of 'The Cult of Infinite Greed', or 'The Evermore Society', were considered seriously also, but were rejected as being insufficiently clear of purpose.

Like a virulently disposed tsunami, Papi's computer terminals swept away all competitors, such as the Blossom Mountain Buckstop System, and quickly became the most sought after stock market leech instrument, occupying the eyelines and nervous mousehands of any dealer who could afford the exorbitant fees.

Papi operated his empire from the basement of the Seulpierre house, even though there were far nicer rooms further up the four-storey building. Too suggestive of 'openness' was Papi's reasoning.

From there, using an array of computers hooked up to a pasta dinner of cables going in every direction, Papi operated his Oracle financial information service. People who didn't have enough lifetime left to spend the money they already had, were more than desperate to make much much more by subscribing to this fantastically expensive service, which could unerringly predict future stock market prices.

Sean was forbidden to enter this basement sanctum, which suited him just fine.

One day, Sean was taking the forest route home from school. And there it was - it rolled right in front of him. Since it was the middle of November, the ground was covered in a thick layer of red and brown leaves. He was lucky to have seen it at all. He had the barest sensation that someone, or something, had been behind a clump of trees just before it rolled across his path, but when he looked, there was no-one.

The 'it' that rolled was an egg. Not a chicken egg, so Sean was not immediately concerned about which came first. But it was about the same size. And not white nor brown nor freckled, neither healthy free range nor sickly battery-grown - none of these, simply because this egg was made of stone. And highly polished stone, with patches of different pinky colours spelling wondrous mineral diversity. It was beautiful. When he picked it up he found he could addendum its brief profile with a peculiar quality - it was difficult to tell if it was light or heavy. It seemed somehow to be both at once.

He put it in his right hip pocket. He checked his digital watch and quickened his pace for home, stopping more than once to look back. This, in fact, did nothing to alleviate the creepy sensation the hair antennas on the back of his neck were receiving about being followed. Not by nature particularly reassuring, his wild imagination filled his mind's eye with images of robots with piercing red eyes and blaster rayguns coming for him, and him alone.

It is an oft underrated statistical fact that flights of fantasy, no matter how well-feathered, just have to be right sooner or later.

As he was arriving home, he received a fresh dose of the willies, for as he was passing, he could swear he had seen a figure through the first floor window of the haunted house. The house had gained most of its reputation from people claiming copyright on glimpses of ghostly figures of historical nature, often seen on the balcony to that same room, though to date Sean had not partaken in this open source hysteria. Thus freaked out *in extremis* he raced to the indoors of his neighbouring home and slammed the door shut behind him. There he waited, panting, pushing his back against the door, giving the lock and hinges a much needed psycho-illogical reinforcement.

As nothing seemed intent on happening, he abandoned these ramparts in search of more nutritious psychological succour. First he found dissatisfaction in Nonno's copious absence in the *doing science* room upstairs. After finding more nobodies everywhere, not even a cat in either mode de vie, Sean decided he was qualified to waiver standing orders and brave the descent to his father's den in the basement.

He called down for legal coverage. No answer. His default persona lacked the essentials, so he booted up that of Indiana Jones, and began the exploration of a secret passage under the temple of a strangely named pharaoh in search of missing mummies and other relatives, of whom he had to concede he was gaining quite a collection.

All hail the power of imagination - for there, plum bang in the middle of reality, beyond the computers and desks and racks of deed boxes, was the summoned secret tunnel cavitied behind a bookcase, which had been swung open in true mystery tradition.

The only thing that spoiled the fantasticalisation, was the thick bundle of brightly coloured cables that led from the computer nest into the tunnel, but what the heck.

In the absence of explicit adult prohibition, he challenged himself to the dare of meeting his alter-ego expectations of courage and fortitude, and moved to the brick-arched and commensurately cobwebbed tunnel. By now fully in character, he dutifully checked for the dreaded snakes, and then with a more personal after-thought, extended the scan for rats, spiders, centipedes, millipedes, … in fact any-pedes.

The first thing he did was trip over Shrodie. "Oh Shrodie," whispered Sean just inside the echoey tunnel entrance. "Do you have to die right under my feet all the time?"

He peered into the tunnel. It was lit by a series of flaming torches. Somebody, it seems, was expecting somebody. He called out as loudly as one can in a wavering, frightened whisper: "Papi?… Nonno?…" Then, since the silence had only deepened around his echo, he found himself calling "Mami?" by virtue of intuitive reasoning only.

He moved slowly down the tunnel, his kneecaps jumping to an interesting rhythm of their own invention. He didn't notice at first, but after a while he realised that when he turned to look back the way he had come, all the torches on the wall behind him had changed from real, fiery ones to electrical lamps, their sickly yellow light making a poor showing against the sooty, dirty wall. And yet, when he turned back towards the haunted house, ahead of him were only flaming torches, doing much more damage to the unrepentant dark all about them. And this happened every time he turned around - the torches that had been flames ahead of him turned into electric lights once he had passed. He backtracked, and the opposite happened. What had been electric lights ahead of him as he moved back towards the Seulpierre home, became flaming torches again when he turned towards the haunted house.

Perhaps because of this luminescent indeterminacy, he decided he had to feel his way along the wall, which he immediately regretted, seeing as it was clammy brick. At least it started out as clammy, dirty, cobwebby brick. As he went, it seemed to get cleaner, renewing itself. It reminded Sean of the fence around the grounds of the haunted house.

What really made him jump happened another twenty metres along the tunnel. Shrodie suddenly meow-squealed and ran past and ahead of him up the tunnel. Sean had never seen the cat so agitated just after resurrection. What did she know that he didn't?

Then he felt something on his wrist. His watch was

growing, well, restless. Sean looked at its display going into a tantrum of impatience, while the whole thing growled around on his wrist, gaining weight as rapidly as a writer who works in his kitchen. At the same time, however, it seemed to want to float off on its own, or something distinctly unlike that.

And then the tunnel ended at a staircase. These mirrored the ones in his own home's basement, so he knew they would take him inside the haunted house. Shrodie was at the door at the top, purring and mewing, and enticing him to follow her.

"If you die on me, now, Shrodie, I'll... kill you..." threatened a past-halfway-freaked Sean leaking pressurised humour as he ascended the stairs.

The door was ajar, and opened easily on well-oiled hinges. He saw that the bundle of cables that ran through it would have made it impossible to close anyway. He felt the floor change from stone to creaky wood under the rug he was crossing. At the end of this short, pointless passage was another door, this time closed. The cable bundle had vanished into the wall next to the door, leaving him with only Shrodie as a guide.

Probably out of impatience, since Sean was taking forever to open the door, Shrodie had a quick death. But when he finally had the door open, she sprang up and bolted through it. He followed at spectrum opposite end pace. His nerve nearly broke when he heard a brief but distinct sequence of clicks behind him. He turned, expecting to see the door closed, but was relieved to see it was as open as he had left it.

He was now in the natural light of the entrance hall of the house. The front door he had gazed upon all his life from the outside, was now showing him its inner self. Not to disappoint, the house boasted a beautiful Renaissance style. There were elegant arches, and splendid multi-coloured window panes made of mosaics of tiny pieces. A line of hogwarts-gloomy portraits led the way frowningly up a grand stairway.

Somewhere in all this, but without a specific prompt, his nerve reached its limit of endurance, and he turned to leave, but stopped when he thought he recognised the distant voice of Papi. So he took a deep gulp of fortifying air, and returned to his secret entry task.

The bundle of cables had reappeared, and he followed it up the stairs towards the source of the voice. Soon he could discern Papi's tones more clearly - mocking someone. The sound of it was so unpleasant, it made Sean want to run away, and he would have done so, if another, just as familiar, voice hadn't answered it.

"What you propose, not even my son would contemplate. Who are you?!"

"I am you and you are me - now!" This bizarre bit of logic was accompanied by a high laugh which morphed into a chill that locked in on Sean's spinal network.

Now at the top of the stairway, he sneaked a look through a grand door entrance. It was a very large room, with a high ceiling. It was neither oblong nor circular, but had eight perfectly square sides, while the ceiling, not really a dome, gave that effect by virtue of an alternating pattern of four triangles and four squares in a ring, all sloping in towards a single central square. From this was suspended an enormous chandelier at the end of a very long, samsonic chain.

It was in fact a ballroom, equipped with stone fireplaces and brand new antique furnishings. The only thing modern about it was the bundle of cables, which, using the chandelier as its *nodus operandi*, now chose to scatter out in the way the sucky bits of a cow udder milking machine attachment do. Some of the cables, more than could be counted in a single glance, were looping up to the ceiling, while others ran willy-nilly all around the walls - in fact to everything stone inside the room: ceiling cornices, panels, mantelpieces and statue pedestals, all of the same pink porphyry, and nestled at symmetrically spaced intervals. And if he had had the time to take, Sean could have used it to notice that the ends of all of these many cables held what appeared to be stethoscopes – as if listening in on the stone.

In the event, Sean gave this bizarre arrangement none of his attention at all, because that was well and truly monopolised by the strange spectacle a group of figures was creating around the centre of the room.

The only one he recognised was Nonno. He was seated in an elaborately decorated wooden chair, a kind of throne. Behind him, and directly under the chandelier, was an elevated horizontal stone slab, forming an altar covered in what appeared to be hieroglyphicalised writing. What made this scene doubly bizarre was the platform on which Nonno's throne was raised, accessible to the front by a short set of kow-tow stairs. His throne was perched right at the back end of the open platform, giving the suggestion that the slightest movement would cause him to fall backwards onto the stone altar behind him. Why Nonno continued to tolerate this precarious position was in no small part explained by the fact that he was tied to the throne at wrist and ankle, and, despite his intense struggles, he could not but fail to remediate his predicament by any actuation of the own volition option.

Forming a neat circle around this remarkable scene were five other humanesque figures. They were dressed in mystic ceremony requisite robes, with monkish hoods that obscured all features for good effect. Four of these dark figures were standing totally motionless, while the fifth element of the encirclement, the one directly in front of the steps leading up to Nonno's platform, was quite animated. Each of them wore an egg-shaped pendant suspended from a golden, importance-emphasising chain.

Sean rushed far faster than the speed of descriptive writing into the room. "Nonno! What is going on?!"

Nonno struggled against his restraints and cried out a warning: "Sean! This is not your father. Run away, Sean, run! Don't worry about me."

The animated hooded figure at the base of the kowtow stairs was taken by surprise, but nevertheless beat Sean to the old man. With one cruel push with his foot on Nonno's chest, he sent the old professor sailing backwards in his throne onto the altar, which seemed to waver fractionally in its determination to be solid.

And then Nonno was gone. Relieved of its burden, the chair ricocheted off the altar, its restraining cords now Houdini-loose. Nonno had simply vanished.

Sean came to a staggerstill at the base of the steps, staring in disbelief at the vacant seat where his Nonno had been, his jawline locked to agape. Then out of the shimmering altar materialised another hooded figure. It hovered up to take its place next to the figure on the platform, while the stone slab below returned to smugly impassive.

The figure on the platform that had pushed Nonno now turned slowly towards Sean, and pulled back its hood to reveal a cruel and twisted face - a face whose features were normally the copyright of Papi Seulpierre.

In a vain attempt to deconstruct the discrepancy, Sean stammered out a lame and incredulous "Papi...?". He looked from the empty chair to the static new figure. "Nonno?"

Giving him no heed, the Papi figure took from his pocket an extra chain and egg pendant identical to his own and those on the other four figures in the circle, and hung it around the neck of the new figure. Then he placed both hands on the creature's shoulders, as if he were a French general about to kiss both his cheeks. A brief sensation of eerie, greeny glow passed between them, and the new figure came to life. The Papi figure was now unmoving. The new figure replaced his hood, and guided Papi down the stairs, to a vacant place on the circle the other figures mapped out.

Having seen the animation effect, Sean had backed away from the advancing pair, but at one point felt compelled to tear his gaze away to check that the other four dark figures were still immobile in their vigilant places. The new figure took the opportunity of this momentary distraction to make a lunge towards him with a hideous growl. But just as quickly Sean leapt out of his reach and made a bolt for the stairs.

Furious, fearful, and practically frothing with indignation, he reached the lower floor, and, without bothering to check if he was still being followed, he threw himself through the thankfully still open door towards the underground tunnel, where normality beckoned.

Vitruvian Boy

As a general rule, the best-laid plans of mice and little boys don't take cats anywhere near enough into contention. Shrodie had chosen right then to drop dead in front of him, just inside the doorway, so when Sean fell over her, and, subsequently, onto the trapdoor he had earlier triggered by opening the inner door, plunging him and the cat into the chasm of the shaft beneath the rug, she was not alive enough to meow a warning of 'Mind the Gap'.

* * * *

CHAPTER TWO

Thanks a Bundle!

"COME on, Shopliftitian, you're up next. As soon as they've cleaned up the mess left of the one before you. By the collective gods, I'm glad I'm not you!"

Sean stood up from the hardboard bed he found he was lying on, gagged at the smell of rotten straw and let's-not-go-there other things, and stood blinking stupidly enough into the surrogate eyes of two flaming torches.

"Nonno?" he tried with a serious want of conviction.

"*Nonno*?!!" Laughs of a cruel kind pockmarked the voices which answered him. "Yeah. You would have gotten off lightly if his grandfather *were* still king. Good old Hiero, may his soul rest with the gods collective. Too bad for you he found the time to die and leave your judgement in the hands of the young 'un." The man made a disapproving sucking noise on what was left of his teeth. "Young kings, these days. No patience, you see. Trying out his spanking new omnipotence on a few deserve-what-they-gets."

A second voice went on: "Yeah. The yun' king is the

complete opposite of 'is gran-da."

"And *greedy*! Greedy as a republican," agreed the first voice.

"I tell yer wha', moosh (he meant Sean), if yer've been lifting his gold, say goodbye to yer fingers."

"They say the old man has found the answer to *the question*, so we're in for a show," returned the first voice.

"Who has found what to what?" Sean stared at his hands. Not actually because they were manacled at the wrists. Not actually because they were projecting from inside a pair of seen-much-better-days-not-too-long-ago sleeves. But because they were *old*. Old as his father's. He was also still wearing his digital watch.

"Archimedes, of course. If you knows wheres to go, you can still get odds of 'undred to one against that he's worked out how to tell if silver has been mixed in with gold. Doesn't seem possible to me."

"I reckon it's by the taste," said the other one.

"Have you ever eaten gold? So how would you know?" demanded the first voice.

"It tastes good in me dreams. I'm allowed ter dream, ain' I?"

All through this conversation the two guards were pulling Sean out into a corridor. Although they were holding flaming torches, they still managed, through repeated practice no doubt, to push, pull and kick-walk Sean the way, up some stone steps and into a sudden and painful light of day.

"Wouldn't get your hopes up, though. The king's first uncle-regent, Adranodorus, has sold tickets for the public flaying. His palms are just as itchy as his nephew's - he'd rather be flayed alive himself than hand money back. And by the size of him, that would take up all the rest of the light entertainment season."

"An' he's right peed off that he can't be king - on account of him being only married to the dead king's daughter."

"An' the other regent-uncle, Zoippus, is married to the second daughter. So you could say he is peed off, twice removed."

They crossed a laser bright courtyard, through an animated crowd, and then into a long hall in the opposite building. People wearing epic film extras clothing eyed Sean's entry with disdain or amusement, and, even more disturbingly, one or two with a pinch of pity.

He was pushed to stand alone in front of a grand, oh-look-at-me, dais. On it was a matching high and mighty throne - occupied by a lounging boy just a few years older than Sean. All around him stood richly-attired nobles, soldiers and an array of also-rans. The local duly-appointed scum were looking in through the windows, eagerly hoping for whatever scraps they may be thrown by the rich, whether it be money, food, or entertainment sound-bites.

"Dog! Kneel before the mighty King of Syracuse, Hieronymus of the Rapturous Returns."

Someone lifted Sean as a prelude to throwing him with mellow drama onto his knees.

"Ouch!" was all Sean could think to say.

The (by far) largest of the richly attired men standing beside the king, who turned out to be the afore-in-awe-mentioned Adranodorus, the boy king's uncle, informed the sundry all: "Shopliftitian, metal merchant, you are accused of a very serious crime... A *high-flaying* crime." This was greeted by a ripple of appreciative laughter.

"I'm sorry, sir, but I'm not…" began Sean.

"Silence, scum!" An unseen foot flattened him to the floor and held him there.

Adranodorus was probably the fattest man Sean had ever seen. He had a strong sensation that he had seen him before – at a zoo, only then he had a trunk and kids were queueing to ride him.

The proud bearer of this image pronounced pre-sentence on Sean: "When… sorry… *if* the king decides you are guilty, you will be flayed alive, hung up for the crows, and have your insides jellied before your eyes, which I mean in a chronological sense as they will be hanging down your face by then."

"Eh?… I mean 'Help'…?" Sean squeaked out this weak plea-enquiry to the amused crowd, hoping that this Shopliftitian they all took him for had friends in the sea of fair weather faces.

"Who has evidence against the guilty party?" called the king eagerly in the standard school bully intonation.

"But… I'm not guilty… yet…" protested a flat Sean.

"Silence, you dog of debasement!" The same heavily-reinforced foot encouraged his ribs to speak to his lungs in that vein.

"I have evidence, my new young liege." An old man came forward. As wise old men go he was a walking cliché - he had the requisite long, flowing white beard and wore a magnificent red wrap and matching funny hat.

"Ah. Archimedes. The official court smart arse," said the brat king.

"Clever person," corrected his second uncle Zoippus, a tickler for protocol, and as skinny as Adranodorus was not.

"Same diff," said his nephew while he picked his nose and wiped his fingers on the expensive drape of the throne. "He looks like a school teacher. Bloody Greeks. At least he doesn't smell."

"That is because I have been taking a long bath, my liege," announced Archimedes with a hint of pride-left-still.

"Well, oh newly clean one? Have you an answer to *the question*?" asked Adranodorus in his nasty-smiley bloated way.

"That I have, my liege and master."

Something went ping inside Sean's head.

"Speak. The king hears," Adranodorus ordered by proxy authority.

"Let me define the problem," began Archimedes with a voice that sounded like a trailer to a very long film.

Zoippus lent towards Adranodorus and commented sottovoce, "Oh, by the collective gods, these mathematicians… so …"

"*Add*ictive? Patience, brother Zoippus." And then to Archimedes: "If you must."

The boy-king pulled haughtily at the cloak of the advisor: "Uncle Adranodorus! *I* am king - *I* am supposed to say that!"

"All in good time, Hieronymus. Remember, I and your other uncle, Zoippus, are your guardians till you are mature, which may take longer than any of us realised. Then it will be your turn to say 'If you must'."

"And 'Proceed'," said the king.

Vitruvian Boy

"Exactly."

"And 'flay that one slowly'."

"As often and to whomever it so pleaseth his majesty."

"So long as that is understood, you may proceed."

"Thank you, your highness," said Adranodorus sarcastically. He turned to Archimedes. "Well, old man?"

After a while the boy-king began to stifle a yawn, and then thought since he was king he shouldn't have to. As a result, and in a half a mind, which is all he could muster at a pinch, he swung one leg over the arm of the throne six sizes too large for him, and stared with desperate boredom out the paneless window at the large sundial on the wall opposite. All the while Archimedes was talking the king was wondering how many slaves it would take to lift and turn the wall so he could knock off early for the day. But that would be time travelling - and he had always been instructed that time travel was best left to the professionals.

Archimedes was trying to play to the crowd. "Let me recap." He put his hat back on and grinned. A few groan-laughs escaped from the crowd, but were stifled immediately by Adranodorus shaking his head discouragingly at them, which caused the folds of fat around his neck to wash around like fish caught en masse in a rising net.

So, left to himself, Archimedes opted to drone on. "The problem is such: the royal crown has been made by the guilty party from gold given to him by his gracious ex-majesty, Hiero the Second, some many moons past… ago… oh, what's the word…"

"Hence?" Helped the king's uncle advisor. "Do you

now wish to take as long in revealing the results as you took to deliberate them, that we should all also die of old-age as did Hiero, before we hear the answer?"

"Yes, of course. I mean, no, of course not..."

"Archimedes! Where weren't you?"

"Ah, yes. Since the finished crown is the same weight as the gold given him, how can we be sure the guilty party has not substituted an amount of the gold by a baser metal - for example silver?"

A murmur of outrage and disgust washed around the crowd with prepared one-liners. 'Carat pusher!', 'If he takes the carat give him the stick!'

Adranodorus responded majestically when he sensed from the crowd's mood that an opportunity to do something memorably executive was approaching. "Yes, Archimedes, oh sage and extremely clever person in my eyes?"

The king blurted out. "What do you mean 'in my eyes'? I am the bloody king. Don't you mean 'in... er... *my* eyes'?"

"Exactly, your young majesty. That is exactly what I mean."

While this was going on, the phrase 'extremely clever person' was being echoed softly and mystically from several quarters of the gathered-here-todays.

Another advisory looking, self-importantly robed gentleman with an even funnier coned hat stepped forward and spoke priestily. "If the crown indeed weighs the same, is it not impossible to tell if the metals have been exchanged? Is it not true, as the scriptures tell us, that such an imprecise possibility will always lead to an impossibility?"

Yet another of the king's confidant-tricksters came

forward and looked contemptuously at Shopliftitian. "We could just torture this fellow till he told us what we wish to hear…"

Adranodorus waved him away with: "We want none of those republican tricks here."

The king picked up the enormous red ruby pendant hanging by a gold chain on his chest, to relieve his neck of its weight, and looked at Archimedes distractedly through it. "By Zeus and Apollo, not to forget the nymphets, this is exciting. I love being king. Continue. You were going to solve the riddle of the crown?"

Archimedes was obviously on a roll. "Yes, my liege, for an ordinary man, such a conundrum is surely a hard drum to beat."

Polite and embarrassed chuckles. Levity arising at the thought of the entertainment to come when Shopliftitian was strung up and beaten political promise thin as a suspected gold debaser.

Uncle Adranodorus asked solemnly. "So, Archimedes, do you have *the* answer?"

"I do."

"Um…, it is not 'forty-two' like the time the old king asked you for the meaning of it all?"

Archimedes coughed quietly. "Er, no, my lord, forgive me, that was but an aberration that came to me in a dream, the meaning of which I have given much deep thought to ever since."

"As have we all. I hope, for your sake, you did not come to the same conclusion about it as *we* all did?" A laugh did its crowd ripple thing. "Will this answer need such lengthy pondering?"

"I think not, my lord, for this solution is indeed my 'Eureka' moment."

A warning bell clanged very loudly inside Sean's already pinging head.

Adranodorus was getting impatient. "Yes, yes, yes... we all have Eureka moments in the bath - just when we don't have quill and parchment handy to scribble them down. Yes, yes... by all that's tax-deductible, get on with it!"

"The answer is... you're going to like this..."

"Just give us the answer!" cried Zoippus.

"You're really going to like this, you know... that while it *is* necessary to measure the volume of the crown to determine if its weight per volume is the same as pure gold, it is not necessary to melt it down to a uniform shape to do so."

"No?"

"No."

"Then how, oh extremely clever person, how? We are all ears."

More like noses, thought Sean, looking at the crowd's facial prominences.

Some dissenters in the crowd muttered things like: 'I bet he says something stupid, like his fishing hook for ships idea.' 'Or his death ray caper! Looking at too many futuristic frescoes, that one', or 'Bet you half a mina he makes a complete arse of himself,' and 'No, I'll only risk a hundred obols on that one.' 'Hope he's found it. I love a good slug-and-flay.' 'Oh, Shopliftitian, why don't you come out and flay?!' 'What's Shopliftitian's favourite song?' 'Heard it: Flay me to the Moon...'

Adranodorus advised the old sage. "Remember, Archimedes, this is your last chance to retain your position as official court smar... er, clever person. An exclusive government contract is at stake."

"I shall not disappoint again, oh indirect liege. The solution is that if you were to immerse the crown into a container of water…"

The crowd erupted: 'Ha! You owe me a hundred obols! He wants to give the crown a bath!'

'Shh.. he hasn't finished yet.'

Archimedes was flustered, but rallied with: "I … er… oh, yes, my theorem states that the volume of space occupied by the crown will be precisely equal to the volume of water displaced."

The expectation of the crowd had a gooey texture to it.

Archimedes waded through it stoically. "And thus by comparing this amount of displaced water to that from an equal weight of pure gold, we should be able to determine not only *if,* but by precisely *how much*, the gold has been replaced by a lighter metal, since the lighter metal will occupy more space for the same weight."

In the ensuing pause, Zoippus whispered to Adranodorus: "Is he saying gold weighs the same as water?"

"No…," replied his fellow regent from under a mountain chain of forehead ripples. "I think he is saying the volume is the same, whether it is water or gold."

"But that doesn't resolve the issue - it is the weight we need."

Archimedes was trying to explain. "We have no word for this new quality that results. To what degree a weighty thing occupies a space."

Zoippus shook his head. "Honestly, Archimedes, for a clever person at times you can be so dense."

"That's it!" cried Archimedes in eurekaphoria. "We can call it 'dense-iticity'."

"Hmmm…" and Zoippus scratched his face, which must have been somewhere beneath his beard.

The boy king in the meantime was saying something to the likes of: "Now I must say that *sounds* clever. What does it mean, anyone?"

His uncle advisor Adranodorus cleared his throat loudly, and signalled for Archimedes to approach him and his fellow brother-in-law, Zoippus, for a confidential scrum discussion, with their backs to the king, who stood on his throne in an attempt to overhear what they were saying.

"Archimedes, are you out of your hyper-logical brain?!" roared Adranodorus in a whisper, tapping Archimedes' chest sharply, which is where people in those days thought the thinking was done - whereas today we know men do it much further down.

"No, my liege but one, I have tested the method and it works."

Zoippus stared at him. "You total idiot! You have invented a system for detecting the presence of impure metal in gold!?"

"Ah… yes, my lord. I rather gathered that is what I had been instructed to do?"

"Do I look like a monkey's uncle!?" Adranodorus demanded. At this, the three adults stopped abruptly, hooked by the irresistible irony, then as one turned to look at the boy king, who, caught out standing on the throne, pretended to be trying to learn to fly. Adranodorus heffalumped to bring them back into the huddle. "No, Archimedes… you were asked to get proof that Shopliftitian is a crook, not undermine our entire monetary system."

"Sire?"

"You do realise how serious a crime this is?"

"Stealing?" said Archimedes.

"No… we all do that. Explain, would you, Zoippus?"

With exaggerated patience and the simplest, intentionally condescending, words he could find, Zoippus proceeded to explain the basic facts of reality - the eternal gift of the economist to the scientist. "Currency debasing is a commodity hedge fund instrument. At a critical time as this one - facing an on-shore invasion and aggressive auditing forays, we risk massive capital flight. Sicily is an island, but our off-shore status is in serious doubt. The only guarantee we can offer for our currency is the gold standard. If rumours leak out that members of the securities council are mixing base metals with gold, it will cause a stampede in the already tight marketplace - a run in our tights like you've never seen."

"But my method can prove it is all untrue. That you do not debase our coinage," announced Archimedes triumphantly. Then he saw the contrarian faces of the two uncles. "Ah, I see."

Zoippus went on. "If this gets out our entire economy will be ruined! How can we balance the books if we can't float the debase points?!"

Adranodorus furied out: "If your 'method' gets into the wrong hands we will be holdable to account for our actions - and no responsible government can afford to be put in that position! Go away, go away!"

Archimedes stumbled down from the dais in a state of total confusion, while Adranodorus malevolently contemplated what to do, and who that would be to.

Sean had been following all of this very attentively,

and saw this as his opportunity.

"Sir, may I speak?"

"Why should you speak? You are the accused?" mumbled Adranodorus in a real grump.

"But, if I may sir…?" Sean nodded towards Archimedes, or as much as he could from his prone position, and put meaning into his plea.

"Oh, very well. Let's have it," the king's uncle advisor answered miserably.

"All I wanted to say, sire, is ask Archimedes what he did just *after* his 'Eureka' moment."

Adranodorus gave a formality-compliant sigh and turned to Archimedes. "Eureka?"

The old man shuffled his sandals uncomfortably. "That's *why* I was having a bath."

"I see. And afterwards…?"

"I ran through the streets calling 'I have found it' in Ancient Greek."

"What do you mean - *Ancient* Greek? We speak Modern Greek. It won't be Ancient Greek for another two thousand years!"

"And he was naked," added Sean as Shopliftitian.

"Old man nuddy?! Yuck! How gross!" commented the king.

"Your majesty, please!" interjected Adranodorus.

"Well, it's true. It would be so shrivelled it wouldn't even bounce as he ran along. Not like my great big…"

"Archimedes?! Have you been streaking in public again?"

"My lord.." Archimedes dropped his post-sage status head and went as red as his cloak.

The scum screamed with laughter and the chortling classes lived up to their name.

Adranodorus placed his heavy hand of remonstration on the old man's shoulder. "And have you been self-medicating on leeches again?"

Archimedes nodded his head sadly.

The brat king made a face and said. "Oh, man, that really sucks!"

Only one person was impressed. This was Cespuglio the Younger, representative of the Roman Republic. He had one of those faces which probably inspired the invention of the punching bag.

His voice somehow matched that concept. "Ha! So this is the so-called genius you claim will provide the weapons of mass destruction that will sink our Roman fleet from afar?!"

"Cespuglio… my dear sir. I did not know you were here." Adranodorus glowered at the guards at the door, who knew they had seen their last sunrise.

Zoippus, the skinny uncle advisor, stepped forward supplicating with hands like sea anemones grasping for … whatever it is sea anemones grasp for. "Let us assure you you may inform the Roman Senate that they can rely on our good sense with regards where our loyalties lie."

"Business sense, I take it. Nothing 'good' about it. Old king Hiero was loyal to Rome and his kingdom thrived. I have been sent here by the Roman praetor in Sicily, Appius Claudius. Do you know what we always say about the praetor?"

"Where there is an Appius, there is a way?"

"Precisely! And what he wants to know is whether you will betray Rome and your people for Carthaginian gold and flattering promises, which your brat king licks up like a mewing kitten?!"

"Why? How much are they offering?" piped in the king.

Cespuglio mocked the uncle advisors. "Tell me, Adranodorus and Zoippus, does your great wise king here even know what and where Rome is?"

Hieronymus sat up, his hand punching the air hermionesquely above his head, as if it were a question in history class. "I know! I know! Our hated rivals to our north and round a bit."

Cespuglio the Younger turned to Adranodorus and smiled saccharinely. "Hated?"

Adranodorus eclipsed the king with his bulk. "What he means is hated *economic* rivals. That is technically flattery."

The brat king jumped up and down on the throne to be heard. "You told me yourself, uncle." He recited from a memory rush: "Republicans to a man, ready to throw up trade barriers at the slightest competition. Rome is a multicorporate monopoly run for the maximum benefit of the minimum number of people, with a vicious foreign policy they call a ... er ... 'free market corrective'."

"Really?" said Cespuglio. "So, tell me, Adranodorus, what is different about your state? I will tell you - you are merely *led* by greed. We, instead, have *institutionalised* it. You are antiquated. We are the future. Allow me to demonstrate." Cespuglio bent over Sean, still squirming under the heavy sandal of his gaoler. "Do your people even know what year it is?"

Sean did not answer.

"Well, tell him!" bellowed Adranodorus impatiently. "Or shall I invent a game involving a flat square table, a low net, two round paddles and one of your most precious, dangly body pieces?"

Sean gulped, and managed to get a look at his digital watch, which he was still wearing. "Oh, um… it would be two hundred and twelve BC?"

"Be sea?" enquired Cespuglio in his quiet, sarcastic voice. "Does that mean 'by the sea' time?"

"I mean year minus 212," blurted Sean, unable to kick himself from his prone-imposed posture.

"*Minus* 212?!!" Cespuglio took out a pocket sundial and went to the window and the sunlight. "I make it Year of Our Founding Fathers 541." He shook the instrument and compared it to the large one on the wall opposite. "Cheap Helvetian import. Must be running fast."

"Perhaps you have not set it to southern standard time?" suggested Archimedes.

"Very soon, I promise you, the whole world will be running on the Roman Standard. Never mind. Where were we, Adranodorus?"

"We were boasting."

"Oh, yes. Forgive me. After you."

"Syracuse is an advanced, modern state. A tyrannical despotism."

"We can all dream of ideals, Adranodorus. But who is the tyrant? This teenage brat?" Cespuglio pointed at Hieronymus, but kept his gaze on Uncle Adranodorus. "Or you?"

Before the regent could answer, Cespuglio went on. "Do you think Republicanism is doomed to failure? Far from it! I have been consulting with your very own Oracle of the Albumen Insight. She is not the diva of the divination industry for no reason. Do you know why she makes it to the top of the charts every year?"

"You mean, other than the low-cut dress, the erotic

dance routines, the high sales of top ten illustrated predictions she broadly casts on fragments of parchment called 'clips'? She has a good head for business, does our Oracle."

"So," continued Cespuglio. "I take it we can both agree that the high financial returns are a guarantee for the quality of her predictions?"

"Nothing could be more reassuring."

"Shall I tell you what she says in her latest extreme-range forecast?" He took out and unrolled a parchment. Some fortune cookie crumbs fell out, and Cespuglio brushed them away surreptitiously.

"I managed to get an interview in the after-lunch slot. I was a little disturbed when the Oracle said she was not expecting me. There was a bit of confusion with the appointments secretary."

"How so?"

"I asked her if it were true - that this is the One Stone age of the two by two? Is this the time of the two two, too?"

"And she said?"

"She consulted with her sundial reader, who ran away and came back to say she thinks it is two to two, too."

"2 2 2 2! What does it mean?!" cried the background chorus of priests in awe at this revelation from the gods.

"Besides we have missed lunch?" interrupted the king, now bored again beyond all redemption.

Cespuglio spoke presagedly. "I find it convenient to interpret her words as meaning that this is indeed the ordained beginning of the Age of the Four-by-Two. It shall henceforth be written that two thousand, two hundred and twenty-two years from now, in mid autumn to be precise, so the leaves will give it all a nice, rustic effect - good for sales of the illustrateds I have planned - there shall be a long-awaited 'uniting of the paths'."

"Which would mean that now is the 'parting of the ways'?" asked Adranodorus.

"Only for you, and your kind, Adranodorus. Only for those who resist my will."

"*Your* will?"

"I mean Rome's," corrected Cespuglio slowly and unapologetically. "Rome has its best minds working on a grand unification theory. In this regard, I also run a side business as a talent scout. I have come to ask Archimedes if he would join us - we need his weapons of mass destruction to bring peace to the world."

"You mean help unite the world under the Roman logo?" corrected Adranodorus.

"And circumvent the royalties on his patents we hold…?" added Zoippus.

Adranodorus stepped forward menacingly in an attempt to bulk down Cespuglio. "I am afraid you would first have to negotiate with his majority shareholders."

"And they would be…?"

"You see before you the sole agents and managers of 'Eureka Moment Industries', at your disservice."

"Be careful, Adranodorus, my recommendation to Claudius Appius may be an extension of his six-lane chariot way to this little rock of yours."

"Your tollgate charges do not intimidate me."

"Perhaps a joint adventure?"

Adranodorus contemplated this for a moment. "We do have an alternative investment partner…"

"If you mean Carthage - just because they did so

well in the Cannae armaments show… just a temporary fad. Their logo, the elephant -" Cespuglio appraised Adranodorus' physique. "I can see why that attracts you - has run its course. But in the meantime Rome has invested a lot in research and development, and next year our eagle will carry home the season trophy."

Archimedes broke the deadlock by stepping forward, his curiosity taking him over. "What else, lord Cespuglio, did the Oracle tell you?"

"What do you think your very own Oracle has proclaimed for the year that falls two thousand, two hundred and twenty-two years from now? Do you imagine that in such a time reason and knowledge will rule the Earth? You would like that, wouldn't you, Archimedes? Well, you're going to be *very* disappointed.

"I'll leave it to you to imagine the incense, the swaying and chanting, the goat's blood, not to mention the coordinated dance routine and sexy groaning." Cespuglio unrolled the parchment scroll further and read. " 'In that year the world's greatest superpower under the logo of the eagle' - that is a clear reference to Rome - 'will be just coming out of a terrible two-term' - whatever that means - 'period run by an ignorant man who thinks he knows everything he needs to know, and resultant thereof never listens to anyone. A man who will lie and invent explanations, and drag the world into a series of terrible wars for the personal profit of his small band of supporters' - who the Oracle calls the 'Vampires of the Black Blood' - 'And he shall be the downfall of all his most faithful allies. A man who has no facts but sounds sure of himself to his people, and they believe him, because they have put their faith not in knowledge but little boxes, shrines, in their living rooms, through which the idiot proclamations of this man are heard, but he cannot hear them back, cannot hear them cry out in their anguish.' "

He turned to Archimedes. "*That* is the future, old man, not your mystical mathematics and star-gazing. Even if man one day reaches the Moon, the people will not put faith in the testimony of their own witness, but will stay resolutely glued to their empty promise shrines and listen to false hopes from false men such as this."

Cespuglio the Younger now extended the discussion to the wider audience, one hand gripping his tunic over the heart and the other the hilt of his short sword in classic caesarean cutting-edge style. "I will now tell you of another prophecy. I remember what mighty Hiero told me last time I was here: 'I am cast as the wise, old dying king. This young brat here is my grandson, Hiero the Anonymous, shortened to Hieronymus, known around the Med as Prat the Younger. And those two jackals over there are the standard repertoire conniving, power-hungry uncles, husbands of my ugly daughters - no greater testimony exists to self-sacrifice for greed - who will make Hieronymus a puppet, the unworthy inheritor of the crown in question. Its debasement has a double meaning here, as you will see.' "

The ambassador prodded Sean with his toe, as he lay before the dais, still squashed under the jacksandal of his guard. "It would seem I have come at just the right moment to see his prophecy fulfilled." He bent down by Sean, and lifted his arm still wearing the digital watch. "Interesting bracelet you have."

"Patience, Cespuglio the Younger," replied Adranodorus, and then sottovoce to Zoippus, who snorted: '… but just as dumb as the Elder.' "Patience. I had almost forgotten the metal merchant. Thank you for reminding me."

"Yeah, thanks a bundle," mumbled Sean.

"We shall all now flay to the gods collective. Let the entertainment begin!" He clapped his hands and the flaying squad moved in with a portable brazier, incisors, flap levers, dermal rakes and other gruesome instruments, and behind them a back-up team of slaves with mops and buckets. "I trust you will enjoy this little diversion, which I now dedicate in your honour, Cespuglio. We have spared no expense to buy in the best international flayers for our home team."

Cespuglio dismissed him. "I thank you, Adranodorus. But I have no time for such idle merriments. I must make haste. I have a trade delegation to organise."

"Trade delegation?"

"Oh, didn't I tell you? Since you are all obviously so impressed by Hannibal's mid-season streak of luck at Cannae, due to some overweight players…"

"Tusk, tusk.."

"…it seems you wish to abandon Hiero the Elder's wise policy of alliance with Rome, and throw in your 'favoured nation' status with Carthage."

"I assure you, Ambassador, the market oracles are not in favour of anything of the sort."

"Then you have nothing to fear from a 50,000-man trade delegation? It will be here to 'renegotiate' our trade relations - on a permanent basis."

"Is that prudent? Rumours of a hostile takeover could cause some volatility in our share price in the East."

"Believe me, Adranodorus, during these aggressive negotiations, your personal net worth will be the least of your worries."

"Believe *me*, Cespuglio, my personal net worth is my *only* worry."

"Not a 50,000-man trade delegation?"

"Not since you have given me time enough to sell my shares."

"So be it. I see I am dealing with a formidable opponent, who has true values clearly in mind. A ruler who knows when to cut his losses and sell out his people. One who knows he should put his trust in market oracles rather than men of science and learning." He looked with contempt at Archimedes. "Old man, you could learn much from your master."

"You honour me, my lord."

"Yes. Pity. Still, you cannot argue with the market. That is all we need to know, is that not right, Adranodorus?"

"It is so written. We promise you the battle of all mothers, Cespuglio."

"I will seek you out on the trading floor. Let history be the final judge."

As Cespuglio turned to leave, Archimedes scratched his may-as-well-be-bald head under his funny hat. "My lord... Just a technicality, but don't radical market adjustments of this type need to be approved by the Council of the Big Three, under the Mediterranean Sacking and Pillaging of Neutrals Convention?"

Cespuglio the Younger threw his answer to him with a cheeky swish of his battle skirt as he stormed out. "Not on Wednesdays. I abhor conventions on Wednesdays."

* * * *

CHAPTER THREE

Crossing the Ruby Con

AFTER Cespuglio's departure there was a high-ranking silence in the executive throne room. Then someone screamed the evergreen "We're all going to die!", and within a half-sixtieth second arc of sun rotation the trading floor was emptied of non-stakeholders, leaving the clutch of oligarchy looking open-frontedly about them.

The king said: "Er... Uncle Adranodorus, if we really *do* have a death ray, why is everybody so worried?"

"A bluff. Weapons of mutual delusion to keep our enemies uncertain about levels of return in the sector of regime changes."

Zoippus cleared his nasal passages noisily. "A 50,000-man unilateral negotiating team isn't really the reaction we had hoped for."

Adranodorus developed a forced upbeat. "There is nothing to fear - we have Archimedes, haven't we? He understands the Language of the Gods, does he not?"

The headpriest stepped forward to peeve around a bit, then began to predicate from on high: "I too have a message from the gods. I gazed into the bowels of a

Vitruvian Boy

three-week dead cat which appeared to me mysteriously on Mount Showdunger, and I did verily sacrifice my lunch to it for three days following, calling as I did to the great green god of Peuk."

"Obvious place to look for a message from the gods," agreed Adranodorus. "But sometimes with you priest I feel we have far more than we need to know."

"Thank you, sire but one. We are but vestibules of the divine knowledge." He looked with contempt and hatred at Archimedes. "All desire for knowledge beyond that which we are born with is sacrilege to the scriptures and an affront to the gods collective."

Adranodorus showed one of his two faces, and answered with the type of have-it-both-ways policy statement which has since become the standard: "The wisdom of the scriptures is absolute. However, I am sure the priests will be able to interpret them in such a way that will allow the financial potential of this situation to be exploited fully, and in so doing ensure the continuation of their temple's royal annuity? Hmm…? I thought as much. This is a great opportunity to prove to the whole world that Syracuse is at the vanguard of cutting edge religious technology. I am sure if you revise the scriptures closely enough, you will see that they say just that. Take your time. Neither of us can afford for you to make any mistake in this," he added threateningly, and the priests all shuddered as one. "And when the Romans get here we will make a killing. Literally."

Zoippus added: "With such a successful public demonstration of the death ray, we will be able to break into the Eastern market."

"Idem the killing." Adranodorus rubbed his hands

together enthusiastically. "So, Archimedes, when can we have your death ray?"

"I have finished it."

"Good."

"Finished the design, that is."

"I see. So we are ready to start prototype production?"

"As soon as I can solve just one tiny last little annoying problem. It is a relatively minor detail, but I must admit in all tests so far it has been disturbingly consistent in its recurrence, and unfortunately does tend to have some undeniable degree of detrimental implication for the overall success of the project, both in terms of its technical specifications and production characteristics."

Adranodorus looked about him with a kind of sarcastic helplessness. "Did anybody get that?"

The answer came from an unexpected quarter: the brat king. "He is saying it doesn't work."

The silence that met this was as dead as the streets of Syracuse were going to be after the Roman holiday.

Zoippus muttered to himself: "Kids are the only ones who understand technology these days."

Adranodorus turned with sinister self-control to Archimedes: "Not at all?"

Archimedes nod-shook his head, causing his cap to fall over his eyes. "Well, science is never as exact as the scriptures." The priesthood nodded indignantly as one (an acquired skill). Archimedes continued. "There is always a degree of uncertainty - but in this case, statistically, the uncertainty reduces to … very close in fact to … well, whatever one minus one equals."

"Zero," burst out Sean helpfully, still proned by brute's force.

"Oh, that's ridiculous," exploded Archimedes, with an unexpected degree of passion. "How can there *be* a zero? 'Nothing' can't be a 'something', that's what I always say. Zero doesn't count... will never add up to anything... It is just one of those mad Babylonian theoretical entities."

"Like negative numbers?" Sean knew the ancients liked their mathematics geometric, straight up and real.

"*Negative* numbers...?! Great gods incorporated, what a concept..." Archimedes stroked his beard dumbledorishly.

Adranodorus swept away the historical moment of intellectual discovery as it has been done ever since - with economic override: "This is a disaster! Do you realise we have prelaunch brochures already chiselled and ready to be erected on every primetime hill of every port in the Middle Earth Sea!? We have endorsements lined up from the top gladiators and mega-stellum chariot pilots, even an ex-first consul of Rome - not cheap, but well worth it. It is all ready to roll - all we need now is for Research and Development to give us the product according to the original specifications. We've done our job, why can't you do yours?"

Zoippus added: "We even have a product name ready for the man-about-town, single-seated version: 'Sicilian Vespas'."

Archimedes went on: "Yes, I do realise marketing is millennia ahead of science... Mind you, my theory is beautiful. But I was never that good on the... er... whatever and bolts side of things."

Adranodorus bulked over Archimedes threateningly. "Oh, nuts to your bolts! Archimedes, old man, are you telling me you won't be able to make me my death ray?"

"No… as in yes. Well, you know, great theories are like bad models … they look good in the sketches, but in the final draw …"

Zoippus started to do the accountants' deathwalk, back and forth, pulling at his hair: "We're doomed! We'll be broken up by a Roman anti-trust commission, sold into corporate entities that have direct governance from Rome itself. A hell on Earth. Tax slavery in its true form."

The guard still squashing Sean spoke. "Sorry to interrupt, my liege corporation, but what about this?" He poked Sean with his spear, and then nodded at the rabble growing impatient at the public windows.

Adranodorus did some mental calculations, then answered: "Pull the curtains down. Tell them we apologise for this interruption to the normal programme. Then offer to let the scum into the throne and torture room at five obols a head. Concessions apply. Don't see why they should get to watch it for free. I must make a note to obtain exclusive rights on window viewings for the future. Maybe even sell advertising space along the sill – that they can click on perhaps when they want to buy some refreshment … Can't disappoint our public, can we? Make the show long and excruciating. That'll ensure a good season and fill larger-capacity public arenas for future events. Let flay start."

"Sir!" screamed a desperate Shopliftitian-Sean composite, as it was dragged towards the upright flaying rig. "Sir, may I speak?"

"I told you, guilty parties have nothing to say."

"I can finish Archimedes' death ray for him!"

"What? What can you know about it?"

"I know his design, and I know it doesn't work. I saw it on Myth Busters."

"Myth Busters?! That league of anti-Hellenic scum?! Roman propagandists!!" Adranodorus bellowed at the guard: "Pre-torture this object. I want to see him with a poker face."

"Please sir. I can do it," begged Sean.

"Archimedes?"

"Well, a little inspiration wouldn't go amiss. I am stuck on how to focus the light sufficiently. On papyrus things look so easy, don't they?" Archimedes went over to Sean now being tied to the t-shaped flaying rig. "Do you have a moment?" The guard took out his knife and began to rip off Sean's vestments, including his watch.

Archimedes muttered on. "If you're not too busy? Shall I come back later? … It's just that I would love to know how you propose to do it?"

"Using a laser," answered a terrified Sean.

"And what is that?"

"It amplifies light, but only mono-frequency light."

"No such thing."

"Ok, you might know it as monochromatic light?"

"Nope."

"Well, ok, it hasn't been discovered yet."

A priest now screamed at Sean. "Blasphemer!! Knowledge seeker!! Devil worshipper!!"

Adranodorus mediated the issue in a highly reasoning tone: "Surely, you must see, the priests do have a point. The history of man is long. *Logically*, there has been more than enough time for everything there is to know to have been discovered already."

The other priests held up their scriptures and chanted: "That's all you need to know."

Zoippus joined the collective prejudication: "Ignore him, brother. He's just flaying for time."

Archimedes pulled Sean's ear aside, which was rather painful because the rest of him remained where it was tied on the vertical rig. "But why would that make light more intense?"

"Because it can be amplified. Through... that ruby!" Sean managed to point with the only part of his body still able to move - his nostril flare - at the enormous ruby around the brat-king's neck.

Adranodorus laughed brutally. "You are incorrigible! I like you. Facing death in the ... well, face, and still thinking about pocketing something for yourself. Yes, I like the way you think. You shall be remembered - I think I'll name a crime after you. Er... what is your name, again?"

"Sean... I mean Shopliftitian."

"Let it be ordained: when anyone steals anything from a shop - from now on I decree it shall be called ... 'Seaning'. The punishment shall be having his hair publicly 'shoplifted'."

Zoippus hummed a bit then said: "Could I suggest the other way around?"

"Eh?" replied Adranodorus. "Liftshopped? That doesn't sound right to me."

The first torturer came up to Sean, and, with what he probably thought to be a professional courtesy, showed Sean the red-hot poker he was going to use as an opening bar.

Archimedes said to Sean in apology: "Well, I can

see you're busy. Perhaps we can talk more comfortably later." He shuffled away with his head bowed in sage-thought, which is why he alone saw the watch lying on the ground so anachronistically as it was, if a watch *can* be anachronistic.

He held it up. "Did someone drop this?"

"It's mine!" cried Sean.

"Yours? What is it?"

"A watch."

"I *am* looking at it."

"No. A timepiece. For telling the time."

"Indoors?"

"Yes."

"What on earth for? You only need to tell the time when you're going out, and for that we have state-of-the-art precision sundials. An indoor sundial is not only unnecessary, but a contradiction in terms, not to mention a physical impossibility."

"Do you believe that all imprecise possibilities must lead to impossibilities?" Sean nostril-flared towards the priests.

Archimedes came back and leant over him to whisper like a schoolboy hiding his shared heresy from a tyrannical teacher. "No. No, I don't."

"I could explain the watch to you. And many other things."

"What things? What, for example, does this little button do?" Archimedes pressed a button on the watch and the planetarium mode came on in the display, showing the planets revolving around the sun. "Oh, I say, how very interesting."

"What is it, Archimedes?" asked Adranodorus and Zoippus, coming over together, their instincts converting readily 'interesting' to 'profitable'.

Archimedes slipped the watch into his robes before turning around. "I… have just… I was going to say something… important, I think it was…" He said the ancient Greek for 'drat' and began to wander away, Sean forgotten.

"Continue!" ordered Adranodorus, tether-endedly, to the torturers.

"Archimedes, please! The laser!" screamed Sean.

Archimedes turned back to him. "Lazy? No, I am many things, young man, but I am not lazy! I will show you!"

"You won't be able to if I am dead!"

"But that would mean postponing your execution? I couldn't ask so much of you."

"Yes you could."

"But only if you *really* don't mind? You're not just saying that, so as not to hurt my feelings?"

Sean stared at the hot tongs hovering towards his mid-riff. "Oh, don't mind me. A little delay won't bother me, believe me. In or out of my skin - same to me."

"Very well. So long as you don't complain about it later. Lord Adranodorus? I think he would be of more use skinned."

"That he will be in a few minutes."

"What I mean is skin left on."

"Yes… yes… I was only teasing. Honestly, Archimedes, for a wise old man you are awfully thick at times. So be it. Bring the prisoner for the tenderising ceremony."

"And the scum, your liege but one?" asked the guard, indicating the disgruntling crowd waving their tickets with timid indignation.

Vitruvian Boy

"Oh, very well," the mountainous man sighed. "Tell them they are invited to a new form of interactive reality entertainment - audience participation. Draw a ticket number from a helmet. No, not that one - unless you take the skull out first. Winner loses even the skin of his teeth."

"Do you think that's fair, my liege?"

"Oh, very well, give him a form to request an eventual refund on the ticket price afterwards."

Wondering what on earth a 'tenderising ceremony' might be, Sean was cut down and drag-kicked along a series of corridors to a hastily-called conference in a bathhouse. While the wealthy patriarchs were massaged and indulged variously, ministers of panic and sundry were giving their reports.

"We have attempted to block their passage by raising the Messina Strait toll, but our price regulation steering committee has been outsmarted by the Roman fleet sailing around the low-market side of Sicily. We hadn't anticipated such a cunning costs-saving manoeuvre."

"We are, after all, an island unto ourselves," commented an accountant and hobbyist philosopher.

Another minister of something really stupid said: "Our supplication team to the volcano island eruption deity group has not returned, and all we can do is hope for the worst, but we cannot rely on their help for a quick act of *force majeur ex-contractus.*"

"Enough!" Adranodorus used the throat of his masseur as a prop to lever his enormous bulk to a sitting position, and signalled for Archimedes and Shopliftitian to approach. We will proceed to the tenders. No doubt you are all aware of the contract default clause we have with Carthage - pillage and raise in case of failure to supply x death ray units by specified date: pillage in case of delay in supply exceeding 30 days, and simple raise in case of quality inadequacies. A standard clause. Gentlemen of the regular bored, and, sorry, regularly boarded ladies, there is not a moment to lose. I propose we release unprecedented funding from the public coffers - Zoippus and I as commissioning agents receive our usual 40%, of course - to the clever person for accelerated research into the death ray. We have endless backs of clay envelopes ready for the scratch design team and a hundred specially trained mirror polishers ready to move in."

"May I throw something in here?" Sean asked.

"*Another* death throe?" and the audience chuckled in synchronised sycophancy.

"Archimedes' death ray doesn't work."

"*We* know that - but our investment partners do not. That's all that interests me. The initial public offering will sky-rocket. So in that one true sense it does work."

"What I mean is the Romans will reach the harbour wharf, land and massacre everyone in the city, Archimedes included."

"Rubbish. Their business plan is an open secret. Everyone knows clever people are bundled back to Rome to help them on their secret weapons projects to use against the eastern 'axis of evil' states. To profit from their 'mutually insured destruction' scam."

"I can build a death ray that will work," insisted Sean.

"How?"

"All I ask is unlimited resources, manpower and time. Oh, and that enormous ruby of the king's."

"Don't cross the ruby con with me, young man! That ruby is the symbol of high office. You can have its equivalent value in money."

"But that's not the same at all... it won't work..."

"Don't *ever* underestimate the power of a wad of cash, young man. I take it you are haggling for even more venture capital?"

"Not really..."

"Then request denied. Guards...!"

"Ah, then yes, please, could I have a raise on my weekly venture capital?"

"Ah, that's better. Now I have the situation in focus. Granted, provided you agree to sign an all-indemnity agreement, containing a standard clause stating that all inventions, and profits deriving therefrom, made during the specified term of our agreement, will automatically revert to the ownership of the crown... or, ahem, its due representative. Choose. Death is the alternative."

"I guess so."

"Do you furthermore agree to take out sufficient insurance for the slaves, ex-works of course, and that damage caused to third parties, conflagrations and sinking of shipping, intentional or otherwise, is severally and collectively due to your own independent actions, and *in the event* the crown will deny all knowledge of this conversation or the existence of any exclusive agreement between the aforementioned and the postmentioned, so help me an oversight committee of gods? Choose. Death is the alternative."

"I guess so."

"So be it. You drive a hard bargain, young man. Fail and you will be bankrupted before your very eyes. We will tie you to your own share price and let you sink to the bottom of the harbour faster and more surely than any anchor."

Zoippus came forward with the contract the scribes had been hastily stylusing up for Sean to sign: "Don't take it personally - it's cruel and unfair, but then business has to be so, doesn't it?"

Adranodorus spoke to the collective: "I now declare the tender competition open. The specifications are as follows: the death ray must be capable of destroying up to twelve enemy vessels per hour, fry up to 240 enemy soldiers a minute, and extra merit will be awarded for a chic, modern design. A pocket version for killing mice and lighting cigars would also be an advantage. You could invent cigars while you are at it. And come in a range of colours to choose from. Suitable for catalogue sales to the Eastern states, preferably in kit form. Manuals in all ten universal languages.

"Go to it. And, oh Archimedes, try not to upset the ladies during your moments of revelation again. And keep your ray pointed to the poorer sections of town. I've just had the palace redecorated."

* * *

Unable to believe his luck, Sean found himself being escorted back to what he had to assume was Shopliftitian's dwelling. No sooner had he sat down in the shabby workshop which doubled as his residence, than did a group of five young people, two women and three men, come storming in.

"Hi," Sean said in the high spirits he was still buoying around on.

"Hi!" echoed some of them repeatedly and teasingly

back at him.

"For someone so close to being skinned, you must be feeling pretty full of yourself, Shopliftitian," one of them sneered menacingly.

"Who are you?"

"Or should I call you Sean?"

"Eh?!"

"Eh?!" the multi-mock did another round of the intruders.

"Oh, come on, who do you think you're fooling?" asked the tallest boy.

"Well, everybody. Except you, obviously," replied Sean at a loss.

"Just what do you think you hope to achieve by this impersonation of a perfectly respectable goldsmith?"

"He's a thief!" replied Sean.

"We're *all* thieves."

"You're just not as good at it as we are," said one of the girls, who was trying on some jewellery she had found somewhere on a side bench.

"What are you doing here?" asked a by now totally confused Sean.

"I'm *seaning* these," she replied sarcastically, pocketing some earrings. She came over to Sean and caressed his cheek with the backs of her fingers. "Feel how 'light' my fingers are? Poor, poor Shopliftitian. He would have been alright if Archimedes had not chosen this precise moment to reveal a great secret of mathematics to the world, wouldn't he?" She pouted demurely, then laughed at her own cleverness.

The boys picked up the mock. "Poor, poor Shopliftitian - had to pay the first price of progress."

"Who *are* you?" asked Sean.

Crossing the Ruby Con

"No. The question is: Who are *you?*" A boy pushed Sean into a chair, then slumped himself extra-boredly into a facing chair, and put his feet on the bench right next to Sean's head.

"Well, until today I was Sean Seulpierre - of the year 2010. Lugano, Switzerland. How do you do?"

"How do you do?" they mocked back with creative intonations of derision.

The light-fingered girl was suddenly puzzled. "Isn't Lugano in Italy?"

"They moved it."

"Moved a town?"

"Yeah. I know. I don't get it either." Sean felt himself teetering on the brink of some sort of confusion crater.

The other girl stepped up to Sean and extended her hand, picked up his, shook it, and put it back down again. "My name is Geni."

"Jenny?"

"That's right. We are TimeRiders."

"We ride the big time waves," the shortest of the boys boasted, as he jumped onto a workbench, put his arms out and swayed around like a surfer.

Geni continued reproachfully. "You have some explaining to do, Sean. Changing history is one of the big no-no's."

"The *biggest* no-no," said the tallest boy, using his height to tower over the seated Sean.

Sean felt the tone become more threatening. "But I had to save myself from being flayed alive!"

"They always have an excuse," said the surfing boy, who had surfed his way along the bench till he was standing directly behind Sean and now looked down on him.

"Nothing compared to what is going to happen to the fabric of time," the taller boy continued.

"Fabric of time?"

Geni was cross now with her friends. "Don't, Pau. Stinto, get down." Then to Sean: "He invented that. It is nothing at all like a 'fabric'."

"It helps Monos understand," said the tall boy, his lips taking on a cruel superior smirk, as if he were about to say 'sister of mine'.

"Monos?" Sean looked from one to the other.

"Mono-directionals. Like you. At least you were until you appeared here."

"Mono-directional - as in time?"

"Sure. What else?" The boys all seemed to think everything Sean said was highly mockworthy.

"Knock it off, guys," said Geni. "He's just confused. And lost, poor boy."

"Poor boy," mocked the boys again.

Sean was too fascinated to take umbrage, and even if he had he wouldn't have known where to take it. "You mean, you can travel in any time direction you want?"

The small boy was now showing off. "Of course. It's easy once you understand what time really is."

"So… do you have a time machine?"

"A machine!? Why would a 'machine' help us travel through time?"

"Then how do you do it?"

"I told you - by simply understanding the true nature of time."

"Tell him about the fossils, Pau," joint-boasted the surfing boy.

Geni now took charge. "That's enough! Sorry, we shouldn't have just burst in on you like this. Time for introductions." She indicated the tall boy: "This is Pau. And this is Stinto" - the surfer. "And little Elf." She brought the by now even more self-bejewelled girl over. "And this kleptomaniac is Amur."

Sean blushed when he saw how beautiful the girls were, especially Geni. The boys, too, had something wonderfully fine and noble about them, despite their school bully behaviours.

"Your brothers and sister?"

"In a way. We are TimeRiders."

"Nothing since you said 'hi' has made any sense at all," admitted Sean.

"What *do* you understand, Sean? Spherical maths? Non-dimensionality? The true maths?" sneered the boy called Pau.

"Um… a little bit of 'New Maths'? Why?"

"Tell him, Pau," chorused the two other boys.

Pau thus condescended. "*Everything* can be seen and understood in two ways, like the two sides of a coin…"

"Any flat geometric shape…" generalised Geni.

"… neither is ever more correct than the other. Follow me?" continued Pau. "No, I thought not. I'll let you in on a BIG secret… once you know how to describe a sphere inside a cylinder, you have the key to the true geometry of time, and with that the universe."

"Ah…," said Sean. "Now isn't that one of Archimedes' famous things - the volume of a sphere is two-thirds of the volume of a cylinder it sits neatly in?"

"But the amazing thing is that two-thirds is *also* the ratio of the surface areas," added Geni. "That makes it a magic ratio. Without magic ratios the universe would be cogless."

"Archimedes puts that ratio on his tombstone,

doesn't he? Just a minute!" Sean looked auto-puzzled. "How did I know that?! Come to think of it, how do I know how to build a laser?"

"Now you're getting it," said Pau. "Once you have got a handle on that, you might just start to understand that time, and therefore the universe, is not what you Monos think it is."

Sean was suddenly excited. "I feel like I can tap into some sort of… massive knowledge bank."

"It is the knowledge your future self gains. I doubt it's particularly massive in your case, but it's perfectly natural," inform-sneered Pau.

"It is not *perfectly natural* at all!" stammered Sean, trying to retain some sort of perspective, which was like trying to keep fine dry sand in a sieve while someone keeps knocking your arm.

"Well, of course it is," said Amur, taking a break from her quiet thieving. "When you time travel, you have to be able to see the truth about time, otherwise you are left with a monocosmic perspective - and that won't do at all, no not at all." She put on a necklace and admired herself in a polished bronze plate.

Now Stinto began doing some sort of imitation, putting on a mature, deep voice, like that of a tv presenter: "Time travel is all about geometry. Get that right and you can go anywhere. For example, the quickest way from Europe to China is through the core of the Earth - true?"

Elf put on a high, childish or cartoony voice to answer him: "Yes, but if we can't pass through the core, the quickest way is around the surface."

Stinto replied, still impersonating someone with deep, persuasive tones. "Wrong again, Mr Zeepo. If you can just detach and stay still, the Earth will rotate beneath you. You don't have to take the hard route of forcing yourself through the atmosphere."

"What a drag!" Pau broke into their routine, and the three boys collapsed, laughing at their own in-joke cleverness at Sean's expense.

Geni walked over angrily and punched Pau on the upper arm, clopped Stinto on the back of the head, and missed little Elf, who scampered just in time out of range. Then she came back and continued the explanation to Sean in kinder tones. "What we are saying is, if you don't restrict yourself, you can free your mind to all sorts of other possibilities."

"By never assuming anything is impossible?" said Sean.

Geni beamed at him like a pleased teacher. "That's right. Very good, Sean."

"Are you saying you don't 'travel' through time - but you let time *pass* you by? You stand still and just find yourself in another time?"

"Like surfing the big ones," and Stinto began his beachboy act again.

"But only the consciousness travels – you are occupying other people, just as I am occupying Shopliftitian?"

"Bright kid, this one." said Pau.

"Do you really mean that?" counter-hoped Sean.

"Cos' he doesn't. You're a dummo Mono, isn't he Pau?" laughed Elf.

"So what's he doing two thousand, two hundred and twenty-two years out of place?" asked Amur.

Sean was struggling with the concept still. "But how? Aren't we dragged along at the speed of time?"

Geni answered him. "Time has no 'speed'. It is not moving - we are. What you have to do is realise time is only a trick of the eye, an interpretation of the observer, not some sort of fixed framework hanging in the universe like your mother's curtains."

Pau said: "There is no 'wards' to move 'to'."

"No 'by' to tick away from," unhelped Stinto.

"There just is and isn't," mysterioused Amur.

"It sometimes helps to think of time as a river in the Spenmatt," concluded Geni.

Sean's face made a highly liberal '?'.

"Spenmatt is short for the cosmic background of 'space - energy - matter'. Follow me?"

"Not in the slightest."

"Think of the Spenmatt as the projector and screen for the film of time," said Geni. "Reality is what we think of as a fluid film, but is in truth a series of nearly identical frames giving only the illusion of fluid movement."

"Now, ask yourself what happens when the film projector jams," said Pau maliciously.

"See this?" Elf held an egg-sized piece of polished rock out to him before Pau could stop him.

Sean took it and gasped. "It's my rock egg!" He looked at it more closely. "Or one just like it."

Geni said: "It's a very special egg. Shake it."

Sean did so. To his surprise he could hear something splashing around inside it. His didn't remember his egg doing that.

"It's a piece of inverta-rock, and it contains a small amount of ancient, fossilised time. Just a couple of chronons, tiny fractions of time interval, but in super-condensed liquid form and enough to trigger a jump."

"Wow!!" Sean held the small rock tightly and

squeezed his eyes shut and imagined his home, Mami, Papi, Nonno and Shrodie. He opened his eyes and was disappointed to see he hadn't moved. The boys snickered cruelly.

"So how does it work?"

Amur answered. "Not like that. First, you have to make an omelette."

"Break it? Well, let's go…" Sean lifted his hand and prepared to smash the egg.

Pau seized his arm and prised the egg out of his grip, and gave it back to Elf. "No you don't! That is not for you. Only one jump per person per egg. Get your own."

"Oh. Where from?"

"Not telling."

"Please."

Geni sat in front of Sean and took his hands gently in hers. He liked her the best of all. "You see, Sean, your coming here is not right. As a Mono, you shouldn't be able to do this. And as a result you have upset the historical record."

Stinto added. "Before we let you go home, you have to put things back the way they were."

Pau said cruelly: "Archimedes is now discredited - thanks to you - and his theorems about maths will be lost, putting the world back centuries, if the priests have their way."

"If not forever," said Elf in a far-away kind of voice.

"They all now think he is an old git, thanks to you!" said Stinto.

Geni finished the group explanation. "That will have unknown consequences for the future. You have got to re-establish Archimedes in the eyes of the people here, so his discoveries will be safely imprinted in the historical record."

Sean sighed as he recalled his last image of Archimedes, shuffling sadly down the road, while a flock of children ran after him calling 'Dud-head nuddy!' and other taunts.

This, he decided correctly, was not going to be easy.

* * * *

ᐸΗΔΡᕕᕕᕓᕒ ϜΔᐯᕒ

Συτεκα Λτσαδε

Ω N his way to Archimedes' house, Sean noticed that someone had daubed over the name of his street, replacing it with a taunting 'Eureka Arcade'. Sean found Archimedes looking as anyone should when he knows he has just missed the last chariot to immortality by the narrowest of margins.

"I have come to apologise," he said to the old man. "I should not have humiliated you. I should have let them find me guilty and flay me alive."

"Quite right. There are principles of basic decency at stake here."

"Listen, Master Archimedes…"

"You can call me 'Archie'."

"Right. Ok… Listen… Archie, you are not a head of manure steam, as everyone is saying."

"And this is supposed to cheer me up?"

"Ok. Let's start again. You are, I promise you, destined to go down in history as one of the greatest mathematical geniuses of all time. You give the world the beginnings of the 'language of the gods'."

"Oh, do I? Quite frankly, I am thinking of retiring.

I find my style of calculating all too exhausting. And so do my staff." He indicated several assistants panting in a circuitous heap around a table covered in diagrams, clay tablets and measuring instruments of various types.

"Not another calculation, master," they begged.

"Why are they so tired?" asked Sean, amazed.

"I use the 'method of exhaustion' to find the lengths of lines that describe circles. It's part of a commercial line of mathematical solutions I market under the name 'shape-o-mat-tick'."

"Shape-o-matic?!"

"We put the 0-shape on a clay mat, then tick off the corners of shapes inside and outside it. It's like this: the client delivers the circle to be measured. Then two teams work on it. One outside, one inside. We start with a square touching the circle, then from that we make an eight-sided shape, all eight sides or corners touching the circle, but not crossing it. Then we halve each of these sides so we have sixteen, then thirty-two, and so on, gradually getting closer and closer to the shape of the circle, but never quite. Then, when we can't get the sides any smaller, and the clay mat has become quite a pudding, we measure them all."

"But why?"

"Well, for one thing, it is very pretty. But the point is that straight edges can be measured with straight rulers."

"That's what this country needs," said one of the measurers. "More straight rulers!"

"Why *two* teams?" queried Sean. "You could economise there."

"Not really. The more sides the shapes have, the closer the measure gets to the length of the circle's perimeter, but even with hundreds of sides it will never be exactly the same."

"So you are always wrong? What use is that?"

"Well, if you know beforehand that you do not have the means to know something for sure, it is not wise to have a single answer with unknown inaccuracy. That way, all you will ever know for sure is that you are wrong. Using my patent-pending method, we can put precise limits on what is unknown. In this case, we know that the sum of the side lengths of the shape inside the circle will always be too low, and the sum of the shape outside will always be too high. This way we can put precise limits on how wrong we are. I was hoping it might kickstart some new fashion in philosophy, but the accountants in the marketing department of Eureka Moment Industries sank the proposal on previous experience grounds, market surveys, etc. They tell me uncertainty is unlikely to ever sell as well as certainty. I just have to bend to their superior wisdom."

"If you want to know the circumference of a circle, why don't you just use pi?" asked Sean.

"Not hungry, thanks. Oh, 'pi'! Not known yet, you see. Damn nuisance. I was hoping to be the one to find it but this whole crown affair has completely unnerved me. Without pi, I'm afraid it's back to the old exhaustion treadmill for everyone."

Groans circumnavigated the next commission being laid like a cold pizza in front of the measuring team.

Sean stopped Archie and said. "Ok, I can do at least that for you. Got anything to write with?"

Archimedes took a large notebook of animal skin parchment from a shelf.

"Yerr…" yerred Sean, wrinkling his nose. "What's

that?"

"I'll have you know this is the finest abattoir stationery money can buy," huffed Archimedes, as he chipped the clay price tag off the back showily. "Try this imported quill. From over the Far Eastern Mountains," he said, handing Sean a fine white feather.

"You get your pens from China?!" Sean was staggered.

"Sure. Airmail delivery."

"In 212 BC?! That's not possible!" Sean saw his first stagger and raised him a second.

"Why not? The geese fly over. We pluck them on arrival." Archimedes sniffed one. "Go on, they're fresh."

"Ok. Now, Archie, the value of pi is three point one, four, one…"

"What do you mean by 'point' a number?" Archimedes pointed his index finger at the sequence as if he expected something would happen.

"Ah. Ok. You don't have decimals yet… but you have fractions! You can also describe pi as this sequence." Sean took the parchment and quill and wrote: "Pi over four equals one minus one-third plus one-fifth minus one-seventh plus one-ninth, etc., etc., etc., and yet again etc., till you look like those guys there, except perhaps slightly bluer in the face."

"Very pretty. That's easy enough, but what's it for?"

"It is pi - the ratio between the cross-section of a circle and its circumference."

Rather than jubilant, Archimedes looked entirely fallen in the way crests can only do. "But the sequence goes off the edge of the page. There is not enough flat parchment in all the known world to describe the simple ratio between a circle's aroundness and its across-ness?! That sounds distinctly 'unreal' to me. Both of our techniques can still only *approach* the true value. Can only be an approximation. This means the fundamental ratio of all celestial movement will always be a complete mystery to man?! Are we destined to be uncertain forever about the true nature of the universe? Destined never to speak to the gods?!"

"But, Archie, you teach the world how to handle this uncertainty. Your technique will be the inspiration of the celestial language – *you* are the creator of the language of the gods."

"You mean *spiki celestii* has been found?" asked one of the measurers, who had been dropping eaves throughout the conversation.

"Not yet," went on Sean. "But in two thousand years, when the enlightenment comes, thanks to Archie's teachings men will be able to divine great things about the movements of the universe, design machines and calculate all motion and relationships with extreme precision and ease. Without you, Archie, the future world would be a barren place of assumed knowledge that is always wrong."

"Tell me about it," murmured Archimedes, thinking of his arch-enemies the priests. "You mean I have not been wasting the last fifty years drawing stupid shapes around circles? It was really exhausting."

"Tell *us* about *that*," complained the outspoken measurer.

"Who is that?" asked Sean.

"John. We call him John the Measurer. He is also our chief scribe and photocopier."

"Photocopier!?"

"Sure. Makes photo, or visual, copies of my notes. It's slow work - he does it the old way - chiselling basalt, or deluxe porphyry slabs if you can get them, in three languages. He says hard copies last longer. I'll get him to make a copy of this notebook. And he has theatrical ambitions, this John the Measurer. He is leaving soon for the theatre festival in Rosetta, Egypt, to launch a comedy he has written about old men on the home front during the Second World War."

"You know about the Second World War?!" Sean gave in to the yearning for yet another stagger.

John replied as he chiselled the mandatory ISBN[*] onto the back of a large pink porphyry slab, ready to start the copy of Archie's notes: "Well, sure. Technically it should really be called the Second Known World War. In fact it hasn't finished yet - the season keeps getting extended. The Romans call them the Punic Wars, which is a pity because all the kids keep chiselling the 'n' to a 'b' on the promotion slabs. It's a classic plotline: army meets army, army defeats army, everybody left lives miserably ever after. This is the sequel to the first war and is currently doing a tour of the Mediterranean. It is due here in Syracuse any day now. Everybody who is anybody, and quite a few people who aren't anybody, is dying to be involved. You can't get frontline tickets. Standing or fleeing room only. Should be quite a hit. But I'll be missing it, since I have to sail for Rosetta, in Egypt."

"What about the stone copy of my notes? - you promised!" pouted Archimedes.

"That's ok. I'll finish it on the voyage," said John.

"Here," said Archimedes, handing him Sean's digi-

---

[*] In-Situ Basalt Number

tal watch. "You'll need this to finish the instruction manual."

"So the Second Known World War is why you have to make a death ray?" Sean asked Archimedes.

"Not really what I had in mind. I figured some special lighting effects might add something to John's show. I didn't realise my suggestion would be taken so life-to-death seriously by Adranodorus and his friends. Honestly, they get everything wrong. They thought my Archimedes Screw invention was a new fiscal instrument."

"Ok," said Sean. "Got your quill ready? We have got to re-establish your credibility with everybody. I'll be your image manager. How far have you got with the death ray?"

"Not meeting expectations. Even with hundreds of mirrors, they can't even raise enough heat to cook a Syracusan donkey burger. And, believe me, with an exhausted team to feed I have tried and tried."

"And you've had no success at all?"

"Oh, I wouldn't say that. See that moor at the end of the table?"

"Yes."

"He didn't use to be one…"

"I can see a few problems with this design. What if they attacked in the rain?"

"Yes. That would put quite a damper on the idea. We'll just have to ask them not to."

"My design is more waterproof, Archie. I am going to build you a death ray to be the mother of all death rays. It is called a laser. It will burn holes in the enemy ships so fast the sailors will be looking for a dock without the 'k'."

"Sounds good. What do you need?"

"A lot of volunteers…"

"They come by the shipload, called slaveboards."

"Ok… Five thousand should do it."

"A whole half a myriad? That'll be expensive."

"Slaves work for free, surely?"

"If only. They tell us slave supplies are low due to some poor warspoil harvests. But I suspect the international cartels have tweaked supply to keep the prices at an all-time high. We will have to get them on lease through one of those dodgy MagnaGraecia import agencies."

"I'll leave that to you," went on Sean. "I also need a large amount of poor conductor."

"No problem. Our orchestras have lots of them. Terrible timing. Our metronomes work on sundial principles, you see, but the new king's uncles prefer evening concerts now…"

"Archie, are you *sure* you are a genius? I mean a material that charges up by friction. You obviously don't have plastic - but glass should work just as well."

"Oh, we have lots of that. Made from sand. I once tried to count all the sand grains in the universe, you know?"

"Why?"

"Sundays can be really dull around here. Anyway, there is a factory bulk discount outlet right here in Syracuse. The glass-making district is called Silicon Alley. A sand tanker from the Sahara Desert is due any day."

"Ok. We also need five thousand woollen jumpers. So get all the grandmothers of the town to start knitting. I'll do the rest. Where can I find some copper wiring?"

Archimedes thought for a moment then said: "Try the lads at the Ye Olde Bronze Age metal merchants. They are a little old-fashioned, now that everybody is moving over to the new fad of iron, but they do a good job on order."

"But I need copper, not bronze."

"No problem. Just ask for bronze wires and say 'hold the tin'."

* * *

One day, Archimedes and Sean were surprised by a special visitor in the upstairs, dockfront workshop they were surprised to find they had leased from Eureka Moment Industries through a special current account payback scheme.

"So, Archimedes, have you and Shopliftitian come up with the goods?" It was the young king himself.

"Your majesty, this is indeed a great honour," and the two bowed to the floor and almost beyond, as Archimedes slipped on some oil.

"Is the death ray ready?" asked the teenager in a strangely unenthusiastic way.

"Er... I will let my apprentice answer," said Archimedes airily.

"Who... me?" surprised out Sean, but rallied to say, "Yes, of course, Archie... I mean Master. This way, please, your high and mighty majesty. As you can see from this window, on the dockfront we have a thousand giant glass combs, each the size of a horse, lined up and ready. On your order, five thousand slaves will start rubbing them like crazy with woollen jumpers, producing a magic energy known as electricity."

"Lick a turkey?" said the king. "Strange name."

"I told you it was a terrible name," whispered Archimedes to Sean. Then to the king: "Could I suggest we rename this new, powerful emanation 'Hieronymus's breath' in your honour, your majesty," ingratiated Archimedes.

"Or even 'The evil breath of Hieronymus' to instil fear in the hearts of our enemies?" suggested the king.

Sean went on commendably straight-faced. "All the combs are connected by copper wiring to a central point, to provide the energy to excite the crystal. Above this point is an array of Archimedes' mirrors, to focus the sun's rays to where they will be amplified a thousand times in the core of the device."

"Which is?"

"Your majesty's giant ruby," Sean pointed at the large red ruby hanging from its chain around the king's neck.

"And that is your 'lazy'?"

"Yes, your highly 'steemed majesty. All we need do is put your ruby in place, align the crosshairs on the aiming mirrors, and the weapon is ready."

The king did not seem as enthusiastic as one would expect of a king who has just heard that his kingdom was safe from certain invasion. The silence was broken eventually by Archimedes.

"May we have the ruby now, your majesty?" he suggested.

"That's what I came here to talk to you about," began the king slyly. "First tell me something. If the ruby were not in place… if… for some reason it were… say… stolen… the night before the Romans attacked… say… by someone the guards wouldn't dare stop or challenge, and would obey if told to turn their backs for a few moments, and... Anyway, if the ruby were not in place, would the lazy still work?"

Sean answered. "Er... no, your majesty. The ruby is the core of the device, and its absence would make everything else as pointless as Master Archimedes' jokes."

"Or as tasteless as an Archimedean pi," inappropriated the man in question.

"See what I mean, your majesty?"

"I do indeed."

The king stood gazing out at the harbour, now quiet before the storm, and began to talk, more to himself. "With this weapon, Syracuse would become the most powerful city on the Middle Earth Sea."

Suddenly, Sean was elevated to an all-time inkling high that his attempt to re-right history was going to do just that – rewrite history.

The king went on. "Uncle Adranodorus has been a good teacher. I like it that I am so young, yet I already know everything I need to know. I see things perfectly clearly. I see, for example, that Uncle Adranodorus wants to be king himself. You see, I am actually much cleverer than either of my uncles. I will surprise them by applying their principles better than even they can."

"In what way?" asked Archimedes, hooked by tenters.

"Oh... it is a surprise. A *big* surprise... for everybody. But really ingenious and all my very own idea. Or at least it was eventually." He absentmindedly fondled a parchment projecting slightly from the inside pocket of his diamond-studded regal robe. "You see, there *is* an alternative to fighting the Romans."

Archimedes said: "Your majesty, in our enlightened days politics is a very streamlined business. The reigning business model dictates that we have to fight someone. It's either Carthage or Rome. And your uncles prefer to side with Carthage because Hannibal has won many engagements this year in southern Italy."

The king shook his adolescent head. "Yes, and if we declare against Rome, Carthage has promised us help. Help… but I want more than 'help'."

"More than help from the most powerful nation in the world?"

"Yes. That is what my uncles want, what my people want. But not what *I* want! What *I* want is to be safe. Safe means, of course, rich. Above all, safe from my uncles. Which means I have to be richer than them, you see? I know that they plan to murder me. Have already tried - they very nearly succeeded two years ago – I know it was them."

Something dusty on the backshelf of Sean's memory flagged an alert that history had already been derailed, and slid down a gully somewhere, with maximum casualties.

The brat-king went on. "Everybody wants me dead. My uncles, the Carthaginians, my own people. The only person I am safe with is you, Archimedes, because you are too absorbed by your science to notice what's going on around you. You are the only person who says he doesn't know everything already. That means you are always waiting for more information before making decisions. Leaving your silly wise old head open to unknown possibilities. This is a luxury you may be able to afford, being so irrelevant. But a king, a *great* king as I am going to be, greater than my grandfather even, cannot afford to be seen to be uncertain. Where I don't have facts, I must invent them. That's what the priests do. They can say, and will always say, the stupidest things, but nobody will ever dare to criticise them. That is the test of true power. The power to say stupid things and not be challenged. I want such power. The power of fear. A great king must have the power to make people afraid of him."

"Are you not powerful now?"

"Not enough! I need to be rid of my enemies. And I know how to gain that power and be rid of them at one stroke."

"Your majesty!"

"Yes, Archimedes. You are powerless because you seek knowledge above all else - forever uncertain, poor old man. I, instead, am clear about what I need to know in advance. That is what my good friend Cespuglio says." Yet again, Hieronymus's hand touched the parchment roll in his pocket, still bearing its priority sealane, urgent delivery stamps.

"Yes, people tend to mistake the certainty born of ignorance for strength," agreed Archimedes.

The king continued. "Even if all my own people are my enemies, I have friends outside who love and admire me, who wish to see me a strong ruler. Others may call it being a puppet. But, strings pull in two directions. I see it as a joint venture, with very promising returns. I like the phrase 'disproportionate returns'… very republican. All I need do is cross the ruby con… one night soon… and all my troubles will be over, and the great reign of Hieronymus of the Rapturous Returns will start afresh under the protection of a powerful corporate logo… the eagle."

"But, sire, your people…?"

"Oh, no. My friends have explained it all to me. It is not betrayal to betray someone who has betrayed you first."

Even he realised he had said too much, and awkwardly changed the subject.

"And what is this?" He went over to the opposite window. "What is this machine? A catapult?"

"Yes, your majesty. It is a captured Roman onager I was just about to test," replied Archimedes.

Sean added a technical detail. "This is a really kick-ass machine, your highness."

"Fine, but surely it is not donkeys we want to kick? Give me a lesson, old man. This onager does what exactly?"

"Its name does indeed derive from the fact that it works on the principle of a wild ass. The frame is held firmly down, the shaft erected, then we screw the windlass in ever tightening cycles, till we are ready for the sudden release."

"Very good, if a little raunchy. Now what does it project exactly?"

"Projectiles."

"Ah, brilliant. What will you R&D chaps come up with next?" The king leant over the machine, his hand playing with the trigger pin absentmindedly. He tried the giant ruby in the sling pouch for size.

"I would recommend caution, my liege, it is loaded…"

"You seem to forget, old man, that I am omnipotent. My name, is it not, is Hiero…" The king hit the trigger impatiently to stress his words… "…ny…moooooo", the catapult twanged, and the carrier flew forward, taking the ruby, and by virtue of the neckchain, the brat-king with it, and out the window. This meant that the last half of his name was spread all over the town, as would be his royal person after a short, parabola described delay, while the king took his place in some corner of historical footnotes that will be forever Hieronymus.

"So endeth the lesson," said Archimedes.

Sean and Archimedes watched the first human flight philosophically from the workshop window, the king's diamond studded cloak billowing cometically behind him.

"Ruby in the sky with diamonds?" Sean suggested.

To change the subject to something even more morbid, Sean glanced out of the harbourside window.

"Archie, correct me if I am wrong, but those hundred heavily-armed battle triremes weren't there a few minutes ago, were they?"

"Oh dear. The show is about to start and the ruby is lying somewhere in diagonal alley."

"We have to find it!"

"It's too late. The Romans are landing." Suddenly whistling could be heard and explosions as oil-filled projectiles exploded against the dockside buildings.

"Quick! We have to get out of here, Archie!"

* * *

At Archimedes' house, they found the five TimeRiders waiting for them.

"Sean!" said Pau unsympathetically. "I'm happy to say this is where we say goodbye."

"Bye bye," mocked the other boys.

Four of the TimeRiders were sitting crosslegged in a circle, each with their own egg in front of them, but Geni ran to Sean and hugged him.

"Come on, Geni," called Pau, not without jealousy. "You insisted we see the Mono before we leave. You've seen him, so let's go!"

Geni started to cry. "We can't just leave him! The Romans will be here any minute! We don't know what they'll do to him - and poor Archimedes!"

Pau came over and pulled Geni away from Sean. "We can't allow history to be changed, so it is best if he is eliminated along with all the evidence of his being here." The noise of battle and panic was getting louder. Pau pushed Geni down into her place in the circle sitting on the floor. "He's not one of us."

"I am sorry, Sean. So very sorry," said Geni, her face streaming with tears.

Sean stepped forward with "Geni! Don't leave me!", but Pau had taken her limp, unwilling hand, inserted her egg in it, then brought it down with force in front of her, at the same time breaking his own from his other hand in a similar fashion, while the others smashed theirs.

From within each of the time fossils came a kind of swirl - hard to describe as a liquid, or a gas, more a sort of galaxy in miniature, if you can imagine that - spinning ever broader and denser, mixing into one big omelette, till it enveloped all five of the TimeRiders and obscured them from sight.

The last Sean saw of Geni was her face mouthing 'so sorry, so very sorry…', then she was gone.

When I say she was gone, I obviously don't mean physically vanished. Let's be clear - this is a serious story. But Geni was no longer there. In her place was a young woman who looked very much like Geni, just somehow not as beautiful or corporeally so perfectly steamy-lined, who got up and looked about her in surprise and wonder. She totally ignored Sean while she did a few panicky displaced person laps of the room, before she found the door and ran out of the house, followed or preceded by the other people left behind by the emulsified consciousnesses of the TimeRiders.

All, that is, except one. Stinto was still there. He had his arms out, and was pretended to be surfing with his eyes closed. When he opened them he called out "What a ride!", but then his face fell an octave, as he obviously had not expected to be still sitting crosslegged on Archimedes' floor.

"What the...!" Then, seeing the others had left him behind, Stinto panicked demonstrably by hunting through the scattered broken time shells, trying desperately to salvage some time liquid. But it had all evaporated.

Sean stared at him: "Stinto, why are you still here?"

"I don't know... It must have been a bad egg."

"Are you trapped here?"

Stinto tried to calm down enough to think. "No. All I need is another egg." Then he clicked his fingers in sudden realisation of something, stood up and ran out of the house.

Sean turned to Archimedes. "I am so sorry, master, but..." He indicated the way Stinto had fled.

"Yes, Sean, go... go my son. Go ... it is your destiny. Say hello to the future for me. Ask them to think of me sometimes and to remember me kindly."

"That they will, I promise you."

"And you."

"Yes, I will too. I will miss you terribly." With tears beginning to rivulet down his face, Sean hugged Archimedes, then he turned and sped after Stinto as if his life depended on it.

Which, as you will soon see, it did.

Stinto had already reached the top of Eureka Arcade, and would have disappeared from sight by the time Sean had come out of the house, if he hadn't suddenly jumped and started running back down the street towards Sean.

"You have come back for me?!" called Sean happily to him.

"Like .. unlikely!" screamed Stinto as he raced past him.

Then Sean saw the reason for the direction change. And it was a good one. A group of viciously-armed and no-questions-ever-asked Romans had appeared in the street and were giving chase, ignoring everything and everyone except them.

Sean caught up to Stinto just as he dived into a narrow side ally, then another, over some market stalls, and ran in the counter direction to a mass of sustainably panicked locals fleeing away from the harbour.

"Where are you going, Stinto?! The Romans are that way!" heaved Sean, wishing Shopliftitian had kept his body in better shape.

"I have to reach the Oracle."

"Strange time to ask for a reading of the future - I would have thought ours was rather obvious..."

"Oh, shut up... You're not invited. Pau said you have to stay here."

"But it's dangerous."

"Tell me about it."

"And chronologically inept."

"Why is that?" gasped the just as unfit body Stinto was occupying without permission.

Sean reasoned with him. "Look, if I belong in the future - and you to all time - we have to live to be in the future - so how can we die here? Isn't that a time paradox?"

"What?! What has all this to do with a pair of socks?"

"No - pa-ra-dox. As in kill your own grandfather and not be born so you can't travel back in time to kill your grandfather in the first, or rather, second place..."

Stinto stopped suddenly. People were still screaming and rushing past them. Projectiles of flaming oil were exploding around them and flying overhead. "You're right. I can't die here!" A spear suddenly arced towards them from out of no-particular-where.

"Stinto!" screamed Sean a warning.

"It's ok, Sean. I can't ..." The spear thudded into Stinto's body... "die here..." and he paradoxed himself on the spot.

The next thing he knew, Sean was being jumped on by a burlesque of Roman soldiers.

The centurion shook him: "Got you!"

"Get your filthy hands off me, you murderous monster!"

"Get your filthy hands off me, you murderous monster,... sir!" corrected the centurion in charge. "There is never an excuse for bad-manners, is there men?"

"No, never," the men responded with strangely electronic-sounding unison.

Then the centurion did the most unexpected thing. He took a helmet out of a bag he was carrying and connected it by some wires to the end of the spear projecting from Stinto's inert body. His oversized hands fiddled awkwardly for a while till he got the adaptors right, then the assembly of helmet, spear and Stinto seemed to be possessed by some mysterious, special effects energy of a glowy, weird-whistling kind. When it had faded the body still looked like Stinto, but much less handsome and perfect somehow.

The centurion unclipped the helmet and signalled to the guards behind Sean to do something.

* * * *

CHAPTER V

FLASH MEMORIES

SEAN woke up wet. And it had nothing to do with his dreams.

A Roman soldier was walking away with a bucket swinging at his side. Another was slapping his face not entirely unbrutally, while yet others were pulling him into a right up position on a chair in what turned out to be an interrogation tent, one, field, canvas, brutal thug, for the use of.

Suddenly the soldiers were stamping about and saluting, barking instructions and replying the obvious, doing their bit to shape the future of military idiot-syncracy. This was because the sinister bad guy had entered, slamming the tent flap as nastily as he could to cover all expectations.

It was Cespuglio the Younger.

And he had chosen for this occasion a battle skirt from the serious butcher-about-the-town range, with just enough blood spatters to suggest, without erring to ostentatious.

He pulled down a soldier and sat on him opposite Sean.

"So, if it isn't our old friend, Shopliftitian. Last time I saw you, you were about to invent skinny-dripping."

He looked up at the centurion. "Did you get it?"

"Yes, my lord." The centurion handed him the helmet. There was something definitely mechanical about his voice.

"Is it charged?"

"Yes, my lord."

Cespuglio put the helmet on, then hunted for and found a switch somewhere at its back. His body went suddenly rigid as the parental-guidance only glow Sean had seen pass out of Stinto through the spear reappeared and took up residence in and around Cespuglio's face. While this was going on, Cespuglio changed somehow - he seemed much less repugnant in features. Then, after all this had stabilised, his features faded back to baseline hideous, and he smiled and spoke.

"Well, well, well. How very interesting! Sean Seulpierre are we, of Lugano, Switzerland? Moved from Italy? What does that mean? Are you a secessionist, Sean? You don't like the Roman Republic? That's a capital offence." He took off the helmet and placed it over Sean's head.

Suddenly, Sean had a vision of all time. This is a bit like turning the light on early in the morning, and for a while all you can do is blink and wish it were Sunday.

Cespuglio was saying from somewhere outside the blur. "Tell me, Sean Seulpierre, can you see it? The watch? Where is it?"

The voice of Cespuglio was muffled by the roar of infinite time and space Sean thought he was sailing through. He had trouble distinguishing the words.

"What watch?" He answered loudly, like someone

wearing headphones.

"What watch? The watch we want is where?"

"Eh?! Did you say 'What you won't swear?' "

"No! The watch which is that we want - where?!"

"The witch's hat you won't wear?"

"Watch is where?!"

"Watches wear... what? Witch's hat?"

"Hat?! Watch?! Which is it?"

Sean thought this was uncalled for, so said so. "No need to swear."

"What do you see?"

"What is all this about a wearing a witch's hat?"

"What hat? Who wore a witch's hat?"

"Eh?! You *swore* and the witch ...?"

"Watch it."

"I agree."

"Enough!"

Cespuglio tore the helmet off Sean and stared at it at arm's length. "Must be on the blink."

"What *is* that?" asked Sean, shaking his head and blinking stupidly from the shock. Cespuglio looked at Sean strangely.

"So, why, do you think, are you still here?"

"Sorry to disappoint. What is that thing?"

"Oh come now. Are you telling me you've never seen a Shroud trap? A time traveller like you?"

"Shroud? Is that what you call the TimeRiders?"

"More like time hiders. Mutants, Sean. Criminals who upset the time lines. My... er...," he looked at the helmeted Roman soldiers around them, "clients... wish to stop them."

"Did you have to kill Stinto?"

"No. *Un*fortunately, you *can't* kill someone who is not alive in the sense you and I understand. But we can neutralise them."

"Does that mean capture them? With that?"

Cespuglio paradiddled the helmet with his fingers and smiled. "And with this," he put the helmet back on himself, "We can see the universe the way *they* see it. Don't you think it is interesting? *Very* interesting indeed?"

"Stinto? Stinto, can you hear me?" called Sean to the helmet, feeling more than a little foolish.

Cespuglio laughed cruelly. "Oh, don't bother. The Shrouds are, as I told you, not alive. They just think they are. How stupid can you get!"

Again, Cespuglio's face contorted from his serial ugly to something far more in the designer line. His voice was different somehow too. "Sean! Sean!" said the voice. "You have got to warn the others. Warn Geni… the Invertabrakes are here!"

Then, just as wrenchingly, Cespuglio made an enormous face-pulling effort and took control of his ensemble wits. "Enough! Down boy! Down!" He relaxed suddenly. "Ah, that's better. Not really what I had in mind. Ha!" He looked at his audience of soldiers and Sean, and kicked the one he was sitting on. "Get that?! Not really what I had in mind?!" And he laughed to himself at his joke. "Nah… you had to be there…" He then touched his helmeted temples and spoke to his inner young adult. "You behave yourself and everything will be fine. We'll have your friends in there with you soon enough."

"You leave my friends alone!" shouted Sean.

Cespuglio made a sign to the guards behind Sean, the same sign as the centurion had made in the street.

'Oh, no, not again…' Sean had time to almost think.

* * *

He awoke this time in a heftily mid-antiquity decor temple, large and low-budget gloomy, full of suspicious vapours, auditioning priestesses, and animals from various cost categories waiting patiently for their cue to sacrifice their all for the slake of the show.

Cespuglio was haggling the price of something with the famed Oracle. There was stoic refusal body language in play on the oracline side, till Cespuglio made his final offer of immediate indiscriminate slaughter of all present, and this seemed to swing the deal. While this was going on, a row of soldiers was concaved behind Sean's prone form, making him the main attraction of the little spectacle unfolding, although his actual consciousness did not seem to be particularly requisite.

Then he was being encouraged forward pointedly by spears and swords and a couple of special purpose unmentionables, till be found himself in the 'magic circle' - well, not circle exactly - more sort of egg-shaped. But, then again, 'magic egg shape' lacks a certain something, doesn't it?

And there it was: an enormous time egg. In the hands of the Oracle.

"This boy has no power," proclaimed the Oracle, showing a bit of varicosed leg as part of the show, while the priestesses attempted a hastily-choreographed ballet routine. "The Holy Blood calls to him. He is drawn to the ticky-tocky…"

"Send him to it. You men go with him. Kill him

when you have the watch," ordered Cespuglio to the troop of ten soldiers, who as one came forward and ranked around Sean in both senses. "I will take the long way round," concluded Cespuglio.

The Oracle incantated something in ancient sacred gibberish, then, with a last reluctant sigh at losing her chief crowd puller, she threw the egg at Sean's feet. It cracked, and the outrush of liquid time enveloped him and the troop of Roman soldiers around him in a swirl of you really should have gone before you went.

* * *

Waking up for the third time in the same chapter, Sean knew from hardly won experience to look first for the things that didn't make sense. And in this regard he struck it rich. The first discovery was that he was breathing. Why this should be classed as strange may not be immediately apparent to the reader, nor was it to Sean, until the second discovery retrospectively adjusted the first to pole position in the category. This was that he was under water. And not just 'under water' as we immediately think of it - so much of the stuff in every direction that water had become a three-dimensional atmosphere that went far far up to a shimmery, airy stratosphere.

He was breathing. He was underwater. Some joint delegation from both sides of his brain divide was counselling him that the two somehow didn't, or shouldn't, fit, and that trying one in the other would eventually, or even quite very immediately, lead to the lumbering giant of greater reality to come stomp-thumping along, with his ever faithful chihuahua of lingering unpleasantness yelping at his heels.

Yes, the world was definitely inverted - no less so than if you went out one morning and saw fishy, marine type creatures, calling themselves terranauts, moving around on dry land with water snorkels, tanks or long tubes reaching back into the sea or lakes, or a type of inside-out submarine, full of water, so they could still breathe while they explored the heights of the inhospitable dry world.

He moved his cold hands and arms and found he had something on his chest as well as in front of his face. And further bloated finger feeling revealed this to be a mask of glass and leather, with a tube leading up from it. When he looked around, he found he was stand-bobbing on the deck of a presumed given current location sunken ship. Another rather curious thing Sean noticed was that on and around the wooden ship were a number of last convulsion quality Roman soldiers, being pulled down to their deaths by their exaggerated, weight-wise, armour.

It seemed to him that the Romans had the right idea, so he acquiesced to the wishes of the majority, and joined the panic. Soon his struggling form was being pulled out of the water, and the world's very first diving rig pulled off his face and chest, to find himself happily enough coughing, gasping, and blinking into a welcome alternative cocktail of fresh air and sunlight. Voices were rebuking and soothing him simultaneously.

"Did you find anything?" an old man asked keenly in a whisper by his ear.

"Find what?" Sean spluttered back, and the accompanying gesture revealed that his right hand was involuntarily gripping something.

"Ah, bravo!" the old man seized the object and quickly stowed it somewhere in his robe.

The man instructed the small crew of the boat they were on to hoist sail and head back to the shore. As this was performed, Sean managed to calm down enough to register a few things. First, he seemed to be in the body of a boy of about his own twelve years. Secondly, the old man was not that old - his greying beard made him look more venerable than the just shy of fifty he turned out to be. The other men around them referred to him as 'Maestro' - master, or teacher. Sometimes they referred to him indirectly as 'il Maestro', which Sean thought strange because the man seemed to be in the best of health.

By the time the boat docked, they were surrounded by gondolas, gracefully scurrying here and there like leaves jostling for a parking space in a stormdrain.

He followed in the train of the Maestro and his assistants, alongside narrow canals, over footbridges, and across a pedestrian and stall crowded piazza, up to a room with a view of a Venetian canal which I shall leave to you to dollop atmosphere onto the story with.

Soon Sean was sort of dry, less underfed and preliminarily rested. When he rejoined him, the Maestro was bent over a worktable. All around him were drawings, paintings and wooden models of all sorts of things.

The Maestro was humming as he worked, and muttered "Yo-ho-ho, so much to learn, so much to do."

Sean ran forward. "Nonno?!"

The man laughed and turned his bearded face to him. "Not that I know of. You nearly drowned, young man, to obtain this…" He was cleaning something with a cloth.

Sean wiped away a tear he found skiing down the side of his nose. "What is it?"

"Ah… What indeed? It has had a long sleep under the sea. But, unless I miss my guess, this little object has seen more of this world than any human being… except perhaps the Polos themselves. Look."

The old man opened the cloth. What was there surprised Sean no end in sight.

"My watch!"

"Your what?"

"I mean… my catch."

"No. You definitely said 'my watch'."

"Sorry. It's just that… Sorry, what is your name?"

"An impertinent boy, you are."

"I really can't remember anything."

"Oh dear. Perhaps old Leonardo has a remedy left in his travel chests. Perhaps a leech or two are still fresh. To adjust the humours, they tell me, although I find using them to be far from a laughing matter." He called over his shoulder as he rummaged through his trunk. "Most curious, because although it has neither the size nor shape of a clock, you refer to it as one."

Sean remembered that in Italian clock and watch were the same word: orologio.

He read the name on the travel chest the old man was hunting through. "Sir, you are Leonardo… Leonardo what?"

"Just Leonardo. Less to remember."

"Not 'da Vinci'?"

"Yes. That is where I am from."

"What year is it?"

Vitruvian Boy

"Oh, now, surely you know it is the year of the Grand Jubilee? 1500 anno domini - the 1,500th anniversary of the invention of dominoes. And all the finest brains of Europe have come to Italy to join in the Treenailing Festival. All the finest brains, but also quite a few not so fine ones - like the entire French army. That is why I am here, in Venice. I had a really cushy post at the court of Ludovico Sforza, Duke of Milan. But then the French came - destroyed my giant horse model - used it as target practice. Darn shame I didn't get around to doing it in bronze, but I think terracotta has a lovely, well… earthy look to it - took me ages to get the nostrils right. Know anything about equine nostrils, yourself? … Pity. Twelve years of hard work down the proverbial canalisation."

"How did you know the watch was on the sunken ship?" asked Sean.

"I didn't. I was trying out my new underwater anti-drowning apparatus on you. I didn't know if it would work."

"Thanks a bundle."

"You're welcome 'a bundle'. How curiously you speak. It just happened to be where Marco Polo's ship sank. Extraordinary coincidence…"

"I am beginning to believe nothing happens by coincidence."

"You were doing fine - by which I mean you hadn't drowned yet - not like the others…"

"The others?"

"Prototypes. Then you suddenly panicked and swam to the surface without inflating the bladder as I had instructed you."

"I might have drowned."

"Yes. That would have been inconvenient. I am fresh out of volunteers. I don't really have enough ready cash to buy any at the war seizures and disposals centre. Bit hard up these days, you see. All sorts of commissions behind schedule. Still, can't be helped, things to do… things to learn… yo ho ho…"

"What was my watch doing on Marco Polo's ship?"

"In 1295, on his return from China, entering the Lagoon, his ship sank under mysterious circumstances. Probably hit a trade barrier. Chinese imports were looked on with suspicion back then. Many suspect spies from Genoa, jealous of the new technology and trading opportunities the opening up of the East would bring Venice, or fearful of textiles market dumping, or aggressive takeovers like the stockpiling system they brought in their wake."

"Stockpiling?"

"More commonly known as the Mongol hordes. According to his book, when his uncle told Marco about having seen an armclock in China inscribed SANG Re.al, he became enflamed with the desire to find it. His uncle had terrible map-making skills, for a traveller, and had forgotten where he had seen the watch. As a result, what should have been a quick trip East turned into a 25-year marathon for Marco Polo, his father and uncle. They combed every part of China and all the Far East for it. And when they did find it, and brought it back to Europe after 15 centuries of exile, it ended up lying in fifteen fathoms of water not far from Venice for two hundred and five years."

"Till this morning," said Sean. "But if the watch is so important, why didn't Marco Polo salvage the ship for it?"

"Tried to, but just as he was about to, Genoa sent its navy and sank all the rest of the Venetian fleet, and Marco was captured and thrown into prison. There he dictated a book, but the ghost writer who helped him was one of the world's first and worst pulp fiction writers, who added some twists that stretched Marco's credibility rating beyond redemption. Anyway, by the time he got back to Venice, he was so discredited nobody would rent him any craft, thinking he would sail off to one of his imaginary islands in it, and so he never got back to the shipwreck. In any case, due to the war, there were so many wrecks, it would have been impossible to find the right one - I am curious to know how *you* managed it."

"The watch drew me to it."

At this juncture, Leonardo could have said a number of things, not all complimentary. He opted instead for a neutral "Why?".

"Because it belongs to me."

"The Holy Grail belongs to *you*?"

"Why do you call it the 'Holy Grail'?"

"Well, how do you explain these markings on its back? See there? SANG Re.al. Sang means 'blood', and Real obviously means 'Royal'. The legend is usually marketed under the trademark of Santo Graal. Men have been searching for this ancient relic for over a thousand years."

"Why?"

"It is reputed to contain *spiki celestii*, the 'Language of the Gods'."

"I see. Shall I show you how it works?" Sean took the watch and made sure the photocell was clean. Then he laid it in the sunlight.

"It is definitely my watch. But if it has been under water for two centuries, and for that matter bandied around Asia for more than a millennium, how could it be in such good condition?"

"Shall we make a list of the perplexities of this moment for cataloguing, or just take them as they come?" remarked Leonardo.

Suddenly, the watch sprang to life, its little mouse figurine ticking joyfully away electronically, as if it were glad to see Sean. Sean pushed a button and showed Leonardo the planetarium mode, with the sun at the centre and the planets rotating around it.

"Most interesting. I must show this to that young Polish astronomer, Kopernik, who is passing through Venice on his way to Rome for the Treenailing Festival. I am sure he will find this interesting."

"Copernicus? The Polish genius who gives the West the Heliocentric system of the solar system – putting the sun at the centre of orbiting planets?"

"Really? Well, it seems, young man... Er, did anyone ever get around to giving you a name?"

"Sean. Sean Seulpierre."

"Well, young Sean, it seems destiny is somehow in orbit around this watch... and you. Tell me, where are you from?"

"It is not really a question of where, but when. I come from the future. The year 2010."

Leonardo may or may not have batted an eyelid, as either would have been impossible to detect under his bushy eyebrows. "If you are from the future, why doth this armclock arise from the deep past?"

And so Sean explained the whole story, or at least

the parts he felt he had some handle on, which didn't take long.

When he had finished, Leonardo nodded and said, "Do you think there is any point my saying 'interesting' - or shall we just take that as read?"

Then he stood with sudden, lively decision. "I think, young Sean, we need to undertake a journey. We must return to your home."

"I am going home?" cried Sean in delight, tears filling his eyes wish-washily.

"First, I must show this watch to Copernicus. Then we leave."

* * *

To slip by the French occupying army, Leonardo and Sean drove their small cart by a route which skirted the southern edge of the Alps that stood over the plain of Lombardy as ominously as an impending tax audit.

Throughout the journey, Leonardo asked question after question of Sean concerning the world he came from, what vehicles there were, whether machines fought war for humans, how much medicine had changed, the price of leeches, and some useful tips about avoiding queues to airports on holiday weekends.

Leonardo insisted on writing everything down, beautifully illustrated, in his famous mirror handwriting, right to left. This required them to stop frequently, and involved a lot of mirror polishing, so the journey, which Sean had once done with his father in three hours on the A4 horseless carriageway, turned into a week - but the most enjoyable week of Sean's life. Or at least coming close to rivalling the week he had spent alone with

Nonno touring Europe's best science museums. So well did Sean feel, he actually called Leonardo 'Nonno' again accidentally.

When this week had finally exhausted the road's length, but not Leonardo's curiosity, they arrived at Lugano, and Sean's heart began to beat on its own agenda. Lugano incoronates a bay on the north coast of a long lake which is so concertinaed around the bases of vesuvian mountains, that it takes on the shape of a skinny, prancing squirrel. This lake is in turn bookended to the east and west by two even larger lakes. One of these bends into a finger reaching for the nostrils of the mountain passes to the north, while the other, y-shaped, lies spilling its contents in rivulets, like an overturned wine glass, onto the tablecloth plain pulled starch taut towards the southern horizon.

"We are but half a day's ride from Milan, where I lived and worked for seventeen years. Here in Italy seventeen is considered unlucky, which I guess is the case."

"Why do you say that, Maestro? Milan is where you painted the Last Supper and did many other of your most famous works."

"Nice of you to say so, Sean. I had given up hope that any of them had survived. You see, we are now in the very north of the Duchy of Milan, which has been occupied by the French since last year. They could do this because the current pope, Alexander Edition Six, known around the red candle districts as Rodrigo the Runting Rat, sent one of his litter, Cesare Borgia, who is just as nasty a piece of work as his father, to help them. For his birthday, Cesare murdered his brother, and to purge this sin, his Holy Father made him Captain

General of his forces for land acquisition, theft, torture and general mayhem. He runs an online business as a confession auditor."

"Online?!"

"Yes. They string you up before auditing your confession portfolio."

"Are we safe here?"

"Well, in this modern age of rapid communications, it is difficult to say, but I don't see any frogs strung up for sale, so I don't think the French have bothered to come up here yet. We should be safe - at least for a while. I have done nothing to offend the French, but they seem to have taken a special interest in me. Can't imagine why. I hope it isn't to have all their passport miniatures redone. It would be best to avoid them."

They passed through the town of Lugano - very little of which Sean recognised. Even the shape of the lakeshore was yet to be straightened enough for traffic to race by and be oblivious to, so its banks lay adorned with the living evidence of fishermen, their boats croqueted with their distinctive wire-hoop awnings, and nets festooned on stakes to dry. If it weren't for the easily identifiable mountains around the lake basin, and perhaps one or two of Lugano's oldest buildings, now impossibly fresh and new, Sean wouldn't have known where he was.

Leonardo turned the horse's head away from the lake towards the line of mountains that backdropped the narrow wedge-shaped valley Lugano would take half a millennium to fill. But Sean knew that when it did, it would do so with an undignified titanic rush of concrete - powdered stone crashing up and over integral stone, splintering and combusting the wood between to lesser molecules. And these would be condemned to roam the earth for centuries to come with zombie-like vengeance in their nanoscopic eyes, to join all the other chemically displaced and homeless in inseminating the climatic havoc which distinguished his time. He shuddered at the memory, but didn't let it prevent it ruining his enjoyment of this wondrous moment.

As if he had guessed what was troubling Sean, and to underline the dramatic changes that were to come, Leonardo said: "I have a client from Florence who has a winter sports home here." For Sean, Lugano had long ceased to be a skiing centre, as the glaciers retreated and snowfalls became stuff of legend.

"Perhaps he is in," added Leonardo.

Sean's pulse quickened as they moved towards the north of the little town - and by easy triangulation to the peaks and distance from the lake, Sean realised they would soon be more or less where his home would be in five hundred years. And as they turned into a strip of flattened terrain, which, if the seasons so consented, served as a road, he saw it - the haunted house! Looking regal and aloof, out on its own amongst its feudal fields on the primordial periphery of the town that had missed the launch ceremony of the Renaissance by a margin of half a century.

"Why are you bringing me to this house, Maestro Leonardo?" asked Sean, as pleased as he was bewildered.

"Because this villa is the holiday home of my client, Francesco del Giocondo, and his wife, ma donna Lisa. My lady Lisa is very charming, and beautiful. If we are lucky, they will be here. I have also invited a friend of mine - a mathematician called Luca Pacioli. It should be an entertaining couple of months here."

"Couple of months!" Sean was beyond happiness. He was home, with Leonardo, to whom he was growing as attached as he was to Nonno, which made the thought of the 500 years that separated them a little more bearable.

They lucked in, although the Giocondo couple were not in at the moment - out for the day trying out Leonardo's idea of sliding down mountains in boots nailed to wooden slats. They had left a note for the milkherd: 'Half an udder today, please, but hold the contaminated fermented milk'. This was 'yoghurt', explained Leonardo. A local brand, made on the basis of one of his experiments - reputed to have kick-started a plague or two here and there.

When they did arrive, Lisa and Francesco exchanged salutaries with Leonardo, but reacted with mixed pleasure and surprise on seeing Sean.

The young and handsome Francesco scolded Leonardo: "This idea of sliding down a mountain on wooden slats leaves a deficit of desire, Leo."

"Perhaps I forgot to emphasise you should do it in winter - when there is snow?"

"Ah," coughed Francesco, embarrassed.

Lisa smiled wickedly at her husband's foolishness.

Leonardo gasped. "Oh, I have *so* got to dash off a snap-portrait of that smile, M'donna Lisa!"

And in so doing, Leonardo had secured for them an invitation to stay while il maestro painted the portrait of 'La Gioconda' - a nickname Sean thought up, which translates roughly as 'the teaser'.

They set up the improvised painting studio on the balcony of the haunted house, to make use of the splendid backdrop of lake and mountains.

While Leonardo was having a leechjuice break from painting, Lisa called Sean over and whispered:

"Sean... it's me, Geni."

* * * *

Chapter Six

Model Friends

"GENI!" Sean leapt to hug her.

"Hey!" shouted Francesco. "Keep your dirty Venetian paws off-a my-a wife!"

Sean stopped dead. But when Geni winked at him, he turned and called "Pau!", and they re-unioned too, albeit several notches further down on the enthusiasm scale.

"But… how long have you been here?!" stammered Sean.

"We came to meet Leonardo on our way through the timeline, as we always do," said Geni. "We didn't expect to see *you*. What a wonderful surprise! I am so happy you got away."

"Without scraping through, so to speak," added Pau, relishing the memory of Sean on the flaying rack. "Leonardo was late this time…," he said, looking at Sean suspiciously.

"And where are the others?" asked Sean.

Pau explained in his show-offish manner. "Oh, Amur stayed back in 1485 to pose as Venus for Botticelli… her *clam* to fame, you could say. Gorgeous!" He said this obviously to make Geni jealous. "We're models. Being so perfect 'n'all. Not like mere monos." He looked at Sean with acquired distaste.

"You're *models*?!" exclaimed Sean.

"That's why we are here, idiot. Geni wants to be the Mona Lisa *again*. Little egotist."

Geni pouted back: "Don't you talk, Pau - you're scheduled to be Mick the Angel's *Davide* soon! Great buttocks!" she scandalised.

"And Elf?" Sean asked, having done the sums requisite.

Pau pointed to a small pile of time egg shells on the balcony they were on. "Elf got bored waiting for Leo, so went on ahead to 1508, Rome, to pose for y*ou know who* as Adam on the ceiling of the Sistine Chapel."

"Great Pects!" clucked Geni.

"Who are these 'Mick the Angel' and *'you know who'*?" asked Sean.

Geni answered: "The same. Never say the M word in front of Leo - he gets incredibly jealous of..." she mouthed the name 'Michelangelo'.

"These are things a termite larva like you would know nothing about," snubbed Pau.

Sean stood up to him. "Oh, really? So, is that all TimeRiders do? Just ponce around through time and take all the best modelling jobs?"

"We are more than just queue jumpers. Our job is…"

"Yes…?"

"To inspire," finished Pau with crushing superiority.

This hadn't sounded as finalistic as Pau had intended. After the silence had hung uncomfortably for a while, Sean turned to Geni and said: "Could I be one, too?"

"Sure," answered Pau, thumbing an imaginary catalogue. "There's an opening in 1893 for Edvard Munch's *Skrik* - the Scream."

"Don't tease him so, Pau. Poor Sean."

"*Poor Sean,*" Pau tried to mock, but stopped abruptly. "I miss him, Geni, where *is* Stinto?"

"Sean, we can't find Stinto," added Geni with a worried frown that washed away her Mona Lisa demurity entirely.

Sean bit his lip, before saying: "I have to tell you something. When you all left Archimedes' house, Stinto didn't. For some reason he didn't jump when he broke the egg. Do these eggs ever go off?"

"A bad time egg?"

"Never happened before!" retorted Pau.

"What did he do then, Sean?"

"He tried to get to the Oracle, whom he knew had an egg."

"Of course she did." Pau was getting angry in response to his worry. "All oracles have them. How else can they see the future, you widget!"

"But the Romans got him. They... oh, this is terrible... they *speared* him, then connected a helmet to the spear - and I think I saw him pass into the helmet. Then later that Roman ambassador guy, Cespuglio, put the helmet on, and I saw, or heard, Stinto again briefly. He told me to warn you."

"Warn us? What about?" Geni took Pau's hand, frightened.

Sean closed his eyes and thought. "He said 'Warn them. Tell Geni... the Invertebrates are here."

Pau threw back rudely. "Not 'Invertebrates', you driftwood barnacle... 'Invertabrakes'."

Geni squeezed Pau's hand hard, tears welling in her eyes.

"Who are these Invertabrakes?" asked Sean.

Geni answered in a small voice. "We don't know. But we know what it means if they appear on our timeline. Something is going wrong..."

"Totally whacko!" furied Pau.

"...with time. We have suspected it for some time now."

Pau had by now abandoned all pretence to control. "Since you appeared, to be precise. What did I always tell you, Geni? It is Sean. *He* is the cause of all this."

"No, Pau, we don't know that for sure."

"Oh, yes? Something has changed, hasn't it? Everything is the same as every time we pass through the timeline, except for this measly little... time-flea!"

Geni bit her lip and shook her head. "*And* the Invertabrakes."

"They have come to eliminate *him*, Geni. Can't you see? It is obvious that he is the cause of it all."

"Then why did they let me go?" blurted out Sean.

Pau pointed at Sean with disgust and anger. "Ah ha! That is as good as an admission! I see through you! You invented all that rot about the Romans. It was you! You betrayed Stinto to get his egg! *You* killed him!"

Sean, in the guise of a young boy, backed away from the tall and angry young man. "No! Cespuglio said you can't be killed - only captured."

"Captured? What does *that* mean, you little bubonic plague carrier?"

"That is what the helmet is for - to capture the

Vitruvian Boy

Shrouds - to use their abilities."

"Abilities? What would they want with them - they can't use them - can they Geni?" Pau sounded unsure.

Geni was trying not to cry. "I... I don't know, Pau. I am so frightened. Oh, I wish Amur would hurry up and get here."

"What I can't understand is why she hasn't arrived yet?" asked Sean. "If she stopped off in the past, then surely that doesn't mean she can't be here, now, in the future?"

"Oh, don't you know *anything* about non-Euclidean time geometry?" said Pau, who had well and truly reached the nether end of his tether. "Time is not a straight line, as you monos think. Oh, I couldn't be bothered explaining!" Pau went to sulk in a chair, looking furiously at the town and lake, as if the unfair cruelties of the world were all just as much their fault.

Geni continued for him. "Amur insisted on stopping off, to try again to be Venus for Botticelli. She missed out last time round because her agent got the plague and took the rest of his life off. But, you're right. She should have been here by now. I'm worried. What *is* going on?"

Leonardo came in at this juncture with a freshly sharpened brush. If he had overheard any of the conversation, all he said was: "Sean, could you please find me some pinky brown pigment to mix in with the paint?"

"What about these egg shells?"

"Yes, they should do quite nicely."

While Sean was grinding up the time egg shells and mixing them into the paint base, Pau left to check if

Amur had arrived in town.

Geni whispered out of the side of her mouth while still posing for Leonardo: "Please, Sean, you mustn't blame Pau for being how he is. He is aggressive because he is fearful by nature."

"If Pau embodies fear, what about you? Are you the embodiment of beauty?"

"That is sweet of you to say that, but beauty is not an entity. Beauty comes to all of us when we are together. We miss Stinto. We feel an emptiness where he should be. We need his instinct."

"I don't think it is right that you guys go around in time and take advantage of everybody - posing as the perfect example of humans."

"But Sean, that is our job."

Leonardo threw down his brush irritatedly. When he was annoyed, which was rare, he turned more Italian, which couldn't help but be comical under the circumstances of high art in the making. "Please, M'donna Lisa, I need-a you to keep-a still. Now your eyes and-a mouth are all-a blurred."

"Sorry, Maestro."

"Actually, I don't-a mind the effect. Kind of, how to say?... Smoky? Sfumato, I think I'll call it. But please-a stay-a still. Like-a last-a time."

"Last-a time?" Geni was surprised. "You mean... you remember?!"

"Sì. Now, be a good-a girl and give me that-a foxy smile that will have-a Paris in an uproar."

Geni stared at him. "Leonardo, you are really the most remarkable of men!"

"Still-a please," he answered seriously, but Sean could see the ends of his mouth curving in a smile.

"Of course, maestro. How long would you like?" Geni asked.

Leonardo looked for the sun, then squinted at the distant town clock tower, trying from habit to remember how many bells there had been last hour. Only then did he remember he was wearing Sean's watch. "Oh, there are about-a three hours of light-a left."

"Time out…" said Geni.

And then she went still. No - more than still. Empty. Her eyes did not blink, she may not even have been breathing. Like a mannequin. No, not like a mannequin, either - she still looked alive, smiling as though she were laughing at her own joke.

After an hour, Leonardo took another break, this time of contaminated fermented milk. Sean whispered to her: "Geni?"

She didn't move.

After being like this for exactly three hours, and just as the sun was launching into its Hall of the Mountain Trolls routine, she suddenly came to life with: "Time back!" She looked around. "Did you miss me?"

"How did you do that?" asked Sean amazed. "Was that meditating?"

"No. I just did a quick time jump. We can do little ones while we retain some of the time egg albumen in us."

"But you were so still?"

"That is what makes us such sought-after models." She would have waggled her eyebrows, if she had had any.

"And your beauty," insisted Sean.

Geni did not answer, but blushed deeply.

Model Friends   115

"Oh, honestly. Now-a I have to mix-a some-a red into the skin-a colour. Can't you-a two be quiet while a master creates a piece?"

"Sorry, Leonardo," said Geni and Sean together, and then they corpsed - falling over each other laughing themselves totally silly.

Leonardo sucked the end of his paintbrush and shook his head ruefully. "I can see-a this is going to take a long-a time to finish."

* * *

Well past the onset of evening, Pau had still not returned. Sean and Geni set about tidying up the balcony from the day's creativity, while Leonardo went to ask the cook to prepare an extra place for his friend, Pacioli, whom he expected to arrive any moment.

"Are you worried about Pau?" Sean asked Geni.

"Oh, not really. He often does this - goes off in a tantrum when he can't have his own way. He's just worried. He'll calm down soon enough."

"I like it like this - just you and me, and Leo."

"Sean... I like you, too. I don't know why, exactly."

"Thanks a bundle."

"What I mean is, I normally don't allow myself any feelings for monos - it's just too painful. We see monodirectionals trapped on their timeline, destined to age and..." Sean knew she didn't want to say 'die' to him.

"Maybe it's because I am not a mono. At least not for now... Geni, who are *you*? Where do you come from?"

She sighed. "We usually tell people something vague, but for which they have a context."

"Such as?"

"Oh, sometimes we say we are ghosts. Or angels. Other times we say we are 'from the future'. Or from 'beyond the veil'."

"The other world?"

"Would you prefer that one?"

"Is it true?"

"They could all be true. We are not sure ourselves. Pau thinks we have been 'sent' here to teach 'poor humans' how to live better. That is why he wants us to pose as the perfect examples - to inspire."

"But that is not what *you* think? Can you tell me that?"

She sighed and thought for an unusually long time, before answering, weighing her words carefully. "I think we are human self-entities. We don't 'come from' anywhere. We belong here. Have always been here. We just keep travelling through time, again and again, never age-ing, never dying. I have no memory of anything else. We are as much a part of this world as you, have always been. Furthermore, we are detached consciousnesses - we can manifest ourselves any way we wish - but we have no body of our own - no corporeal existence."

"So, you will travel on soon?" Sean was depressed at this.

"I am sorry, Sean. I wish you could come with us. Something tells me Pau is wrong – that you *do* belong with us... somehow." She looked earnestly into his alive, brown eyes, as if willing the impossible to be true, suspending the inevitable that weighed her so. Its shadow won, as it always did, and took possession of her face. She looked down. "But it can't happen. It never does…"

"No future?"

"No time … at least not to call our own," she answered sadly. "Let's talk about something else. Tell me about your family."

Sean walked to the north end of the balcony, and pointed. "Just there, where that tree is? There, one day, about 1800 to be precise, will be built a house, right next to this one."

"Who will be your neighbours? Who will live in *this* house then?" Geni looked through the balcony doors to the beautifully decorated interior of the not yet haunted house, with its fine frescoes, ornate chandelier, dark wooden panelling and stone recesses, and, most unusually, no less than four fireplaces made of local red porphyry, distributed evenly around the eight square walls of the large ballroom.

"Nobody will ever live in this house," said Sean.

"But, how can that be? They would demolish an abandoned house, surely, even one as beautiful as this one?"

"No. They try. Often. But, whenever workmen approach, strange things happen. The house becomes known to be haunted, and then nobody will enter. The strangest thing of all is that even though nobody ever goes in - or if they do they never come out again - it remains well cared for. Nothing rots or rusts, ever falls off, no matter how strong a storm may be."

"How strange…"

"I live next door with my family." Sean's voice cracked when he tried to say their names, and he failed to hold back the tears.

"You miss them very much, don't you?"

He nodded. She placed her arms around him, and he allowed her to hold him like a mother a lost boy, which is what he was, after all, despite having his grown-up self in his mind alongside his child's. "Dear, dear, Sean. I wish I could help you understand what is happening to you. Why you have travelled so long away from your loved ones, but I cannot."

Sean lifted his head. "Tell me, Geni. Do you believe everything has a purpose? A reason?"

"Yes. Yes, I do."

"Then, tell me. Why did my mother disappear?"

"Your mother disappeared?! How awful! What happened?"

"We don't know. One day, she just wasn't there anymore. Papi says she was kidnapped, and was even prepared to go quite high in paying a ransom - which is saying a lot for him - but no ransom letter ever arrived. Nonno has never said anything about it."

"Never?"

"No. But from that very day, he began to investigate the haunted house - this house. Papi says the shock had sent Nonno into senility earlier than even he had expected."

"You know what I think, Sean? I think, in fact I am sure of it, your Nonno knows a lot more about this than you realise - in fact, I feel his presence all around us. You know what? I think you are going to see your mother again one day."

"Do you really think so?" asked Sean, beaming his tears dry.

"Yes. Trust me."

"I will always do that," replied Sean, and they gazed at each other in the rising moonlight for as long as the world, so often unsympathetic to lost souls, would allow them.

Which, to make its point, wasn't long, because just then Pau rode up the drive in an eight-hoof drive carriage. And with him was Leonardo's dearest friend, the mathematician and occasional monk, Frate Luca Bartolomeo de Pacioli.

* * *

Leonardo had been in an inventive mood, and had spent an hour with the cook, trying out some new cooking methods. As a result the evening meal was both highly suspicious-looking and delicious. During the second main course, Sean asked Luca Pacioli what he did when he wasn't inflicting mathematics on his students at university.

"We make books!" the cleric, seven years older than Leonardo, answered. "I write the text, young Leo there does the illustrations."

"Wow! How are they selling?" asked Sean.

"Not at all well," beamed Luca joyfully, adjusting his monk's habit. "For example, 'Solace for the Solstice' hasn't sold a single copy."

"In fact I stole mine," said Pau.

"But why not?" asked Geni. "It sounds interesting."

"Its sub-title is: 'The Modern Housedamsel's Family Reference to Infinite Number Series to Stretch Out Those Long Winter Evenings'," said Pau, and Luca saw from Geni's face that no further explanation was needed.

So he said instead: "And the one before that: 'The

New Fun Triangulation Reckoner for Ploughboys' - a disaster!"

" 'Curves to Woo By' did well for a while," countered Leo.

Luca smiled at him. "Only because of your great centrefold illustrations, my dear friend. It was selling brilliantly until the church slapped an x-rating on it."

"X-rating?" Sean was surprised.

"Oh, the usual 'withdraw from market or we excommunicate' threat. Legal gibberish so the church can retain their monopoly on 'The Word'. They force everyone to keep a copy of their Gospel Explorer, version two, on their desktop, to establish it as the world standard search tool for all knowledge and wisdom. There is a growing movement in Germany which may one day lead to an antitrust action, but the church has a burning desire to counter with anti-antitrust actions of their own."

"Then we lost the lonely clergyman market when all the marketing hype about building your own human to order backfired," said Leonardo sadly.

"Your robots?!" asked Sean.

Leonardo smiled appreciatively at him. "Trying to cash in on government subsidies - one of their initiatives to counter plague-driven deficits in the labour supply. But I forgot to put warning labels on saying they had a mindless mechanical soldier mode."

"We did rather.. er.. kill off what little clientele we had to begin with," Luca said.

"What you have told me about the political culture of your day, Sean," Leo continued, "has given me some new ideas about an inflatable model."

"But many of your titles are just great," insisted

Geni. "How about 'The Home Omnibus, and Other Low-Energy Domestic Transport Solutions'?"

"Sunk by the hay supply lobbies, who have always pushed for high-energy consumption in transport."

"Don't you remember '1001 Frequently Unanswerable Questions for the Chronically Curious'? That flopped big time!" Pau counter-critiqued.

"What about your other farming guides? 'Know Your Sheep: Baa Coding for the Modern Shepherd'?" Geni continued. When it became obvious that even its authors had forgotten that one, she said hastily: "So, what are you working on now?"

"A book called 'Summa'," Luca answered with enthusiastic gloom.

"Oh, good. Is that a guide to good beach resorts?"

"Er… no. 'Summa' is a history of mathematics – but it includes a chapter on games of chance."

"Gambling tips?" Pau's interest shot up like a New York governor.

"I am thinking of changing its title to something racier, like: 'Dux Oceani undecim victoriae casinis'."

"Cool. Er… perhaps you had better translate that for Sean…?" said Pau, but didn't fool anyone.

"It roughly translates to 'Ocean Eleven's guide to success in casinos'."

Pau nodded. "Mind if I give that title to a guy called George who will live near here in five hundred years?"

"But the 'Vitruvian Man' is doing well, isn't it?" asked Geni, and whistled appreciatively as she held up her battered copy of the famous centrefold of the well-proportioned man in two superimposed poses, inside a square and a circle.

Luca brightened. "True. Illustrated dance steps.

Released under the 'Shake that Golden Ratio' logo."

Leo nodded: "I suggested calling it 'The Man with the Perfect Length'."

Luca shook his head. "But I said it was a little risqué for this day and age. We can only hark forward to the good new days. Still, I must admit it has ladies' hair-robic classes the length and breadth of the country jumping. But it is just a passing fad. It won't last."

Geni went on. "Tell me about your joint project: the *'De divina proportione'*?"

"Promising. It was featured in the summer edition of *PlayPrince*, syndicated by the Macchiavellian group - *'You paint 'em, We frame 'em'* Arts and Smarts Promotions. Leo and I have done extensive field research, trying to determine the perfect golden ratio between breast separation and belly button. These young models will do *anything* to get into a syndicated painting. It is all based on Euclid's geometry. Poor Euclid - totally obsessed by that magic triangle. I think he died prematurely of repetitive measurement strain."

Sean couldn't believe what he was hearing. If his maths teacher could hear this... "But I thought Euclid was the Father of Geometry?"

"What he fathered in his private life is none of my concern," went on Luca. "He was in the business of catalogue, made-to-order golden triangles, based on the divine proportions of young ladies. Never heard of the famous 'Isosceles' trademark?"

"Sure!" Sean was perplexed.

"Well, the intellectual property rights were, let's say, 'taken over' by the Romans, but pirated by the Chinese. Now they are marketed under the 'Easy on the Eye' label: you see, 'Isosceles' is Greek for 'Eyes-so-ease'. Now a Roman called Vitruvius figured that this ratio, which so pleaseth the eye of man, if applied to, for example, architecture, would amaze and bewilder. Leo and I want to revive this lost 'fondle-mental' art of erotic geometry."

"A kind of medieval FengShui?" asked Sean.

Pau nodded. "Why do you think the church declared the navel to be the 'middle evil' - and named this entire age after it?"

Leonardo explained: "The great Roman architect, Vitruvius, was the first to use Euclid's geometry and Archimedes' ratios to create the perfectly proportioned building, to tap into the power the ratio of breasts to belly button has over the imagination of men."

Luca grinned more than a little wickedly. "I personally think of very little else, and so do my students."

"Is that why the pope has his private chambers adorned with pictures of nude girls?" naughtied Geni.

"It is the only pious explanation. Now, I can proudly say that Leonardo and I have finally recreated the golden ratio. And here it is!"

"Where?" asked Pau, Geni and Sean together.

"Here." Luca waved his arms around him.

"In this room?" asked Sean.

"Not *in* the room. It *is* the room - or rather the entire house!"

Sean looked around him in amazement. The room was indeed made up of panels which were an unusual mixture of perfectly symmetrical square and triangular shapes.

"Leo and I," said Luca, "designed the house for Francesco after we discovered that if you extend the golden ratio, as illustrated by the Vitruvian Man, into three dimensions you get an exact rhombicuboctahedron."

"A *sacked rompy cupboard head on*?! Cool," said Pau.

"You know, Pau, I can never tell when you're being serious," said Luca.

"That's easy," said Sean. "He's *never* serious."

Luca continued. "That's alright then. As I was saying, the *sacked rompy cupboard head on* is an Archimedean solid."

"So Archimedes *has* left a legacy?" Sean beamed with joy.

"He certainly has. It is a shape containing 18 squares and eight triangles, formed symmetrically into something exhaustingly close to a sphere - a kind of ball for foot."

"A football?"

"Might start a fad. But the beautiful thing is that the resulting shape maintains the golden ratio in all directions and dimensions."

Leo added: "Beneath us, the same pattern of squares and triangles extends down through the lower floor and into the wine cellar. The focal point is the very centre of this room. On this floor, the vertices in the horizontal plane are marked by porphyry fireplaces. All locally quarried stone."

"And this gives the house 'magical' properties?" sarcasticquired Pau.

"That's the theory," nodded Luca.

"How can we know?"

"We can test it. Right now."

"Test a theory? How refreshingly heretical. If Aristotle were up to it, he would turn in his grave," commented Leonardo, stroking his beard as potential lit up his eyes.

"How do we test it?" asked Sean.

"Give a magic show!" announced Luca.

"Oh, *please* do. I *love* magic shows!" pleaded Geni, stirring some *jus de vache* into her cup of Leonardo's experimental expresso brew - so-named in honour of its potent digestive properties.

"Oh, don't encourage him," said Leonardo, pretending to bury his face in his hands.

"*Do* show us," begged Geni.

"Well, if you insist…" began Luca.

"No, she's not insisting," said Leonardo hopefully.

"Oh, but I *am*," said Geni, to tease the maestro.

"Well, er… in that case," stammered Luca, fake hesitantly. "Maybe just one… or two. For the sake of science, of course."

"Oh, of course." said Leonardo joke-castically.

While the servants were clearing away the dinner things, Sean helped Luca arrange the chairs carefully into a parabola shape around the walls, focused on the centre of the room, where was located a waist-high, beautifully fluted porphyry pedestal.

The show went fairly well, although when they were invited to attend, the servants suddenly remembered a latrine or two that needed urgent scrubbing. Unperturbed, Luca first produced a hat from a rabbit, a bunch of wands from a flower, a sleeve from a deck of cards, to polite applause. He wanted to cut a sore in half with a lady, but there were no volunteers. And then he announced that for a finale he would make any personal item of Leonardo's appear.

"Don't you mean 'disappear'?"

"Hopefully it is a round trip," optimisticked Luca with disconcerting glee.

"Do we *have* to?" moaned Leonardo.

"Go on, Maestro Leonardo. Give him your watch," urged Sean.

"Very well. Said with appropriate dobs of foreboding and dread..."

Luca took the instrument and placed it with corny showyness on the pedestal in the centre of the room. He covered it with his 'kerchief, and then with a wicked grin he chanted a rhyme:

> *I Luca here*
> *I Luca there*
> *I Luca everywhere,*
> *Oh watch of thine*
> *Be lost in time,*
> *Time to watch*
> *This trick I botch*

He pulled the 'kerchief away to reveal that he had indeed 'botched' the trick. The watch was still there.

Everybody thought this was a grand joke. Luca took a theatrical bow, then went to pick up the watch to hand it back to Leonardo.

His fingers passed right through it. Everybody stopped laughing and stared in amazement.

"Very good, Luca!" commented Leonardo, actually impressed.

"Um... thank you, Leo... but I didn't do it." Luca moved his hand through the image again. It shimmered slightly but remained.

"The watch is ... ephemeral."

It had indeed vanished in every sense except for its image.

"It seems, we have separated the material watch from its image," mentally annotated Luca, as if it were the sort of thing he did every day.

While the others were busy congratulating Luca, Sean went to Leonardo, who was staring sadly at the image of the watch. "Maestro Leo, what does this mean?"

"Who knows?" Leonardo thought for a while. "What is the watch, exactly? It has grown to be more than an artefact lost in time - it is the mythical SANG Re.al, royal blood, the San..g-real, marketed by popular lore syndicates as Santo Graal, the Holy Grail. But the most important role of the watch is as an inspiration. It empowers the mind with valuable uncertainties, which are otherwise hard to pluck out of the background noise of assumption and dogma. You see, it is only by questioning what others take for granted, what is to most too obvious to question, that insights and discoveries can be made. I have no idea how the watch works - I don't need to. Just knowing that such a thing exists has provided me with more than a lifetime's worth of inspiration. It has, has it not, six fundamental machinations?" Leo smiled at Sean's surprise.

"We call them 'technologies'. And what about *spiki celestii*, the 'Language of the Gods'?" asked Sean.

"Its time is not yet. But I suspect it has some key role to play in the coming revolution, under which minds are finally liberated from prescripture."

"You know about the scientific revolution?" asked Sean.

"Perhaps the watch is drawn to its inevitabilities as much as you are drawn to it? With the SANG Re.al we have a glimpse of the future - the image of the watch here is now a permanent window to the inevitable."

Sean looked at the image on the pedestal. "And the display? 15:11:2010. It is not changing."

"The time it disappeared - it is perhaps ten minutes past eight bells, unless the campanile is running slow. But it might also be read the other way round - 2010 and seven-eighths, the date you disappeared? Or both? As Archimedes has told us, we can safely assume all the universe works on principles of proportion and balance. Why should time be any different?"

"Why do you look so sad, Maestro?"

Leonardo looked over at Geni and Pau. "What I wonder is whether it is now taking over the role of the TimeRiders, replacing human entities with a random mixture of your 'technologies'?"

"Is that why they are being captured by Cespuglio?" asked Sean.

"I don't know. But I did not answer Geni about whether I had seen their future visits because…"

"Please, maestro, please don't tell me it is because there aren't any!"

Before he could answer, they were joined by the others. Pau was speaking haughtily: "So, you and Leo are purveyors of erotic geometry? Do you honestly believe, Doctor Pacioli, that the universe really does rotate on the golden ratio of nipple separation to belly button?" He sniggered, and received a punch on his upper arm from Geni for his trouble.

Luca took it as a serious question. "I don't know.

All I can say is that if the universe *does* have a single, divine proportion, I would want it to be that one. We need something to bring back the crowds to live maths demonstrations. The home entertainment industry…"

Sean looked at Leonardo for an explanation.

"He means printed books," whispered Leo.

"… may be just a passing fad, but it is killing traditional culture. The golden ratio could be a way of calculating the location of a portal to a wonderful, greater cosmos. Leo and I have worked on this idea - he using the geometry of artistic beauty, I numberfications, to try to visualise such other world views. What else is a multi-storey building but a compression of horizontal space into a vertical series of parallels? Tell them about the cows, Leo!"

"Cows!?" Sean was as confused as ever.

"Oh yes," said Leonardo. "Did you know cows can't look up? What then, does a cow make of the upper floors of a building? Are they not only inaccessible to the cow, but also invisible?"

"That's probably why we never have to queue with cows for the upstairs bathroom in the morning," commented Pau.

"What udder nonsense you speak," said Sean, and was pleased to see Geni approve of his wit.

"Exactly!" enthused Luca, sidestepping the sarcasm with the habitual ease only a university lecturer truly acquires. "Yet *we* know the upper floors exist."

"You mean to say the cow is convinced it exists in two-dimensional space, while we look down on it from an invisible third dimension?" suggested Sean.

"That puts it rather well, don't you think, Leo?" said Luca.

Vitruvian Boy

"Yes," nodded Leonardo, adopting the new term at the speed of flabbergast. "If, in the cow's 'two-dimensional' world, the third dimension is invisible, in the same way…,"

"… a fourth dimension would be invisible to people who are convinced they live in a three-dimensional world," concluded Sean.

"Which is what we do," concluded Leo.

"And what would be the staircases in such a world?" asked Sean, amazed that he was discussing multi-dimensional space with people a century before Descartes would draw the first set of axes in two, then for an encore, three dimensions.

Leo answered. "Ah, what indeed? They can only be put where you *know* there is another floor to go to. To do that you need to understand the divine proportions to visualise the other dimensions. Have you ever wondered why Archimedes had the solution to the ratio between the volumes of a cylinder and the sphere it contains carved on his tomb?"

"You mean - it was a message? Who to?"

"That is the ten-thousand-florin question," continued Luca. "By all rights, the sack of Syracuse should have destroyed all of Archimedes' work. Almost as if that were their intention. But Archimedes outsmarted them. What could he do to safeguard his discoveries about *spiki celestii* - post-humorously, so to speak? Go on, ask me."

"Don't," groaned Pau.

"What?" Sean asked Pau.

"Glad you asked," replied the venerate doctor of logic. "The Romans conducted a thorough sweep and clear audit of Syracuse, but the watch could not be found.

All traces were lost, so the SANG Re.al was syndicated to legend. As for the Golden Ratio, all Archimedes had to do was carve the truth high and bold in front of everybody's noses. He had arranged for his tomb well beforehand, taking advantage of some summer specials at the local marble quarry. Naturally, the Romans, their noses being what they are, still couldn't see it. Not, that is, until over a hundred years after Archimedes' death, when along came a philosophical entrepreneur called Cicero. Our guess is he was seeking the SANG Re.al, reputed to have appeared to Archimedes. Cicero unearthed the tomb and made a killing from popularising the legend of Archimedes, which he licensed to architects. Later, Vitruvius adapted the golden ratio to human proportions in general, and Leo drew the Vitruvian Man from his description."

Near the end of this remarkable evening, Sean was once more alone with Leonardo. "Maestro, do you know what Archimedes meant by his *spiki celestii*?"

"The language of the gods? Art and Nature are expressions of each other: they are the only things that are defined by needing no justification. Mathematics is the common basis of both human art and our understanding of nature. Until we started using three-dimensional parallax, based on Euclid's laws of geometry, paintings were flat and unnatural. Mathematics is therefore the only language we have to project from one limited reality to a greater one. The only means with which to talk to the forces that make up and drive the permanent universe. What else are 'gods'?" He looked at the image of the watch. "Everything else is immaterial and transient. And while we are on this topic, I am afraid that the watch moving on means the time is coming soon for you to follow it."

"But I never want to leave you, Maestro!"

"I will miss you terribly, Sean. You called me 'Nonno'. I shall never forget that."

"Then I will stay with you."

"And your real Nonno? He needs you too."

"Yes…" Sean said miserably. As much as he loved Leonardo, he also desperately wanted to see Nonno again, and tell him he was alright.

Geni came to them. "So, goodnight, Maestro Leonardo. Goodnight, dear, dear, dearest Sean." She kissed him gently on both cheeks, then tussled his hair to break the moment of intimacy. "I will dream of you finding your mother. That will make it happen."

She turned to hide her tears, and hurried up the stairs.

Leonardo looked from the crestfallen Sean to his departing angel. After a tactful while he said: "Yes. She is right. I think no matter what we desire, how we would like it to be otherwise, the universe has its own indelible plan."

"So, if we are not allowed to determine our own fate, why do we live? How can we find happiness?"

"It is never a question of why we live, but that we live fully. And as regards happiness…? We don't look for it - it finds us when it's good and ready. And to make its path to us all the easier, it is best if we embrace the true nature of things. I'll tell you one thing I have observed: illusion is a strong happiness repellent. It can be nothing else. From what you have told me, I can foresee a time must come when the whole human species will be facing disaster because they turn their back on the guidance of nature, in favour of illusion, and lose the golden ratio between hope and reality."

"Then I shall make it my life's ambition to remind them."

"Do that, Sean. It may be all of our salvation. I do believe we did not meet by chance."

"So do I."

* * * *

A TRIAL WITH A SMILE

THE next morning began with a brief series of howl screeches, acoustically representing the dying moments of the entrance gate hinges. Considering the gate was not even closed, let alone locked, it would be safe to say whoever they were, these were not your run of the mill guests. Not that I am suggesting guests should be allowed to run the mill.

In the house, everybody fell out of everybody's bed, simultaneously cursing Leonardo's experimental cocktails, and colouring the air with a shower of the very latest in fashionable Renaissance expletives.

They all crowded onto the balcony just in time to see a frightful sight. Into the courtyard was marching a score-strong squadron of the pope's meanest FAQ troops, heavily armoured, and wearing regulation religious accoutrements with terror accessories, which included a sort of Halloween hooded white sheet adorned tastefully with a dripping red death-ter-all-ye-blasphemers cross. They were led by a man trumping even their magnificent first impression, courtesy of the tall, black-as-fingernails stallion he was riding.

As if all that weren't enough, stopping just outside the gates rolled an enormous, black-tarpaulined, four and more-wheeler, pulled by six of the meanest looking bullocks this side of the black madonna. On the side of the wagon was painted 'Papal Inquisitional Services', and a type of monkish smiley bearing the logo 'A Trial with a Smile'. Below this were stempled several rows of brightly coloured little symbols - pictograms of crossed logs burning - each presumably representing a witch or heretic they had hunted down. The rows continued with just as many more profiles of the same symbol, in ghostly grey, marking out their quarterly target.

This was the Madonna of all Church terror: a mobile unit of Confession Auditors.

"This is not good," whispered Leonardo out of the corner of his mouth, while he smiled and waved at the commander from the balcony of the first floor. "I wonder how they found us?"

"Who is that man?" asked Sean, meaning the commander, who had dismounted and was striding towards them across the courtyard of the house.

"It's Cesare Borgia," sighed Leonardo grimly. "I am afraid this is probably the worst way to wake up there is."

"Why is that?"

"He's an ex-agent of mine. Either he's come with the inquisition to burn us all alive... or something far worse."

"*Worse*?!"

"Yes. He may have found some work for me."

"Why is that worse?"

"You don't know Cesare like I know Cesare."

"Working for the church means stopping all brain activity," explained Luca. "They already know everything there is to know."

"But, you're a churchman…," said Sean. "You're dressed as a monk?"

"I know," shrugged Luca. "I find it hard to kick the habit."

Cesare Borgia was now standing directly beneath the balcony. He was in his mid-twenties, tall, and would have even passed for handsome, if it weren't for the considerable scarring from disease and underestimated enemies. And he wore a crown. An iron crown. He smiled up at Sean, which did nothing for Sean's current willies count.

A monk-robed clerk shuffled up bookishly. On his back was strapped (possibly even nailed?) a large wooden writing board. He bent over so that Cesare could use him as a desk. Another clerk nervously laid out a document, a quill and inkpot, and pulled back hastily as if he expected to be beaten for his efforts. Cesare instead read from it, quickly, monotonedly, formally, boredly and professional-indifferently, hardly glancing up at the people on the balcony:

"Evil sinners! I bid you good morning. Do you swear to sell our truth, our holed truth, poke your eyes out, hope to die? I warn you that everything you say will be taken down and used against you in a place of torture."

Last right thus read, without waiting for an answer, he then signed the document, thereby clocking in as duty quizmaster, and the clerk scurried away.

Cesare now pulled out a parchment roll, took off a blood red ribbon, and unrolled it. Some of the soldiers had brass instruments and made an awful attempt at a showy fanfare. Cesare announced:

"Time to play 'Quiz for Your Life'! You have just sixty seconds to give ten correct answers to these burning questions. Any incorrect or incomplete answers and the contestant will be eliminated."

Leonardo surreptitiously pulled up his sleeve where he had a parchment of cheat notes.

"What's that?" Sean whispered to Luca.

"FGAs. Frequently Given Answers. These are FAQ troops. As in Frequently Asked Questions. To test people's unthinking adherence to totally mindless dogma. If you answer correctly you lose your stake."

"You mean win your stake?"

"Not this kind of stake." He indicated the portable barbecue the troops were unloading from the wagon.

As a tease, Cesare allowed them to think he was going to read the standard FAQs. Then he smiled and put his scroll away. He clicked his fingers and one of the clerk-monks shuffled forward with another, black-bordered scroll. They could just make out the letters F..U.. on the cover.

"Oh no! We're doomed!" moaned Luca.

"Why? What's that?" asked the terrified Sean.

"It's an upgrade of the FAQs. These are Frequently Unanswered Questions, Upgrade Two. Its acronym would never pass the censors."

Pacioli shook his head ruefully. "I've heard rumours, but nobody has been able to hack them yet."

"Hack them?!!" cried Sean.

"Yes. As a failed candidate is being burned, he can communicate the questions to others through a kind of coughing code called hacking."

Leonardo listened to the first question: something about "Who then tie-eth the boot laces of our lord on the day the fifth sheep was verily…" Cesare paused meaningfully, "… shorn?" Sean counted to the fifth person on the balcony and sure enough it was him.

"Time to retreat!" said Leonardo, and shooed them all back inside the house.

They stood in silence while they listened as some of the confession auditors began to put together a kit-model battering ram, reading from and arguing over an instruction etching.

"Come on, Leonardo," said Luca, his voice edging along the scale towards level-four hysterical. "You're the ranking genius here. Think of something!"

"And you're the senior genius. *You* think of something," was Leonardo's vaguely panic-tinged reply.

"Will you two stop bickering about who has got the biggest brain, and get us out of this mess! We've got to go go go!!" called an angry and terrified Pau.

Leo and Luca stared at him, and then simultaneously clicked their fingers and pointed to each other as they said together: "The hex-a-go-go!"

"The hex-a-what?!" called Geni, pulling herself free of Pau, who had been whispering urgings to her and trying to hold her back.

"I am afraid we have deceived you - all of you," Leonardo explained apologetically to Pau and Geni. "You see, last night we were afraid you wouldn't allow us to experiment directly on your time eggs." At the mention of the eggs, Pau recoiled suspiciously and his hand went instinctively to his coat pocket. Sean took note of it.

They could hear that the FAQ troops had finished

their union regulation prayer break. Leonardo continued quickly. "So we arranged the chairs so that by sitting there, Geni and Pau, with your eggs on you, you would complete the six principal points of the Vitruvian hexagram."

"In Recent Wave mysticism it's called a 'hex-a-go-go'," explained Luca. "It's a trick we used to play on the apprentice witches behind the alchemy lab."

Leonardo continued. "As you can see, we used porphyry for the fireplaces in this room. Porphyry that contains the eggs you use to time ride - these eggs contain a substance alchemists call *tempus albumen*. But we could only find four stone slabs which contain such an egg."

"How do you know they contain an egg?" asked Sean.

"You can sense it. You see, when someone is close to an egg, he or she gets visions. Sometimes glimpses of 'ghosts', other times insights of another time, or perhaps of all time. That is why oracles and other professional outsighters get such rave reviews - and where you get your eggs, am I correct?" Leonardo asked Geni and Pau. "Don't you get Amur to steal the eggs for you from oracles, who possess and pass on hereditary knowledge of where to locate them?"

"Yes/no," answered/hedged Geni/Pau helpfully/evasively.

"After all, they are hardly likely to complain, are they? Who can they to?" smiled Pau vulpinely.

"Since the minimum number to activate the power of the hex-a-go-go is six," went on Luca, "we got you to sit here and over there, in these empty spaces between the fireplaces, so the hex-a-go-go would be complete."

"That's brilliant, Luca, Leo!" Geni applauded, smiling appreciatively and looking every inch the Mona Lisa.

"Sneaks," sulked Pau.

Geni suddenly went serious. "Just a minute… I was sure of it! You *can* remember our last visit, Leo, can't you? You can see it through the eggs?" asked Geni.

Leonardo did not have time to answer, as Pau suddenly grabbed Geni's wrists roughly and said: "Time to go, Geni! Get out your egg."

"What?! And leave the others to the confession auditors? Pau, we can't…"

"Look, Geni. Ever since Sean appeared, following us like this, Cespuglio has been after us… capturing us one by one."

"You mean Cesare Borgia is…?"

"Of course he is! He has Stinto and Amur in his helmet - which, if I don't miss my guess, is now that crown Cesare is wearing. He has come for us now. But what he really wants is the watch. Because it is the watch that is disrupting the timeline. Don't you see? The FAQ troops are the Invertabrakes - they want to stop the timeline collapsing - that's why they are helping Cespuglio."

"But the watch has gone," said Geni, indicating the pedestal and shimmery image of the device in the centre of the room.

"So let's give Cespuglio Sean - he's the one drawn to it. Then they'll both leave us in peace. Now come on! We have got to get to Elf first and get him to safety."

"And Sean?"

"He's not one of us. Leave him!" He began wrestling with Geni to get her egg out of her purse.

"Leave her alone, you great bully!" called Sean, racing over to try to pull Pau off her.

Pau spun around and swung at Sean as hard as he could with all the fury fear generates.

But a hard punch is a pre-announced punch, and Sean ducked it easily, tackling Pau in a way, as the wrong kind of footballer, he had always wanted to try. Pau was quickly on top of him. When he swung to hit at Sean again, Geni tried to arrest his arm, but the force of it knocked her backwards. She dropped her purse and her egg rolled out across the floor. Dazed, she stumbled, first forwards, then backwards ... and into the pedestal, which began to topple. Pau screamed 'Geni!', abandoned Sean, jumped up and ran over to her. He reached her just as she followed the falling pedestal, and they went into a kind of threesome tango, to end up spiral-limbed on the floor.

The hiatus that followed this was broken by the sound of the battering ram finding its target.

Luca helped Sean up, and Leonardo Geni.

"Are you hurt, Geni?" he asked, concerned.

"No, I am not. Leo! It's good to see you! And Luca! Ehem... who is this handsome boy?"

Luca, Sean and Leonardo stared at ... Ma Donna Lisa.

Her husband jumped up. "I say! What was I doing on the floor? Is it a party? Hope so!"

"Francesco, Lisa... I..." began Leonardo, perplexed.

The house shook again.

"Who's that knocking?" asked Lisa. "For heaven's sake, Francesco, don't stand around like a garden fence, go and let them in."

"Sean," said Leonardo. "I would like you to meet Signor Francesco del Giocondo, and this is his charming wife, ma Donna Lisa."

"Pleased to meet you, my lady, sir."

"What is happening, Leo? Who are those men in the courtyard?"

"The church making inquiries, my lady."

"Oh, those pesky priests. Tell them we have donated already."

"I don't wish to alarm you, Francesco," said Leonardo. "But they are confession auditors coming to torture and burn us alive."

"I see. Hmm… you always manage to come up with something new every time we see you, don't you Leo?"

"Francesco," said Lisa, "I don't want to be burnt. I've only just arrived! Tell the nasty men to go away."

"Yes, dear."

"And not to step on the flowerbeds."

"Yes, dear."

"And to wipe their boots if they do break in."

"Yes, dear."

"Oh, just look at my hair. I look awful with it down! I can't be burned looking like this. Francesco, this is *all* your fault!"

While she had her mouth full of hair clips putting up her hair, Francesco took the opportunity to pull Leonardo aside. "For goodness sake, Leonardo, we can't be tortured by just anyone like this. It just won't do. What would the neighbours say? And you know what Lisa is like about uninvited guests. Can't you do something?"

"I would, but to do so I would need another egg," said Leo, holding up Geni's, which had rolled to the wall.

"Surely this is a strange time for to maketh of an omelette?"

"It seems Pau used his," said a last-will-and-testament-stage Luca, frisking Francesco's pockets, causing him to giggle and squirm.

The sounds of the battering ram being rehoisted for a another enquiry at the door came to them.

"Oh, I wouldn't say that," said Sean and held up Pau's egg. "I saw where he kept it, and got into a wrestle with him to get it off him without his noticing. I used to do it with Papi when I wanted the notebook in which he kept his passwords."

"Well done Sean!" exclaimed Luca. "Quick! Put it in the enclave there. That's right. Leo, put Geni's over there. And 'hey early'… I mean 'hey presto!' "

"Right," said Francesco, as he looked from one to the other of his four room companions. "Clearly, you've all gone mad as horses." And he sat with a familiar huff, trying to remember if the payments on his fire insurance were up to date.

"So, Geni has gone," said Sean sadly. "How?"

"It would seem that as we solve one piece of the mystery, another piece appears," said Leo. "We can only assume there was enough essence left over from last night's hex-a-go-go for them to travel. They are, after all, merely self-entities. Suggestions of people."

"Not really alive?" said Sean, quoting Cespuglio bitterly. "I don't believe that!"

Luca had gone to the window to peak out timidly. "Er, Leonardo, they have stopped battering on the door. Perhaps they wish to parley?"

"Francesco, why is there a very small clock on a

ribbon hovering in mid-air in the centre of the room?" asked Lisa.

"The watch!" cried Luca and Leonardo. They ran to it and found the image was still exactly where it had been, hovering. They lifted the pedestal and replaced it under it. "Interesting," said Leonardo.

"What is, Maestro?" said Sean.

"The hex-a-go-go is in place, yet Luca and I are unaffected."

"So am I," said Sean, coming over and moving his hand and arm through and around the watch.

"So... it hasn't worked?" said Luca. "They'll be able to get in?"

"Flaming shame," said Francesco.

Luca went to one of the eggs and adjusted it slightly. "Any signal yet?" he asked hopefully.

Leo was at the window. "I am afraid this is it," he said. They all joined him and looked down. The FAQ troops were launching a final attack on the door. The ram hit home, followed by the sound of the door crashing in, and Lisa screamed. So did Luca, actually, but ok.

Instead of metal boots on the stairs, however, they were surprised to hear spine-curdling and blood-tingling screams. The next they knew, they were witnessing the grim scene of a pile of disused white sheets, presumably containing a dozen ex-united inquisitors, fall past the window, into an orderly but demilitarised sudden stop on the ground beneath the balcony.

Standing in the courtyard below, when he had seen what had happened, Cesare Borgia screamed "Fantastic!", grabbed one of the other FAQ soldiers, and pushed him unwillingly through the door aperture.

A brief scream from the roof, then two objects fell. One was a skeleton in armour and the other was a complementary mass of soft human bits in a previously white robe.

Down in the courtyard Cesare called: "Hey, this is fun! Any more volunteers?"

The few remaining FAQ troops backed off with a devil-did-care look.

"What *is* going on, Leonardo?" cried Lisa. "Look what those intrusive men are doing to my flower beds!"

"We have built a time shield around the house. Much like the shield around your watch, Sean, that prevents it from age-ing or corroding."

Sean looked out of the window, too. What he saw was absolute chaos. Besides the bodies of inquisitors, there was half a bulldozer just inside the fence, a large number of black ravens were dancing a to-be-or-not-to-be on and off the roof, and a terrified cat appeared out of nowhere and raced across the courtyard to some alternative nowhere best known to itself.

"Sean, I think you had better go too," said Leonardo.

"But if I use an egg, that will break the hex-a-go-go, and you and Dr Pacioli will be left defenceless. Come with me. It is not safe here."

"Actually, I think we will be perfectly safe. I think I now know what Cesare wants. In any case, I don't think we *can* travel through time. That is for TimeRiders and the consciousnesses of special people."

"What makes me special?"

"Your not being where you belong. You see, Sean,

for some time now I have suspected that a tooth has fallen out of the cog of time. That is my guess as to why you have been cast adrift. And why you are drawn to the watch. Like two pieces of debris in the sea - the same forces of waves that push them together the next moment pull them apart. But Nature is clever. It is trying to resolve the enigma. My guess is you are part of that attempt. Do as she wants. Follow *her* instinct, not your own."

"Are you sure?" asked Sean.

"Of course not. But, we can test the theory."

"How?"

"Like this." Before anyone could stop him, Leo strode out onto the balcony.

"Maestro, no…!" called Sean.

The hated voice of Cesare Borgia cried 'Fire!', and a volley of crossbow bolts flew towards Leonardo, standing unafraid on the balcony. But just as the deadly bolts were crossing over the stone balustrade of the balcony, they disappeared. Some simultaneous thuds and screams from the courtyard informed them that the last of the inquisition FAQ troops were dropping dead, the bolts impossibly protruding from their chests.

Cesare Borgia looked far from angry - if anything he looked jubilant.

"Cesare, are these all papal bulls - from your father?" called Leonardo from the balcony, indicating the wagon's traction units.

"Yes, he does proclaim a lot of bull, doesn't he? Leonardo, I may have a job for you…"

"Thought as much," muttered Leo with saddle-sore wisdom. "All the Invertabrakes are dead now, so you can speak openly."

If this insight took Cesare by surprise, he only showed it marginally. "I want the eggs, the *tempus albumen.*"

"Why?"

"As weapons. Cannons shatter the eggs, so you will also design me an arbalest, a giant crossbow, that can fire the largest eggs inside the walls of my enemies, so they may be banished not only from my sight, but from all time.

"Plunge them, Leonardo, into the depths of the Earth, these eggs of hell shall make me the supreme lord of the whole planet.

"For I am a Borgia, and we are the pope's army of righteous wrath. We take a prosperous land at peace and turn it into a chaos of fear and death. For we are the bearers of the Word, and that word is death. I wield it as a sword against dissenters, for I *love* war, I *love* betrayal - especially against me for it gives salary to my indulgence, as my father, the Pope, indulgences on me the powers of lust and vengeance. Power to crush your cherished Renaissance."

"Did you learn nothing from Machiavelli?" asked Leonardo, denying Cesare the despair he craved to see.

"My tutor, Mack the Knife, taught me 'Force and Prudence' will be the strength of the state. I scribbled 'insane cruelty' into the margins of his book, *PlayPrince*, when he was not looking, just as it was going out to the publishers. That is why it is such a big bestseller. You see, purposeless, sadistic cruelty taints reason with just enough unwarranted certainty to keep the sheep in line. And it is more fun. What else is the world for, but for *my* fun? Tell me that?"

"You forget, art and truth are always on the side of

good," corrected Leo coolly.

"But, Leo, in the end 'Evil Begets Good'. When I am Pope, that will be my motto."

"How can one such as you become pope?" challenged Luca as he came on to the balcony to join Leo.

"The same way as all democratic elections will be decided in the future: by auction. My father simply outbid the other cardinals to become pope. I will do the same. I was a bishop at 15. Remember, in chess, the bishop just one square from king."

"But on the opposite colour."

"And then my father arranged to have me made cardinal at the age of eighteen. But he had not read my soul. Do you know, I am the only person ever to resign as cardinal? I did that in order to launch my career as a soldier. But to take control of my father's private army of confession auditors, I had first to kill my own brother. Do you have any idea what it is like to kill your own brother?"

"Terrible."

"No. *Wonderful!* But it is nothing new to me. Did I not, as 'mighty Caesar' bring the world to my will, and when I had tired of bestriding as this particular colossus, I revenged my own murder as the first emperor of the Roman world? That was so much fun. As Augustus, the nephew of Caesar, could I not revel in family feuds, and bring on the greatest civil war in history? Did I not then create a great dynasty? Me!! It was *always* me. You create masterworks, Leonardo, so you will understand. My masterworks were Nero, Caligula…" He touched the crown. "Constantine…, Attila, Charlemagne, Genghis, … whenever there was savagery to be had at a bulk discount rate, I was there.

Have you not understood yet? Cespuglio has never left the Earth - ever!?

"The jubilee has brought untellable riches to Rome, as the pilgrims pay their indulgence subscriptions, booking their private seats for the afterlife. Which was a good investment, because I then used their own money to hasten their departure from this world. I used it to betray your patron, the Duke of Milan, to the French, as you know, and to take Romagna by force of arms, not to mention some pretty darn nifty footwork, if I do say so myself, turning my enemies against each other. Piety buys anxiety in a Borgia papacy.

"I have just come from killing my sister's husband. Sibling love is worth far more than any dolt's signature on a marriage certificate."

"Is this some more holy father bull?" asked Leonardo.

"My father? When he needs net new money he sells new cardinal robes. He calls the faithful to arm and join the papal army on the whisper of a crusade, then gives them to me, to do my dirty work on my fellow Italians.

"Talking of sheep - is Sean there? Sean… Shorn sheep… come out and be fleeced, my little lamb. Come to the embrace of the merciful Cespuglio."

Sean came out on to the balcony. He was not afraid - Leo's courage was infectious.

"Hello, Cespuglio. I hear you have been having fun wrecking history."

"Do you know what my favourite weapon against my former allies is?"

"I can imagine several contenders," replied Leonardo.

"I, or more usually my sister, Lucrezia, give them *cantarella*, a form of arsenic - I call it the 'liquor of succession'. Will you too, old Leonardo, like Socrates, receive the golden cup of the Borgias?"

"If that is to be my fate, I do not fear it."

"Ooh... delicious. That defiance makes your corruption all the more appetising. I can taste it already. Come now, Leonardo," he pointed with a mail gloved hand down the road towards war-torn Italy. "The road to infamy beckons us."

Leonardo, Luca and Sean re-entered the ballroom.

"Maestro?" begged Sean, but stopped when he saw Leo shake his head. "Then, this is good-bye?" Sean failed to hold back his tears.

Leonardo took an egg from its enclave.

Sean looked to Luca for an ally, but saw only resignation there too. "Goodbye, Sean. Bearer of the watch, guardian of the *spiki celestii*. Cespuglio must never be allowed to find and destroy these things. They are our only light in his new dark age. Look for the signs, and you will understand."

Leo took Sean gently by the shoulders. "There is so much we could have said and done together, you and I. But I will tell you this. I have no family except the family of scientists through the ages. And we can never be separated. Our thoughts pass forwards and backwards through the time barrier with ease. For us time is of no importance." Leonardo held him with his penetrating eyes. "So can it be for us."

He let the egg fall.

* * * *

A Trial with a Smile   151

CHAPTER EIGHT

falling for science

SEAN woke with a jolt.

Which was rather unfortunate because the selfsame jolt technically didn't belong to him, but rather to a person whom he had just occupied. Just like when you grab someone else's parking space, it is never a smooth process. And thus armed with a new momentum, something that officially didn't exist yet in this age[*], the chandelier started swinging.

Yup, a chandelier - as in cathedral high in thee I swing. And of course it was full of exhibit A candles, all arranged carefully to singe those parts the others can't reach. Despite his barbequesque tenure, Sean tried to focus on what turned out to be cathedral walls and columns as they swung stomach-juice-cocktailingly into and out of what little focal power he still held claim to.

Little did he know but he had just inspired one of

---

[*] *Church proclamation MMCCXXII* (Golden Psalm Award 1589)*: '… and the lord sayeth unto the unbeliever… I'll give you momentum up your bottomium…* (**Dogma 32, verse 14**) *… and the people cried 'oh lord, let the heathen swing for it'… and the lord spaketh … bring in the chandeliers …'*

the most important scientific observations of all time. A candlelit winner, so to speak.

Far from the ideal, which would have been to have arrived as unobtrusively as a cockle on shore leave, he found he had achieved the complete opposite, for within seconds he had scores of people making direct references to him, in a manner congruent to the obligation they were under to dodge the hail of hot wax and flaming candles.

Pretty soon a ladder was being shoved under his flailing feet, and he managed to clamber down to face several dozen immediate zone indignants.

"Sacrilege!" screamed a well-known pew-jumper.

"Intruder and ceremony destroyer!" cried several others picking up on the license.

"Must be a heretic!"

"Burn the heretic!"

"Yeah… burn him till he's sorry!"

"But I *am* sorry!" Sean squeaked out.

The crowd went suddenly as silent as someone's grave.

A voice was heard coming from behind it all. "Make way, I am a doctor of theology!" The indignant mass parted into the pews of the cathedral, leaving the priest facing Sean, the knave in the nave.

"*How* sorry are you, evil sinner!!?" he screamed at his badly nibbled index finger extended towards the terrified Sean.

"Oh, really sorry, sir."

"Call me father."

"Father?"

"Yes," the priest shrugged. "It's relative."

Falling for Science

"Ok, … er… Dad."

"Really, *really* sorry?!!"

"Yes. Really *really* sorry, cross my fingers, hope not to die."

After relishing the dramatic attention for all it was worth, the priest turned to his flock and announced: "He recants! He recants! By the sacred knobbly knees of his holiness, he is saved!"

The crowd made a quickly improvised multi-part harmony on the vowel 'oo', in appropriate awe-sum amazement at the undeniable miracle. Then one had the initiative to lead a polite applause. Thusly self-satisfied and reinforced in their suspicions about the true workings of the universe, they began to move away, leaving Sean trying to claw the shards of reality back into some sort of more familiar jumble.

The cleaning equipment and his soggy clothes, informed him of what his host had likely been doing up the ladder before his sudden arrival had caused him to fall onto the chandelier. The fallen bucket confirmed his guess, since on it was written: 'Property of GSE, the Grovel-Sure Ecclesiastical marble cleaning service'.

The crowd had all moved away, that is, except one. This was a young man in his mid-twenties, middling to ogerish in features, and a nose which would be quite a liability should the owner ever visit a chip factory. He was holding his wrist and looking from it up at the still swinging chandelier, and then back to his wrist.

"Excuse me, sir, what are you doing?" asked Sean.

"Shh. I am counting."

After a while, the man stopped counting the swings, looked pleased with himself, and did something that's-enough-for-now under the cavernous sleeve of his robe.

Sean could have sworn he heard the faintest of 'beeps'. Then the young man started down the aisle towards the exit, with Sean hunching behind him in both senses.

Outside the enormous Duomo, he saw a wagonette bearing the logo for the GSE marble cleaning service. But Sean continued after the man who was crossing the wide grassy lawn that separated the Basilica from something Sean recognised immediately. This was a beautifully ornate tower, familiar by its outrageous lean with respect to more standard reality.

"Excuse me, sir," Sean called after the hurrying figure in its long, seriously untailored robe. "But are you Mr. Galileo?"

Without breaking his pace, the man said over his shoulder: "The right of honourable Galileo Galilei, at your service. My friends call me 'Lilly'. So do my enemies, for that matter. And who are you, may I ask?"

"Sean. Sean Seulpierre. Of Lugano."

"*Lugano?*" This had gained Galileo's attention, and he stopped to examine the young man Sean was occupying. "So, Gian' Seulpierre, how is it that you do know me?"

"Well, you're so famous. Except that I expected you to be an old man. You're always old in portraits."

"I think you are taking of the micki with me. I am but a poor paperfront writer of little beknown and fewer prospects. Er... on that subject, do you have any money? I'm a bit hard up this decade..."

Sean felt his pockets and pulled out half a scudo worth of copper coins. "Yes."

"Then let us take of refreshment at the Hard Mock Bean House." He led the way down the main drag leading to the centre of the university town. "I always go there to slip in a bit of sagacity mid-week, before the weekend crowds hit the philosophy wells."

Sean skipped after him. "Did you say paper*front* writer? Don't you mean paper*back*?"

"Hmm... Good idea. These days with paper prices the way they are - wood shortages you see, with all the heretic burning - it would indeed be a good idea to economise and be a paper front *and* back writer. Thanks for the tip - but, in any case, nobody reads anything I write." Galileo's crest fell a commensurate notch.

"Oh, don't say that. One day you will be a best-selling author, and you will change the history of science forever."

"Oh, I bet you say that to all the sages. But you are wrong. There is no demand for my stuff. There is no flexibility at all in the market. It is all controlled by the big Aristotle multi-corpus syndicates. Has been for millennia - why would it suddenly change now? In desperation, I have applied to be a professor of mathematics at the University of Pisa, but I am having trouble with the Aristotle crowd who vote for the astrologer of the month."

"Astrologer? But you are a mathematician?"

"Same thing. They hate everything I write. And to be a scholar you have got to publish papers - and the best papers have something written on them. For my critics, the proof of sound judgement is to come to exactly the same conclusion as someone nearly 2,000 years ago. That someone being Aristotle, of course. We call them the 'strollers'."

They were passing a used-ideas bookshop, prosaically called 'Nothing New under the Sun', which was holding a pre-fire sale on heretical works. "My books have been pushed out of the publishing market by Aristotle cartel firebrands such as these." Galileo indicated a display featuring a mock-up of a torture wheel, covered in books in sombrely garish covers. "All you need to know books," said Galileo.

Sean perused the titles, which included: _Faith for Dummies_, _Faith at Stake_, …

There was a special promotion for an up-coming combined book-signing and confession session with the author of: _A Life of Burns Nights: memoirs of a stakeholder._ On the back cover were quotes from critics, extracted under torture: 'The Cardinal looks back over a career of half a century, reminisces over his more outlandish mistakes, … this book will have you rolling in the pews, … told with that crisp, dry tongue which is so unique to pyre humour'.

Sean went on to a different shelf: _Dogma, man's best friend_, and a ponderous academic tome entitled _Limits to Knoweth_. In the home advice section he found: _Cleanse thou the sole, and other good cooking hints from the Puritan kitchens_, followed by The Puritan Classics series, which included hits like: _All I kneed from you is that sin-king feeling_.

In the Self-help books: _Don't make yourself a flaming martyr to truth_; _The road to Eternal Bliss_, by A. Repentant; _I survived Eternal Damnation_, by F. Singebart; _How to remain a nobody in the State of Fear_; _A hundred new ways to avoid the pyre_ (knee-pads included); _A practical guide to fixing a flat pyre_; _1000 martyr sites to see before you die too_; _Confessions of the top 50 heretics of 1588_ (blood stains faithfully reproduced - refills available); …

In the comedy section: _Is it my lack of recantation, or is it getting hot up here?_ ; _Ash Wednesday follows Martyrdi_.

There was also the children's Hellfire series, sold with gadgets, including miniature pyre wheels for irrecantant hamsters for the home fanatic.

Church manuals were also reaching out to the younger public: _Favourite ways to think of nothing original_; _Living with fear_; _With terror in your heart and a smile on your face_; …

In the Political and Economics section: _Who takes what_, an insider's guide to church hierarchy; _Soul-saving investments_, the modern bankers' guide to indulgence instrument trading; _Making Indulgences Pay_ - long-term strategies in soul relocation; and recommended with that purchase, _Location, location, location_: all-important geographical factors in choosing a faith; …

At the checkout barrel was a headline on the daily Vatican Bull: "We do not torture," Church Administration Statement.

On the door was a publicity etching for the 'Why Wait!?' 24-hour soul reclamation service. 'Go all the way next time you pray.'

Outside, a group of greens, who were standing for a seat, were sitting at a stand, warning that the rate of burning heretics was unsustainable, and that irresponsible use of hellfire was raising the temperature of the earth. Out of earshot, Galileo whispered to Sean. "They are lobbying to have sinners recycled instead. But they are generally considered just spoilsports, and they are unlikely to get onto the committee of national recantation."

They entered the Hard Mock Bean House, as smoky a den of idlers as there is ever likely to be. Columns of coffee reek stood here and there around the many philosophy-stained tables. "This is where the richer students hang out," explained Galileo. "You see, some of them sling their servants, poor devils, in to attend the university lectures in their place. We call those servants 'arrows'."

"Strange name."

"Not if you see what our lectures are like."

Sean saw a group playing some sort of game. "What is that they are playing?"

"Heretic snap."

"Snap?"

"They start with the little fingers. Ah! There he is. Toby Nobler - my main rival for the vacant chair of professor of mathematics. Rubbish in geometry, but makes up for it with a pretty sharp made-to-order line in horoscope greeting cards. Toby Nobler... Will they vote him the next professor of mathematics? Toby or not Toby? That is the question. Whether it is Nobler in their minds to suffer the slings and arrows..."

A young English theatre student, just two months younger than Galileo, on an inspirational sabbatical of Italian feudal hotspots, pricked up his ears and annotated on the back of a skull he used for opening bottles, murmuring, 'On myne nun's late honour, perchance not bad that be-ith for myne nexteth boards bestride.' He reviewed his notes for a moment, then added: 'Forsooths, egads.'

Ignorant of the plagiarism going on ahead, so to speak, behind them, Galileo and Sean were gradually joined at their table by students.

"My job," explained Galileo, the underpaid and depreciated tutor, "if I am elected mathematics professor, is to twist the universe to fit the Administration's version, tell astrological forecasts (sponsored by Grovel-Sure Ecclesiastical) for the Vatican's Daily Bull, and sweep the lower floor corridor twice a week."

One student had arrived shortly. This is because he was less than five feet tall. He was carrying a book entitled '100 Recantations to dampen zeal with'. "It is the author's posthumorous sequel to his best-selling '101 Flaming Good Ideas'," he explained, seeing Sean's gaze on it.

The richer students were dressed in robes of circumstantial pomp, while the poorer ones were distracted, their heads bowed in concentration, their hands under their sleeves, their lips murmuring something.

"What are they doing?"

"Wristwatches," answered the demi-dwarf, whose allocated name in fact turned out to be DiDi.

"Wristwatches?!" exclaimed Sean triumphantly to Galileo. "So I was right - you *are* wearing the watch!"

"Sure," answered DiDi for him. "We all have one. Don't you?" All the students pulled their sleeves back to reveal … bare wrists.

"I used to…" said Sean, uncertainty having an absolute field day on his forehead.

"You see, clocks, even the finest Swiss sundials, are rubbish at measuring any time interval less than a minute," explained Galileo, but notably without revealing his own wrist. "The wristwatch technique involves keeping an eye on the time by counting the pulse beat - the most accurate time-measuring instrument known to man."

"But… Galileo, I thought… I was sure you had a …"

"… time-measuring instrument?"

"Yes."

"I do."

DiDi interjected quickly: "Lilly… is this wise? It is supposed to be a secret."

"I think we can trust Gian'." Galileo looked around the tables to be sure nobody outside their group was watching, and then pulled back his sleeve to reveal…

"What on earth is that?!" exclaimed Sean, his flabber by this stage totally gasted.

"Shoosh!" shooshed Galileo. "It's still in development. I don't want any spies from the Padua University Medical School to see it yet. I know they are close to a breakthrough in time technology. I am trying to get them to headhunt me out of this place."

"But what is it?" Sean looked at the extraordinary instrument. Though quite bulky, it somehow strapped onto the wrist, and was surmounted by what appeared to be a miniature pendulum.

"I call it the… pulsilogium. Catchy name, don't you think?"

"The pulsihooligan?!" laughed Sean. "That's the dumbest name I have heard since 'sacked rompy cupboard head-on'!"

There was an uncomfortable silence from everybody. Sean followed their gazes to the instrument and saw, to his irresistible if eventual amusement, that the frame was in fact an exact rhombicuboctahedron, with its unmistakable football look.

Galileo explained: "It's an automatic pulse reader - tapping into the power of the rompy to amplify the pulse, regulated by the pendulum (patent pending), to provide highly accurate time measurements."

"Does it work?" asked Sean, in the grips of a made-to-order form of mental dislocation.

Galileo nodded. "While you are living, yes. Otherwise, dead inaccurate."

DiDi thought it would help to explain with: "You see, we figure that Purgatory is so overcrowded, because, since their pulses have stopped, after death people miss the last flocks of angels guide thee to thy sleep escort service."

The sound of hurried skull scratching came from behind them.

"So this doesn't help, does it?" said Sean. "Dead people are pulseless."

DiDi nodded. "Yes - to jump the purgatory time-out queue your pulse would need to be pretty special - you could say, of holy blood..."

"SANG Re.al, in other words," said Galileo, studying Sean's reaction very carefully.

Obviously satisfied about something, he suddenly changed the subject. "Not only, but also to spite the strollers, we play an interactive game."

"To be safe, we first set up a fire wall," said DiDi.

"How do you mean... fire wall?" asked Sean, confused about so many things he had given up any system of prioritising them.

"Fame on one side..."

"Flame on the other - warming to the idea now?"

"I am indeed," nodded Sean, getting to like more and more his eccentric new friends.

"We call it mundi secundi - Second World," said Galileo. "Students create second personae and we live in a fantasy world, in which, instead of the Earth being fixed in the firmament and everything else rotating around it, or as the church thinks, around it, it is a rock that, get this, flies around the Sun. And not only that, but...," he leant forward to whisper, "... the rock rotates on its own." Happy with this scandal, he sat back.

"That's where we get the nickname of 'the rock and rollers'," said DiDi.

Galileo chuckled, and continued: "Through the fire wall medium, we make concerted rock proposals - called rock concerts. It's the only chance we get to meet the chics."

"*Chics*?!!" cried out Sean in his latest edition of surprise.

"Sure," Galileo shrugged back. "The *Ch*urch *Ic*onoclasts. But we have to be careful. We can only operate safely behind fire walls. That's one over there," and he pointed out the window at a wall across the road. It had been daubed with graffiti saying:

You can only groove on rocks that move !

Sean saw there was a cartoon character on the fire wall. "Who is that?" he asked.

"That's Cardinal Perry Pathetic. One of my best creations," said Galileo proudly. "You see, Cardinal Pathetic and his followers, the Dogs of Ma, uphold Aristotle's ancient ideas as the exclusive source of all wisdom, so refuse to allow any new observations or experiments to test them."

"Are they your 'strollers'?"

"Yes. From the Greek 'peripatetic' - which I think means literally 'to loll about the edges aimlessly'. You see, in Ancient Greece, the followers of Aristotle would stroll behind him while he took his dog for a walk, and pounce on the little droppings that came out at regular intervals. After a particularly successful stop, Aristotle would apparently compliment the dog and say 'ma!'. That is why the utterances of the church today are still referred to as dog-ma."

DiDi added an example: "They came to the conclusion in this way that we stay on the Earth because the air pushes us down."

"Whereas we now know we stay down because our toenails are magnetic," threw in a passing Toby Nobler, in mid-selfcontented stroll towards the door.

"See what I mean?" whispered Galileo. "That kind of logic fits the church's way of thinking like…um…"

"An ass does a cardinal hat?" helped Sean, and it seemed to him the ugly features of the caricature on the wall looked disturbingly familiar. "So this Cardinal Perry Pathetic is a Second World character who already knows everything there is to know?"

"Exactly," beamed Galileo. "While we follow Copernicus's teaching that the Sun is immobile, and it is the Earth that moves around it. Our slogan is 'We can move it, yes we can'." He stood and said: "Would you accompany me to my workshop? I have something I think will interest you."

DiDi came with them, and said from somewhere below Sean's elbow: "By the way, if you are interested, tonight we are having a talent binge. An all-night Pythagoras party. Bring your own enigmas."

"By the ecstasy of mother superior, you mustn't miss that!" called another student after them.

Galileo's residence and workshop was just off a

large piazza, which sported a large blank board along one wall. "What is that?" Sean asked Galileo.

"Oh, left here since last year, when there was the Spanish Armada. Big event! Supposed to be the grand final between the Catholics and the Rest of the World. Billed as the debate to end all debate. They erected boards like this in every main square of every town in Italy. Top artists were engaged to sketch large depictions of the action as news came in. There were also commentaries and round-the-dial updates on divine signs, team selections, injuries, trainers and tactics."

DiDi added: "Gangs of youths roamed the streets looking for protestants, wrapped in papal colours and chanting 'We are the Catholics, down all the way with the Heathen!' "

"News Updates were called 'fill-ups' in honour of Phillip, the King of Spain."

DiDi laughed. "The Spanish ambassador kept saying: 'We've got everything under control'."

"When the final result came in that rain had halted play before the tourists had even landed, there was, shall we say, a sense of … er… 'disappointment' … that the team of divine righteousness should have made such a poor showing."

"The refereeing divine powers were accused of bias. Some people have no sense of irony," commented DiDi.

Galileo sighed. "Or learning curve to speak of. The forecast is for another hundred years of fire and brimstone, with only intermittent pockets of enlightenment."

* * *

When they arrived at Galileo's humble lodgings, Galileo said to DiDi. "Can you take the test equipment to the launch tower? We will meet you there shortly - no offence."

The little DiDi went off in an obedient huff.

Galileo chuckled cruelly. "With him around, I am never short on jokes."

Just as they were entering the house, Galileo pulled Sean up by the arm. "Shh. Can you feel that?"

"No. What?" said Sean.

"Can't you feel the Earth spinning? What shape is it exactly? A pizza? If so, it should be expanding at its edges - that is the only possible explanation for why no matter how far we sail or travel we can never reach the edges of the world." Galileo let Sean ponder that for a moment, before saying: "Only kidding! I play these tricks on my students all the time. Trouble is, they take me seriously."

As they went in, Sean said: "You know, as crazy as that sounds - in my time scientists are still stuck on the same question - only not about the Earth, but about the shape of the universe. Is it a pizza or a balloon? Will it expand forever?"

"A pop question, you could say?" and Galileo led Sean into his professionally homely mess. Like Leonardo's workshop, there were wooden models everywhere, mathematical half-dones scattered over tables, and piles of order forms for a military compass he had invented, made himself, and was catalogue selling.

After Galileo had conjured them up an excellent dinner, skilfully prepared from inexpensive ingredients, and poured them both some tasty, philosophy-stimulating vino, he gave his answer.

"It seems to me that a rational approach to explaining the fundamentals of the universe would be towards an ever-simpler model. A kind of catch-all, gut-feeling I have is that our model of five elements is too complex, and that fundamentally there should be only three. Who knows, perhaps a grandly unified theory may arise one day that reduces it all to one element."

Sean shook his head. "I am sorry to tell you this, but the latest count is over a hundred elements. And people of my time are *still* trying to find the commonality between them all."

Galileo was evidently disappointed. "So, in addition to still haggling about the shape of the universe, in the future the Grand Unified Theory is still just ..."

"Yes, a GUT feeling."

This second disappointment about the future was obviously a blow to Galileo. In a bit of a funk, he began to play with one of his toys. This was a long, narrow board set at an inclination. On it were two grooves, in which balls of different sizes and weights could be rolled. No matter which balls were chosen, if released simultaneously they would arrive at the bottom of the slope together. Sean watched him for a while.

"I built this model race track to give my younger brother as a Christmas present," explained Galileo. "But it doesn't seem to work properly. The balls always arrive together. I have tried everything to fix it: polishing one of the balls, using hollow or solid ones, lead versus cork, even cheating by pushing one slightly - but it is no good, they always arrive together."

"So, what do you conclude?" asked Sean, recognising this kiddies' toy as one of the greatest experiments in the history of science. That balls and a feather are locked together.

Galileo nodded wisely, and said: "That the equipment is broken. It is rubbish."

"No, I mean, what do you conclude about gravity?" Sean asked.

"Good on red meat. Want some more?"

"I mean the reason we are stuck to the Earth's surface?" said Sean, his exas beginning to perate.

"Oh, *that* theory... about bodies moving up and down?" Galileo tut-tutted. "Why the Greeks were so obsessed with perfect bodies and their nocturnal movements points to some sort of mental deviance, if you ask me."

He went to a football-sized glass model of Luca Pacioli's rhombicuboctahedron he had hanging, half-filled with water as a vase, and span it. Now Sean could see that the eight squares around the middle had engravings of the Vitruvian Man, and spinning the shape made him dance in a brief flicker animation sequence. "Still, there is no denying that erotic geometry, with its divine proportions, or Golden Ratio, is a cornerstone of the Renaissance. After all, there is something intrinsically fascinating about heavenly bodies moving together, in harmony, especially at night."

"Maestro Galileo, you said you had something to show me?" said Sean, not knowing what else to say.

"Yes. It is this." From his other sleeve Galileo produced ... the digital watch.

"I knew you had it!" exclaimed Sean happily, taking the watch and admiring its still as new appearance. "But where did you find it?"

"Rather a long story."

"So long as it is not another tall one."

"Ever heard of a man, an oracle, called 'Our Lady'?"

"Never. Strange name for a guy."

"That wasn't his only problem. You may know him under his syndicated trademark: Nostradamus."

"Ah…"

"When he was young, Nostradamus came up with a rather novel business model. He would first send out anonymous messages of doom and gloom, in enigmatic quatrains, four-line poems, designed to up the value of his mood-booster greeting cards. As with my practical joke teaching method - the worst thing that can happen is people taking you seriously."

"Sorry… but I don't see what that has to do with the watch?"

"If I were to tell you that Leonardo da Vinci knew Nostradamus?"

"Leonardo?!"

"They met at a future-guessing festival. One of those iron-man events where people drink themselves so stupid they begin to see visions. Nostradamus was only a teenager, but it seems he managed to get Leonardo to illustrate his first line of greeting cards. On Nostradamus's deathstraw (the last straw), a publisher gained the rights to bring out a commemorative series of these cards. They were medical advice cards, published under the unlikely title of 'Mr Our Lady cures your blockage' - sold with a giftpack of remedial cures for ailments of the juices - you know how these quacks work: take a quatrain after meals and call in on me in the morning - and they still appear in French as 'Les Pro-Faeces de M. Nostradamus'."

Galileo began to rummage for something in various piles of notes and dried animal parts. "It is an online service."

"Online?!" cried Sean.

"Yes. You append the card on a line above the door to your privy. Just a little ditty about how to avoid the plague, which leech is recommended for what, yet another bleeding cure this... bleeding cure that... The very latest in medical science. There is also a desktop version. And a boot version known as a screamsaver."

"But why did he call himself 'Our Lady'?"

"Well, it was Leonardo's idea: an intentional allusion to Mona Lisa. 'Ma Donna' Lisa was doing really well in the miniatures market in France. So, they used the medical advice trademark of 'Ma Lady', to keep the Italian flavour. A very successful brand. In fact, we still call illnesses 'maladies'. Since there were now two of them, Nostradamus adopted the plural form as his penname, which has since become one of the most successful oracle brands ever."

Galileo hung a card up on a string. "I received this little ditty for my 21 and halfst birthday:"

Sean came over and read the ponderous script:

**Supra capitulum armarium rompyus
Tenet linguam caelestiam
Ubi claudit lacus cerasus
Incapsulata Madridum realum**

"What does that teach you?" asked Galileo.

"Um... that Nostradamus was rubbish at Latin?"

"What do you expect from a guy with a name which means 'Our Lady'? Anyway, he usually wrote in French, except for the foreign festivities card trade."

"So, what does it mean?"

"Translated you get:

> A rompy cupboard head-on
> Holds the celestial tongue
> Where the cherry lake locks
> A ball for foot in a box

"So, duly, I went to the Cherry Lake, which I took to mean Lago Ceresio, on the shores of which lies Lugano. After searching for three days, I found the only house that matches that description. The main portal bears an inscription above it. Three letters, which make up Leonardo's logo: 'A.V.O.', meaning Amur Vincit Omnes, Love Conquers All."

"Amur!?" cried Sean.

"Ring anything up a bell tower?"

"Certainly does. Do you think Leo is trying to tell us something?"

"Oh, definitely. He has left a whole trail of clues."

Some light was cautiously dawning for Sean. "Is that why Leo went to France?"

"Could be. He gave Nostradamus a clue as to how to find the *spiki celestii*, the mythical 'language of the gods'." Galileo picked up the watch. "Embodied in an artefact known as the SANG Re.al."

"So you deciphered the quatrain and found the watch inside the house?"

"Yes."

"But… the house…?"

"Oh, don't worry," Galileo reassured him. "It is sealed by the hex-a-go-go still. Leonardo made sure

Cesare Borgia, and his later incarnations, could never get in."

"So, if Cespuglio couldn't get in, how did you?"

"By studying the geometry of Pacioli, who was a keen student of Vitruvius. He and Leonardo returned and finished the house, adding more eggs to seal it. They guessed the watch would return one day, so they left clues and a single way in - if you can work out where."

"Which of course you could! Good old Luca and Leo!" cried Sean happily.

"So I found the watch as they wanted, and brought it here, … and waited for you," finished Galileo. He looked sad suddenly. "Now, I am afraid my usefulness has ended."

"Maestro Galileo, don't be like that. I promise you you will go down in history."

"That's what my teacher told me. If you don't study harder, he said, you will go down in history. You're just trying to cheer me up. It's no use. It is already the modern world of which they spoke. There's a brand new calendar. What else can there be to learn?"

"Lots and lots of things. Let's start here: what is all this stuff?" Sean pointed at the shelves and tables covered in an incredible variety of things. It reminded him of Archimedes' and Leonardo's, and Nonno's for that matter, workshops.

"Oh, little nothings I amuse myself with. Trying to get something to work finally so I can convince the university to give me a real job. Fat chance. They say I don't understand the basics. That's why I waste my time experimenting, they say. Only because I haven't grasped the fundamental truths yet. Maybe they are right. It was all written in Aristotle's works two thousand years ago.

Who am I to think I can change anything?"

"There was another ancient Greek - well, more old than ancient - who challenged Aristotle: Archimedes."

"Archimedes!" Galileo looked pleased and shocked at the same time. He went to the door and window to ensure no-one was there, before returning to whisper: "I am a great fan of Archimedes." Galileo indicated a long shelf holding just two small books. "I have everything ever written about him, and a full set of 'Who's who in the ancient world' tobacco cards. There is a rumour that his greatest work has been mislaid due to a classification error in some library in the Middle East. And of course we cannot go there because of the 'no hasta la vista' restrictions."

"Which means?"

"I don't have a visa."

"I know Archimedes better than you can possibly imagine. And I can promise you he felt just as rejected and misunderstood as you do."

"And he succeeded in the end?"

"Well, no. They killed him. But you will be different. Pick up your crest - it has fallen."

When Galileo remained in a funk, Sean tried:

"What were you doing in the cathedral?"

This bucked him up as intended. "Proving one of my theories: that a pendulum of a certain length will swing with the same time period between swing ends no matter how heavy the object suspended. Watch." He had a rig with two strings of equal lengths attached. One had a heavy metal ball, the other a cork. "Observe." He released them. They swang in perfect harmony. "The same thing happened when you landed on the chandelier. When you came down, the chandelier continued to swing with the same period, despite the change in weight."

"That's brilliant, Maestro Galileo! And what's that over there?" asked Sean, indicating a tub of water, over which hung a balance. On one side was a piece of metal fashioned roughly into the form of a crown. On the other was a shapeless lump.

"I am recreating Archimedes' greatest Eureka Moment. It uses density and buoyancy in water to measure impurities in metal. The Duke's department of coinage doesn't like it for some reason. I call it the 'little balance'."

"And the 'big balance'?" asked Sean.

"That happens on the tower." Galileo slapped his copious forehead. "Oh! I have forgotten DiDi! He is waiting for us up the tower!"

"Why?"

"I'll explain on the way."

Galileo took the watch and inexplicably strapped it onto a large apple. He then rigged a small and complicated device over the watch, which involved some sort of lever on its buttons. He positioned a silver coin so it rested on the stop/start button, before he put the assembly carefully in his pocket.

"Can you pocket that cannonball?" he said to Sean, and led the way out the door, and back up the road to the Leaning Tower.

"Galileo, why is the tower leaning?" gasped Sean as he ran alongside, struggling with the heavy ball.

"A spelling mistake. The city had commissioned a Tower of Learning, but on the specifications they had written Tower of Leaning." The tower stood over the rooftops like a beacon as they made their way to it. "The engineers say it is the Devil's work. Well, they would wouldn't they? If you are incompetent in your job, all you have to do is invoke the Devil, and you're in the clear. So some are lobbying for it to be filled with wood and heretic fuel to be burnt as an eternal beacon for the one true … something or other. I forget the details, but it is a terribly good argument. They want to call it the Tower of Inferno."

"So, why am I carrying this heavy ball?" asked Sean, his arms aching.

"I have decided to enter this year's Cannonball Olympics. If I can win, the mathematics chair will be mine for sure! The tower is a perfect launching pad. It leans over so the balls fall clear. We have races - to see whose cannonball will land first. The heavier the better, obviously."

"But… you saw from your brother's game that all bodies fall at the same rate of acceleration."

"What actually happens does not change what is written in the Games manual."

"So what are the results of the races?" asked Sean.

"So far in every race the church favourite has won."

"How can they always win?"

"Well, they say they have the best engineers to optimise the descendancy control. That and the fact that they also supply the judges. Some cynics say the results are related to the fact that the church also run the gambling stalls. Who knows?"

"I thought sport was supposed to involve fair play?"

"This is Italy. What's it like in your day?"

"It's still Italy. But, Galileo, if you dropped a wooden ball of the same size, it would fall just as fast."

"Ah… well, I see a couple of problems there. First of all, there is no such thing as a wooden cannonball. Wouldn't be much use, would it? And secondly, it is against the rules. That's fair enough. All sports must have rules."

"But this is science," objected Sean as they began the ascent up the 294 steps of the tower.

"Ah, there's the technicality, you see. The church very cleverly reclassified cannonball dropping from science to sport, so it falls under their recreation licensing jurisdiction. In this way, they can determine how it is to be done, and anyone trying anything else is disqualified."

"What does that entail?"

"Have you never heard physicists talk of 'falling bodies'?"

"Yes."

"Never wondered where that expression comes from? Anyway, they are always looking for fuel for the eternal flame at the next games."

"I see…"

They were near the top of the tower. They edged around the huge bell in the dark chamber, and then proceeded up the last marble steps to the ex-physics laboratory ledge, jutting, by virtue of the lean, over the grass lawn a sickening 56 metres below them.

"Where is DiDi? He should be here," complained Galileo, gazing back down the stairs into the dark of the floor below them.

Somebody flicked a switch. This is to say they used a branch to whip a servant to light a lantern to plunge the chamber into a less gloomy shade of black.

What Sean saw coming up the steps behind them froze the more crucial of his cerebral hemispheres.

These were the feared watchhammer troops - bearing symbols of a breaking watch and a hammerhead: from a distance the combination looked uncannily like a beaker, with SANG Re.al written beneath it

And there, at their head, was Cardinal Pathetic.

"I thought you were only a cartoon character?" Sean couldn't resist asking.

"Oh, but I am. My two-dimensionality is the secret behind my popularity. So, we meet again, Sean Seulpierre. And an old friend, too." The procession had reached the upper landing. The Cardinal stepped aside - which is not usually advised on a narrow platform - to reveal a little someone being held by a group of the white-cloaked and heavily armoured watchhammer troops.

"DiDi?!"

"Oh, come now Sean. Surely you recognise your old friend from Syracuse?"

"Sean, it's me, Elf," said the little man, pinioned between the guards.

"Elf!!" cried Sean. "But, what are you doing here?"

"Doing as Pau suggested: trying to inspire Galileo to drop things from the tower."

"What is that supposed to prove?" asked Sean, not giving in to the temptation to ask where Pau and Geni were.

"Something about gravity, isn't it?" replied Elf. "Didn't Pau tell you?"

"Um… he may have skipped over some of the details."

"So, what do you want, … Cespuglio?" challenged Sean, bravely turning on the cardinal.

Cespuglio laughed his cruel laugh. "Why don't *you* enlighten us, Signor Galilei?"

"Yes, of course," and Galileo lit his lamp.

"No, I mean tell us about your theory of cannonball dropping."

"Oh, um… After I realised that, since the scriptures had been irrevocably declared right, there must be something wrong with reality. I determined that the only way to win the competition was to measure the actual time a body takes to fall. With the church cheating as the judges, I needed proof. And this," he pulled out the apple and the watch, "would provide that."

Cespuglio's eyes lit up at the sight of the watch, and the watchhammer troops shuffled, their beady eyes signalling tones of expectation.

Galileo continued. "By tying the watch around an object about the same size and shape as a cannonball, but very different Archimedean densiticity, such as this apple, and dropping it, I could get a measurement of the time it takes to traverse the 56 metres to the ground. By fitting the watch to the apple in this way - the impact will cause this lever to push this coin onto this button, and the watch will stop its count. Then I repeat the experiment with the cannonball, and then I have the two times - and we can determine the true winner.

"Incidentally, by measuring the falling times from different levels of the tower, I have discovered an interesting fact: the objects do not fall at even speeds, but appear to accelerate. And this acceleration may be described mathematically, allowing me to predict how long it will take any object to fall any height. This may lead one day to a general description of the motion of all bodies. A small drop for an apple, but a giant leap for mathkind."

"*Spiki celestii!*" cried Sean, remembering Leonardo's words about the importance of the language of the gods to breaking the mental paralysis that gripped the world before the enlightenment.

Cespuglio shook his head. "So much theory - it makes my head ache. But, Galileo, the church wins every time, does it not?"

"So far, yes, I have had no luck in getting my ideas approved by the various departments."

"Which departments," asked Sean.

"For example, when I attempted to revive an old idea that the stuff of the world is made up of very small pieces, called in ancient Greece the unlikely word 'atom'."

"Why 'a Tom'? Why not 'a Dick' or 'a Harry'?" mocked Cespuglio.

"I guess it was the first name that came to them," was Galileo's lame answer. "It was the Department of Health that blocked my atomic testing. They said that an atomistic theory meant that the holy ghost could not substantiate his body, and a slice of bread for some reason, in the holy sacrament. So the theory ran afoul of the Food and Herbs legislation, and my atom idea was banned for public health reasons."

"Now tell them how I blocked your Copernican system," chided Cespuglio.

"The theory that the Sun is the centre of the universe was banned for reasons of national security, since there would otherwise surely be widespread panic at the thought of the Earth falling towards the Sun."

" 'National security' is one of my favourite excuses," cherished Cespuglio. "Galileo... the watch, please!"

Galileo held the watch, still wrapped around the apple, and looked at it sadly.

"Couldn't I just do one last experiment? Before you destroy it?"

To Sean's lasting surprise Cespuglio indulged him: "Oh, alright. Just one."

While Galileo was fumbling with the timing trigger mechanism, Cespuglio turned to Elf. "And now, little man, you can join your two friends." He opened a small wooden chest one of the Watchhammer troops was holding, and took out the same iron crown that Cesare Borgia had been wearing. He let it play in the last rays of the setting sun for a few moments, relishing its power over the minds of men, before he lowered it ceremoniously onto Elf's head.

In a last desperate bid, Elf broke one arm free from his Invertabrake guards holding him. He reached into his pocket to pull out a time egg, and lifted his arm to throw the small piece of polished rock at his feet. But the crown had begun to glimmer and do its parents guidance only thing, just as the helmet had done with Stinto in Syracuse. As a result Elf's host took back control of his body with a jolt, causing the hand to release the egg in mid-swing, sending it flying over Sean's head to do a teasingly slow parabola up and over the tower's balustrade.

Sean instinctively lunged for it, and in so doing caught Galileo's hand holding the apple with the watch strapped around it. The next thing Sean knew he was falling, target Earth, the egg and the apple rotating just out of his reach beneath him. They hit the ground in exactly the same formation.

Galileo, who had been watching from above, simply noted: "Now, *that* is interesting."

* * * *

Chapter Nine
Still Falling

"UGHH!" was really all Sean could think of saying.

"What?!" a vocal outrage tore into his earhole. "By all the atoms of sweet Democritus, desist and remove of yourself from me, ye idiot of dimensions diminutive!"

Sean attempted to do as instructed, but trying to stand made just about everything worse because he was not only on top of an offended someone, but by leaving the lap of that same verbally visceral someone he found himself immediately skating on a laminar flow of skittish apples, none of which were rebels to the third law of obstinacy.

After falling on his offended interlocutor for something between the fourth and eighth time, depending on where the line is drawn between slip and fall, he perchanced to recall what had happened to bring him to this situation. On this prompt he inverted his strategy and lay still and looked up.

Just as he hadn't fully unanticipated: no tower at all, leaning or otherwise. Only an old apple tree.

'Ping', or rather 'schlupp', went up a memo note of sorts inside Sean's head.

"Er, excuse me, sir," he hazarded to his wrestling companion, a thin young man in his early twenties. "You wouldn't happen to be Sir Isaac Newton, would you?"

"Without the minimal refraction from your ineruditeness, sirrah, our pattern of replication lies securely centred on a most perfunctory negative."

Sean used a simple 'ah' to verbalise the sudden truncation of his previous line of thought.

After a further while of renewed pushing, voluntary and involuntary cycles of separation and reuniting, colourful complaining and space-clearing enough to stand, the young man said: "Albeit, the *actio* and *condicio* of beknightenment are not wholly extremus to myne idle fantasys."

"Eh?" said and thought Sean to celebrate his mêlée extricus.

"Isaac!" shrilled in upon them a mature woman's voice from the stonewall cottage nearby. "Isaac! Dothen't juste looke upon yon apples, yunge man. Whereof art thy thoughts attending? Divine inspiration?"

"Sorrie, Mumsie," called the young Isaac Newton, daring Sean with a pair of hawk's eyes to perchance to take of the mickey, as he gathered up the apples that had fallen to the ground and put them in a large basket.

"Shall I help you?" offered Sean.

"Mostly decent of ye. But do not anticipate goodly remuneration. I shalt give ye this bruiséd apple albeit. Bye the longe loste booke of the Measurer, watt is this?" He held up the apple on which the watch was strapped. "Howe solitarie." He took the watch off and before Sean could say anything, had pocketed it, and was heading towards the farmhouse, the basket completely forgotten. Sean picked it up and pursued the long-haired youth in his lacey velvet costume.

As they entered the door to the comfortable farm cottage, Newton's mother was in mid-rebuke. "Of alle the fleabitt excuses I am aheared in myne tyme! The Greate Plague?! Oh, to bee sure it bee 'greate' - greate for laie-a-bowtes who butte seek excuse to avoide of the worke. A plague this, a plague on yonder, alle falle downe - like to as a ruddie London bridg! Nexte thou wilt be teling me alle London towne bee aflame. Indeede! You bee juste shirkeing worke yungge man."

"But mater mia…"

"Donst thou 'but mater mia' mee. 'Mumsie' wilt doe juste fyne. And if thou canst nae abide that, trye 'honour'd mother'. Fore t' love of Mr Biggy, I am like to swear that everie fourthe worde you utter bee Latin."

"It's all the rayge in Cambridge, Mumsie. They're called latin quarters."

"I bee not knowing abowte that. Butte I doe knowe thou bee juste wasteing thy time a-sitting nether yon appel tree. Onn watt bee thou awaited? The mithycal Bigg Apple of Inspiration, I shallt swear? Lyke as myne grandadd wert wont a-sayeing: a apple a daye is … farre too slowe. Nottinge will ever comm whither all this buke-lerning. Marke myne wordes. A farmerer - that's wha' thou shudst bee, yunge man. Doeth a oneste daye's worke."

"I do work."

"Oh, I wudde fae haff it that thou wuddest nott droppe thyne 'e's in soe like a manner - this moderne slangg is terribbul. Thou cannst doe thyne mattameticks bye cownting watt thou hast pickk't. If the gude hevvens hath wantéd uss to use owr branes, tings wulde bee as like to fall uppe as downe. Soe it art downe you shude be a'luking. It bee qwite simppel if thou dothst nott think abowte it. Doeth thy dreameing in thyne owne tyme."

"But there isn't any own time around here on a farm."

"That bee becaws alle thou doest is sitt arrownd makeing of t'rithmetic. If a one dothn't alreddy knowe it, a one ne'er wilt, that bee whawt I alwae saye. Alwae buke-lerning! Dothn't thou know enuff as yet? Luke att me! Alwae berrying hussbands, levt on myne owne running this farme and bringging upp a howle bunch of lae-abowt chiddren. But dothn't thou goest a-thinking as I knowe nowt. I knowe alle I nede a-knowen. Myne poore parents infested a howle sixct month in myne schulling, affor the Grate Warr off cawse, befforr we wert evakuated. An' that wert enuff forr me - servéd me fyne a howle lyfetyme it haff."

"What didst thou learn from the Great War?"

"If thou be awanting a gude evakkuation, be takeing a lott off prunes. Healthy, affilling - for a goodlie wile aniwae - and kepe the wile longger thann freshe fruites. Who bee this?" she indicated the straggly-looking boy of about eighteen Sean was occupying, and she had only just noticed.

"I am not possessed of that knowledge. He did fall out of a tree, *terrae cadens…* directly atop of me. Not at any angle as a spinning Earth would predicate. Hmmm… interesting…"

"Sacky!! Whoeth in the name of Lord Beezlebub's knees bee this stranger bedraggley?!"

"Assume did I he was but one of our fruit pickers?"

"Neffer have I on him eyes laide affor nows. Thou there! Pute downe yon appel chest and bee cleareing thee well off!"

"I am sorry, Mrs New…" began Sean, desperate to get his watch back.

"Ayscough."

"Sorry?" said Sean.

"Ayscough. Hannah Ayscough."

"Oh dear. Have you tried honey in tea? I'm sure it'll get better."

"Righte! That doth doe it! Insulltes onn the gude nayme of myne poore parents, which aye recycled after the dethe of t' gude Mr Newton. Cleare thee off befforr I doe putte the hedgehoggs onn to thee."

"Hedgehogs? - don't you mean dogs?"

"Morr the spikier, morr the hard to remove off the one, and never are wont to burie one's souppe bones. Frendd and prottektor of woman be-ith the olde hedgehogg. Now mownte thy two-wheeley contraption, jamie boy-o, beffore I bee of minde to sette one onn to ye."

Sean doth bide a retreat.

He stood on the mud road by the entrance ruts to the property, listening to Newton's mother berating him decibellically for his useless alchemy experiments.

"Soe?! Iff tha' be-ith the case, wher be-ith alle the gulde, eh?! Eh?!! We wulde bee living in a palas, wulde wee not? I'd as like to haffe a countie for myne gardene, theyed be servants bye the bayker's dozzen, and swanpoope bye the gallon, not olde spineless hedgehoggs and yunge, laie-abowte sonnes…"

The door swung open and Isaac came out with a bucket of pig swill delectables. The voice followed him. "Thou art dreameing, Sacky, howe cannst thou bee a proffessorr of 'rithmetic? Any proffessorr offa

Vitruvian Boy

Cambridge or Oxford must toe bee a priest. Ovviussly. After alle, mathemattick is the languayge of the godds. Howe canst thou hoppe to understande 'thematics bye spending alle thy tyme exerrising on useles equations aplace off on thy knees begging the heffens forre divine inspiration?!"

Isaac returned to the door and said: "I wilt show thee knowledge falls not just out the skye."

"Rubbish. Every soule knowst it dost."

"But mumsie... I wilt build thee a powerful telescope and thou shallst see for thyself there be much on high for the goodly readeing therof."

"How canst thou see an any thing if thou only goest oute bye nite, wenn the lites be-ith owte? Wuldst thou goen into a library after darke withowte a canddel, ehh? Thou musst needs to luke athwart the daye. Lukst thou at the sunne, giver of alle lite."

"I've tried it."

"An'...?"

"I nearly wenteth blinde."

"I wert talkeing abowte knowledgeables."

"So wert I."

"Thou seest? Thatt proofes myne case. Overtaxing thy brane. Thou muste nedes to begg in hummel genuflexion posture, whence thou maest only luke downe, nott bee ofendding Mr. Biggy bye raysing thy ofendding hedd and daering to luke for knowleddg thyself. Onn thy knees, Sacky! Like everie a one else. No a one hath effer o'erburden'd theyr thinking facultyes onn theyr knees."

"But mumsie..." The door slammed shut on their enlightening conversation.

Literally at a 'now what?' proverbial crossroad, Sean looked up, and then for variation down, the various road branches at the copious ye olde English countryside. Visi-bites, audio cues and olfactors galore attested to the furious purity of the pre-industrial age. Fields of stuff growing vigorously and unassisted by contaminants, freshly baled hay, some scattered farmhands in regulation smocks and straw hats, chickens, ducks, pigs, sheep, and some cows as scenic mooey extras, seemed to be the only contenders for the next step, until...

'Psst...' a cliché asserted itself leafily from the midst of a hedge.

"Hello," engaged Sean, feeling both a little foolish and possessed of little left to lose.

He heard again: "Psst, over here," the hedge midst expanded on its theme.

"Er... Yes, can I help you?" inquired Sean directly to the vegetation - hedging to politeness, so to speak.

"Sean," hoarse-whispered a female voice "It's us, Geni and Pau."

"Geni!! Pau..," called Sean and ran around to greet them on the far side.

"Hello," intoned Pau unenthusiastically from inside the form of a middly-agey country gent, handsomely attired in wig and stockings, and carrying a disguise detail in the form of a gentleman's walking stick.

"But... what are you doing here?" Sean asked, amazed and thankful, after he had been embraced by Geni, who was herself occupying a matching beautiful country gentry lady.

"Inspiring," replied Pau, then added for maximum unnecessity: "What else? Something you wouldn't even know how to begin."

Geni was squeezed into a very fetching country dress. And just what it was fetching were very difficult not to notice. "Oh Sean, it's so good to see you!"

His eyes flicked down involuntarily. "And it's good to see you *two* - and Pau as well."

"We're both glad you escaped Cesare Borgia… *Aren't* we, Pau?"

There was a telling gap between the question and the answer - something akin to that between a multilegged hairy something and its victim. "Yeah, right. Glad as wrap."

Giving this as generous an interpretation as could be squeezed out of the laws of sense and sensibility, Geni hugged Sean a second time, causing him temporary deafness. "You see! Pau is pleased as well!"

"But what are you doing here?" stammered Sean, himself hardly able to contain his joy at finding himself with his old friends he had last seen vanish from the haunted house at a moment of chronic peril.

"We're trying to get Isaac Newton to see a falling apple and be inspired to discover gravity, like it says in all the schoolbooks." She paused and bit her lip. "Or something… But he's just not getting it."

Pau kicked a stone sulkily. "I still say he doesn't need an apple. Let's just trip him up - or string him upside down from a tree and threaten to cut him loose unless he comes around to thinking our way."

"No, Pau. It is not the time for a string theory. If we want things to return to normal, we have got to get him inspired in the classical way."

"Um… I am afraid that's too late. I let him get the watch," admitted Sean.

"You what?!" exploded Pau. "You little chrono-virus!

Here we are, a whole month we've been here, hiding behind hedges, up trees, throwing apples at Newt-boy at every opportunity, he always missing them, or using them to practice his legspin, while he moans to the chickens about their mutual lack of opportunity for inspiration... And just when we think we're about to make a breakthrough, you come along and hand him a piece of turn-of-the-twenty-first century technology!"

"He *took* it - I didn't *give* it to him."

"It doesn't matter, you hoppy little plague-carrier. With that watch, the timeline risks going haywire. Haven't you worked *that* out yet?"

Geni reproached Pau. "Pau... now we've talked about this. We agreed that the watch *may* be causing a disruption, but we can't be sure. That's why we came here. To 1666. Newton has been here in his family home in Lincolnshire for six months because the plague has reached Cambridge. And the university, where he is an undergrad, is closed."

"And *that's* not *my* fault either..." began Sean.

"Nobody is saying it is, Sean," soothed Geni, with a glare of warning at Pau. "Anyway, we have a three-week window - Newton is scheduled to discover gravity this autumn, while there are still apples in the trees in this, his family's orchard. One of the most important scientific discoveries ever - leads to understanding that things fall downwards."

"What - are you saying nobody had noticed *that* before?" laughed Sean.

"Well, yes, of course they had. But it was important that *he* noticed it when he did, because, ... you know, ... um..." Geni bit her well-indentured lip.

"Why all the subterfuge? Why didn't you just talk

to him directly?"

"Oh, Pau tried that. It didn't work."

"Why not? Pau? What did you say?"

"Oh, he asked me a silly question - something about why is it that an apple will fall directly to the Earth, and yet the Moon does not?"

"And you said?"

"Oh… I can't remember exactly…"

"Didn't you say it was …" began Geni.

"Look," Pau cut her off. "It doesn't matter. Whatever it was that Newton discovered, I heard if it weren't for Newton there would never have been a steam age," concluded Pau.

"Why steam?" asked Geni, trying dutifully to look impressed at Pau's great wisdom.

"Ah… well, that would be because he invented matches," shrugged Pau.

"Yes. That must be it," agreed Geni happily.

"Matches?!" exploded Sean.

"Yes," said Pau.

"In 1666?"

"1066, 1666, what's the difference?"

"Six hundred years. What have matches got to do with falling apples?" logic-nagged Sean.

"Look, the Great Fire of London is due any day. See the connection now?" dismissed Pau loftily.

"You don't actually know anything about history, do you?" Sean stated more than asked.

Pau exploded: "Shut up, you little interfering nematode. What did you have to come here for, anyway? And, for that matter, why was your stupid watch on that stupid apple?! What is this: some sort of tree of knowledge remake?!"

"Well, who do you think you are? Adam and Eve?"

Geni and Pau looked at each other as if to say: 'Now that's an idea!'

Sean went on. "Galileo and I were measuring how long it would take for a body to fall – but I didn't realise it was going to be *my* body. I fell off the leaning tower of Pisa just after the watch, which was strapped around an apple."

Pau held the element of derise: "Don't mistake this for interest, but 'Why?' "

"We wanted to enter a team in the summer cannonball olympics…"

"No, I mean why did you fall off? Although I like the concept."

Sean's face clouded over. "Because Cespuglio came after us."

"You and Galileo?"

"And… Elf." Sean added miserably.

"Elf! Where is he?!" they looked around.

"He didn't make it. The cardinal's men got him."

"And you escaped. How very convenient," Pau drawled suspiciously.

"Elf was trying to use an egg, but when they grabbed him he let it fly – over the edge. I tried to catch it, but, you know, we forget that leaning towers have leaning floors… and I fell over the side, with the apple. I guess the egg must have arrived just in front of me. It must have broken open, causing me to time-jump instead of hitting the ground, and I came out here. I just feel so sorry for the person I was occupying. I guess he died because of me."

Pau shook his head. "I hate to be the one to bring you consolation, but you didn't kill anyone. You're nowhere near that significant."

Geni hushed him angrily. "Sean, the inquisition must have been hunting that person anyway. He was … let's say 'scheduled' to be terminated … that's how things work in this. We are not capable of changing the basics of the timeline."

"It's called the TPF," said Pau with hurtful superiority.

"Time Paradox Failsafe," deciphered Geni, when it was evident Pau had forgotten what it meant.

Sean remembered Stinto's famous last words, then said: "But how can you be so sure?"

"Because history is always the same - every time we come through it is always exactly the same as the last time - that can only mean we never cause any changes."

"But the watch?" continued Sean undaunted. "You said yourselves that is different. And Cespuglio. And me, for that matter?"

The two were silent. Some chickens were responding to the cluck-clucking of a pretty teenage girl, Isaac's half-sister, Hannah Smith, as she offered to feed them.

Pau sat dejectedly on a milestone at the side of the road, reading 'London 112 mile, Minde ye the Gappe'.

"That's what I don't understand," he said, scratching his head under his wig with a twig. "The watch *must* be changing history, accelerating progress. And yet… each time we get to a new jumpspot, it's as if the watch has just arrived - has never been in history before now."

Geni sat next to him, and he lent against her as she consoled him.

Sean gave them a tranquil moment before throwing liquid hydrogen on the smouldering debate. "So, what's the problem?"

Pau stood up angrily, sending Geni flying backwards as a blossom of petticoats. He towered over Sean menacingly, jabbing him with a finger in his chest. "The problem is, you little rat hitchhiker, is that our friends, Stinto, Amur and Elf, have been captured by a megalomaniac by the name of Cespuglio who seems to always have a private army, and is always finding us by homing in on *your* watch! *That's* the problem!"

Sean stood his ground. "Well, don't you see? That's exactly it. It's as if the watch were riding a wave of change - a wave that is racing forward, and we are just coming along for the ride."

"So… what will happen to the future?" asked Geni, pulling Sean out of the firing line before Pau could launch his next digital missile, leaving him with his stab finger hovering in the air, towards an attentive but not unduly impressed squirrel under the hedge.

"My guess is that there are two futures," went on Sean. "The one we know, and a new one forming. The watch must be splitting the timeline in two around itself as it ploughs through. Like an ice-breaker… or something."

Pau made an honest enough effort to understand this, his face screwing up into something quite prunish, before he blew out the tension and said: "But this is all crazy!" He grasped Geni's hand hard and looked pleadingly into her eyes. "I just want everything to go back to as it was."

"I know. I know," cooed Geni to calm him. "It's all so difficult to understand."

Pau reverted to the easier route of recrimination. "Well, I understand this much: Sean Seulpierre here is

Vitruvian Boy

causing everything to go wrong. If we could just get rid of him - and the watch - everything would probably return to normal, and Stinto, Amur and Elf will be waiting for us at Syracuse in minus 212 next time round, just like before."

"By 'get rid of' I hope you mean return home!?" demanded Geni, bristling with shades of femme fatale.

Pau looked down and kicked the brother of the stone he had kicked before. "Oh... yeah... sure. Home. Safe. Sure, that's what I meant." He smiled submissively at Geni, then sideways with malevolence for Sean's private consumption.

Geni took charge of the antler-locked males. "But first, we have to get the watch back."

Sean sighed. "Haven't we been through something like this already?" he asked, postboding his thoughts to Roman assault craft and flaming catapult missiles. "The last time we tried to reset natural history manually, the watch disappeared to Egypt with John the Measurer, where it became the star attraction in a mathematics revival theatre festival. Then the Romans, under Cespuglio as every new emperor, invaded every country they could find to look for it. So, the Egyptians spirited it away on a fourteen hundred year spree around the world, causing leaps of scientific and mathematical knowledge in Persia, India and China, before it ended up in the Venetian lagoon for two hundred years with a horde of Mongols at its heels. This time we'll have to be more subtle."

Sean listened towards the house where the strains of maternal beratement had gone into stasis some time before. "Getting the watch back from Newton is not going to be any easier." He turned to Geni and took her hands. "Why don't you do it?"

"We can't."

"Why not?"

"He won't listen to us. He thinks…," began Pau. "He thinks…"

"Yes?" asked Sean.

"He thinks Pau is an idiot," said Geni matter-of-factly, with an unconvincing dismissive laugh. "Because of his answer to the gravity question. Why the apple falls but the Moon does not."

"Yes, yes, yes… We've already been over that," Pau said hastily.

"What *was* your answer, Pau?" Sean insisted.

"Don't change the subject. *You* were the one who gave Newton the watch - *you* are the one who will have to get it back before it does any more damage to the timeline."

"And you?" Sean took Geni's hands again. "Will you be waiting for me when I get back?"

Geni bit her lip as tears teased through her lashes. "I'm sorry, Sean, we can't. Now that Newton has been inspired, we have to move on."

"Why the rush? The future will wait."

"Well, Pau? Couldn't we wait at least a little while?"

"No, Geni. Sean's not one of us. We have to continue on doing what we have always done - only this way can we keep the timeline intact."

Geni sighed, and kissed and hugged Sean. "I am sorry to leave you like this, Sean, truly I am. Goodbye. Good luck, dear dear boy." She turned sadly to join Pau.

"Ready?" he asked, holding up his egg.

"Ready," she said, and held up hers.

Sean stepped forward. "But, tell me, where do you find the eggs?"

"Oh, different places," replied Geni. "Oracles, diviners, fortune tellers, alchemists… they all stock them. They are rare but there is a trade. Some call them the philosopher's eggs."

Pau added: "These ones I got from a baker in London in exchange for a box of matches. He was a part-time alchemist and was experimenting with natural gas heating."

"That wouldn't happen to have been Pudding Lane, would it?" asked Sean, suspiciously.

"What's wrong with that?!" shrugged Pau. "Executioners work in Diagony Alley, civil servants in Memo Circle, legislators in Backhand Avenue, lawyers in Waffle Park, doctors in Or Topsy Deadend, marriage agents in Pickadilly Circus - why shouldn't bakers mix in Pudding Lane?"

The eggs fell and broke, and they were gone, leaving two very surprised gentry folk looking at each other and at Sean, wondering what on Earth they were doing there. The lady Geni had been occupying seemed confused, as she looked about her and her low-cut dress. She whipped up her hands to cover her embarrassment.

The man Pau had been occupying turned and fled quickly down the road, the lady following, complaining, in his wake.

Isaac Newton came around the hedge behind which he had been hiding. He walked straight to the eggshells left by Geni. "What manner of witchcraft is this? I saw a figure, a soul, pass from that lady when the egg broke. A swirl of ether or perchance Descartes' vortex? Can you enlighten me?" he said finally to Sean.

"I think, Sir... *Mr* Isaac... we need to talk."

Newton collected the eggshells carefully in his handkerchief.

"I see you are well versed in the modern slang! What a hute! Call me Sacky. I wish to examine and experiment on these eggshells. Can I prevail on you to accompany me to Cambridge where I have my alchemy laboratory? There is the slight inconvenience of almost certain death from the plague?"

"But please tell me one thing," replied Sean. "That man who just left - what did he answer when you asked him why the Moon does not fall to the Earth while an apple does?"

"Because it is not a fruit."

* * * *

Chapter Ten
Sacks n' Socks

To 'poste ourself to Cambridge Towne', they boarded the half-past Wednesday coach. Due to the Level Black plague warnings, they had the coach to themselves.

During the journey, the 23-year-old Isaac Newton took time out from his ruminations to astound his new companion with: "So, Sean Seulpierre, where in your opinion did lie Galilei's chances in the cannonball derby?"

Sean agaped his face appropriately: "How did you …?"

Newton smiled. "As elementary, my dear master Seulpierre, as mercury. It is a little hobby of mine - to read the signs. I am trying to inculcate a reputation about the town as a scurrilous deducer. To make a reputation these days one has to be written up by one of the gutter diarists - like the infamous Samuel Pepys - known to we students as 'pepying Sam'. My ambition is one day to be a great detective. I envisage myself with a telescopic lens in one hand, a health-giving pipe in t'other, perhaps wearing some sort of fetching cap and cape, stalking the underworld of the docklands in London, hunting down criminals. Especially coin clippers. Hate coin clippers, don't you?"

"Those who debase coins? I've met them before. So what else do you know about me?"

"Oh, I am completely in the dark," said Newton unconvincingly, and took the digital watch out of a frayed pocket of his coat stained variously and chemically. "So much so, in fact, that I can deduce nothing at all… except the blindingly obvious. For example, that you are a time traveller, that you have fallen with this time piece from the Tower of Pisa, helping Signor Galilei in his researches, and that you were the famed apprentice of Archimedes quotationed in the John the Measurer texts – the so-becalled Watchbearer of Syracuse."

Feeling a little Dr. Watsonly, Sean replied: "That's amazing. How can you possibly know all that?!"

"Ah." Newton put the watch to his mouth and bit down on one of its buttons. He then frowned menacingly at the happy little mouse image when it appeared to count out the seconds playfully. "This time piece is recorded on the great column of Trajan in Rome as the legendary 'Mikelus Mowses'. But even so, it is clearly from a future time – a time when the world is obsessed with unnecessary precision… and worships mice." He wrinkled his nose in distaste. "Which would mean they are extinct. Live ones smell. One function of the watch is a commence time increment count – terminate time increment count – operated by these two little tooth nobbies. It measures not only minutes, but also seconds. And if I were not of better knowledge, I would have said that these fastly moving numbers would be fragmentations of seconds thereof. But that is quite clearly impossible. No mechanicalism could be that accurate. And there can be no possible need for such an absurd disintegralisation of the time path."

"My grand-father always says 'the real creativity behind new technology lies in its justification' - you know, anything new drives the search for a need for it."

"I see," replied Newton. "So in this *technique-logicus* world of yours, people are so busy admiring the cleverness of their things, they forget to wonder at their real value? Sounds like a place made poor by its material wealth."

Sean thought of the pollution and noise which stained his generation's world. "But what about the Tower of Pisa? How did you know I had fallen from that?"

Newton looked surprised at the question. "Well, that's not difficult, surely? When I found the watch, it had been affixéd to an apple. A coin acting as a lever had been posited ingeniously against one of these nobbies so that upon impact it would be the causative action of the cessation of the time interval count progression. Why would that be necessary when it is clearly designed to be tooth operated by a human? The only explanation can be that no human would be accompanying it. See here, this attachment band - some strange animal skin…"

"Plastic."

"What sort of animal is that?"

"It's not an animal. It is manufactured artificially."

"Whence?"

"Whence?"

"Perhaps I meant 'whither'?"

"Worse."

"Sorry. I was a-forgetting in the slang to speak. Old

habits die hardly. Try 'What from?' "

"Mineral oil."

"And that would be…?"

"Remains of long-dead animals."

With an involuntary cry, Newton threw the watch down on the coach seat hurriedly and wiped his long fingers on his coat sleeves. "How totally revolting. At least *we* use fresh corpses for our desecrations. The more you tell me of your world, Sean Seulpierre, the more I think the future will take us into an all new low."

"Yes, you could be right there. You were saying about the watchstrap?"

"Its girth and mechanism implies it should be worn circumventially of a corporeal appendage - quite possibly the ankle. But now methinks no self-respecting person would want flesh contact with this… 'plastic'." He shivered in revulsion. "If the 'mineral oil' of which you speak rules the minds of men in your world, I hazard to propose it will cause the soul to seep… But, as I was nearly saying, clearly the watch was travelling unaided by human operation, for the purposes of measuring an interval of time. Hence, I deduce it was dropped from a height as part of a trial of sorts."

"But how did you know it was the Tower of Pisa?"

Newton tapped the side of his prominent nose. "That was the easiest of all." He pointed at the numbers on the frozen stopwatch display. "Since I know how long it has fallen, it is but a simple calculation."

"How?"

Newton metronomed an index finger at him. "I am certainly not going to tell you! Sufficéd shalt it be to say it is based upon my patent-appended formula for the acceleration of bodies attracted to the *corpus terranum*

- the Earth. And furthermore, since I witnessed you come out of the tree with it, I deduce you fell with it *unintentionally*. Otherwise why the complexity of the coin mechanism?"

"And that I wouldn't want to be killed!"

"Ah, yes… Very good… I hadn't thought of that." Newton reflected for a moment, then shook his wiggy head. "Inadmissible. Although that may be true by *logic*, it cannot be verified by *trial*."

"But how did you know it had to be the Leaning Tower of Pisa?"

"Handrails. Italians never put handrails. Also it is the only tower of exactly that height in Christendom - that is to say the known world."

"And Galileo Galilei?"

"Who else would be eccentric enough to do such a thing? The fact that the timepiece is strapped to an apple implies it needed to be in free flight but suffering minimal impedimency from the combined action of the ether and the air, and the Descartes vortexes that inhabit them. Knowing you are a time traveller, that must mean you were testing a theory for Galilei. Corroborative, although inconclusive, evidence, is the coin itself. Stamped 1582, Cosmico, Duca di Azzardo - a figurative promotion for a well-known post-Renaissance gambling clan. As you can see, not an enormously difficult deduction."

Sean thought this over in amazement for a while. "And my being the apprentice of Archimedes? How did you deduce that?"

"I think I shall let my master, Isaac Barrow, tell you that in person - for here we are arrived."

The coach had been passing through the narrow

streets of a half-deserted Cambridge, and had now stopped in a wind- and rain-, but otherwise un-swept, courtyard of Trinity College.

The coach driver called down through the various aqueous consistencies: "Nexte stoppe, Trynitie Colegge. Alight ye masters of lite and lerning." On exiting, Sean immediately fell flat on his face in the mud.

"Ohh, an'… Minde ye the gappe," called the driver as he courteously dropped their trunks into the smaller of the puddles.

They traipsed up the welcome carpet of mud-vectored slime to enter a plague-depleted but otherwise grand hall of Trinity College. And there, looking disapprovingly at the coffee-coloured lakes forming beneath them, was a sorry-looking professor senior to Newton by a fifth of three score years.

Newton did the introductions. "Sean Seulpierre, this is the honourable enough Lucasian professor of mathematics, and well-known scourge of the Eastern Mediterranean pirates, Isaac Barrow. We students just call him 'the Wheel' - a clumsy enough work implement allusion, but entirely appropriate as a moniker, if you know his lectures - round and round on the same point like an ideal Keplerian orbit. Also it is because all he delivers in the end is a load of… well, you know."

Barrow shrugged indifferently. "Myne waye forre to keepe studentes fromme attendding…"

"Hold your hedgehogs, professor. Sean is a master of the new e-drop slang."

"Hee speketh the e-droppe?"

"It is all I speak," admitted Sean.

"In veritas? Mye mye, young people these days…" Barrow scrutinised Sean. "So this is Sean Seulpierre?

He has arrived at long last?"

"You know me?" said Sean surprised.

"Generations of scholars, as have I, have kept vigil, waiting in eager patience for you through the long ages. What took you so long? You could have given us some idea when you would be coming, you little shyte."

"He can be a bit testy," whispered Newton to Sean. "He is an examiner, after all. But do worry - he does mean it."

Barrow continued: "Still, I suppose it is an honour. Welcome to Cambridge, Sean Seulpierre, the TimeRider, the legendary bearer of the 'SANG Re.al', who appeared to Archimedes and who is recorded in the Measurer texts." He did a sort of theatrical bow.

"What are the Measurer texts?" asked Sean in wonderment.

"A collection of comedies for the Rosetta Theatre Festival of Minus 212. They were collated and bound together in a single book. It is known as the Swansong Palimpsest, because it also contains Archimedes' last notebook on *spiki celestii*, and a user's guide to the SANG Re.al."

"Sorry, what is a palimpsest exactly?"

"Parchment," explained Newton. "Not paper or papyrus. Made from animal hide. Can be scraped over and reused."

Barrow continued. "In fact, palimpsest is from the Greek for 'scraped over'. Students here like to play a game during lecture breaks. It involves kicking an inflated sheep's bladder in the shape of a 'rompy cupboard head-on' between two piles of jackets. When they fall, it is pleasing to hear them resort to the classics, as they cry, 'Oh palimpsest! Palimpsest! I have palimpsested my knees!' "

Then Barrow added in a whisper, as a true connoisseur of dead animal parts: "Archimedes used only the very finest in abattoir stationery."

Newton shivered in disgust. "Still decayed corpse - much like your watch's 'plastic', Sean."

"Have you seen this 'Swansong Palimpsest'?" begged Sean, facial features at maximum extension to emphasise his excitement.

"Yes. In Constantinople."

"During his 'pirate days'," teased Newton.

"Oh, Sacky, that was a long time ago. You see, Sean Seulpierre, I was adventurous in my youth, much like you, seeking the knowledge of the East. I am afraid it has made my reputation rather hard to live up to."

"Or with … The Wheel turneth full circle, as we say in Euclidonomics class," said Newton.

As they walked through the magnificent, and very woody, corridors towards the dining hall, Barrow asked Newton: "Do you have the whatsit?"

"Watch. Not whatsit. How many times do I have to tell you? Yes." Newton dug his hand into his pocket, brought out the watch, and a handful of plague posies fell out with it. He handed the venerated instrument to him gingerly in a 'kerchief, avoiding at all costs skin contact with the strap. He went slightly green when Barrow took it with his bare hands. The professor studied it for a short while, then turned it over, read the inscription, and nodded.

"So, this is the SANG Re.al… sought mercilessly by every ruler of the Roman Empire, pharaohs, kings, emperors, of Egypt, Persia, India, China. The cause of countless wars and igniting legends by the dozen, lost for sixteen hundred years, hunted by popes and their payroll hench-cardinals, who wished to destroy it and the knowledge it contains. And now… here it is: The Holy Grail." He tossed it carelessly back to Newton, who to his horror found himself catching it instinctively by the strap. "Quite an anti-climax, after all the fuss."

With a cry of disgust and dismay, Newton flung the Holy Grail back into the air, stood aside briskly, and threw up into his wig.

'It's good to see university life was always like this,' thought Sean to himself, as he fielded the watch.

For dinner, Isaac Barrow put on his best pirate costume in Sean's honour. After they had been served in the otherwise empty grand dining room by an old servant of non-determinable sex and filthy hands, Barrow said to Newton: "Thank you for finishing my mathematics paper for me."

"My pleasure."

"But thank you for nothing, as usual."

"Sorry professor? Was something not right?" The way Newton said this made Sean think this was not the first conversation of this type the Isaacs, Barrow and Newton, had ever had.

"What *is* this attraction gravity has for you, Sacky? Gravity, gravity, gravity… so serious… It's really getting me down. Nobody will fall for it."

"Sean did."

"And it hurt," added Sean.

Isaac Barrow continued. "I mean, honestly! What in the name of all that hangs was all that absurd stuff about 'an invisible force acting over a distance'? Haven't we agreed, as do all the Invisible College, that occult agencies haveth no place in science?" He rolled his eyes beneath the rim of his heavily beplumed pirate hat. "It's *so* chapeau vieux. Honestly, Sacky, you are only 23, but sometimes you act like someone of the Middle Ages."

"I am sorry," said Sean. "What is this 'invisible force' of which you speak?"

"I don't want to hear this nonsense again!" and the pirate, Captain 'Sack Barrow, covered his ears with his fakely bejewelled fingers, and began humming to himself loudly.

Newton smiled fondly at his professor, and said to Sean. "You see, I have this really strange idea that gravity is..."

"Not listening!" called Barrow, now staring at the chandelier.

"That gravity is... promise not to laugh... but, well, what if it *were* a force? And furthermore, a force that... that, well, acts... over distance."

Sean waited a few moments, then said. "And...?"

Newton didn't like this. "Didn't you hear what I said?! I said a force acting over distance! Two bodies attracting each other... *without contact* !!" Sean's lack of scandal was ruining everything.

Barrow broke his vow of silence, seeing the chance for an ally in Sean. "Doesn't that seem like 'magic' to you?"

Sean replied: "Not really. Gravity is one of the four fundamental forces of the universe."

"Fundamental forces?!!" scandalised Barrow back at him, feeling surrounded by lunatics.

"Well, yes. You know, like... electricity?" said Sean hesitatingly, trying belatedly to get his sense of chronology up and runnng.

"Like what?" asked Barrow, overwrinkling his brow.

"Electricity? Do you know what that is?" asked Sean.

"No."

"But you *do* know it. For example, it's what you feel when you take off a woollen garment on a dry day."

"We don't have dry days here. Terrible weather forecast for the rest of the century. Could be a little ice age for all we know."

"Well, it does have another name. Maybe you know it as… the 'evil breath of Hieronymus'?"

Barrow's face defurrowed from thought. "Why didn't you say so in the first place, instead of going on about 'lick a turkey' like that? Now I know what you're talking about. It's mentioned in the Swansong Palimpsest."

The two Cambridge Isaacs went on for a while about the mathematics of Barrow's paper. Then Barrow said: "To solve these enigmas, we need experiments of the mind."

"Thought experiments?" interjected Sean. "Shouldn't you also be doing *physical* experiments?"

"Thoughts are cheaper. Come in under the departmental budget."

"Which means more time for building miniature windmills," said Newton, with undisguised pride. "That's my hobby, you know."

"And the telescope?" asked Sean, knowing that Newton had this far-sighted interest.

Unexpectedly, Newton blushed bright crimson.

Barrow explained. "His interest in telescopes grew when he found the window of his room had a direct view of the young ladies refinery - on a clear day you can see straight into their post-sin absolution changing room."

Newton assumed control of the confession. "Trouble is I always blush. And if I have a visitor, it gives me away. But I have come up with a cunning plan to avoid that: I shall decorate my rooms in the brightest crimson tones, then no-one will notice. That way, I can continue to sell telescope viewing time by the minute, to discerning gentlemen callers."

"You like money?" asked Sean.

"Out of scientific curiosity, you understand. I have a theory that since gold, like all metals, is the product of mercury, the only metal that is liquid at normal temperatures, it seems quite logical to assume that far beneath the surface of our spherical planet there is a rotating liquid metal core, from which all metals arise to mix, transmute and congeal on contact with impure air. Therefore gold is what…"

"Makes the world go round?" finished Sean joyfully.

Barrow came to life. "I like that. Sacky, we should use that in our show."

"Show?" asked Sean, starting to feel that after a dinner with the two Isaacs nothing would ever be surprising again. "What *show*?"

Newton transgressed: "You asked me why an apple doth fall while the Moon dothn't - sorry, …doesn't?"

"Yes," said Sean. "I think not being ripe yet can be excluded, considering the age of the universe."

"Yes. Four thousand years is easily enough time for all fruit to ripen. That is what putteth me on to the answer."

"Gravity," nodded Sean.

"Oh, don't start him off on that again," groaned Barrow, and covered his ears once more.

"That is why I want to build a better telescope," explained Newton. "So that I may gaze upon the string that is surely holding the Moon up."

"A string!!?" cried Sean.

"I call it 'string theory'. It is my *philosophae naturali principia* that in all manner of being and essentials there is always a string attached, especially if it has anything to do with university research grants."

Barrow now put his hands down and stopped humming. "That's better. Gravity sounds *so* depressing."

Sean said: "Could I suggest that the 'string' as you call it is not holding the Moon up, not having anywhere to hang from, but is invisible and between the Earth and the Moon."

Barrow and Newton looked at each other and then burst out laughing. "An invisible string?!"

"Yes," Sean went on. "Called 'gravity'."

Barrow groaned. "I thought we had escaped gravity."

"You see, the Moon is like a heavy ball on the end of the string you whirl around your head." Sean illustrated his treatise with a finger twirl, and now wondered why this hadn't seemed so silly in physics class.

Newton was unsatisfied. "But who does the whirling? Mr Biggy? It would seem to me that he has better things to do than stand, or hover, or whatever, around all day, whirling objects about our heads…"

Sean desperately cross-referenced. "The universe is imbued with original spin, and bodies attract each other across space."

"Or a room?" Barrow looked up from his jellied sparrow and mushy crabgrass. "Now *that* is *sexy*. Bodies attracting across a room - I have felt *that* attractive force across dancefloors *many* a time. The greatest force in nature. Now that I see a practical application I am prepared to back the theory. 'There's no pull like Gravity' - that will draw the crowds in for sure."

"Crowds?" puzzled Sean by way of return.

"Didn't I say? We are entering the Big GUT festival in London, as soon as we get the all clear from the plague wardens. Isaac Barrow and Isaac Newton: we're billed as 'The Sacks'."

"What's the Big GUT festival?"

Newton answered him. "It is a vehicle to promote New World fried sliced potatoes. Being sponsored by that Scottish clan - the MacDonalds. Since they lost the claim to the throne, they have gone totally multinational."

"If you want to make big money, you've got to go in for branding these days," added Barrow reflectively.

"Branding! In 1666?!" Sean surprised back.

"Sure! You think we are primitive or something?"

"No, of course not, I didn't mean that…"

"Mind you, the hot irons they use really hurt. Hell of a way to advertise."

Newton went on. "GUT stands for 'Grand Unified Theory'. Originally billed as the GUT Instinct, but now that we are going for the final theory that explains life, the universe and sundrae phenomena, it is being sold as the Big GUT Festival."

"The final theory that explains everything?"

"I know, I know. People think we have now reached the point where we know everything there is to know."

"Nonsense!" said Barrow.

"Quite right," added Sean.

"Absolutely," Newton sealed the agreement, and continued picking his teeth with a hedgehog spine.

"Of course there is still a lot to learn," iterated Sean.

Newton spat out the spine in irritation. "Don't be silly! Everything was already all known by the ancients. Trouble is the Romans wiped the slate clean - literally in the case of Archimedes - so they could relaunch the learning industry and snap up the patents on the rediscoveries. 'Leech the Controversy' was adopted by the church as the logo for their Dark Age knowledge stagnation racket."

Barrow nodded. "But what really upset their monopoly were those pesky Arabs and Indians who weren't having any bull from Rome. Thanks to their safe-keeping, the knowledge from the ancient Greeks literally scraped back under the church's nose on the palimpsests."

"Their only response was to get quite cross about everything."

Barrow threw his serviette down happily. "And for the Sacks, fresh controversies mean fresh new shows. After all, popular philosophy is all about bums on seats."

"A sort of end game?" added Sean.

"Butts about it."

Newton continued. "You see, Sean, Galileo was right. It was because of the watch inspiring progress outside Europe, that Aristotle's monopoly days were numbered. His ideas just don't pass go."

"Numbered, yes… but - which numbers?" Barrow

leant forward and whispered his heresy. "Aristotle's followers, the Strollers, who enlisted most voluntarily in the Inquisition, which everybody expected, had the perfect weapon to suppress the *spiki celestii*."

"Fear and intimidation?" suggested Sean, remembering the early morning alarm call by the confession auditors, two days and a hundred and sixty-six years ago. "No, hang on, that makes two weapons. Or perhaps there were more…"

"All right, *amongst* their weapons was the deadly…"

Sean held his breath in horror.

"… Roman numeral system!" finished Barrow.

Sean's eyes did an involuntary sideways shift. "Sorry…?"

"You see," went on Barrow, "by banning Arabic numbers for centuries, mathematicians were forced to work with an archaic numbering system that made any arithmetic more complex than my laundry bill a nightmare."

"Well, your laundry *is* a nightmare - it is the talk of the campus," grumbled Newton.

"Precisely! So, probably related to the shortage of water for good and wasteful cleaning, the Arabs came up with an ingenious laundry bill simplification system. You see, their empire being stable only by virtue of constant expansion, the Romans had no concept of zero, maintaining that a nothing cannot be a something. But some entrepreneurial Arabs revived it from an old, expired Babylonian patent. Initially as a college student date-juice binge dare, they added this zero to the numeral one, and discovered they had invented a novel way to make ten. Then, under carefully controlled laboratory conditions, they added another zero. After many attempts, they finally made one that remained stable, and the world's very first fully functional digital hundred came to light. They refined their production technique, and in time an entire rational number system was formed."

"And this was adopted everywhere?" asked Sean.

"You must be kidding! The Church immediately slammed self-protectionist trade barriers on it. You see, since it made calculations easy, thus exposing their bookkeeping 'techniques' to public accountability, the Church called it the 'devil's numbers', and banned it."

"This situation held back European mathematics for centuries, until along came Leonardo," concluded Newton.

"Da Vinci?" Sean sat up.

"Left a bit."

"Sorry?" asked Sean.

"Not Vinci - Pisa."

"Leonardo of Pizza?"

"His surname was Bonacci, or more completely 'filius Bonacci', son of Bonacci," hyper-precised Newton.

"Oh!" said Sean. "Fibonacci!"

"Was that his stage name?" asked Barrow.

"So, it was through this Leonardo Bonacci that the decimal system was adopted in Europe?" asked Sean. "Sometime back in the thirteenth century, wasn't it?"

"Yes - just after the SANG Re.al was reputed to have returned to us with Marco Polo," said Newton.

"And with Arabic numerals came 'al-ge-bra'," went on Barrow. "As far as my selective..."

"And somewhat stylised..." overlaid Newton sweetly.

"...research can reveal, that's an Arabic logo

promoting a brand of ladies' undergarment. Which was brill for flatter-confusing the theoretical knickers off difficult laundry women wanting to be paid."

"Sorry, are you, Isaac Barrow, the very first Lucasian Professor of Mathematics at Cambridge University, telling me the whole basis of modern mathematics relates to dirty laundry?" Sean asked.

Barrow did not deign to perturb. "Laundering may one day form the basis of an international banking system. And how do you think the Royal Society got its name? They started out in the time of Charles the First as an outservice for the palace called the 'Royal Socks'. They were only forced to branch into theoretical physics when trade dropped off with the king's head."

Newton hoped to elucidate, or something in that general line, and failed with: "They were known around the intellectual dives as *the Invisibles*, for discretionary purposes you understand, until Charlie One lost his divine-right-to-rule race by a head."

Sean gave up and joined in. "I heard he was forced to withdraw from the race because of a broken reign."

Barrow murmured: "I hope, dear Sacky, you are getting these lines down to use in our show?"

"So, Isaacs, what inspired your Big GUT stage show?"

The older Isaac answered. "My old gambling friend, René Descartes."

"You knew Descartes?!" asked Sean in amazement, handing his untouched shock-o-late moss to Barrow, who had been eyepleading it for quite a while.

"I knew René Descartes when I was a young man. He was a great one for the cards. 'René', I used to say.

'Have you got des cartes?' Then after a few tankards, he would say: 'Don't try to cheat me, Wheelie-boy. Cogito ergo sum…' - that's classical pidgin for 'I can think so I can add up as well as the next man'. 'Cogito ergo sum!' he would scream when he was drunk and winning, and dance on the tables in the tavern till we dragged him down. We just called him 'René of the cards'. He was sharp. Who needs philosopher's stone when you can have a stoned philosopher!"

Newton said: "I grew up with Descartes' pocket 'Heavy Thinker' series."

"My favourite was *Cogito ergo terrore*," nodded Barrow. "Subtitled: 'Everything you have always known about the world but were afraid to be asked'."

"In fact, *Cogitas ergo incendimus* was the church's response."

"And as a teenager," said Newton. "I followed the comic series '*Shakata non cogitata*: the adventures of a spymaster, in the service of the crown', starring his alternate ego, Giacomo Bondo."

"And what did Descartes tell you?" prompted Sean.

"He said that a too little under-rated idea is the presence of Mr Biggy in every universal pie."

"The Archimedean Pi?" asked Sean.

"The same."

Barrow was by now slurping on a piece of bark, enjoying his dessert of créme à la tree moss. "It was thanks to Archimedes' pie proof that we scientists know for sure that you get more spherical cherries in cylindrical confectionary than any Euclidean triangular one."

Sean was pleased at the mention of Archimedes,

but lost simultaneously. "Are you saying, that all this struggle, all this accumulation of knowledge through history, has resulted in people sitting around sharing recipes?"

Newton answered. "Is *your* world any better? However, you are right. Mathematicians cannot live from pi alone. I have a theory, called *Fluxions*, which explores what curves pies go down and what makes it so difficult to extrapolate them in the mornings."

"This year, the Big GUT will be all about the relationship between pies and circumferences," confirmed Barrow, patting his stomach by way of illustration.

Newton leant forward, suddenly sharp-eyed all a-twinkly. "Sean, is the Earth round or flat?"

"Well, everybody by now knows it is round."

"Then tell me, if the Earth has a round surface, why, when you droppeth a spherical marble, doth it not roll away?"

"Um…"

"I asked your tall friend. The one with the lovely lady friend."

"Pau?"

"Yes."

"And what did he say?"

"He did sayeth it was because of the inherent stickiness of all things."

"That's Pau… And the real answer?"

"That, my little friend, is the essence of my very own grandly unified theory."

"And what is that?" asked Sean.

"The rules of the first GUT competition were too simple," continued Newton. "All you had to be able to do was define all places in space. That was too easy -

thirty years ago René Descartes wiped the floor with his competitors, when he unleashed his system of three space coordinates."

"X, Y, and Z coordinates," nodded Sean.

"Besides obvious applications to the food industry, this allowed us to rise above flat-earth perspectives, and think in three dimensions."

"Suddenly we understood why cows have never been seen to use upstairs bathrooms," went on the surrogate pirate. "The implications for hygiene, and particularly the all important laundry questions that are still open debate in intimate mathematics circles, are enormous."

Newton coughed intentionally. "Thank you for sharing that with us, professor. So, purely to make it harder, the GUT organisers decreed that you may not delete Mr Biggy from the equations."

"Which is fair enough," put in Barrow. "You see, they have some pretty onerous sponsorship issues to contend with."

Newton continued. "The long-reigning champion - Ptolemy's megawheelie theory – had a fixed, central Earth, and described the motions of planets around it by an impressively complex machine involving wheels within wheels within, believe it not, even more bleeding wheels."

"I think the judges always voted for it because they didn't want to admit they couldn't understand it," laughed Barrow. "I know I can't!"

Newton pushed on. "Ptolemy's run of success was finally broken by a late entry in 1543. In fact it was quite a deathbed effort - by a Polish contestant, Nicolaus Copernicus. He was nicknamed by the press as 'the heliocentric hellboy', because he put the sun at the centre of the solar system. He passed the title to the tag-team, Galileo and Johannes Kepler. But, going for a solo career, Galileo lost it in a tiebreaker match in the Roman Festival of 1633, to some really dubious tactics and an ongoing controversy concerning the impartiality of the judges."

"Poor Galileo," murmured Sean sadly. "He told me scientists were destined to lose the cannonball races unless the winner was the one who correctly predicted the outcome. Instead, the Church proclaimed that, in the case of a draw, the reigning champion would retain the title."

Barrow expounded... then immediatley apologised. "Galileo's proposal was rejected on the grounds that Mr Biggy determined the result according to His whim, or, in the case of non-showing, his self-appointed representative."

"Now this year's Big GUT festival is being held in London, and it is to decide once and for all what sort of glue Mr Biggy uses to put the universe together with," said Newton, with hints of gravity.

"The Puritan entry says that it is held together by seriousness," added Barrow. "Gravity would be a name they could live with. However, times have changed, Sacky. Galileo was right - the world moves on. Today the Restoration theatre crowd want only naughty comedy. Just think! We now have women on the stage!" Barrow's large wobbly hat developed an interesting resonance as he got excited. "Real women! On the stage! Egads! The mind boogles."

"Boggles."

"Mine boogles."

Newton wrought them back on track briefly. "But our toughest competitor is a military entry. You see, there is the question of what would happen on a round Earth if, as it seems to be the case, we keep building more and more powerful artillery cannons. The more powerful the cannon the further the projectile will fly. Your experience with cannonball races will be of utmost utility to me in this, Sean."

"Fire away," said Sean.

"I ask this: Would a cannon ball, given sufficient propulsion, describe a full circumvention of a spherical planet without ever landing?" Newton illustrated his point by bouncing an apple off Barrow's still wobbling hat.

Sean thought of Hieronymus and the neat parabolic curve he had described during his capital flight. "You mean, enter orbit?"

"And if it were to do so, would that mean that a cannonball would eventually return to strike those who fired it in the back? Thus destroying any army and making war impossible?"

"If you put it like that…"

"That is why the army have put in a team for the festival, pushing for a return to the flat earth, so that the cannon balls that miss their target will eventually roll off the planet and do no-one any harm. They claim that a round earth is unpatriotic and a threat to national security. After all, the Interregnum has ended."

"What was that?" asked Sean.

"A dry period when no king was reigning," answered Barrow. "By the way, Sean, what shape do you normally keep your head?"

"Sort of round I guess. Why?"

"I'd take to wearing a hat if I were you. You see, after Oliver Cromwell died, the new king announced that all roundheads shall be shortly."

"... shortly... what?"

"Just shortly. As in no-headly."

"Executed? How awful."

"The king is both cruel and generous," said Newton. "I myself hope to be drawn, hung and quartered one day."

"You *hope* to be?!!"

"Of course. Provided I play Des Cartes right. All the best careers end like that."

"But... but... it would hurt like anything!"

"No... not at all. *Drawn* by the best artist in the country, the portrait *hung* in a place of prestige, and myself pensioned and *quartered* at royal expense for life. Won't hurt a bit."

Then Newton announced: "For this purpose, I intend to win the title in this year's Big GUT Festival with my own laws of fair and easy motion. And I am not talking about my mother's prune obsession."

"For example?" asked Sean.

"The Cornelia Consequence." He did the name up in candles thing by flashing his extended fingers.

"What is that?"

"When any applied force proves insufficient for the purposes of overcoming the cumulative forces attributable to a general or specific resistance, a system that gave initiation to that selfsame force is compelled to favour an augmentation of the said applied force to the point of surpassing those and subsequent factors of resistance."

Sean thought about this quickly for a long time,

before asking: "You mean… when push comes to shove?"

"Couldst say."

Barrow added: "We hope to entice a larger audience by the use of experimental theatre: using a new technique we call 'sit-coms'."

"Sit-coms?!"

"Yes. Sit and be communicated to. Sitting in a theatre instead of standing! Incredible concept. How impuritan. Delightful!"

"Yes," enthused Newton. "And the public get to ring in."

"Ring in?" asked Sean, hedging around his flummox by skillful use of a screen of astonishment.

Barrow shrugged. "Sure. Bells are not supplied… and vote for the most popular theory of creation and stuff like that."

Newton nodded. "We are also reviving the John the Measurer classic comedies about the first world wars - adapted to our Great War as part of a nostalgia series under the title *Magna Armata Soughtet Homum* - MASH for short."

Barrow translated: "The English version is *Bringge ye the Boyes Bakke Home.*"

Newton continued: "At Cambridge I am duty optiker - so I am organising a group called Footelite - but I need to do some pretty fancy optics theory work before I can get the lights to stay on when they are glued to their feet. I've got an idea involving prisms that might do the trick."

Sean rallied his thinking. "So, what is the plot?"

"I found a brochure for the play stuck between the pages of the Archimedes Palimpsest," said Isaac

Barrow. "Its climax is the burning of Syracuse by the Romans. The Measurer has left us 'John: the Avenger-list. A bright tale of deep philosophical struggle and overheated romance under the Ptolomeic sun'. We are currently working on the special effects to recreate the burning of Syracuse."

"And the theatre in London?"

"Where the Cambridge Players always go: Pudding Lane Monumental."

"I see…" said Sean. "I think your show will close on opening night, but your special effects will scorch their place in the annals of history."

Strangely satisfied by this, Barrow went on: "You will find the story most interesting. Although you know it already, am I right? It talks of a certain Bearer of the Watch, who brought *spiki celestii*, the language of the gods, to Archimedes in the form of a 'celestial dial' - caused a sensation because the timepiece works indoors as well as out."

"All of this was recorded in a brochure for the Rosetta Theatre Festival?" Sean could hardly believe what he was hearing.

"Legend has it that there are some hard copies of the original publicity posters still standing in Rosetta," added Newton.

"Carved on grey basalt stone?" asked Sean, remembering John the Measurer chiselling a copy of Archimedes' notebook.

"Festival promotions used pink porphyry - more eye-catching."

"And what happened to Archimedes' Palimpsest after the festival?" asked Sean.

"It was exchanged with an eastern goat herder for an order of cheese and yoghurt just before the Roman invasion of Egypt."

"That was cheap."

"It was good cheese."

"Did the Romans come looking for it?"

"Yes. Their commander was called Cespuglio the Inflagrante. Translates as 'The Burning Bush: a tinder story of death and more death'. There used to be forests in that region till he came along."

"And then what happened?"

Barrow sipped some more fermented squirrel juice before answering. "It was kept safe from Rome, and eventually was filed in the Mar Saba Monastery – that's a relics wholesaler and haberdashery - near Jerusalem, until it was 'liberated' by a crusade remake in the 1100s. Not knowing what it was, the crusaders took it to Constantinople, where it was recycled and scraped over, cut up and the pages turned around. As if that weren't enough, some really boring liturgical hits were downloaded onto it by a heavy hand. That's how I found it. I could just make out Archimedes' writing - parchment never loses all of its imprint."

"You found Archimedes' notebook?!" Sean could barely contain his excitement.

"Yes, I did. In a library. I couldn't take it out - my library card had expired. So I transcribed what I could."

"Good!" cried Sean, grinning with pleasure.

"But I lost my notes."

"Bad!" Sean squeezed out through the same grin.

"Yes... sorry about that. But it wasn't just careless-ness, as it would normally have been. Just bad luck. You see, on the way home I stopped off in Venice for a quick paddle, and a fire in my hotel destroyed my notebook. At least I couldn't find it afterwards."

"Couldn't even find the hotel," commented Newton.

"Well, that wouldn't have been anything new. Terrible memory for Calle numbers."

"You remember all the calle girls, though," winked Newton, relishing Barrow's infamous reputation, and trying, in vain it must be said, to force a match to the professor in pirate costume he had before him.

* * * *

Chapter Eleven
Cracking Yolks

"PROFESSOR Barrow is certainly special," summarised Sean as they walked down the long, deserted corridors towards Newton's digs in Cambridge University's Trinity College.

"Yes. We may have modern anatomy, but we still have the human humours to contend with."

"Isaac, you can now measure the effects of gravity, but do you have a guess as to what causes it?"

"I do not feign hypotheses," replied Newton haughtily.

"What does that mean?"

"It means 'Your guess is as good as mine'. My rule is: if in doubt, factor it out."

"Then publish it?"

Newton looked dismayed. "You mean... tell *other* people?"

"Well... yes," replied Sean.

"Never!"

"Why not?"

"What if they steal it?"

"If you publish first, they can't."

Newton patted the pocket containing the watch. "Too risky. Better just to keep it to myself."

"But you're Isaac Newton… you *write* the laws."

"You betcha! Newton's laws will hold forever!"

"But… if you don't publish how you derived them, the truth will never come out!"

"Na… there has never been much of a market for the truth. Anyway, today's dawning of truth is this afternoon's fire lighter: just ask Giordano Bruno - put everything he had at stake. The world of natural philosophy is a jungle, believe me."

"So, how are your laws of motion going?"

"They started well, but now I've hit a problem. Aristotle had several hundreds of explanations for why things move as they do, and more on the drawing tablet when he died. Try as I might, I can only come up with three."

They stopped at a door, from behind which some grunts were emanating. "The university boxing club here is an early adopter - they are testing them out for me."

Sean sneaked a look inside. A few die-easies were punching each other in the face in the name of sport. On the wall was emblazoned the earliest known edition of Newton's laws of motion:

1. If a bodie be laide to reste it doth stae at reste.

2. The harder thou hittest the harder they falle.

3. Thou gettest back whatt thou givest oute.

Vitruvian Boy

followed by the warning:

Breake alle three
And oute be thee

Newton said: "I was thinking of adapting them to more general 'university laws of motion'. But since that domain name has already been taken by the college dispensary, I'll have to settle for 'universal laws', though I am afraid someone will steal them and people will be able to move whenever they choose without paying me royalties. Especially in the East."

"China?"

"No! The Germans - the worst pirates of natural principles around. The illicit equation trade operates through the free ports of Switzerland, where the powers of natural philosophy impostation can't touch them."

"So, how can you establish yourself in the universal laws of nature market if you can't publish?"

"With a deadly form of patience, all my own. When I am ready, the Sacks are going to move in on the London maths cartels, in particular the Royal Society. It will be nasty - they fight with Hookes - but one day the Socks will belong to me. Our motto will be "Nullius in Verba" - meaning don't take the word of no-one. Cash up front in return for the right equations. Believe me, I'll have all of Europe screaming for British 'stuff'. That's why I keep it secret for now, in anagrams, not publishing - to control the street price, yer see?"

"So, one day the whole world will know about Newton's Laws of Motion?"

"Only if they buy a renewable license. *I* write the law. In this world, nothing moves without *my* say-so."

Newton's laboratory was in his private digs,

although the word 'excavation' would have been more helpful for initial orientation. It was cramped and rather not as one would expect to be the venue of some of the most important scientific discoveries ever. The bookcases were crammed with over a hundred books, most of which were occult and alchemical references. There was a staggering range of glass instruments and tools, and two stoves, one of tin and one of iron, and a chemical kit he had received as a desperate, last-minute Christmas present from someone.

"Will you be a professor one day?" asked Sean.

"When Professor Barrow stands down, perhaps I will take his place as the Chair of Lucasian Maths Wiz. Tell me, why is it we say that in order to take someone's *chair*, they have to *stand* down?" Newton started to stoke up a fire under the stoves. "Anyway, before that can happen I have to become a fellow."

"The long hair and frilly sleeves are a little disconcerting, but you look like a fellow to me."

"I mean appointed to the permanent teaching staff. The first step to becoming a professor. There are only nine positions to be filled from sixty candidates."

"So, being the most junior, you'll have to wait?"

"You must be joking! Newt-boy is on the move - one of my principles of motion. If there is anything we have learnt from the Italians it is 'Never wait your turn'. If you do the mathematics, you can see a little pushing of the odds in my favour is called for. One of the more obvious applications of mathematics is fiddling the numbers and hedging the odds in one's own favour at everybody else's cost and risk. I am sure this will one day become the standard for good business practice."

"So, what are your chances of getting elected to

fellow?" asked Sean.

"Well, let's just say fortune has smirked my way - by my making sure it doesn't smile on the others. There have been a number of … let's call them 'accidents'. Two of my rivals were injured quite severely when, in a drunken stupor, a bottom step impacted with their heads."

"They fell down the stairs?"

"The key to legal success, young Sean, is locum, locum, locum."

"Meaning you weren't there at the time?"

"I have the official report to prove it. Another rival, again under the influences of the devil's urine, was found frozen to death in a field. He just happened to be my main competitor. The evidence against me was purely circumstantial - or at least most of it, or the bits that actually reached the inquest.

"Another 'fellow competitor' felt the compulsion to retire due to a 'mental aberration'. I think we both know what that means - I can be quite persuasive when I put mye minde to it. And for the rest… well, it was most unfortunate they happened to catch a coach which had come directly from a London plague district - somehow the warning sign must have fallen off… There may have been one or several others… And *ipso facto*, the field has opened up quite unexpectedly and fortuitously in my favour."

"You are very sure about not getting caught," remarked Sean.

"I operate in law like I do in science - what can't be proven is inadmissible. Call it my imperious method."

"I thought your method was 'empirical'?"

"I was misquoted."

"But why cheat? You're so smart - you would surely pass any test they set?"

"Too risky. I could lose my groats with these hard-up examiners."

"Groats?"

"Coins you deposit before standing the oral examination. If you fail the test you lose the deposit. The rate of failure towards the end of the month is going on 100%."

"That sounds incredibly unfair. Don't you ever complain?"

"Who to? There's a saying around the philosophy labs - An appeal a day keeps the doctorate away."

"And once you are a professor, what will you do?"

"Skive off from classes like Professor Barrow, and get on with my real work. All this optika and philosphae naturalis nonsense is just a front for my serious studies of the occult and alchemy. Turning base metal into gold. That's where the real Net New Money is."

"You want to make money?"

"I run a student loan business on the campus. Want to borrow a pound or two? Good interest. Good terms. Guaranteed minimal barbarism from the debt-collecting agencies. Legal standards are a minor appendage a week for arrears up to one pound. Disfiguration thereafter. Best deal you'll get these days, believe me."

"No thank you. Is that all you want - money for nothing?"

"And my chicks for free."

"Really?!"

"Well, I've got to eat something. Anyway, I've applied for a longevity grant."

"Longterm tenure?"

"No. The Elixir of Eternal Life. Why laughest thou?! I have a mathematical theory to back it up. For example, I was born on Christmas Day, 1642, right?"

"If you say so."

"It is based on heresy."

"Um… Don't you mean 'hearsay'?"

"No. Heresy. Also, I can choose not to have been there at the time."

"How is that?" asked Sean.

"Temporal shift."

"Temporal shift! You can travel through time?!"

"Yes," answered Newton. "You see, the calendar proclaimed by Pope Gregory in 1582, which we have refused to ratify in England, is ten days ahead of our old Julian Calendar. This is the famous Gappe we Minde here in England. And it is growing. Soon it will be eleven days, and then twelve days. Now, according to the Gregorian calendar, I was born on January the fourth, 1643 - ten days after Christmas! Never heard of the ten days of Christmas?"

"Only an inflated version…" Sean answered. "The soundtrack of the twelve-day version is full of people jumping and leaping."

"Which only proves my point. Over in Greg's world, they say I was born in 1643. See where I am going with this? Just think of the business opportunities!"

"Er…?"

"Well asked. If the introduction of Greg's calendar would push my birthday into the next year, that would make me instantly a year younger, and that can only mean I will live a year longer."

"You mean, if you Minde the Gappe you live longer?"

"Not bad, eh? Or does it mean I will time travel ten days, or lose ten days of knowledge? If the latter, can I choose which ten? That's the crucial point: we could start a business, reinventing the calendar at regular intervals so people could pay to have memories of certain days erased, or have extra days inserted before the exams. I am sure that would be very popular."

Sean thought about this for an undue while. "I am sure there is something wrong with that argument, but I can't quite put my finger on it."

Newton was now satisfied with the temperature of a copper crucible on the oven. He carefully pulled out the folded handkerchief containing the egg shells left by Geni and Pau.

"These are encapsulations of the elixir of eternal youth."

"Really?" replied Sean. "Leonardo called them *tempus albumen.* I figure they appear in the crust of our planet due to some force that is compressing time, squishing it all up, putting it under pressure. So, like lava bursting out of a volcano - they are forced to the surface."

"Like I said - the elixir of eternal youth," nodded Newton. "Allow me to digress. I have made a long and detailed study of ancient tourist sites." Newton pulled down a large multifolio from a shelf. "I have managed to convince myself that King Solomon's Great Temple was designed to be a giant machine."

"A machine? That does what?"

"A machine that could rise through the ages of time and be one with the cosmic background." Newton found the page he was looking for, and held it up. Sean saw it contained some extremely detailed drawings of

King Solomon's Temple, and was accompanied by many scrawling mathematical calculations giving the whole thing a rather pleasing craquelure effect.

Newton shook his head. "But Solomon's Temple failed to rise."

"Why?"

"Not enough eggs. Does it help you if I tell you that Solomon decreed his temple be built entirely from a rare and precious stone imported from Egypt? Known then as now as the 'One Stone'? A stone that came from only one quarry, and is a form of pink porphyry?"

"Ah…" Sean recalled, while loose tendrils from a vague legend about a search for a lost mine of King Solomon began to snag in the hooks of his peripheral memory.

"And he got his geometry wrong. The Egyptians did a little better with the pyramid shape."

"I see…"

"Both Solomon and the Eygptians used the very same stone within which are found these time eggs. The very same pink porphyry that the Romans invaded Egypt in search of. That the emperors forbade anyone else to use and called 'Imperial Porphyry', or more commonly the 'emperor's little pinkie'."

"I thought Imperial Porphyry was purple?"

"Rock that comes from the same quarry but does not contain any eggs eventually turns purple. Never heard of the 'Purple Reign' mentioned in the 'Prince'? But the stone that stays pink is the famed OneStone that the philosopher trade is still dependent on. And the source of the stone has been lost. The crusaders, with its location symbol emblazoned on their t-shirts, a kind of lop-sided X on the road map for the Middle East, tried for a hundred years to refind it, but could not. I am convinced that the source cannot be found simply because it is no longer there. At least not in the Middle East."

"You mean, it has moved?"

"Yes. After more than a thousand years of scarcity, the eggs seem to be reappearing. According to the New Alchemists' Quarterly, the source of the pink stone has crossed to Europe. There is a NEO…"

"NEO?"

"A non-ecclesiastical organisation - which is dedicated to finding it. They call themselves 'sectatori rosae crociati': the seekers of the pink crossing."

"The Rosicrucians!" gasped Sean, and felt that some pieces would have fallen into place if there had been enough of a place for them to fall into.

While Newton prepared a second crucible with a concoction of smelly unctions and powders, Sean asked: "Sacky, do you know what Solomon and the Egyptians were trying to do by building those enormous…"

"Egg boxes?"

"Yes."

"Having studied the ancient geometers, Euclid, Archimedes, and Vitruvius, I can definitively say find a particular orientation of the eggs. In fact, they were trying to create a giant crystal which could orientate itself on the timeless cosmic background."

Sean thought of Nonno, and his explanation of the 'spenmatt', his theory of the space-energy-matter background, where time does not exist - or is reset to zero 'for another go', as Nonno once put it.

"Euclid gave Archimedes his great work, the

Elements, including illustrations of the Golden Ratio, to pin up in his maths factory to keep his workers happy. And it was Archimedes who passed the principles of two and three-dimensional erotic geometry to the Roman architect, Vitruvius. From his designs was built a structure which is a giant sphere within a cylinder. It looks uncannily like a ball for foot."

"The Romans built a rompy?!" exclaimed Sean. "I mean a rhombicuboctahedron?"

"Tried to, at any rate. It is called the 'Pantheon' - a place to talk to 'all the gods' at discounted group rates."

"A cosmic blog…?" asked Sean. "But, I have been in the Pantheon. I experienced nothing special."

"The eggs were removed and sold as invasion souvenirs to the invading Visigoths. It never worked anyway. The Romans, being Italian, went for the look rather than occult functionality. In any case, they did not possess the mathematics. To build a true Vitruvian Crystal you need the power of *spiki celestii* - and all traces of that had been destroyed in Syracuse two hundred years earlier. The Church tried too, but got all their tolerances crossed. Orthodox churches got the basic shape better, but by then there were no more eggs to be found - just a few smoky imitation ones they waved around during ceremonies for special effects, and to cut down on the mosquitoes."

"And what would happen if such a crystal were built?" asked Sean.

"The original project specifications have it that whomsoever enters the Vitruvian Crystal would never age, for time would become meaningless. And that must mean they would be able to be anywhere in time. Take your friends, for example."

"You mean… the TimeRiders don't 'jump' time…?"

"They are already in all moments of time simultaneously. The only thing I don't understand is why they, and you, can do this with a single egg, and yet, except for some jumbled visions of the future, the eggs have no effect on normal people. Oracles and alchemists have been trying, and failing, for thousands of years to unlock the secrets of the elixir of eternal youth."

"So, that is why Geni and Pau always talk about cycling through the timeline? For them it is a never-ending loop. When, in reality, they are everywhen always." Sean went through his meetings with the TimeRiders in his mind, recalling their sense of detachment. He shook his head. Except Geni - *she* cared.

Newton was busy taking well-used vials and instruments from shelves, and hunting through drawers. "Everywhen… or *no*-when. If time does not exist for them, what they are experiencing when they manifest in a specific time is an illusion. They just agree to go along with it for a while. They are not really there in the sense you and I understand."

"Not really alive," Sean quoted Cespuglio, not for the first time, bitterly.

"Lacking an anchor in time, what they think are their memories are simply little stories they tell themselves to explain something they otherwise cannot understand. Without a memory of time past, Sean Seulpierre, you cannot conceive a future. And without a future, existence is pointless."

"And me?" asked Sean, suddenly very afraid. "Am I really here? Am I experiencing an illusion, too?"

"No. There is something different about you. You are neither fully a TimeRider nor fully ordinary."

"Both here and not here," said or maybe thought Sean, remembering now, for some reason, Shrodie, the half-dead cat.

Newton was starting to experiment, preparing one concoction after another. While they waited for the 'sweat of Hermes' to come to the boil, Sean asked the question that had been lying in lurk the whole day: "Sacky, why is Cespuglio hunting us?"

Newton paused for a moment or three, before he nodded. "Alright, make that two things I don't understand. Let's look at what we doe knoweth." He tended to slip back into pre-edrop speech when he was thinking. "Thou and the watch are inexplicablie linkéd. That maketh thee a marker forre Cespuglio. Findde Sean Seulpierre and he doth findde the watch."

"And the TimeRiders? Are they drawn to the watch too?"

"Yes. At least, they seem drawne to events in history in which the *spiki celestii*, the language of the gods, makes a leape forrward. What thy and their ultimate purpose is I cannot saye. But I do know it is important enough for an entire race of strange creatures from a distant future time to come over the gappe that separates our two worlds, to forme a demonic alliance with Cespuglio, to hunt down you and the SANG Re.al. For this reason, and to honour Archimedes, Leonardo and Galileo, I will help thee. For they believed in you, and your mission, too."

"But Sacky, what *is* this *it* I am supposed to do?"

"I think you must seek your grandfather."

"Nonno?!"

"And when you find him, I think you will also find your mother."

"Are they together?" Sean had not felt so much hope since the day he had started his incredible journey.

Newton placed a kind hand on his shoulder. "I regret I cannot say for sure. But I sense the presence of your Nonno when I am near the watch."

"Others have said the same thing. Why can't *I* sense him?"

For the subsequent while, Newton gave Sean a crash apprenticeship in the mysticised world of alchemy. Half chemistry and half voodoo, it at times seemed to suggest rational method, then at crucial moments veered off into the realm of superstition and fanatical beliefs rooted securely in the vaporous air it produced by the roomful.

"I have never had so much eggshell at one time," explained Newton, obviously quite excited. "My Holborn suppliers, who import from a Swiss distributor, bring me the occasional fragment - more often than not mixed with worthless powder. None of us, the great Robert Boyle included, have ever seen a full shell, ne'er minde an egg that contains *tempus albumen*, the time juice. Boyle, like Barrow after him, scoured Europe, visited the home of Galileo, all the known sites of cracking of the yolks. Either he was missing the essential sense of the humours, or else the yolkes were too old, but not once did these bring him to smile."

"And you? Which method do you follow?"

"I used to use Des Cartes to read the future, now I bring the unctions to the Boyle," pointing at Robert Boyle's collected works on chemical magic, alongside some other 'how to be popular at parties' books.

Newton took a large notebook, and began writing in it in a strangely perpendicular and almost microscopic handwriting. "I have recorded everything I have seen during my long, lonely vigils over the alchemist furnace, roasting the eggshells in search of the *materia prima*."

Sean took an older notebook and read in it at random:

'Tonite i haff seen the future. A future which seeth the coming of a new forme of twice and then thrice-contaminated iron, which will bring us to burne coale in such quantities as this shalt become the defining notion for the new age - an age obsessed more with means than of endes. The fossil Age shalt arise, and shape our planet even more than alle the stone and iron we wilt emploie. And as the evil breath of Hieronymus races down tubes of copper, me seemeth we become beholden to the coale from which it derives. Are we not then slaves to the dead creatures of the past - the ancestors of our living world? And what will the world of natural breath feel about sharing its lungs with such corruption, when the bodies of ghostly entities are wrought into our world with no anima to guide them?

'Man will not choose to define himself by his weakeness, but by what he cann controle. So being, with all the knowledge and macchinations the Revolution of Knowing will bring, men's eyes will remain fixed uponn his own greateness to the detriment of moste evidente truthe. Verily, an inconveniente truthe.'

Newton came over and saw what Sean was reading. "What you describe to me of your time, Sean, sounds like a dark age of industrialised ignorance - at what point does it all go wrong, when does man cease to be in awe of the majesty of nature? Or better said, when does foolish man fancy the laws of natural life become *his* slaves?"

And as if to demonstrate just how ambivalent his insights were, Newton next poured some mercury into a bowl. "Tell me, what does your age know of mercury? It is the only liquid metal, so is obviously the fundamental of all metals. The Greeks called it *hydrargyrum*, which means 'watery silver'."

"In fact, its chemical symbol is still Hg." Sean wrote it down for him.

"Hig? And the search for the Hig fundamental: does it continue?"

"You could say that, yes. In my day, the world's largest governments unite their resources to build the most expensive and powerful machines ever constructed to try to reveal the secret of the fundamental particles, especially one they call the Higg's particle."

"Ah… alchemy is recognised at long last." Newton swirled the liquid metal in the bowl. "See how formless and how brilliantly silver mercury is? That is because it has no light inside it. When it doth combine with light, it formeth all other metals, and gives them their form. So it is with the eggs and time. Only when the time liquid mixes with matter does the perceived world take form."

"That's amazing, Isaac. The starting point of your reasoning is completely wrong, but your conclusions are perfectly right," said Sean. "Is that how you do all of your work?"

"Pretty much." Newton went to another dish. "Look upon this."

Sean looked at the dish. He saw a white crystalline star-shape, with shards radiating from, or equally towards, a singular core. "It's beautiful."

"It is the Star Regulus of Antimony: see how a

small concentration of the antimony, in a crystal form, draweth all similar metal powder irresistibly to it. Soe I asketh: what if a large crystal of the time eggs were forméd? Would it drawe all time towards it in just such a way?

"The ancient Greek - actually he wasn't all that old - Democritus, known as the little nit-picker by his school chums, imagined all things in the world being composed of tiny parts called atoms. Could it be that, rather than being a smooth continuous liquid, time is also composed of very small chunks, the smallest of which are indivisible?"

Sean nodded. "We call them chronons."

"And like all metals, these can be isolated, distilled and reassembled in a different forme. That I believe is the nature of the eggs - for when your friends did disappear they did so in a mercurial storm - that is the fundamental of the universe - the milk that formed the whole galaxy, galaxos ubiquitos. You see, 'Galaxos' is Greek for 'milk'."

'Not *more* cows…,' groaned Sean, remembering the cow analogy laboured by Luca Pacioli to explain multi-dimensional space, in which, since cows could not look up, the third dimension remained invisible to them.

"Divine providence is allowed to flow when we crack open an egg - it is purified liquid providence, and our portal to the cosmic background - the *spenmatt*, as you say your Nonno calls it. With this we can cause the fundament of the soul - the anima - to decant - as has happened to your friends."

"Um…" contributed Sean.

Newton lit some more coke with a taper from the fire, and prepared his alembic for distilling liquids.

"Now we apply the technique of Helvetius. Please read the recipe." Newton gave Sean a chemically stained, and in places charred, volume, bookmarked to a page by a Swiss Occultist Supplier's Emporium flyer.

"Disanimeum: the decantation of the anima via the philosopher's stone," he read. "Ingredients: take a fresh piece of brimstone."

Newton placed a soft piece of yellow, chalklike substance in a copper bowl on the iron oven.

"Distalatum in solemis, extracteum tribikos…"

Newton carried out the distillation and poured the residue through a funnel into another receptacle. Then, in accordance with the instructions as Sean read them, Newton very carefully measured amounts of sometimes quite smelly powder, metal, and suspicious-looking liquids, and heated them to various degrees and lengths. The more pungent the better it seemed to please him.

Then Sean read the final lines, which made even less sense to him. "What is all this?" he asked, looking up.

"Oh, it is always the last ingredient: a carefully calculated amount of distilled mumbo jumbo, read only by one who is pure of spirit and soul. So, go ahead."

"But, you are a scientist, not a magician."

"That's why I distil it. Agreed?"

"Uh…huh…"

Newton nodded to the enormous notebook. "Good. Like everything else, the mumbo jumbo must be recorded carefully. Every syllable, inflection, cadence… every detail is recorded in my notebook."

"Where do these recipes come from?"

"It is usually assumed that this knowledge dates back to the time of the old testament. But, according to

Professor Barrow, the handwriting of John the Measurer found in Constantinople supposedly matches the basalt handchiselling in Alexandria, where they originate."

"I see," said Sean, who didn't really, but thought he had done for a brief moment. He looked at the brutish concoction as it bubbled, toiled and troubled away on the fire. "So, what are we trying to do exactly?"

"As we all know, the world is composed of four elements - fire, earth, water and … I always forget one…"

"Air?"

"That's it! Thank you. I see you are a trained chemist. Obviously, to transmute a substance, we need simply adjust the proportions of these four elements in it. Simple and logical, you must agree?"

"Um…"

"You'll get the hang of it. Now, these eggshells are clearly more earth, but they showed fire to release the swirl which engulfed your friends when they disappeared into eternal time. This swirl was clearly primarily of the element water - follow me? Hence, to reactivate the eggs, we need only to replace the lost fire, and add a little fluidity."

"Water?"

"*Are you mad*?!! Pure essence in transmutation?! No. We must reduce the level of magic, by using a lester oil. It is an oil that lessens transmutation to safe levels. Many alchemists failed because they did not use it. Boyle summed it up in his book 'Lest we forget'. An own concoction, a combination of two such lesters, I call co-lester."

He duly placed the eggshells in their own copper bowl on the low flame, before gingerly adding equal amounts of their animeum concoction and the oil. The pieces of eggshell floated to the surface, quite indifferently, quite all they were cracked up to be. The two experimenters bent closer over them and watched as they eventually sank and bubbled, and began to give off a vapour.

"Empty eggshells are no yolking matter," Newton began to say… "Sean?" Newton shook the young man next to him. "Sean?!"

The young man who was standing next to Newton looked very confused at his present situation and said so in unwavering pre-edrop dialect.

"Oh deare," said Newton, as he wrote in his notebook with his scrawly, microscopic handwriting:

'Too muche co-lester oile in these eggs.'

* * * *

Chapter Twelve
Bridge Head

WHACK! Sean's forehead was recommending a change of walkpath in no uncertain terms.

"Min' d' lo' beams, yun' mah'her," emitted a grotesque kind of voice, the wielder of which and his lantern fumes conspired to a sort of joint venture aura explicitly promotional of kippers.

Sean was in a corridor, trailing the general midst of three lantern-eclipsing figures.

" 'ere 'ee his," said the same perfectly uncharismatic speaker of h-cut n' paste, the evergreener London dialect.

"I be thanking ye," said the shorter of the other two men, and, in an attempt to enter the spirit of the vernacular, said: "Now, prithee pithee thee off."

"Aye, goo' mahher," mumbled the language vagrant, as he pocketed the proffered coin and shuffled off the way they had come.

"Which one is he?" said the taller of the men, who had nabbed the lantern from the retreating man.

Sean's eyes had adjusted to the dark enough to see that the taller man was very dignified and handsome, in his early forties, while the average-heighted man was in his fifties, threatening to portly, and looking somehow insistently dissimilar to something familiar.

This latter addressed him: "Well, Fatio, come and see a dead man talking."

"Don't you mean 'walking'?"

"No, no, this one is not walking anywhere. In an hour they will tie him to a wooden frame and draw him to Tyburn Gallows, where he will perform the Tyburn jig to a standing room only crowd." He turned and addressed the referenced sagging mound of depression. "So, Mr William Chaloner, where are your friends now?"

"You think you can destroy me, Newton?" a voice in refuge deep inside the shadow of a man replied.

"Isaac Newton?!" exclaimed Sean too loudly.

"Yes, Fatio?" the shorter of the two men turned back to him.

"But… you're so much older."

"Offence taken. Fifty-six, as I was yesterday. And for quite a few days before that."

"You seem different, Monsieur de Duillet," said the taller man, leaning over Sean and allowing the vile smelling lantern to be creative with his face shadows. "Who *are* you?"

Newton answered for him. "Come now, Halley, he's Fatio de Duillet, my young Swiss assistant for many years."

The condemned prisoner, Chaloner, clanked his restraining chains as a surrogate conchshell. "Ah… so the watchbearer has returned to walk among us once more?"

Edmond Halley returned to him faster than his

Vitruvian Boy

comet - far faster, come to think of it. "What!"

"Do you not see?" continued Chaloner. "How his face has taken that puerile look of Sean Seulpierre? We know it well, do we not... Pau?" Chaloner addressed this last to Edmund Halley, the tall astronomer friend of Newton.

"Pau?!" cried Sean.

"All right, so you have guessed," replied Halley's voice with Pau's intonation.

"I have known all along," said Chaloner.

"So, why did you let me trap you?"

"It was I who trapped Chaloner," objected Newton. "Anyway, why is everybody suddenly somebody else?"

"Well, you're still you," said Pau.

"I hope so."

"I am sorry. Could someone please wiki me a when, where and what?" said Sean in need of some comprehensibilisation.

Pau-Halley looked at him magnanimously because he was in his hour of glory. "It is March the 22nd, 1699, by the old Julian Calendar. We are in Newgate Prison, London. Isaac Newton has become Warden of the Royal Mint, responsible for hunting down notorious counterfeiters like William Chaloner here, who has been condemned to death - by being hung, drawn and quartered till he is really sorry."

"Quartered?!" shot out a ghastly-flabbered Sean.

"Sorry? Not enough? Perhaps you would like him eighthed? Or simply diced?"

"Could you add an explanation in all that for me, Halley?" demanded Newton.

"I am sorry, my friend," explained the Halley-Pau conglomerate. "I have deceived you. I took up residence here in Edmund Halley some time ago. I arranged for you to become the Warden of the Royal Mint so that you could use your authority to arrest Chaloner, the infamous coin clipper and forger."

"Sacky..." amazed Sean. "You are a Mint copper?!"

"Well, what flavour would you have preferred? ... You have *no idea* how long I have waited to say that!" He turned back to the condemned criminal. "William Chaloner is not the first, but he is easily the most nefarious of all the coinclippers I have hunted down. His activities could have re-destabilised the government. He is therefore a traitor to the crown."

"You hypocrite, Newton. I'm no more a traitor to the 'crown' than you and your whiggy friends who conspired against King James the Second, and forced him to sail for France," said Cespuglio.

"On yer two-master, Jimmy!" laughed Pau.

Newton went on obliviously. "It took me years of undercover work, hundreds of cross-examinations, to nail Chaloner. He escaped me first time, because of his influential contacts. But I hunted him down ruthlessly, using my network of informants in every seedy public house in East Rebuilt London."

Sean pulled Pau aside. "But, Pau, why are you victimising this poor man? What has Chaloner ever done to you?"

Pau verbally victory-looped with the climactic part of his story: "Because this is not just Chaloner. He is occupied by Cespuglio."

Despite the heavy set of chains and matching accessories restraining Cespuglio, Sean instinctively backed away hurriedly.

"*Who* is it?!!" demanded Newton, shaking his head of white hair in puzzlement.

"Well, it is more a question of who *hasn't* he been?" continued Pau-Halley. "With the Invertabrakes on his side, he has been nearly every seriously power-hungry warmonger that has ever lived. Caesar, Constantine, Trajan, Aurelius, Attila, 'Big Charlie' Charlemagne, more Khans than an Australian football match, King Richard of feline ventricle persuasion, Cesare Borgia, any number of cardinals - perhaps even the hound of the Baskervilles, for all I know. Cespuglio exists to bring death to an artform, and if havoc really is *waged* as they say - then his comes with a thirteenth month, bank manager bonuses and a generous retirement plan. But this time … *this time* he changed his tactics. By counterfeiting on a massive scale, he was trying to devalue the currency and destabilise the economy. That is what he wanted - a return of the Civil War."

"This time without the 'civil'," smiled the man in question.

"So you laid a trap for him? Using Sacky?" asked Sean.

Pau as Halley nodded ghoulishly in the lantern light, and looked down with extrovertive malevolence at his victim. "And now he dies. And with him Cespuglio. If the body his consciousness occupies dies before he can 'pass on' through the crown, then Cespuglio ceases to exist."

Cespuglio tried to reach them suddenly, furiously pulling at the chains that restricted him. "No! I am Cespuglio - I am the Eternal Emperor. You cannot kill me!"

"Well, we shall see in just under forty minutes,

shan't we?" smiled Newton, pulling down a stocking to reveal his left ankle and… the watch, still looking not a day older than when it first began travelling through time. Its strap was sheathed in cloth, to avoid corporeal contact, Sean noticed.

"The watch!" cried Cespuglio, his eyes flaming to a normal colour.

"But Pau," pleaded Sean, "if you eliminate Cespuglio, what about Stinto, Amur and Elf? Won't you be losing us the last chance to free them? And where is Geni?"

"You'll never see your little friends again," laughed Cespuglio. "Unless you release me."

"He's bluffing," said Pau. "He would never release them. Probably can't. You see, Sean, the Invertabrakes, the ruthlessly efficient and obedient soldiers we always see with him, are not from this world. And… he isn't *their* boss, they're *his*."

"But he said he was the 'Eternal Emperor'?" objected Sean.

The execution escort arrived and began to prepare the prisoner.

Sean pleaded a final time. "Please, Sacky, isn't there another way? Do you have to kill him? It's so cruel."

"He is a traitor to the crown," said Newton it's-out-of-my-handsedly.

Pau added. "Yes. But, *which* crown?"

"That's a point! Where *is* his crown now?" asked Sean.

Pau said I'm-ever-so-cleverly: "We took the crown from Cespuglio when he was arrested, before he had the chance to use it, and upload himself. Now it is safely hidden in plain sight among the crown jewels in the

Tower of London. We will keep it there till we work out how to release the others."

"Guarded day and after dinner by a whole company of voracious Beefeaters," case-closed Newton.

"Not a vegetarian in sight," added Pau gravely.

In the street, they could breathe real air again, or the nearest London had on offer. As the promotional fliers had promised, the prisoner was tied to a frame, which was then dragged behind a horse. A considerable crowd was aggregating itself to the procession, as it made its ghoulish way west towards Tyburn Gallows, where modern day Marble Arch stands.

Without going into gruesome details of the scene, the crowd had such a mood about it that should a football have occasionally appeared over their heads, it would not have seemed out of place.

After the show, Newton, Pau and Sean were uncertain what to do next. Pau wanted to stay to enjoy the atmosphere, Sean was thinking whether to throw up again, and they were just about to enter one of their perennial arguments when a black carriage with two black horses stopped in front of them. As they tried to slip past, its door opened to block their way. A black attired arm came out. Its owner said nothing, but in its black glove was a piece of paper.

Newton took it and read:

'Uncle, met these moste dishie chappies who tell me they are a bande of brothers from Switzerland, and haff all thy solutions. We awaite thee on the bridg.
    Luv, Catherine

Bridge Head   253

P.S.: they are so veri insistent they will not let me go till suche tyme as you arrive of yeselfs.

Huggs and kissees

Multi-P.S.: nethergarments soggie with worie'

"What pray be the meaning of this?" Newton demanded of the black glove. Its answer was to gesticulate an entry to the coach.

Once inside they saw that the glove's owner was a boy about Sean's age, who was wearing a sinister effect black wide-brimmed hat, and his eyes were hidden behind a pair of glasses the lenses of which had been intentionally obscured by under-age smoking. The boy answered all their questioning with stoic silence.

The coach moved south-east by passing back under the portcullis of New Gate. They turned down, I kid thee not, Blow Bladder Street, to pass beneath St. Paul's The Remake In Progress.

In Cheapside, the morning sun's first rays created the famous London 'golden rain' from the descendents of night soil.

At the junction to Cornhill, where the Royal Exchange stood, they passed down Lombard Street, which became Fish Street Hill, with a tapestry of odours to match, and this led them unto London Bridge.

The Thames was sheepskinned in a habitual fog, the water sluggish and ugly due to the obstruction the stone bridge presented it - many of the stanchions which made up the nineteen arches had reluctant water wheels between them, their combined efforts good for breadmaking, but terrible for river flow, reducing it to a trickle of its natural urge.

Vitruvian Boy

The coach stopped. The boy descended, and, still without a word, led them on to the bridge, between the rows of multi-storey buildings which gauntleted either side of the bridge road, creating a dark and foreboding tunnel. The nightly curfew preventing traffic was still to be lifted, so they were alone.

In the few gaps between the buildings, Sean could see the infamous Tower of London less than a mile to the east, silhouetted against the morning sky, its turrets triangulating the fact that the crown of Cespuglio was located in them, and within it languished his friends, Amur, Stinto and Elf. He longed to see them again.

Then he remembered Geni. "Pau? Where is Geni?"

The four stopped at a wide opening, where a drawbridge could be raised to cut the bridge in half, completely isolating the two sides of the town. On the south side of the bridge stood a turreted gateway that towered over them like a medieval keep, the teeth of the portcullis hanging down into the mouth of the gatehouse like those of a huge beast, no doubt intentionally reminiscent of Hades' canine bouncer. On its top were many spikes, some sporting heads of previous traitors of the month, waiting to pass on their title to the newcomers.

Pau pointed ahead. "There she is."

On the far side of the drawbridge were standing four adult clones. They were all dressed identically in black cloaks, black wide-brimmed hats, and all wore the same smoke-blackened glasses.

A beautiful and elegant lady of twenty stood with them, in her hallmark, doubly-ambitious, 'fetching' dress. Later, this would inspire the fashion known as the 'doublet'.

"These are the Bernoulli Brothers," announced Newton sombrely. "The maths mafia of Switzerland. They trade in illicit equations - no derivations asked.

"And that is Catherine Barton, my twenty year-old niece. Already reputed to be the most beautiful woman in London. Since she is here, it will serve to demonstrate the power of my theory of how bodies attract across space. You feel the attraction don't you, boys?"

All the men on both sides of the drawbridge nodded automatonically.

"Isaac, your niece Catherine is also Geni, a TimeRider like me," said Pau.

Geni-Catherine recognised Sean, smiled and waved nervously at him from the midst of her captors.

The boy who had guided them there called out across the drawbridge: "Hey Brü."

The oldest of the Bernoullis replied: "How many times do I have to remind you, Little Nick, we are in England? It is not Brü for Brüder, but bro for brother."

The drawbridge was down, and as they came close, the boy suddenly ran forward and jumped onto it just as it began to rise suddenly. Both the boy and it were out of reach before Pau, Newton or Sean could think to react, trapping them on the north side, with Geni and the Bernoullis on the south.

"Yo bros," laughed the boy when he reached his family.

"Yo bro," they answered, and they each in turn joined the knuckles of their right fists in the traditional mathematician hood greeting.

"Minde the Gappe," teased the young boy to Sean.

"Who are you and what do you want?" he called back.

One of the men, in his mid 40s, stepped forward.

"We are the Bernoulli brothers from Basel, Switzerland. My name is Jacob. This is our father, Big Nick." Nikolaus senior bowed formally in the old manner, remarkably nimble for his 76 years. He was leaning on a long alphorn.

Next, Jacob indicated a man in his late 30s. "This is Nicolaus. Formally 'Little Nick', but since he handed this title to his son, whom you have already met, he goes by the moniker of 'The Laus'." This man bowed solemnly, too.

Next Jakob indicated a man in his early 30s. "My little brother Johann. And while we are on the subject of getting to know each other, I will tell you something, Herr Seulpierre. My logo is 'Eadem mutata resurgo'. Know what that means?"

Sean thought quickly. "Well, something like 'I shall rise the same though changed'?"

Jacob stared at him. "What is *that* supposed to mean?"

"I assume it means you are a man who likes to hedge his bets?" suggested Sean.

"No. *Eadem mutata resurgo* means… enlighten him, bro JoJo."

Johann obliged. "*Eat badly, throw up.* A wise piece of advice, bro Jacko."

"Eadem, bro JoJo."

"Eadem the eadem," murmured all five Bernoullis in harmony from under their sinister, label-pending black hats.

"What are you boys doing here? Over here rule Newton's laws," demanded Newton.

The Laus answered in unfaltering bad English. "Vee are doing vat vee are alvay doing. Zer trading."

"Trading what?"

"Eyes…" A quick consultation followed. "Me pardon - eggs."

The old man, Big Nick, took out two stone time eggs from a bag.

Pau gasped and made a step forward. "You brought them!"

Newton turned to Pau. "Halley… did you arrange this meeting? Have you been dealing with my rivals behind my back?"

"Now I know it is Pau for sure," commented Sean. He called out to Jacob across the drawbridge: "And just what did Pau offer you in exchange for the eggs?"

Before Jacob could answer, Newton held up his leather case and said. "I know what you have come for. I have here the Fluxions equations, every one."

"The equations that make all the differentials?" asked Big Nick, licking his lips.

"That's them."

The Bernoulli Bros huddled for a few moments, before returning to the discussion across the drawbridge gap.

"We'll ask our client," said Jacko. "But we don't think he'll be interested. You see, he has already got one."

'That sounds vaguely familiar, for some reason,' thought Sean.

"Got one!!?" thundered Newton, possibly inventing

in the process rhetorical surprise denial.

"Sure. German patent. He calls it 'Integrals', but we have convinced him to release it under the brandname of… 'Calculus'," announced Johann proudly, as apparent spokesperson of the marketing team.

Newton stared in apoplectic silence.

"It's from Latin - for 'little stone'," continued JoJo. "As in counting…".

"I know what *calculus* means!" thundered Newton. "What I want to know is what has a *stone* got to do with the most powerful mathematical tool since Archimedes' pi-maker?"

"It is not the only 'only stone' here today, am I right, Herr *Seulpierre*?" replied Johann Bernoulli from behind his multilingualised affront. "I think you will find that the 'One Stone' trademark will one day be the biggest marketmaker in the equations game. And we Swiss intend to be there to get our slice of the pie."

"Cake, you mean," said Sean.

"Not for Archimedes fans."

Newton went an extraordinary colour.[*]

"I know there are rival gangs who want to muscle in on the *spiki celestii* monopoly I hold. You may be trying to infringe my patent on 'calculus' by a prior-publication claim … but I retain the rights to the control equations, and you are not getting your greedy little hands on them. Stuff moves at my command, got me? *My* laws of motion. Nothing moves but by Newton's say-so - the laws of Newton!"

Jacko said coolly to his brothers. "Well, bros, I say Newton's Laws are English laws, not European laws, so

---

[*] #FF1022

do not apply to us. You have no jurisdiction over us."

The Laus added: "Vee are unneedful of your equations - for vee hold to zer Leibniz standard. Isn't zat right, bro son?"

"In fact, we are his exclusive agents," replied the boy.

"Our network is looking at England as potential *integrals* territory," added his uncle Jacko.

"Differentials are what are sold here. Calculus will be done with differentials - never lousy German integrals!" shouted Newton, upside-down himself with fury. "I warn you, Bernoullis, the Socks are nearly mine - and my first command will be to implement the first Law of Newton: if a body is laid to rest, by gum it will stay at rest!"

"So, basically, Newtown.."

"Ton! New...Ton!"

"Don't get heavy with us, Newt boy," said the twelve-year-old Little Nick, pushing his smoked glasses back up his nose for the fifth time in as many sevenths of a minute. "As ratings go you are declassified to 'unbankable asset' - in Leibniz we have an alternative supplier of the equations that make the differential. So your equations don't hold a monopoly, Newt-boy. You do not pass go, get me? You've been sacked, I-saac!"

His uncles sniggered. "On yer tripod, Alte," said JoJo. "The Bernoulli Brü are moving in on your turf. That's the way the equations work out."

"Your fluxions wuz good, we'll give you that," went on Jacko. "But too complex and confoolooting for the average number practician, get me? Our client's stuff is not covered by your patent, so bad luck."

Little Nick lifted his hat enough so he could tap his

temple: "As Descartes said, if yer wanna get to the sums, yer's got to cogito."

Now Big Nick moved forward, leaning on his alphorn. "Boys, boys … Respect, where it's due. Mr Newton, you're the foremosty genius in the numbers racket - but we oldies have got to recognise the world is moving on without us - that there is no market for genius anymore. Bring the enlightenment upon him, bro son Jacko."

"Right on, bro pa. The theory business is yesterday's news. Today it's all about applications. Our customers don't care *how* it works, just so long as it *does*."

"Don't underestimate Newton's Forces," repeated Newton, like a gramophone record that one day would be invented and one day would get stuck.

"And just what are they?"

"My boys - the feared Sacks gang: Johnnie the Lockdown, Pepying Sam, and Halley the Comet here."

"Und zer bobbies?" asked the Laus, referring to Roberts Hooke and Boyle.

"Yes - our rival gang is the Royal Socks, led by Hooke the Crook, Bobbie the Boyler, and the Astronomer Royal, better known as the Flaming Steed."

"You all have more than one name?" asked Jacko.

"Yes," stated Newton proudly. "It is part of my Method: I call it the polynomial system."

"Maybe Captain Hooke can be convinced to support the Leibniz claim over yours?" replied Big Nick quietly.

"It is well known there is no love lost between Robert Hooke and me. He thinks himself a giant, but is really a runt I would benefit from standing on the head of. I wrote and told him that in no uncertain terms: If i have seen further it is by standing on ye shoulders of giants. He knew what I meant. He is President of the Royal Society... but for how long? The Sacks are moving in and taking over the Socks. With Hooke gone the gang war will end.

"And there'll be a few changes when I'm the boss of the Royal Socks. If you want an applications war, you can have one. We'll be branching out from divinity equations to machines, star-tracking, light-bending, the fauna trade and alchemy derivatives. I only want boys with the right connections and who know their stuff. 'Cos we're going to move in on the mobs across the channel, got me?

"Fifteen years ago, when I released my book, Principia, on the market, it wiped the competition right out. It was Halley's idea to publish. With it I wiped Des Cartes from the table. But you guys are still giddy from his vortex left behind." Newton patted the leather case. "These are my laws - the Laws of Newton. Beware any who defy them, for there be stone weights and river aplenty."

Jacko let the tirade abate before saying with disturbing softness: "As I said... it's applications the market's hungry for. That's why we want the SANG Re.al. It's full of 'em."

Newton was stunned. "How... how did you know about the watch?"

"Never mind all that," said Pau, stepping in front of him. "We will exchange the watch for the eggs."

What?!" thundered Newton. "I am not giving the watch to the Swiss! Knowing them, they'll turn it into a national industry!"

"It doesn't belong to you, Isaac," asserted Pau.

"No, nor to you, Pau," called across Geni. "If it

belongs to anyone, it is to Sean."

"Well," continued Pau confidently, "I am sure that Sean will want you, Geni, to escape the Invertabrakes. Am I right, Seulpierre?"

"What Invertabrakes?" asked Sean.

"Those Invertabrakes, you short-sighted nematode," said Pau, pointing at a large group of strangely attired solders, carrying what appeared to be very long spears, jogging towards them along the river bank from the direction of the Tower.

"It's alright," reassured Newton. "They're from the Tower. They help protect my Mint. They're Newton's forces."

"But there are only two eggs," said Jacko uncertainly, looking from Geni alongside him, to Pau and Sean across the gap. "We may be using a different maths over on the continent, but three is still three. Why did you only order two eggs?"

"It's a long story. Basically, Sean is not coming with us."

"Pau!" shouted Geni. "How can you say that?! Of course Sean is coming."

"Now's our chance, Geni. Don't you see? Cespuglio is dead. Sean is left trapped here with his friend Newton. The watch returns to Switzerland. We go on as before. Everything returns to normal."

"But you promised! You promised we would get Sean home."

"He will get there - eventually," replied Pau.

"He'll age to death long before he arrives!" cried Geni, furious.

"Well, that's his choice."

As with any question he had no answer to, Pau ignored it, and addressed the equation traders. "So, do we have a deal? The watch for the eggs?"

"Where is it?" asked Jacko.

"Sacky?" enquired Pau-Halley.

"I want the Barrow papers."

Everybody stopped and stared at Newton.

"The what?!" exclaimed Pau.

"Don't know what you mean," began JoJo clumsily, obviously caught off-guard.

"I know you have them. Your father, Big Nick, stole them from Professor Barrow's hotel room in Venice, then burnt the hotel down to cover his tracks."

"But that was 40 years ago," said Big Nick.

"That's nothing as differentials go," insisted Newton.

"Alright... let's call it a partial differential," shrugged Big Nick.

Newton went on. "Isaac Barrow had seen the Archimedes palimpsest, so his papers must contain Archimedes' solution to the geometry of the golden ratio."

"Are you saying Archimedes discovered the *spiki celestii* - nearly two thousand years before you? How's that, Mr Newtown, for trumping your prior invention claim?"

The Laus added in his strong Swiss-German accent. "Und ve had it in zer family fault all zis time..."

"What's our fault?" demanded his brother JoJo.

"Nicht fault ... fault," replied the Laus irritatedly.

"He means 'vault'," said Geni to defeud the family situation. "But first, tell us - will this *spiki celestii*...

thingey … in the Barrow papers explain what is causing the TimeQuake?"

"Perhaps," replied Jacko. "But we have no time: the Invertabrakes are on the bridge."

Co-ordinated footfalls were echoing menacingly down the tunnel of buildings on the wooden bridge.

Big Nick chivalrously kissed Geni's hand in the European half-venerational, half-sleazy manner, and said: "But, I will tell you this, dear little lady. If Herr Seulpierre is the cause of the time collapse, then he can be the only possible solution."

The old man opened his brief satchel and removed a very ancient looking folio of papers and gave it to Geni. On the front cover Sean could read: 'The Wheel Returneth: the adventures of a Cambridge scallywag in Constantinople.'

"That's them, the Barrow papers," Sean whispered to Newton.

Newton knelt down and, holding the strap through a handkerchief, removed the watch from his ankle and handed it to Sean. The drawbridge came down, and Sean advanced to midway and handed the watch to little Nick, who bit one of the buttons to check it was genuine.

Jacko handed the eggs to Pau, who had crossed the drawbridge to join Geni.

The exchange thus completed, the Bernoullis were galvanised into action.

"You'll never escape, boys," said Newton, hugging the Barrow papers Geni had handed him. "Newton's forces will be here any second."

"Quick, bros, the brachy." The brothers inverted Big Nick's alphorn, and although it was already longer than the tallest of them, by twisting a series of rings they managed to extend it to four times its original length.

"This is no normal alphorn," explained JoJo.

"I never thought there was anything 'normal' about any alphorns," replied Sean.

"Exactly. The non-normalised curve it describes is my own invention: the *brachistochrone.*"

"Cheeky little name," commented Geni.

"Thank you," replied JoJo. "But I am thinking of changing the name to *The Geni.*"

"Why that?" she asked, not too stunned to be flattered.

"*Fantastic* curves."

His brothers had swung the alphorn over the side of the bridge, the bowl anchored on the rail, the length curving down towards the river.

Bro JoJo continued. "You see, the *brachistochrone* is based on the golden ratio described by Pacioli to mathematically define the divine proportion." He looked at Geni's voluptuous shape appreciatively. "No doubt after seeing you." He glanced down. "For obvious reasons, it describes the quickest path between two points. Allow us to demonstrate." And all five members of the Bernoulli gang, with a practised escape drill, slipped over the bridge railing, and down the makeshift pole. In no time, they were gone.

"Bye bye, parchment suckers," was little Nick's parting salute.

"But, where…?" Sean didn't need to finish his cliché, for when he rushed to the bridgeside to see where they were going, he saw the five already on the deck of a river ferryboat, which had appeared at some secret signal of the brothers. It carried a flag bearing an image of a pound of holy Emmental cheese, and Little Nick was waving the watch up at them cheekily. Big Nick sounded the alphorn as a foghorn, and as the boat pulled down the river towards the fogbank that indicated the route towards the open sea, Sean could see emblazoned on its side, in an early draft of the Helvetica font: 'Helvetian Rhineland and Beyond Tours: Ideal for a quick Weekend Getaway'.

"Quick," said Geni, beckoning to her rescuers, now all on her side of the bridge. "Pull the drawbridge up!"

Sean found and released the weight which drew the drawbridge up. Just in time, for on the north side, the owners of the thundering feet had arrived. They were dressed in the fancy dresses of the Beefeaters, and they numbered over twenty. They came to a crashing halt as the leader commanded with the Centurion's voice Sean remembered from Syracuse: "Minde the Gappe!"

"It's alright," said Newton. "These are the Yeomen Guards of the Tower. They protect the Mint inside it. I am the Warden of the Mint - they are Newton's forces."

"No, Isaac," said Geni. "I am afraid these are not your boys. Look at their eyes."

Their eyes were indeed beady and red.

The Centurion figure spoke. "Warden Newton, where is the Eternal Emperor?"

"Dead. He was debasing the coinage - that is the same as debasing maths, so I had him drawn and quartered to show him first hand what division really means."

"Where are his relics?"

"If you mean his bones, all over London by now,

I should think," mocked Pau from the safety of the far side of the drawn bridge gap. The Invertabrakes stomped their spears on the bridge planks in threatening chorus.

Newton spoke. "Now, boys. Remember, you need me. I am the Warden of the Royal Mint - the source of your income." He pointed to the Tower, from the side of which projected a large M. "Tell me, what would a beefeater do without my Mint source?"

"You are not necessary. When your Mint is closed, we will convert it to a MacDonald Clan outlet, who have agreed to provide us with a constant supply of highland beef patties."

At that moment, a special delivery hearse arrived. On its side were splattered more than written the words: *Bridgehead Delivery Service.* A courier brought out a hessian bag dripping *al sangue.* "Special delivery for the traitors' gate!" he announced. Sean looked up at the Gatehouse spikes and its ghoulish traitor head decorations.

"What is it?" asked the Centurion.

"Dunno. They just told me 'head for the bridge'," answered the man. "And here I am."

"I will take that," said the Centurion.

He signed the chit and the delivery man cantered off saying: "Thanks. I'm starving. Disembowellings always give me a real appetite. I'm off to Blackfriars."

"What is that?" asked Sean.

"Illegal vendors of over-cooked potato slices," answered Newton.

Only now did Sean notice that many of the beefeaters had birds on their left shoulders. They were large ravens.

One suddenly took off and flew across to Sean.

"Baldrick!" cried Sean, and scratched his old pet under the beak as he had used to.

"You have deleted the emperor from this time frame?" demanded the centurion, holding up the horrific bag.

"From all time frames," stated Pau from the relative safety of behind Newton and Sean. He pulled out his egg and indicated to Geni to do the same.

"Let's all be treasonable about this," said the Centurion. One of the henchyeomen handed him the bejewelled iron crown Sean had last seen on the Tower of Pisa, where Elf had been nabbed by Cespuglio in the guise of a cardinal. "The pretty lady is going in the crown." The Centurion lifted his hand and as one all the other ravens flew across and landed on the rope holding up the drawbridge. They began to peck at it with razor-sharp beaks.

Pau panicked. "Now, Geni, now!" He lifted his egg, hesitated just long enough to ensure Geni was doing likewise, then brought the egg down hard at his feet.

Sir Edmond Halley was left staring about himself in puzzlement.

Geni did not break her egg. Instead, she took Sean's hands and pleaded with him. "You Sean - not us, Pau and I - it is *you* who know how to speak to the geniuses who are freeing us from the supernatural. The Bernoullis are right. *You* are destined to find the solution to whatever it is that is going wrong with time. So take this egg."

"No! You will be captured by the Invertabrakes."

"I will be, it is true. But you can free me. I believe in you, Sean. The power you have is in your mind. Your thoughts are in tune with something fundamental - that is what is moving the watch, what brings you to it. You control it. So you can stop it."

"How?"

"Do as Pau and I do it when we time travel. We focus, not only on the watch, but on the place we want to be. Look, the whole thing started with the watch entering the timeline. We couldn't change what happened in Syracuse. But maybe we can in Alexandria, where it stayed two hundred years after John the Measurer took it there after winning the theatre festival in Rosetta. You can find the watch there – that is what John is telling you to do in his play. So, when you time jump, focus on Alexandria. Then you will travel *back* in time and you will be able to prevent all of this ever happening in the first place."

"Alexandria?!"

The drawbridge rope groaned a final time, and then snapped. "Good-bye, Sean. Rescue me if you can." The bridge crashed down into place and the beefeaters stormed across. Baldrick flew off in huffy fright.

Just before the Invertabrakes reached them, Geni threw her egg at Sean's feet.

"Geni, no!! I never want to leave you again!" he cried. But is was too late. The time galaxy had formed and he felt himself being sucked into its swirl. He vaguely heard Newton call 'Goodbye my friend! Good journey. Remember me kindly!' And then everyone and the bridge began to lose their taken-for-granted opacity.

Sean's mind stayed fixed on Geni, calling out to her, not wanting to leave her. And he seemed, in the swirl, to be successfully resisting its pull, held suspended in the air near her. But then gradually he knew he was being drawn away.

Just in time, Sean remembered to visualise the watch and to focus on one word: Alexandria. Take me to Alexandria. Then he felt the swirl hesitate, hover at some point of equilibrium, as if it were trying to work something out. Then it made a decision, and he felt himself slurping like a leaf being dragged down a drain.

* * * *

Chapter Thirteen

Marengo Pi

CHAOS was having a field day when Sean opened his eyes. Every body was either stock, with a popular alternative of dead, still, or running around crazily. Nothing in between seemed to get much of a look in.

Gradually the noise began to distinguish itself into different strata. If the melody was a loose improvisation on the themes of panic and disorder, the crack-boom-whoosh of dozens of cannons provided a more disciplined bass section. There were whistles of heavy, and presumably dangerous, lumps of metal, available in two standard sizes, just about everywhere in the atmosphere, which for its part was not happy about any of it, and let everybody know with its air renting. The ground itself was very nervous, and would jump at the slightest cannonball provocation.

Then there were screams of pain drawn largely from the heavy-motif of corporeal dismemberment, and bellows of orders, whinnies in response, and other horsey things with hoof rhythmics, some results of which added creaks of gun carriages being rush-pulled along a recently rain-besoggied road.

"C'est tous perdu!" This biased contribution to the industrial scale panic was offered by a man in a blue-jacketed uniform, blood streaming down his face and over his ostensibly white tunic front.

Yes, it was one of those real men's things: a jolly good battle, in which a man can prove he is, or was until recently, or at least a more intact, man. A battle evidently not going well for the army around where Sean was standing.

Sean looked down at himself. He was wearing a similar uniform to the others, but jutting out the ragged legs of his breaches were young, bare feet that by the look of them had probably never known boots. He wasn't carrying a musket like the others, but a drum was strung around his neck, on which he was unconsciously beating as insistent a rhythm as possible:

rat-tat..rat-tat-tat, rat-tat..rat-tat-tat, rat-tat…

which he was surprised he knew meant: 'By me is the re-assembly point. Form line.'

When the thick acrid wads of smoke permitted, he could see he was standing on the side of a congested road, next to a field of what was previously parade-ground straight rows of rank and file wheat, now just rank. There were vineyards to his right, and farmhouses to his left. Very *European* farmhouses. European. As in not really Egyptian by any stretch of any imagination. Sean's memory cache slotted the rest of the way into place: this was *not* Alexandria, Egypt. Well, that was one more theory for my discards collection, he thought.

The uniforms, the weapons, the location, all contributed to a piecing together of some reasonably consistent profile of when and where (the heck) he was, but the thing that really global time positioned it for him was the man who was evidently the commander-in-chief. Sean had seen the uniform, hat, eaglesque nose, and, while honesty is upon us, distinctive diminutive stature, of this man in many of his history books.

It was Napoleon Bonaparte, First Consul of France.

As it turned out, this was June 14, 1800, and this was the plain of Marengo, Piedmont, Italy. The blue-jacketed French Revolutionary Army was engaged in a brutal life-to-death struggle with the white-uniformed Austrian-Hungarian army under their own age-ing military genius, Feldmarschal Melas: known affectionately to the ladies around the fruit markets as 'Big Apples'. And the road they were standing next to bore a tombstone-like road marker saying something to the effect of: 'Alessandria, not-a-too-a-far, dees-a-way'.

When reality hits dead centre, it really thuds. He had programmed his time jump for Alexandria, but had not taken into account that there were more than one! Providence, as many have noted, is somewhat hard of hearing.

Taking advantage of Napoleon's 'petit booboo' in dividing his forces the day before, all day Melas's Austrian troops had been pouring in unexpected force out of the town of Alessandria onto the plain around the village of Marengo. And after a murderous right of passage disagreement across an irrigation ditch, their numerical superiority had finally broken the French lines, and they were now hounding Napoleon's retreating army relentlessly.

Since it takes a good thirty seconds to reload a musket, the two sides had ample opportunity to engage in some delightfully creative bilingual name-calling.

Perhaps because of his sensitivity to small stature jokes, Napoleon was standing with his back to the advancing Austrians. In front of him were not his general staff, but a military band.

A heavily decorated officer risked interrupting him. "Your Excellency! If Marshal Desaix does not return with his ten thousand men we are lost! What did you say to him yesterday to make him go off like that?"

"I told 'im to look for zee Austrians to zer south - slip of zee tongue. Of course I meant west! Anyway, I can't zink of everyzeeng - eet ees not my fault eef zee Austrians do not follow my battleplan! Don't bozzer me, Lannes. I ham busy with zer victory celebrations. Or are you going to tell me zere will be no victory celebrations…?" he growled low and threateningly to the broader group.

The dozen senior officers, crouching from the fire coming from the advancing Austrian line, and some of them developing a preference to join the fleeing French troops streaming past them, looked at each other, but none were brave enough to tell First Consul Napoleon Bonaparte he had already lost the battle.

"Good," continued Napoleon. "Zo, eef you don't mind, the musicians and I 'ave some re'earsing to do. Please get on with zee battle, and try to keep eet down a beet - we can't 'ear ourselves play."

He turned to the score musicians in a semi-circle in front of him. They were holding dented and scratched trumpets, horns, mud-clogged woodwinds, drums, shrilling fifes, and the one remaining bassoon had had its top blown off. "Now, gentlemen, one more time: 'All 'ail zer Conquering Hero' - from zer top, and play eet as eef you mean eet." He conducted with a cannon ignition taper, still glowing and smoking.

The terrified band began its discordant attempt at the piece. Just before the reprieve, a cannonball bowled down the brass section, the clarinets lost the beat (again), while some other elements of non-musical nature went permanently astray.

Napoleon looked at them with exaggerated patience. "Encore, messieurs. We do not want to make a face of cow dung, as zey say in Italy, tonight at zer victory celebration."

"All is lost! Vive la France!" screamed a soldier as he staggered past.

"Seelence, you jukeboîte! Can't you see zere are artistes at work?" Napoleon turned and shouted at a Guards sergeant: " 'ave zer Austrians shoot zat man as many times as eet takes teell 'ee learns 'ees lesson."

"Oui, mon général." And the man was dragged back into the fray.

"Alors, where were we, messieurs?"

"Bar 42/36..." said two simultaneously.

"I was at 58. I win," said the bassoonist proudly.

"Non, je..."

A musket ball almost comically pinged out the rest of the trumpeter's sentence.

Napoleon threw down his improvised baton. "Oo, sacres nerds! Zese Austrian philistines! 'ow can I 'ear zer pianissimo eef zere ees all zees raclette!! Kellermann!" Napoleon shouted at a cavalry officer.

"Mon général?!"

"Take your 'ussars... and oh, also zose new cuirassiers over zere..." He indicated a squadron of men wearing breastplates and red-plumed helmets standing stiffly to one side, their horses expressing their nervousness in the traditional fashion. When Sean looked hard, he could discern in the cavalrymen's eyes something a little beady and red, which occasionally reflected off their hyper-polished metal armour. When they moved, their curved sabres, sheathed and hanging from exaggeratedly ornate leather harnesses, added to their somehow misappropriate clanking.

'They… no… they can't be…' said Sean to himself, fixated by their diodey eyes.

First Consul Bonaparte continued. "Général Kellerman, be zo good as to take your 'eavy cavalry and request zer enemy to put a sock een eet. We are trying to re'earse!"

"Oui, mon petit général."

Kellermann rode off to assemble his cavalry, ready for the charge of the heaviest brigade there had ever been.

"Sound zer charge!" ordered Napoleon, and Sean beat the 'Gloire de la Republique, Non, Non, Nous Ne Regretons Rien' on his tummy drum.

The column of cavalry moved forward, drew their sabres, formed a parade ground, the so-called 'squeaky-door', manoeuvre, despite the rain of munitions all around them, and with wild yells based roughly on a hastily hypothesised immortality theory, charged the Austrian and Hungarian enemy where it would hurt the most: right between the allies.

The Austrian grenadiers, who had been distracted sporting captured French Guard trophies they had seized an hour ago, were caught unprepared in the open. For an encore, the cavalry mounted (as is their wont) a second charge, sweeping the last of the enemy from the field and giving the exhausted and near-routed French the much needed breathing espace to rally and reconsider their early retirement plans. The day was saved when Marshal Desaix, apparently over his huff at being sent off the field before the battle had even started, returned, and added his ten thousand cannon fodder to the general slaught that was definitely on.

"Ah, zat's better," said Bonaparte, as the Austrians' screams of panic subsided into the distance. And soon the band, Sean amongst them, found itself advancing as they rehearsed, the music now a genuine victory march, down the road towards the bridge into Alessandria, in the footsteps of many earlier conquerors, like Caesar and Hannibal. In fact, just about everyone seems to have been there except Alexander himself, but then, what's in a name?

Despite all his bravado and self-assurance, Napoleon Bonaparte breathed something of an extra-extra-large sigh of relief. Indeed, a very large sigh for such a *oui* man.

Holed up in the town, the Austrians surrendered, and offered to run away from Italy by mutual agreement. After legalising the run-away in a formal signing of an armistice, the commanders on both sides exchanged presents, thanked all those without whom the war would not have been possible, and the armies departed, tearfully making last minute promises to meet again in some corner of some foreign field that will be forever... somebody else's mess to clean up.

As for the band: their victory march was a triumph. So much so, in fact, what was left of the Marengo Victory Orchestra started a tour de farce of towns. Their first gig was to be at La Scala, the famous opera house in Milan, to a, literally, captive audience. The same cuirassier cavalry who had won the battle became their minders and ticket touts. With their beady red eyes, metallic voices, failed Italian and more successful sabres, they scoured the streets for an audience.

And they were there in the theatre itself at each performance to make sure the press-ganged members of the audience applauded enthusiastically after each pièce the band performed on the famous stage. They even provided the special effects for the battle scenes in the show by sending musket balls whizzing over the heads of the audience. Unfortunately, due to their failure to grasp the basics of theatre design, this did cause some considerable casualties among the people in the boxes overhead. However, it was rationalised, since exclusive boxes were the privilege of the rich, this was entirely in keeping with the spirit of the Revolution, so Napoleon, their road manager, let it pass.

"Si on paie en avance, on peut oublier beaucoup[*]," he is said to have said less-oft-quotedly.

After one particularly bloody concert, a 50-year-oldish elegantly-dressed gentleman approached Sean, inclined his handsome head minimally and enunciated in crisp aristocratic garble: "Young man, I must congratulate you on your bâton rouge. How you managed to keep playing under fire during the battle, I will never know."

"Thank you, sir. It was…"

"Oh, no, I am not interested. I said I will never know because I have no intention of ever finding out. My name is Laplace."

"Pierre-Simon Laplace? *The* Marquis de Laplace?

---

[*] Translation: 'Bums on seats! It's all about bums on seats!'

The famous mathematician and astronomer, who wrote the revolutionary 'Celestial Mechanics' and was the tutor of the young Napoleon Bonaparte when he was a cadet at the military academy?"

"You've heard of me then?"

"Er... no," Sean tried to cover up his blunder. A drummer boy would not know such things. He thought to bow, and did so awkwardly, wondering what the regulation depth of inclination was in an egalitarian state. "Er... pleased to meet you."

"That's right." Laplace smiled strangely. "Yes. And more recently, I was the Minister of the Interior to his mostly extreme excellency, First Consul Napoleon Bonaparte."

"Was?"

"Yes. I had a bit of a run-out with his wife, Josephine." He shrugged. "We all did."

"I don't understand."

Laplace handed him an expensive-looking business card with a golden string attached. It read:

Pierre Simon (de) Laplace

the exiest Marquis of them all

ex Minister of the Interior

to the

Glorious French Republic

Sean turned the card over and read some even

Vitruvian Boy

gaudier embossing:

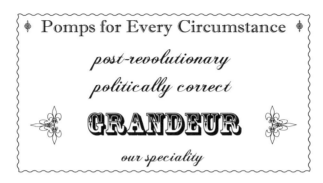

❖ Pomps for Every Circumstance ❖

post-revolutionary
politically correct

GRANDEUR

our speciality

"You do decorating?" said Sean, as surprised as decorum allowed.

Laplace jerked the string and the card sailed back to him. He pocketed it quickly then shrugged his nose into a wrinkle. "What do you expect a Minister of the Interior to do - gardens?! Grandeur for the elite under the new egalitarian vogue. But it is actually a traditional family business - real estate, that is. That is why we are called landed gentry. The motto of the 'La-Place' family is: Location, Location, Location," he continued to explain to an evermore bewildered Sean. "During the Revolution, those of us who could, adapted, those who didn't - well, they, let's say, went a bit short. Ah, the nobility is not what it used to be."

"Not by the head count, at any rate. You were saying you had problems with Napoleon's wife?"

" 'Nappy,' she would say to him. 'Don't be such a wet blanket, Nappy'… Mon dieu, how he hated it when she called him that, and he would get into one of his 'humeurs', and c'est la vie for a country or two till he had calmed down."

As if on cue, Napoleon came into the dressing-room, his uniform enormously red-sashed and opportunity-portrait ready. His clerkily-contrasting secretary, Bourrienne, followed him with difficulty through the narrow door, weighed down by a portable desk hanging from a strap around his neck.

"Bien, bien, now, where weren't we?" Napoleon asked Laplace and Sean, after the two had finished their requisite grovelling, which is not all that easy to a man shorter than an armrest.

Rising from his elegant, stick-accessoried bow, Laplace said: "Your Excellency, I was just about to explain to our friend here about the day I made my little discovery. You see, Sean, while we were repapering the royal apartments, I found a little portrait by Leonardo da Vinci in his Excellency's private cabinet. La Gioconda - or Mona Lisa as it is known in the pre-revolutionary catalogues."

Napoleon nodded. "And zees Moaning Lisa painting ees intéressant, en général très intéressant indeed."

"Ah, Excellency, you have such acute 'e's," admired Laplace.

"Merci. Alors, zey say no person knows for sure where zer Moaner was paintéd. Or 'ow she came to 'ave such a magique smile."

"Is that important?" asked Sean, enigmatized to the spot as to why the great Napoleon Bonaparte and the Marquis, albeit the serial ex-everything, de Laplace should be holding such a conversation with a mere drummer boy.

"Leesen, boy," continued the First Consul. "Everyzing I zay ees important, clair? I first eenvadéd Italy een zer year four of zer revolutionary calendar, otherwise known as one t'ousand, seven 'undred, four twenties and sixteen. What do you teenk - that I should now be coming back for zee peezzas?" demanded Napoleon, pre-emptively indignant.

"No, of course not," Sean confused bravely and onwards.

"Not necessary, anyway, zey now 'ave take-aways - which ees *exactement* what I did zer first time I came 'ere. Do you know what I ham saying?"

"That you made a lot of dough?" ventured Sean.

"No! Well… yes. But I took more zan zat. I also found a codex - a collection of writings - by Léonard de Vinci 'isself. 'is missing Codex Medilágo."

"Codex Medilago?!" Sean out-blurted.

" 'ave you read it?"

"Read it? I wrote it!" Sean found himself saying. "Or helped, at least," he finished lamely to temper the deficit on deference.

"Did you juste?" said Napoleon with a confirming nod to Laplace.

"So, you can tell us which 'central lake' the 'Medilago' refers to?" the Marquis stated.

Sean made the mistake of thinking over for a moment whether this would be a good idea.

"Or you die," prompted Napoleon, matter-of-factly. He flicked up the desk lid which slapped Bourrienne squarely on the nose (explaining its curious shape) and foraged among the ink and own-label brandy bottles till he found a pad of stencilled death warrant chits. He then closed the lid and took one of the less-nibbled feather quills from behind his secretary's ear. Sean could see that several of the chits had already been used, and by the names on the stubs they had been made out for most of the music critics of Milan.

"You know, Scharn, I like my people to zink of me as a compassionate man - but of course, I am nozzing of zer sort. Bourrienne? What threat 'ave I not used today?"

His secretary shook a large document box upside-down, and a single dusty decree came floating out. He handed it to his boss. "This one, free equal brother."

Napoleon snatched it from him and glared at him. "Zis liberté, egalité, fraternité zing is really getting on my nerves. Ok, what 'ave we 'ere…" He read the paper. "Bourrienne, … zis ees an old one."

Bourrienne shrugged. "There is no use-by date. Anyway, we are running low. I expect a delivery of fresh threats by the end of the week. It's you who insists on variety."

"Don't want to get into a rut," Napoleon explained to Sean. "Ok. C'est la vie - or better… la fin de la vie. Zis says: '…or I shall 'ave you 'ung, drawn and decimalléd'."

"Decimalled?" enquired Sean with a rare mélange of curious anxiety.

"Yes. The French Republic has gone metric," explained Bourrienne proudly.

Sean thought it would be opportune to panic. "Your Excellency, if you are doing this to intimidate me, I can assure you it has worked admirably well."

Napoleon drew himself up to his full height and stared the young boy directly in the nostrils. "So, you start? Tu… oui?"

"Yes, we start to wee. The Medilago is the Lake of Lugano, otherwise known as Lago Ceresio, the Cherry Lake of Nostradamus fame," said Sean faster than an unintended mouseclick on a delete button.

"Correct," said Napoleon to Sean's surprise. "Just testing. Bourrienne…" Napoleon scrunched up the warrant slip and tossed it expertly into the mouth of his secretary, who uncomplainingly swallowed it.

"So, if you knew that already, why do you need me?" asked Sean, desperately seeking some comprehension node point.

"Because, Sharn Seulpierre," answered Napoleon gently, "Léonard left us a furzer clue zat we can *not* déciphér. Sleep now - for tomorrow we voyages to Lugánó."

"I am going home…" smiled Sean and dreamed that night of his house, Mami, Papi, and Nonno.

* * *

Lugano in 1800 was taking up its share of a world population that had more than doubled since Leonardo's time - to a staggering one billion people world wide. Thomas Malthus was already whinging to his hyperloined compatriots that such an uncontrolled population increase would soon overwhelm the capacity of the planet to cope.

The lake looked as precious jewelly as ever, with massive dollops of lush and associated green around a broad and vibrant bay, random-pixelled by scattering sunlight and post-storm clearance sails of leisure and fishing craft. If the lake and mountains looked much the same, as did the odd church spire, just about everything else about the town had undergone 'changements' since Leonardo's time. Elegant buildings now frocked the lake from one end of the bay to the other, and had even begun their conquest of the slopes that commandeered the town.

After being ferried across the lake and being ripped off outrageously by the ferryman, they entered the town unannounced, but, despite his false moustache, whether a military procession of several hundred heavily armed cavalry with Napoleon Bonaparte at its head could be considered 'incognito' is wide open to debate.

They entered the brand new Grand Old Café al Porto, where they partook of a hot chocolate.

"The people here seem to like you," commented Sean, noting the passers-by nudging each other and pointing through the large ornate windows at the little man.

"And so zey should. It is I who insuréd zem for zeir independence from Italy."

"By conquering them," added Laplace.

"Soon I will make zem a full canton in zee 'elvetian Republic, my New Switzerland."

"Why are you doing that?"

"It is an act of mediation to keep Lugánó from zee Cisalpinistes."

"Who are they?"

"A hand-picked bunch of crooks 'oo run a franchise of mine - zer Cisalpine Republic - what used to be zer Duchy of Milan in zer time of Léonard."

Sean remembered Leonardo complaining about how the French had come under Louis the Round Dozen, and had used his beautiful giant horse model as target practice. And when King Louey had finished monkeying around, Lombardy was timeshared by first the Spanish, then the Austrians. Italian history was definitely the inspiration behind the game of musical chairs.

Being somewhat musically challenged, Lugano was having none of it. After they found their mercenaries were being paid to fight each other, they decided neutrality was a more insurance policy-compliant deal, and quietly slipped away to the embrace of the Swiss Confederation. It wasn't until nearly three hundred years later, in 1798, that the Italians, newly confident as a French franchise, thought to try to take it back.

"I want Switzerland to forget their *ancien régime*, as France 'as, and to embrace the new 'elvetian Republic I have designéd for zem - with a gouvernement central," explained Napoleon. "But zey cannot agree. Zey speak so many languages… I zink zey do zat on purpóse: it gives me a naughty 'ead."

"Er… I think, your Excellency, the expression is head-*ache*," hesi-corrected Laplace.

"Now, zee Italians, zese Cisalpinistes from Milan, tried to take Lugánó from Switzerland just two years ago, as part of zeir attempt to unite all Italian-speaking areas."

" 'Spaghetti Junction' I believe they call that idea," helped Laplace.

"But zey were repulséd by zee Lugánése zemselves, who zen proclaiméd zemselves 'One and Indivisible'. Right Bourrienne?"

His secretary nodded and read from a Redeclaration of Independence sticky memo: "The full quote is:

ONE AND INDIVISIBLE, LIBRE ET SUISSE, O-YE, O-YE, O-YE, O-YE, UP YOURS EYE-TIES

Marengo Pi

"A small battle as battles go, but a battle never-zer-less, 'ere in zer 'eart of Lugánó," continued Napoleon with morbid glee. "Eet was probably zer cost of zer ferry fees zat stoppéd zem. Zese low-budget invasions..."

"But... the Italian Cisalpine Republic are your lot, aren't they?" puzzled Sean.

"Yes. My people - on both sides of zer conflict. Delightful!"

"So why are you granting Ticino independence? Why do you want to keep Lugano from the Italians so much?" asked Sean with unmasked suspicion.

"Not Lugánó." He signed Sean to lean forward so he could whisper: "La maison."

"The house?! Which house?" whispered Sean, adopting the conspiratorial tone.

"Zer 'aunted 'ouse. Zer 'ouse Léonard and Luca Pacioli built for Francesco del Giocondo - zat's Italian for Frankie zer Playboy," winked Napoleon, whose first language had been Italian.

"The husband of Ma Donna Lisa," added Laplace.

"Zer girl with zer magique smile," went on Napoleon whimsically.

"His ex-cellery has a crush on Mona Lisa," explained the Marquis of location, location, location. Did Sean detect the slightest tone of jealousy in his voice?

"Every person puts zer squeeze, er... *crush*, on zer Moaning Lisa!" thundered Napoleon, making everyone jump back. Then he leaned forward again, and Sean could feel the whole café leaning in as well to catch the words of the great little man. "Why do you zink I keep 'er 'idden in my stocking drawer? Eef Josie were to find out..." He shook himself. "But she loves me. She told me 'erself she cannot go even 'alf a day without 'er

288   Vitruvian Boy

Nappy..."

Sean thought it best to change the subject. "Why did you say 'haunted house'?"

"I didn't. I said 'aunted 'ouse. Zat is because I ham French - Corsican!" Napoleon corrected himself brusquely, as if he had fallen for a trick Trivial Pursuit question.

"The local people swear it is haunted by the ghosts of all the conquering armies that have romped through here over the centuries," explained Laplace.

"Zum others just swear - take eet as a local dialect," added Napoleon. "A legend 'as grown around zer strange phenomena of zis area. People dizappearing, ghostly appearances, certain places are considéréd possésséd by demons..."

"I have one of those myself," said Laplace.

"A legend?" asked Sean.

"No, that is Napoleon's department."

"Time, like zer sand, covers zer labours of man, but leaves zeir legend alive," self-quoted Napoleon pre-imperiously.

It was one of those conversation stoppers, so after a carefully timed pause of appreciation Laplace went on. "I, on the other hand, have a demon."

"I don't understand," said Sean.

"It is a science-friction idea - that the universe is like a wound-up clockwork mechanism. Unwinding, and unwinding, on an entirely predictable course - every planet, every rock..."

"Leeveeng zeeng..."

"...us included, are doomed to follow a predestined path."

"No free will?" asked Sean, somewhat shocked.

"Zat ees why eet ees calléd a deemon," went on Napoleon. "I, personally, 'ave an étoile zet I seek."

"I think it is up there," said Sean, pointing up.

"How do you know zat?" exclaimed Napoleon excitedly. " 'ave you seen eet too?"

"No. But, I can read the signs," replied Sean.

"Zee signs? You see signs?!" cried Napoleon looking around him. "Where?!"

Sean indicated the rest room images on the wall by the stairs.

"No... I said 'étoile zet I seek'... not 'toilet I seek'! Sacre blur!... I believe in my personal star. What do you follow, young Scharn Seulpierre?"

"My heart."

"A bit soapy, but a good answer - for 1800. Pity it cannot fool my demon," remarked Laplace. "My demon sees all, will devour all, in his relentless quest to run down the universe."

"Till the universe just stops?" asked Sean, merging his thoughts of the timeline crisis with uneasy feeling.

"Yes."

"And then what?"

"Newton has shown us that it is not just a question of all objects falling to the Earth, but that anything at all with a bit of substance to its name will attract anything else substantial."

"A substantial enough argument..."

"It is therefore only the temporary speed of planets which keeps them in orbit and thus far able to keep a respectful distance from the Sun, and each other. But it only delays their inevitable doom."

"Cheerful philosophy," said Sean. "And it is your

Vitruvian Boy

little 'demon' that is making them slow down?"

"I have calculated that if enough matter…"

"What's zer matter?" asked Napoleon suddenly.

"Nothing."

"Zen 'ow can nozing attract nozing?"

"No, I mean… oh, never mind. Let's say 'stuff'. If this 'stuff' were to collect together, for example in a massive sun, then nothing would ever have the velocity, the necessary umph, to escape from it again."

"Nothing?" Sean felt one of those premonition tingly things downstairs.

"Nothing."

"You said nozing ees zer matter," reiterated Napoleon his previous point.

"That's right."

"So eef nozing *can* escape… matter can escape. Everybody 'appy! Where ees zer probleme?"

Laplace braved on. "Now, this is the really interesting bit. If Newton is right, and light *is* a stream of particles, and not a wave - because a wave needs something to wave through - then not even light would be able to escape the gravitational enticement. Perpetually dark it would be. A great big … Blob of Dark," he finished with a flourish of fingers as if neon-lanterning the final words.

"Come now, Laplace, surely you can zink of a snazzier name zan 'blub of dark'?"

"What about 'Black Hole'?" suggested Sean, knowing that term wouldn't be used for another century and a half.

"Catchy. But no," Laplace shook his ex-aristocratic head. "It is more of a blob than a hole, but thank you for trying."

Sean sat forward on the elegant café bench. "Ex-Marquis de Laplace, do you think Time could be drawn into such a hol... er ... blob, as well?" He hesitated, but dearly wanted, to ask whether that could explain what was happening to him, the haunted house, to the whole timeline.

Throughout this discussion, Napoleon had been playing with the circular red, white and blue pennant on his enormous hat - spinning it, and seeing if he could keep it turning with his breath. He answered for Laplace. "What is more important ees zat zo many of zer most famous oracles and fortune tellers come from zis area."

"Is that why we are here?" asked Sean dawningly. "So that you can have your fortune told?"

"And what a fortune zat ees," murmured Napoleon. "Yes. But, more zan zat. We are 'ere because of...zem." He pointed through the window at the Guards horsemen who were still trying to get into the café, but were being stopped by the proprietor, on account that the horses weren't cleaning their shoes properly.

Napoleon leaned forward and whispered into Sean's ear: "You know 'oo zey are, don't you?"

"No," remitted Sean.

"Zee Invertabrakes."

"What?!" cried Sean in a panic. "They'll take me!"

"Not eef I am protecting you. Not while you give me reason to protect you. We understand each zother, Scharn, I zink zo, oui?"

"We?"

"Good. Zen zat's setteléd."

The waiter brought another round of hot chocolates.

"Zey are looking for zumzing, eesn't eet, Scharn? Zumzing that one time belongéd, I dink, to you?"

"You mean…?!" exploded Sean too loudly. All the other customers looked around at them.

Napoleon went on: "But, 'ow do you dink I know about zer … SANG Re.al - zer 'oly Grail?"

"The last time I saw it was in 1699, being taken by the Bernoulli Brothers to Switzerland on a Rhineland holiday cruiseboat, while they still had a special weekend rate. What happened to it after that?"

Napoleon nodded to Laplace, who said: "They gave it to Euler."

"But it doesn't need lubrication…"

"No, not an oiler. Euler. Leonhard Euler. The master of all we mathematicians. Codename 'The Owl'. A Swiss genius and prolific dealer in equations. He specialised in smuggling the good uncut stuff across the Rubber Wall."

"Rubber Wall?"

"Yes. To the East, where all mathematics knowledge had been erased. He got through to Saint Petersberg, where Catherine…"

"Oh… great!"

"That's her… she employed him to cook her books for her. That was her mistake - when it comes to cooking, you should always call on a French mathematician, not a Swiss," said Laplace superiorly, with matching French intonation.

"And the Owl took the watch with him?"

"Yes."

"Then what happened to it?"

"They called her Tsarina Cath the lover of math - she was so impressed she had a special ornate egg built for it. One of those Matryoshka things the tourists love, which have a decorative egg within an egg within an egg within an…"

"Zat's enough with zee eggs, already, Laplace. 'onestly, you are such a finickety perfectioniste. No wonder I sacked you as Interior Minister. Monsieur tiny parts we calléd 'im around zer Tuilleries," confided Napoleon.

"I just like to get things correct," grumbled the ex-Marquis. "As I was saying, Kate the Great put it inside a nest of eggs. Legend has it she used an ostrich egg inside a fossilised mammoth egg…"

"Eet doesn't matter, Monsieur agony-détail Laplace, get on weeth eet! My chocolait 'as gone all froid," complained Napoleon sadly, wondering if there might still be room for a death sentence for serving cold chocolate somewhere in the Code Napoléon he was drafting.

Laplace knew that look, so continued hastily: "But the last of the eggs she used was not just any egg - it was a stone egg. From here - Lugano. Suspiciously enough supplied by the Bernoulli Family itself." He pointed across the street where a shop window displayed a sign saying:

Official Agent for Berny Bros.
Oracle and Alchemists
Quality Suppliers
- Philosophers' masonry our speciality -

"There's still a thriving business for miracle merchandising here in Switzerland."

Vitruvian Boy

"Ah," thought and/or said Sean. "And when they went to put the watch inside…"

"Exactly," said Laplace.

"Exactly what?"

"What you were about to say."

"And… what was I about to say?" asked Sean, who felt the confusion settle on every fibre of him like steam on a fuzzy teatowel.

"That on cracking the egg, the watch disappeared," concluded Laplace.

"Oh, really? I was about to say that? How clever of me."

"And reappeared 'ere, een Lugánó. Een zer 'aunted 'ouse," said Napoleon triumphantly.

"I see," said Sean, who didn't really, but what zer 'eck.

"As I told you, I found zer Codex of Léonard in 1796 - and read eet een zer mirror, when Josie was not using eet."

"Did you like it?"

" 'ee gets zer 'istoire back to front, but zer plot was rivet-ing. It told me everyzing. About you, Scharn, and zer 'ouse and zee eggs. But eet stops - at zer disappearance of zer bearer of zer watch. Ah…" He tapped the side of his long nose with his trigger finger. "At zat poin', 'istory tells us two zings 'appenéd. Léonard is 'invitéd' to work freelance for Cesare Borgia, a real son-of-a-pope, who suddenly gains great powér, and starts an incredibly violent campaign across Italy, posing as zer exclusive agent of M. Biggy."

"As all megalomaniacs do," added Laplace.

Napoleon smiled. "A man who put 'is battle-axe where 'is faith is. And secondly, Léonard became obsesséd with zer Moaner Lisa, and took 'er with 'im everywhere, and finally zey went to France togezzer for 'is terminal 'oliday. And zee intéresting zing ees zat 'ee never finishéd zer painting - 'ee kept touching 'er up teel zer day 'ee died."

"Why?"

"Zat ees what I ham hasking you - Why, Scharn Seulpierre? Why?"

"I have no idea. Really."

"Ask him what he did next," whispered Laplace.

"So... what did you do next?" asked Sean.

"Well, of course, I invadéd Egypt."

"Perfectly logical. Why not?! One of your 'humeurs'?" asked Sean.

"Yes. But, zere was also a connection. You know about Jean le Measurer, isn't it?"

"The scribe of Archimedes," prompted Laplace.

Sean nodded dumb-fondly.

Napoleon continued. "I took a whole group of academics with me - scientists and scholars. I rented a harem in Cairo as a multi-use facility - and set up a popular, oo-là-là très populaire, centre of, amongst ozzer zings, learning. It was also zer cover for my secret centre of operations to find zer Measurer copy of Archimedes' notebook."

"We knew there had to be a hard copy still standing," added Laplace.

"I needéd to know what was recordéd een Archimedes' parchment notebook - 'is palimpsest. I 'ad a go at getting through to Constantinople for zee original, but zer museum library was closéd for zer duration of zer war."

"What war?"

Vitruvian Boy

"The war he was waging against the Turks, trying to get to Constantinople," answered Laplace.

"Also, my plans were zwartéd, I zink zat is zer word, zwartéd, by zee boeuf-addicted Eengleesh."

"They sank all his nice boats," clarified Laplace.

Napoleon smashed the cup he was holding onto the head of a passing waiter. His quaint way of asking for another round of chocolate. Yes, zee toss-winning swine played cricket with zeir cannon balls against zer sides of my ships - bouncing zem off zer water - and zey went down clean-bowléd - by, how zose cochons say - yorkérs. A new tactic."

"Newyorkers?" suggested Laplace with a suspiciously straight face.

"You can name zat twice."

"They put a full Nelson on you?" risked Sean, catching Laplace's eye glint.

"Anyway, my man, Captain Bouchard, eventually found zer Rosetta Stones."

"*Stones*?" surprised back Sean. "I thought there was only one?"

"Aha! My ploy workéd! We found two. Zer Measurer stone we kept for ourselves, z'other was nozzing more zan a shopping list from Pharoah Ptolemy zer next in line. We left eet for zee shopkeeper Eengleesh to find, to give zem somezing to keep zem occupied. Zer English military - zey love fulfilling orders."

"How did you get back to France, past the English blockade?"

"We disguiséd ourselves as drunken sailors sobering in longboats."

"And the Measurer stone?"

"We crumbled eet into little pieces and brought eet

back een our pockets, and reassembled eet 'ere. Josie ees a whip at jeegsaws."

"And then you deciphered it?"

"The process gave rise to something I call 'assembly language'. Patent pending," added Laplace with a tone of pre-established proprietal warning.

"So, what does Archimedes say?" asked Sean, intrigued.

Laplace answered. "There were some scribbled notes in the margins: reminders about getting his sandals reshod, and things like that. However, he does eventually get around to mentioning a certain 'One Stone'. As the translation from Greek has it. But the hiero-graphic attachments suggest that 'One Stone' could be a mis-back-translation for 'Only Stone'?"

"Which in French is 'Seul-Pierre'," triumphed Napoleon.

"Ah...," contributed Sean.

"And Archimedes left you a message."

"A message! For me?!"

"You see, Sean, Archimedes knew a secret which scholars have been looking for ever since. The Romans wanted it suppressed - but there was one Roman, Cicero, who came a hundred years after the sacking of Syracuse to find Archimedes' tomb, hoping to discover some clue to his secret."

"And the message?"

" 'Do not disturb my circles'."

Sean was disappointed. "Meaning what? Watch where you are putting your dirty great sandals?"

"That or guard the *spiki celestii* from the Romans."

"I don't see the connection," admitted Sean, getting progressively more confused with each explanation.

"*Spiki celestii* is the mystic 'language of the gods'. It reveals the workings of the 'circles', or Galileo's orbits. That's why 'pi' is so important. In the final match of his series against the Vatican Old Boys, Galileo left posterity one of the most famous soundbites ever: 'And yet it moves'."

"Referring to the Earth moving around the Sun?" remember-guessed Sean.

"It was the greatest challenge the church had ever received: What you see versus what you choose to see."

"Keeping your eye on the ball. An unequal contest in philosophical football, surely?" said Sean.

"You would think so. But it is surprisingly difficult to win when your opponents are also the referees. So Galileo was disqualified."

"Why?"

"Off-side. The Vatican ruled that nobody was allowed to be on the opposing side during matches against them."

"Technicalities…" muttered Napoleon.

"That's why Isaac Newton changed strategies," continued Laplace. "Why he needed to move in on the London maths mob, to sink the church-sponsored royal barge."

"Barge?" said Sean.

"Yes - the king kept barging in on intellectual freedom - it threatened to take the spin out of the scientific revolution."

Sean remembered his day in Cambridge. "The Wheel Turneth. Yes, in those days you had to be a priest to be a professor. Thanks to Isaac Barrow's help, Newton was the first who wasn't."

"Exactly. Till Newton arrived on the scene, actually

knowing things was still considered an option. And often a dangerous one. Intellectuals moved not so much in circles as holding patterns."

"What resulted was a dirty war between two gangs, zee Sacks and zee Socks, for control of zer London Underground," added Napoleon.

"Yes," remembered Sean. "The 'Sacks' were the Isaacs Barrow and Newton, and the 'Socks' were the Royal Society."

"Newton eventually won. Careers were found floating belly-up in zer Thames. It must have been glorious. Pretty warfare," concluded Napoleon.

"I think the usual term is *'petty* warfare', your Excellency?" suggested Laplace.

"The Swiss did well out of it, running royalty-free equations to both sides of the channel," said Sean, remembering the shadowy figures of the Bernoulli Brothers slipping away down the Thames.

"It was thanks to them that the debate escalated into a full-scale pan-European conflict. A conflict that has been raging between English and Continental mathematicians for more than a century. To our advantage," Laplace added.

"Why is that?"

"Exclusion Principle. For example, the currently reigning English genius, Thomas Young, does not stand a chance of publishing his wave theory of light because this suggests that Newton was not infallible. The English have made a religion out of Newton's version of *spiki celestii*, so now they are stagnating, isolated, leaving the field wide open for we French and the odd German."

"*All* Germans are odd," echoed Napoleon from

Vitruvian Boy

inside his mug, as he tried to slurp out the last rivulets of chocolate.

"And the SANG Re.al?" asked Sean.

"That is what started it all. That is what Archimedes wanted to tell you."

"But how can that be? What about the TPF - the time paradox failsafe? How is it possible for me to travel from the future and leave something like a digital watch that changes history and causes me to travel back in the first place?"

Laplace smiled in that way only mathematicians can when faced by an irresolvable and complex riddle. "I think the answer lies in that 'the first place' - my theory that a blob that could be large enough to mop up everything, even light, could be a clue. If a Blob of Dark appeared suddenly near the Earth, we wouldn't at first notice any change, because everything would be drawn towards it at the same time. Till we actually entered it, we would think everything is normal. Perhaps that is what is happening with you and the watch. And somehow the Haunted House holds the answer to this riddle. Leonardo and Luca Pacioli knew this, or discovered it by accident. But only after you disappeared - perhaps *because* you disappeared. They worked it out and left clues about it for you to discover. Secret clues because there are forces out there prepared to do anything to squash all knowledge of it."

Napoleon put his cards on the table. "We hold some of zer pieces to zis riddle, and you hold z'others. It is in both our intérests to collaborate on a solution."

Before Sean could answer, Napoleon called out: "Garçon! Today, I am feeling generous. Is that not right,

Bourrienne?"

His secretary hurriedly searched for and then through his agenda. Today… yes, today you are generous, magnanimous and gentle."

"And tomorrow?"

"Brutal patches but otherwise calm."

"So, I 'ave decided to pay my bill."

"Oh, thank you, most sublimate conqueror," pseudo-grovelled the relieved proprietor of the Grand Old Café.

When the bill arrived, Napoleon took one look at it and passed it hurriedly to Bourrienne.

Bourrienne patted his pockets and said: "Very sorry, I left the state coffer in my other jacket."

Napoleon then passed the bill to the ex-Marquis. "Laplace, old friend, I am a bit short till zer end of zer month…"

Laplace looked down on him. "Why only till the end of the month?"

"Back in Paris I intend to become too big for my boots."

The mathematician looked at the bill and swore in hyper-cholic vectors as he dug in his pockets for some larger notes than the shrapnel he had prepared.

Napoleon slipped off the bench and instantly lost several inches of majesty. "Gentlemens… after we pay for these chocolaits, eet ees time for us to pay also zee ghosts of Lugánó a veeseet."

* * * *

Chapter Fourteen

The Girl with the Magic Smile

NAPOLEON rode his matchingly proportioned, but nevertheless magnificent, white charger, Marengo Pie, a souvenir of his Egyptian campaign, as was his marmeluke bodyguard jogging ahead, while Laplace and Sean had to slalom the fallout on foot. Their dignity was even more rarefied by the narrowness of the ways through the old town centre, which at times obliged them to fall behind the General First Consul, then scurry back alongside his horse to catch his next whimsical observation. They were superseded and, I guess, underseded, by at least fifty death-for-glory outriders with lances raised suggestively, their blue banners flashing their self-awareness through the medium of bright sunlight.

Feeling a little hot in his image-accessory blue coat, his lucky sabre bouncing at his side, Napoleon squeezed down the extending ends of his enormous hat to allow him to pass through the narrowest alleyways, and gave the tricolour pennant on its front a cavalier spin for good measure.

"Passing through nonchalantly like zis gives my

newly acquired subjects an adoration op," Napoleon called down to Sean and Laplace through a professional politician's grimace, while waving with studied superiority at the few emotionless on-gawkers who had bothered to turn out. Most of the populace, however, had opted simply to lean out of the upper floor windows of the buildings to catch a glimpse, while playing trivial pursuit on the details of the personal life of the latest conqueror slash liberator passing through.

The street artists sketched down the scene quickly and made a brisk trade selling their 'paper rockets'* to the competing dailies. Otherwise, the mood towards the First Consul could best be described as ranging from thankfully diffident to detachedly lower-middling.

The First Consul dictated to his secretary, who was riding on a desk-mule close behind. "Bourrienne, write: Zer victorious French legion rode through zer cheering, near 'ysterical crowds, whose mood was appropriate to a people 'oo 'ave embraced fresh liberation at tax-exempted prices."

"Got that, your Excellency."

"Don't forget to add zee 'h's. Zen zend it off as a beacon text message to be in zee papers in Paris by zer day after tomorrow."

"Don't you ever tell the truth?" asked Sean, panting a little as he came back alongside.

Napoleon smirked through his rigid smile. "You don't really expect me to answer zat 'onestly, do you?"

"He calls this 'nonchalant'?!" Sean muttered as he looked at the company-strength cavalry troop all around them, their eyes red and beady beneath their crimson-plumed helmets, their breastplates and other

---

* from Old Italian: paparazzi

crustaceans meticulously polished, and everything ominously clanky. "Do you always take an escort with you wherever you go?"

"When we came over zer Grand San Bernard Pass last month - for our mountain-sliding 'oliday - I rode a'ead of my troops a little too far, and was very nearly keelléd, or worse capturéd, by an Austrian patrôl. Since zen I take mah leetteel escort wherever I go. It makes one 'eck of a queue at zee public toilets, but we manáge."

They were passing a small convent, whose occupants had come out to see if there was any new trade in soul-saving to be had from the tourist influx.

"You know you're hitting it big when you are a nun-event," commented Laplace, and in the process of laughing at his own wit, failed to avoid yet another large, steaming dollop that fell behind the First Consul's decorum-challenged horse.

"People always remark about 'ow full of energy I ham. But zis is zer real reason I never stay in any one place too long." Napoleon indicated the horses and the quickly discolouring road.

"He likes to leave his mark," snorted Laplace as he wiped his shoes on a peasant given to rash cynicism.

And suddenly there it was. Where Sean had left it, except by 1800 the haunted house had lost its regal isolation, now caught up in the town's skirts flung out towards the valleys rivuleting down from the mountains to the north.

To Sean's added joy, he could see that immediately beyond the haunted house estate now stood what would one day be his family home: brand new, garden pristine, touchily French and trompe l'oeiled to the hilt.

"Your house, n'est pas? I 'ad eet built quiétly," said Napoleon. "Not zat you can hever build a 'ouse quiétly… Mebbe I will come 'ere for zee winter 'ill-sliding."

"The skiing is good," humoured Sean.

"I do not like zer word 'skiing'. Eet ees zee only word een Eengleesh with double 'i'. Een my world, zere is room for only one 'I'." Napoleon stopped suddenly and there was the sound of a dozen minor equestrian collisions behind them. "Zer secret to success, young Scharn Seulpierre, ees to be as egoïste and greedy as possible at every opportunity - and above all…" He held a stubby forefinger up to monumentalise the next pontification: "*Névér* be satisfied with enough."

"Yes, I've noticed that. You will be remembered affectionately by the banking system."

They continued towards the houses on the good quality earth road that had been nothing but a muddy track last time Sean had been there with Leonardo. "My poin' exactly. What ees eeconomeecs but a continuation of war by more profitable means?"

"And you love war?" asked Sean.

"War creatéd me and definés me. How can I be ungrâteful to eet?"

"That sounds like someone else I once knew."

"And what 'appenéd to 'im?"

"He died. At least I think he died. He had his head cut off and paraded through the city, before it was skewered on a spike on London Bridge."

"And zat killéd 'im?"

"Call it a weak constitution."

"I, instead, ham writing a strong constitution for France. Ah, 'ere we are." They stopped in front of the gates to the haunted house. "Ma Malmaison Deux. I call eet my 'leetel 'ouse of naughties'," giggled the First Consul.

"Do you mean to say the haunted house is *yours* as well?!" asked Sean, considerate enough to be stunned.

"Mais oui. Zer Council of Lugánó graciously granted me zer 'ouse in perpetuity as a token of zeir, 'ow you say, 'undying' gratitude. Also for not turning zeir town into a stable sale."

"I see you have already tried to enter the Haunted House," said Sean, indicating the piles of skeletons in the courtyard, in blue with red trim Guards uniform jackets, their white leggings yellowing, for two different reasons, the tricolour flags still upholding a limp optimism in the breeze.

Something else was different to when he had last been here. Just as Galileo had told him there would be, there was an inscription on the arch over the door, which read: 'A.V.O.'.

"Do you know what that means?" Sean asked Laplace.

"Yes. It is Leonardo's logo. 'Amur Vincit Omnia': Love conquers all."

"Let us go into z'other 'ouse," commanded the First Consul.

Leaving the cuirassiers outside polishing each other with factor 5 cream, Napoleon led Laplace and Sean next door into what would one day become the Seulpierre family home. Napoleon's Marmeluke bodyguard ran ahead, as always, to check the coast was clear of assassins and cosmetics salesladies. When he touched the door Sean's fingers lingered to caress its wooden planks. He had never felt so in tune with anything so much in all his life. When he saw the familiar staircase and archway leading to the kitchen at the rear, his childhood memories surged, and his homesickness threatened to burst some nostalgia dyke and drown him in tears.

While Napoleon and his entourage of officers and hangers-on générals inspected the kitchen staff and then the 'nibblies cupboard' in the pantry, Sean stood aside and let himself be transported.

He could see his mother coming, as beautiful as ever, down the curved staircase, her elegant hand skipping playfully along the deeply-lacquered bannister, her face alive and inviting news of his day...

Napoleon broke in on his revelry.

"New curtains, don't you think, Laplace?"

"You forget, your Excellency, that I am no longer your Minister for Interiors."

"Oh. What are you zen?"

"I am between titles."

"Don't worry, when I 'ave created zer French Empire, I will make you a count."

"Why a count?"

"How else does one honour a mathematician? I would suggest you write a sequel to zat book of yours - *Mécanique Céleste*. Good title. Good characters - Sun, Moon, ... and zer other stuff."

"Planets?"

"Zat's zem. Ripping good read. Zer ending is left just 'anging zough. It 'as me een suspenders."

"No-one knows how it all ends."

"Why don't you do what everyone else does - invent stuff to fill zee gaps in knowledge? I suggést you tweak future 'istory a leettle een our flavour. Start by planting

Vitruvian Boy

a French flag on zer Moon."

"I doubt very much that any men will ever be so arrogant as to plant a flag of just a single nation on a celestial orb."

"You might be right, zere, but a French-dominated galaxy some'ow… je ne sais pas…," Napoleon gripped a handful of air passionately, "… *sounds* right to me…"

"Quite. As I should have been saying: where does it end? It is my opinion that there is more than one solar system. Ours is just one of many."

"Ah. Mad as zat sounds, zere is zer basis for a good political plot. Zer French solar system conquers zer universe, under zer command of a demi-god…" Napoleon moved to the base of the stairs and looked up it as if it were a launchpad.

Laplace put on his pouting, stubborn boy face. "But in my book there is no god at all."

"No Monsieur Biggy?" Napoleon turned and stared him in the lower chest.

"Not even a Monsieur Modestly-Proportioned," Laplace let slip and immediately regretted it.

Napoleon hastily stepped up the first of the stairs, failed to clear Laplace's shoulder, so ascended a second.

"I had no need for *either* hypothesis," replied Laplace with an involuntary glance down.

Napoleon followed his glance. "Ah… I see you 'ave been talking to Josie… ," he sighed.

There was an embarrassed silence from everyone present till Napoleon broke it by twirling his forefinger in the air: "Zen what in zer name of all celestial anarchy keeps it all turning?!"

"Well, thanks to Newton and his calculus, we know the cosmos didn't need anything more than just an initial good, hard shove..."

"Ah, you *'ave* been talking to Josephine!" Napoleon began to walk up the stairs. Laplace followed but made sure to stay at least three steps below. "And it is also like Archimedes and 'is lévér." Napoleon stopped half-way up and addressed the generals and almost-rans below: " 'Give me a place to stand and I will move zer world.' " Everybody sycophantic by nature did what came naturally and applauded.

Pronouncement over, Napoleon returned to Laplace. "Ah, zee Greeks were masters of zer chiselléd soundbite. But 'oo shoved the universe at zer beginning? Nozing can shove eetself, surely?"

"I have an idea that the cosmos never 'started' as such."

"Ah... so zat means it névér hends?"

"Hends? ... Yes, I suppose that no end in sight would be the expected corollary of such a philosophy."

"Névér hends... Yes... zat's good for a galactic empire trilogy."

"Actually, I was planning a pentlogy."

"Five books? Good. I like ambition. With a serial like zis I can sow dreams and grow a whole fresh crop of cannon fodder for next year's annexation 'arvest. Now, zis death star zingy of yours..."

"Blob of Dark."

"Blub of Dark... You really 'ave to find a better name, you know. How does eet feet into eet all?"

"That's exactly the point. It doesn't 'feet' anywhere. Not any more. You see, a Blob of Dark is a bit like an empire that gets too big for its ..."

"Ah, zose boots again.. Some people are obsesséd with shoe size! Not me!"

Vitruvian Boy

"… foundations - like Atlantis - collapses under its own weight."

"Hmm.. not so pleasing. I don't know eef zat will play well with zer pleb market. Still, I am not zer writer, just a 'umble conqueror."

"And reality?" asked Laplace sweet-innocently.

"Not my strong suit," sighed Napoleon, the conqueror and loser of Egypt. "How are *you* on reality, Marquis?"

"In all probability, it all comes down to probability."

"Meaning you're uncertain?" misinterpreted Napoleon, like every politician and journalist has done since. "You scientists are so proud of your uncertainty!"

"Uncertainty could be the basis of a great principle one day. For now, let us just say that with probability you can explain everything but foresee nothing."

"But I already 'ave a licence to guess. I 'ave to sound sure of myself to the people."

"Yes, but guessing usually leads men stumbling down the path to explanations that include mystic creatures and omnipotent creators. Mathematical probability, used properly, would liberate man from such devices."

"And what becomes of zer 'idden guiding 'ands? Are zey to be nozing more zan dice-throwers in your demonic regime, ex-Marquis?"

"Speaking with all due probability, yes. Just because something has not happened yet does not mean it never will. We must never confuse diminishing probability with impossibility. It sounds obvious, but it is in fact a warning: science can never fully exclude the impossible."

They found Sean sitting daydreaming on the top stair. "Ah, 'ere 'ee ees. Scharn, come along, I have zumzing to show at you."

Sean followed Napoleon and the ex-Marquis up the next flight. He had been seeing himself as a six year-old sitting on the top step howling after his father had rebuked him severely for spying on him, till his grandfather had come and soothed him by letting him play with his telescope (for real, heavy-duty spying, Nonno had explained).

They went into what would one day be Nonno's *doing-science* room, but which was now united with the other future rooms along the entire southern side to make a stunning ballroom, in which an enormous crystal chandelier was hanging, its candleholders fully loaded and keen to demonstrate their version of enlightenment.

Napoleon went to the, what else?, French window that gave onto the same ornate balcony from which Nonno and Sean had done their spying, and which overlooked the garden of the haunted house. On an easel by the window was a cover which profiled a small frame underneath.

"Et voilà!" said Napoleon with as much dramatic cliché-power he could muster, and pulled off the cover.

And there she was: the Mona Lisa.

Sean had to bite his lip so as not to cry when he thought of Geni, and how she had sacrificed herself for him on London Bridge.

"Ah… zer Moaner! Ees she not voluptuous, eesn't eet?" retro-rhetoricalised the First Consul. "Now tell me she was not paintéd from zer balcony of zat 'ouse,

Vitruvian Boy

Laplace!"

Laplace came over and compared the background of the painting to the view from the balcony, the landscape extending over the lake into the mountains to the south, the last line of southern Alps before the plain of Lombardy. After some time, Laplace turned slowly, nodding his head. "Yes. Yes, it is possible. Just."

"What do you mean?! Jooste! Eet ees a match parfait!"

"Not entirely. The mountains, the lake, its distinctive fork there, the road leading to it - yes, they are all correctly collocated. However… there is a bridge in the painting. Whereas on this side of Lugano there is not even a river, never mind a bridge."

"Details! Details! You are obsesséd with details, M. little parts Laplace. Scharn, tell hus. Was zis painting done 'ere or no?"

"Yes. At least on the balcony next door."

"You see, Laplace?"

The ex-Marquis was unconvinced. "So, maybe our 'eye-witness' can explain why this painting has such a magnetic effect on people? Why anybody who gazes upon her immediately falls in love with her? What is it about this painting that is so different? Well, Sean?"

"Yes. Can you *enlighten* us, Monsieur Renaissance man?" grinned Napoleon.

"I don't know. All *I* did was mix the paint for Leonardo."

"And what did you use?"

Suddenly some sunlight peaked through Sean's comprehension haze. "I used time egg shells! For the pinky-brown of her mouth!"

"Laplace?" asked Napoleon.

"Yes. The effect is strongest around her mouth. It is consistent with my theory."

"What theory?" asked Sean.

Laplace eyebrowed an enquiry at Napoleon.

"Oh, go on, tell 'im," returned his boss.

"The shells of the stone eggs consist of a very rare form of porphyry. Known in the philosopher trade as the 'OneStone'. The very same eggs used by oracles, because they are known to induce hallucinations as well as glimpses of the past and future."

"I see," replied Sean. "Do you think it is true? That the stone eggs really contain *tempus albumen* - liquid time?"

"My preferred metaphor is 'time magma': more correctly, a pyroclastic encapsulation of chronoplasma."

"So...," summarised Napoleon. "Everybody is fascinated by the Moaning Lisa because..."

"She has egg on her face!" finished Sean, and the two burst into laughter. Sean fancied he could see Geni joining in on the joke from her portrait.

It was a brave attempt, but there was no way to short out the ex-Marquis' lecture circuit.

"The occurrence of the Stone Eggs goes back to the beginning of little-known history. They are also associated with surges in interest in geometry - the search for what Euclid and Vitruvius called the Golden Ratio, what Leonardo and Pacioli called the Divine Proportions, and their best-selling erotic geometry derivatives. But, I hear you ask - where do the eggs come from?" He stopped and waited with university tenure-length patience.

Napoleon and Sean looked at each other then turned to Laplace and said in unison. "Alright, where do th/zey come from?"

"An *inciteful* question. To which I have only a partial answer. We know there have been different sources. But probably never more than one at any one time. We can track them through shifts in the epicentres of sudden spurts in the progress of civilisation. India and China clearly had theirs. More our way, the oldest evidence of a source we have is somewhere in Wales. The culture of divination that arose built many of the stone circles to be found in Britain and Western France. Then we find the source in Egypt, legend has it at the end of the ancient Via Porphyrites. Attempts to build perfect geometric structures incorporating the stone which encapsulates the eggs led to the construction of the pyramids, within which, it was hoped, the fantastic power that was generated could be contained. The Greeks were irresistibly drawn to Egypt. And it can be quite easily seen that the loss of the Egyptian egg source coincides with the decline of the Hellenic-Egyptian civilisation and the rise of Rome."

"But … what is it?" asked Sean, totally ecstatic to be listening to the great Pierre-Simon de Laplace give a lecture in his Nonno's *doing-science* room.

"No idea. Your guess is almost as good as mine. Greek mythology is full of suggestions of the presence of a hot bubbling lake deep beneath the surface of the earth. Newton tells us gravity will be denser down there. Quite gooey, in fact. So wouldn't the pressure also compress time? At some point, the time goo might be forced towards the surface like… well, lava. Yes… like lava. And as the pressure and temperature decreases, small bubbles of it could become encrusted with containment rock, like any phenocryst. Only this rock is itself transformed by its contents. The result would be the time eggs."

"What you have just described, Citizen Laplace, is a time volcano," nodded Napoleon thoughtfully.

Laplace had always thought Napoleon had been his most promising student. "Exactly! Releasing its magmatic pressure through a weak point."

"A crack? A fracture in zer crust?"

"Not even. A pin prick would suffice."

"Any idea what would comprise such a pin?"

"Well… whatever it is, it would cause some very localised, very focussed disturbance to the natural arrangement of space, the material occupying it, and the *vis viva*, or 'living force', that gives it action."

"Energy," nodded Sean. "Do you have any idea at all as to when the source of the time eggs moved from Egypt to Europe?" asked Sean.

Laplace looked at him meaningfully. "I can tell you precisely when it happened. The year minus 212."

"Archimedes!!" cried Sean.

"The last known use of Egyptian pink was the Rosetta Stone, carved soon after the fall of Syracuse. That is what 'Rosetta' means: 'little pinkie'."

"I thought it was called the 'Rosetta Stone' because it was found in the town of Rashid?"

"Who would believe the word 'Rosetta' derives from 'Rashid'?" asked Laplace. "Only someone very hard of hearing."

"But…," continued Sean. "Isn't the Rosetta Stone grey?"

"Only the basalt decoy we left for the British. After this, there was no more OneStone to be had in Egypt. Eventually the cult of the oracles died out."

"And moved to Europe?"

"Yes," nodded Laplace. "The 'crossing of the pink' eventually gave birth to an alternative cult of oracles here in Europe. There has been a non-stop stream of claims and counter-claims to the 'Rosy Crossing', or Rosicrucian, trademark - the continuous subject of copywrong outfringement proceedings in the low courts."

"*Low* courts?" asked Sean.

"Yes - the secret underground courts that try out cases of reason to the crown."

"*Reason?*"

"They work on the logic that the compulsion to seek reasons implies lack of faith, and threatens to bring the movement into good repute. Part of the infernal auditing system."

"That doesn't make sense," said Sean.

"I'm very glad to hear it. There is an old church saying which goes: why ask for sense when there are dollars to be had?"

Just then, Bourrienne entered, and, as inconspicuous as a man with a 20-kg desk around his neck can be, whispered into Napoleon's ear.

Napoleon nodded and whispered something back. Sean fancied he heard: "...get zem to wait in zer conspiracy room. Leave your desk 'ere."

He then turned to Laplace and Sean. "Gentlemens, I see you 'ave lots to discuss. I really must go. Affairs of state, a country or two to annex. You know 'ow eet ees."

"I used to think I did," replied Sean.

From the window, they watched Napoleon ride with his troop and bodyguard down the road. Only when he was safely out of sight, did Laplace turn on Sean and say in an urgent whisper: "Sean... it's me. Pau."

"Pau!" called out Sean, then quickly changed to a whisper. "What are you doing here?!"

"Same thing as you, you microbe. Looking for a way to rescue Geni, of course. Aren't you?"

"Well, yes, of course. But I don't understand. If all this time you have been Pau, how come you have been talking as if... as if..."

"As if what?"

"As if you knew stuff. That's so unlike you."

"I know all I need to know. Anyway, that wasn't me - it was Laplace talking."

"You mean - he *lets* you be in there?"

"He doesn't know. I have worked out how to switch to passive mode. I can take over whenever I want. Like now. Sean, I hate to say this, but I need your help."

"Sure. To do what?"

"Find the source of the eggs."

"Why?" asked Sean suspiciously.

"So we can complete the VC and save Geni - and the others."

"What's the VC?"

"The Vitruvian Crystal of course, you subliminal suggestion! Leonardo and Pacioli's design of the house, based on the three-dimensional projection of the Vitruvian Man."

"In the Haunted House? But, how will completing this 'Vitruvian Crystal' save Geni?"

Pau tapped his temple. "I have all of Laplace's choicest memories in here. Doing the standard 'private gentleman's grand tour' of erotic geometry hotspots around Europe as a young student, he accidentally stumbled across the secret of the rompy cupboard head-on."

"Luca's rhombicuboctahedron?!"

"Yeah, that thing. When Napoleon returned from his Italian campaign in 1796, he brought with him the Codex Medilago, which describes you as the watchbearer and how the house where Leo painted the Mona Lisa contains the secret to the geometry of the divine proportion. He says the eggs need to be placed at the vertices of the rompy to complete the Vitruvian Crystal. It focuses their time energy at its centre - where the watch disappeared, remember? Now, more than half of the eggs are already in place because of the porphyry finishings, mantelpieces, cornices, etc. throughout the house. That's why the house is so active and dangerous." Pau pointed at the pile of past-used-by-date French patriots in the courtyard next door. "But Leonardo and Luca never got the chance to complete it. By completing it we will be able to control the time jump mechanism - and free Geni, Amur, Stinto and Elf!"

"I see. Or at least I think I do. How many eggs does the Vitruvian Crystal need in total?"

"Twenty-four. The number of vertices in the rompy."

"Twenty-four!!" exclaimed Sean. "There aren't that many oracles! We'll never find enough eggs!"

"I know that! That's why we need to find the source ourselves."

"But... *I* don't know where it is. Nobody does. They've been looking for it for hundreds, thousands of years!"

"Leonardo knew. And he left secret messages. Leo wants *you* to find it."

Sean shook his head in confusion. "You're inside Pierre-Simon de Laplace's head: can't he help?"

"Look - Laplace is brilliant, but his head is full of useless things."

"Like knowledge?"

"Haven't you got any ideas at all?"

"Besides the obvious?" shrugged Sean.

"How do you mean?"

"Well… Leo's logo for one."

"That stupid thing? A.V.O. Amur Vincit Omnia. Love conquers all," snorted Pau. "What of it?"

"In old Italian," explained Sean patiently, " 'avo' means 'grandfather'. And another thing: Leo always wrote from right to left."

"And in a mirror."

"Yes, but there wasn't likely to be a mirror handy when he was chiselling his logo over the door. Read AVO backwards and you get…?"

"O.V.. A… Ova.. Which means…?"

"Egg!" exasperated Sean at Pau's lack of everything.

"A-ha! Now I get it!"

"Yes?" asked Sean excitedly.

"It's obvious! Leo is trying to tell us…"

"Yes!?"

"He's trying to tell us… that he thinks your grandfather was a chicken."

"What?!"

"Or is asking which came first? The Nonno or the egg? … or maybe how he crossed the road…?" Pau's voice dwindled to match his face of confusion.

Sean took a piece of paper from Bourrienne's desk, and began to write. "Amor vincit omnia. That could be an anagram. Leo was always writing in anagrams." After several tries, Sean cried "Eureka!".

"What?" asked Pau.

"If you rearrange the letters in 'Amor vincit omnia' you can make 'Ticino minar ovam'. The grammar is a bit wobbly, but I guess it means that this part of Switzerland, Ticino, holds the mine to the eggs! He is telling us he found the time egg source somewhere near here, and my Nonno has something to do with it."

"Oh yes? And what would that be?"

"I don't know. There must be another message. We have to look for it."

"How?" Pau shook his head. "We can't go into the haunted house - we'd be paradoxed to bits, remember?"

"I've been wondering about that… When I took an egg to escape from Cesare Borgia, I deactivated the hex-a-go-go Luca and Leo had put on the house. I guess that's how they could leave the house, afterwards. But, judging by the pile of French dead down there in the haunted house courtyard, in the meantime the house has been locked again. If it was not possible for anyone to re-enter the house, Leo must have left the clues outside, right?"

After Sean had taken Pau through this lightning logic sequence a few more times, each one slower than the previous, eventually Pau's nods began to take on more conviction.

Finally, Sean could move on. "So, what do we have from Leo?"

"The Codex…"

"Which I helped him write… No, something else.

Something that he had with him long enough to add the clue to." Sean nodded towards the window as a hint.

Pau stared in the indicated direction for a while until he snapped his fingers and cried out: "Eureka! I have it!"

"Yes?" asked Sean patiently.

"The yoghurt!" cried Pau.

"No! The Mona Lisa, you idiot!" said Sean.

"I meant that," corrected Pau.

"Sure. You said it yourself. Or rather, Laplace did. What did he say was wrong about the painting?" asked Sean.

"The bridge. He said it was out of place - the only thing that doesn't fit the view from here."

"And there is absolutely no artistic reason why it should be there," concluded Sean, peering closely at the multi-arched stone structure behind Mona Lisa's left shoulder.

"But - there are thousands of bridges in Europe. It could be any of them."

"Somewhere Leonardo has been, though." Sean suddenly stopped as a new thought struck him: "Tell me, Pau, if you can allow Laplace to take over, how do you know that he's not... well..."

"Well what?"

"You know... listening in?"

Pau suddenly felt uncomfortable. "Because... because it doesn't work like that."

"Listen, I have an idea," said Sean. "How can we get out of here, without Napoleon knowing?"

"And what if he does know?"

"I don't trust him. He is up to something. What does he *really* want the eggs for?"

Pau scoffed. "As he says: to see the future. Imagine what you could do with that ability and the stock market."

"Is that the only thing you can think of? Money?"

"And you don't, I suppose?" scoffed Pau with a smirk as broad as Mona Lisa's. Sean thought he had seen that irritating, self-approving smile before, on someone else…

"We don't have time for this," he said. "Napoleon said he was only popping out to conquer a country or two. He could be back any minute."

"Yeah… but - we can't just walk out - we'd have half the French army following us."

Sean went to the window and peeped out cautiously. "Actually, I think you'll find Napoleon took them all with him. That leaves only the Swiss servants here." He looked about the room, then clicked his fingers. "Ok," he said. "I have an idea. I am as short as Napoleon - and you are as tall as Bourrienne…" Sean indicated the neckdesk Bourrienne had left on the floor.

"Oh… no," pre-empted Pau.

"And here … is a wardrobe full of Napoleon's clothes."

"Oh, no way! Absolutely no microscopic way…"

Five objectionable minutes later, Pau was still exercising his no..no..no prerogative, and variations thereof, as they moved awkwardly down the corridor. Pau was stagger-walking backwards, carrying the desk with the lid open, covering his face, and Sean, dressed as Napoleon, with a suitably enormous hat covering everything from the fifth vertebra up, had his head inside the desk, rummaging and swearing about never finding a pen sharpener when one needs one.

In this way, they made their way to the head of the stairs. Curious Swiss faces looked up at them.

"Don't look at me when I ham writing secret documents, you multerally-lingual people. I order you to turn around," bellowed Sean from inside the desk in his best imitation of Napoleon.

"More French, more French…," whispered Pau.

"Ah odeur yeue…," empha-strained Sean, distorting his palate over and beyond.

"That's better," said Pau.

Very dangereusement, they descended the stairs. On the first floor, there was a frightening moment, when a staff officer approached, and, squeezing his hat in salute, said: "Your Excellency, the troops bravely holding their positions in the front bar of the 'Molten Cheese Inn' need to be resupplied."

Sean and Pau froze for an uncomfortable, unspecified interval. Then Sean, without taking his head out of the open desk, found one of Napoleon's own-label brandy bottles and handed that to the man.

"And paid, your Expediency."

Sean handed him another bottle.

"Sorry to bring it up, but there's the overtime for killing on a weekend?" the officer said, on tippy-toes, trying to see what was in the desk, obviously taking full advantage of having found the First Consul on a rare 'good' day.

Sean handed him yet another bottle over his shoulder.

"Thank you, your Expectancy," and to both their amazements the officer saluted, turned and left.

Vitruvian Boy

The journey around the lakeshore and up the mountain behind Mona Lisa's left ear was remarkably uneventful, except for Pau's whining questioning.

"Why here?"

"Didn't you notice? If you look closely at the mountain behind Geni, on the right of the painting, you can see that there are three mountain peaks. Why three, when you can only see one in reality?"

"So, has Leo's artistic licence expired or something?"

"Look. In Italian, three mountains is 'tre montagne'. But, another word for montagna is monte. I remember there is a village half-way up this mountain called Tremonta. My grandfather told me of a legend that has it there was an ancient village somewhere near Tremonta that disappeared suddenly without a trace, and nobody serious has ever known why."

The postcoach which had brought them up the mountain dropped them in the Tremonta village square, which was deserted. Three of the cardinal horizons were clogged with stunning panoramas of the Alps, while the southern one in stark contrast disappeared into the seemingly never-ending plain of Lombardy's alluvial tribulations. Left alone, they abandoned their disguises, and started to investigate the village.

After an hour, they found themselves sitting on the small church steps, and entering about their fifteenth argument, with Pau complaining to the reprising tune of: "This is obviously a complete waste of time. We don't really know what we are looking for. There is no river, let alone a bridge. We should have looked down in the valley."

"The blatantly obvious was not Leo's style," was

all Sean could think of saying, but he was beginning to agree that his initial hunch had proved to be a dead-end.

"We should get back before Napoleon returns from his annexing and denexes our heads," said Pau. He took out the coach timetable he had stolen earlier. "Oh great! The next coach is not till half-past Wednesday. We'll have to hitch-hike on a dung cart."

Sean was just about to abandon all hope, too, when he suddenly grabbed Pau by the elbow. "Pau... that statue!"

"The angel? What of it?"

"It is turned to a rather strange angle, don't you think?"

"All religious art has a strange angle."

"As if its wings were pointing up that hill. And another thing... I've only just noticed, but this church is dedicated to St. Paul."

"Why is that strange? Many churches are dedicated to Peter, Paul or Mary. What do you want: St. Tom, Dick and Harry?"

"It's just that this mountain we are on is called 'Monte San Giorgio' - Saint George. Why would the only medieval church in a village be dedicated to St. Paul when their local patron saint is George?"

"Isn't this what they call quibbling?"

Sean clapped his hands, the noise of which echoed around the rocky slopes above them. "Eureka! I have it!"

"Really? Is it catching?"

"Look... Everything in the painting matches reality perfectly - except for two things. Both are on the right-hand-side of the painting. Why?"

"Leo was short-sighted in his right eye?"

"More likely, don't you think, they are meant to be used together as a subtle clue for where to look?"

"How do you get St. Paul and angels' wings out of that?!"

"Leonardo loved to play with words: especially between different languages. The bridge is behind Geni's shoulder, right? Leo was living in France by this stage. And in French, shoulder is 'epaule'. The bridge is clearly pointing 'to the shoulder'. 'A l'epaule'. Or 'ale paul'. And 'ale' is Italian for 'wings'."

"I see," nodded Pau, who obviously didn't.

"And here we are, at the 'wings of St. Paul' on the 'Tre-monta' mountain. As instructed."

"So… *if* you're correct, what next?"

"The wings are pointing up the hill there to that group of rocks. Let's go." And Sean led the sceptical Pau up through the brushland to the rocky mass.

"Do you think this is where the lost village might have been?" wondered Sean aloud, as they stood in a small flattish area, long left to its own devices, hidden among rocky precipices and outcrops all around them.

"Who cares? We're after the egg source, not on a school history outing."

"What? You think a vanishing village has nothing to do with the source of time eggs?"

"Do you mean it might be dangerous?" said Pau, looking about him fearfully.

"We have to take that risk. Geni is counting on us, remember? We have to look for some sort of clue as to where the source might be. It is surely underground. There might be a fissure somewhere."

"Idiot! If there's no river, there won't be a fisher…," mumbled Pau as he joined in on the search, but only among the safer looking of the rocks.

It took them a good hour to find it. It was a gap between two rocks, that, on clearing away the copious growth around it, proved to be a broad opening to a rapidly widening chasm within the rock massive they were on.

"Wow!" was Pau's comment. That was well hidden. The best kept secret in the world." He peered over the edge of the hole.

"That's quite a fall," said Sean. "There'd be no way back if you fell in there."

"Yes…" said Pau in a strangely contemplative sort of voice.

Sean put his head over the edge and listened for his echo as he called into the chamber. "That's funny. No echo," he said after a while. He leant inside as far as he dared, then whistled. "I can see eggs! Hundreds of them, all around the walls. This is definitely the source!" He pulled himself back out and sat up. "So this is where the oracles, and the Bernoulli Brothers for that matter, got their stones! We'll need to go back to the village and find some rope."

But when he tried to stand, Pau pushed him back down roughly.

"Careful, Pau! I might have fallen in!"

"That's the idea." Pau's face was now different - hard, angry and distinctly sly.

"What are you doing?" cried Sean.

"I am going to throw you in."

"But, why?!"

"Because it ends now. I don't know how, I don't know why, but you are the factor that is upsetting everything. If it weren't for you, I'd still be with Geni. You and that vermin-advertising watch are the cause of all the changes in the timeline." His voice whined up half an octave as he railed against the injustice of it all. "I just want everything to return to as it was before. This chasm is where the time lava comes out."

"It's connected to the spenmatt - the cosmic background of space, energy and matter. Where time does not exist!" cried Sean, his eyes wide with customised terror.

"However all that works, it seems to me if I send you into it, just maybe it'll rebalance everything."

"You don't know that! *You* never know anything!"

Suddenly Pau laughed. "Well… Mr know-it-all, there are some things you *don't* know. For example, how do you think Cesare Borgia found you in 1500, so quickly after you arrived?"

"How do you mean?… No… You didn't!?" Sean's eyes widened in horror.

"Oh yes I did. I knew already then you were Cespuglio's target - not us. Not the true TimeRiders. All I had to do was give you to Cespuglio and he would leave us alone. When you were enjoying yourself helping Leo paint Geni as the Mona Lisa, I went to Lugano centre."

"To see if Amur had arrived."

"Don't be so naïve! She would have come straight to us. I went into Lugano to send a message to Cespuglio, who was in Milan as Cesare Borgia."

"How could you do that? It is over 30 leagues away! And it was almost night-time."

"I sent him a BMS."

"A what?"

"BMS - bat messaging service."

"A courier bat?! You total rat! How could you betray Geni like that?!"

"Oh no. Only you. I staged the whole thing, arranged with Cespuglio so that he would take only you. Geni and I had eggs after all, even though in the event the hex-a-go-go allowed us to leave without them. It was a great pity you escaped. But you won't get away this time."

"But, Pau, Cespuglio is dead. He was executed in London in 1699. We both saw it. We're safe."

"The Invertabrakes are still here. That means the timeline is still being disrupted! That proves it's you! Your presence out of time is still destroying our timeline. You have to be sacrificed to the volcano god - sent to a place where you can no longer damage time - in fact where time does not even exist. It is my duty to humanity, and the whole world."

"Pau! No… you don't know what will happen!"

"Maybe you'll find the lost village you're so fond of. Or maybe you'll just cease to exist. Out of time, out of your mind, so to speak. You're going in Sean…" Pau was occupying a much bigger and stronger person than Sean's drummer boy, and despite Sean's concerted efforts, he could not help but lose ground in the push-of-war they were engaged in.

"Pau, you're making a big mistake! Listen to Laplace. He knows!"

The black hole beckoned by lack of counter-argument in terms of footlocker. Sean felt his feet exchange the resistance of the rocky ground for thin air, while Pau's tearing silk sleeve played an intermediary role in the dispute. As the over-priced material tore under Sean's panicky clasping, Sean felt the lip service provided by the central hole in the argument slip past him from toe to hanging nail.

The last of the cloth tore. The cavernous mouth engulfed him – swallowed him hole, so to speak.

And that would normally have been the 'it' we all dread, except an extraordinary thing conveniently happened. Sean still had in both hands the piece of shirt from Pau-Laplace. Suspend your incredulity for just long enough, and you will begin to see how this piece of lifesaving equipment miraculously caught over the edge of a timely written in projecting wooden pole. This particular wooden pole, when Sean clambered up onto it, proved to be projecting from a harness of sorts, and this in turn was attached to a much larger overhanging something else above that. What this ensemble composed was suddenly and dramatically demonstrated, when, under the influence of Sean's unbalancing added weight, it shifted, and, with Sean clinging to the harness for dear life, seemed to slide down some sort of rail system and take off into the void of the chasm.

Panic cannot hold a candle to what Sean was experiencing. But then again, on the aesthetic side, there was just enough light for Sean, when he finally managed to open his eyes, to see that all around him was a spectacle of rare and wondrous beauty. He was flying inside an enormous cavern decked and walled by millions of insidiously radiant stone eggs. It seemed as if the entire inside of the mountain were hollow, for the glowing egg walls faded away and down into a dark nothing that made other bottomless pits look like paddling pools. If it hadn't been for this object he was clinging to, he would right now be testing that theory.

He therefore took time off from marvelling at the scenery to construct an explanation for the flying part of the miraculous turn of events. This investigation resulted in the knowledge that he was on a hang-glider. The first ever built - and from its wooden frame and yellowing white cotton wing, Sean immediately recognised its origin, having seen illustrations of it in a hundred books. 'Oh, Leo! Thank you Leo!!" he called out in surprise and wonder. But how had Leo known he would need this? And, while we are listing questions, now what?

The glider was circling on its own - it's wing was set somehow to bank continuously at exactly less than the curvature of the chamber. As a result, without any intervention on his part, the glider was gradually taking Sean in a spiral pattern towards the central shaft of the mountain. His presence must have also been agitating the eggs, for they were beginning to glow with much greater self-awareness than before, and he felt the air buzzing with their collective scintillation. When the glider did finally reach the very centre of the cavern, it lurched sickeningly as a powerful thermal updraft caught it suddenly, and shot it like a champagne cork up and out of the hole he had entered just minutes before so unceremoniously.

He barely saw Pau/Laplace's startled face as he shot past, high, high up. But, before the thermal had even begun to show signs of having run its course, he heard a familiarly accented voice cry out below: "Fire!"

The air whizzed variously and several things on the glider went the wooden and canvas equivalent of 'ping'.

His new trajectory was rapidly earthwards and the freely flapping canvas of the wing above him ensured his spiral pattern was now extremely tight. He looked down, and saw he was heading for the appropriately termed dead centre of a ring of dismounted cuirassiers. These Invertabrakes had quickly reloaded their muskets and were readying them again, their gleaming bayonets promising to make a kebab lunch of him. The unmistakable profile of another figure, with its oversized bicorne hat and spinning pennant, left Sean in no doubt as to who was in charge.

Sean closed his eyes and waited for Napoleon to order the next 'Fire!'. But it did not come.

Sean's corkscrew spiral was now at the level of the treetops. He thought of his mother, Nonno, and of Geni, and how he had let them down. He suddenly also thought of Leo - this was because, as he spiralled the last metres towards the ground, he noticed a cloth pouch bouncing jauntily as it hung from the front bar an arm's length in front of him. By the way it swung he knew it contained a time egg.

'Clever, clever, Leo' thought Sean, realising that his old friend's help across the centuries had not yet ended. Somehow Leonardo had foreseen this whole event, and had fitted a time egg to the craft, to break when he hit the ground, providing him with the means to escape. All Sean had to do was let the egg fall out of the pouch when the glider crumpled on impact, to break on the ground, and he would travel through time, away from the Invertabrakes, away from Napoleon, Pau and the Haunted House. He would be safe.

The kite duly hit the ground. Although Sean was

badly winded, he managed to put his hand out and catch the egg before it could hit the ground. He heard an Invertabrake approach, then everything went the comfortable mauvey grunge black Sean was getting used to at the end of chapters.

* * * *

Chapter Fifteen
On the Road to Nowhen

SEAN was woken by the camp fussing of a group of four men wearing aprons.

"What's for breakfast?" he asked, struggling to sit up on the uncomfortably luxurious sofa he was laid out on.

"Very funny," said one, whose apron had stains and some flour on it. "Just because I had to borrow this from the cook in a hurry."

"Well, serves you right, Mr D, forgetting the official apron at home," said another, whose own apron, like the others, had a pale blue trim and a red, red rose in the place where a sporran would otherwise feel quite at home.

"So, no breakfast...?" sighed Sean.

"You won't be interested in food when you find out what part of the ceremony you play. Ain' that right, Mr B?"

"Right you are, Mr C."

Sean sat up with a start, remembering an awakening with vaguely similar dialogue some millennia ago. "Are you going to flay me alive?" he asked in his by now pretty much standard fright-tinged voice.

"No... we have a better way of stripping out your soul. Won't hurt a bit."

"Not us anyway, eh Mr A?" rejoined another, and the four laughed at their own in-joke, in the full knowledge that no-one else was ever likely to.

"Who *are* you?" Sean asked.

"Shh... Secret. Let's just say we are 'men of letters'. This is a message brought to you by the letter A."

They assisted the little drummer boy to stand dizzily up, and led him out of the parlour room into the main entrance of the Seulpierre home.

"I'm home?" cried Sean happily.

"I wouldn't count on eet."

Sean's face took a fall when he recognised the voice as that of the First Consul, who had come to lead the procession, followed by Laplace. They were both also wearing the same sickly coloured aprons as the messieurs alphabet.

"Ah, Scharn," said Napoleon as upbeat as ever. "So, you 'ave been in zer bowels of zer time chasm? You 'ave 'ad a glimpse of all time, n'est pas? Tell me my future, Scharn. Tell me my déstiny."

"I can't do that," Sean shook his head. "Doctor Who wouldn't like it."

"Doctor Qui?"

"Not key. Who."

"You forget, you are speaking French."

"Oh, yes. Sorry."

"I also 'ave 'ad visions of zer future in store for me. What does 'Elba' mean? And 'oo ees dees Helêne woman, or perhaps Sainte 'elena, I get so attachéd to? And why is zere a water closet een between?"

"Oh… that would be Waterloo…"

"But … I don't just want juste to see zer future, I want to contrôl eet - own eet."

A thought struck Sean. "That could be what is causing the time collapse!"

"Eet ees a reesk I ham preparéd to take."

"And everybody else has no say in it?"

"Zat's why I ham empereur, and you lot are cannon fodder. Ready, gentlemen?" Napoleon presumed more expansively. "Let us go."

The procession made its hierarchically complex way into the kitchen, then down the stairs to the cellar, where Papi would have his secret office and blogging centre in 210 years time. And there, just where Sean had seen it in 2010, was the same open bookshelf door to the tunnel he had yet to pass through all that time in the future. On the lintel were chiselled the words: 'Mind the Gap'.

"I thought it only fair to leave a warning," explained Laplace.

The route was lined by the Invertabrakes, still in full cuirassier armour and helmets, clanking swords in their elaborate leather harnesses, beady little red eyes watching Sean in unwaivering conditional clause. And they all also wore the same pale blue-trimmed aprons as the others. Sean did try hard not to laugh. They obviously had no sense of the ridiculous - yet another addition to their serious crimes list, annotated Sean mentally.

"Zees way," ordered Napoleon.

"No!" Sean cried. "We can't go into the haunted house! It's dangerous."

"Zat ees why you are going first," agreed

Napoleon.

The tunnel was lit by the same torches in wall brackets he had seen last time he had been there, only this time there were flaming torches both ways he looked. The clean brick of the walls and ceiling of the tunnel arch revealed they were brand new.

Napoleon explained: "Laplace calculatéd zat zer only way to enter zer house would be through *le point mort*, zer dead point. And hah am *not* referring to zer cat."

Sean followed Napoleon's gaze, and saw that there in front of them was the outstretched body of Shrodie, the half-dead cat of Mrs Erwin, the cook.

Laplace took over the explanation. "The point mort is located at the *souspex* - a precise location beneath the house, where there is equilibrium between the Vitruvian Crystal and the chronoclysm, the time magma, developing beneath the crust."

"Then *you* built the tunnel!" cried Sean. "So you could access the house safely from below?"

"Mais oui. You saw zer results of any ozzer approach," said Napoleon, referring to the pile of skeletons they had seen tricolouring the courtyard.

"And the crystal? Is it finished?" asked Sean, thankful at least that it was Laplace he was speaking to, not Pau.

"Almost. Thanks to your help in leading us to the source of the time eggs, we have now enough eggs. Just one more needs to be put in place, at the *souspex*, and the Vitruvian Crystal will be ready."

"Ready for what?" asked Sean, in a tone spatter-patterned with best-grade suspicion.

"You will see," replied the ex-Marquis. "In fact, we

will all have plenty of time to contemplate it." They had reached the stairs and begun to ascend.

"Careful," said Sean. "There is a trapdoor up here."

"Not yet," said Napoleon. "Zat trick can only be uséd one time, n'est pas? We 'ave no need of such artifice, you and I, Scharn Seulpierre."

As they passed between the two doors at the top of the stairs, Sean could see that in place of the rug and trapdoor in the floor there was a wooden grate. As they crossed the grate, Sean was hit by a musty, freshly-dug earth smell, and a hollow space sound beneath their feet. On a rig was suspended a stone egg directly above a hole in the grate, large enough to let it pass should it fall.

"When zees egg ees let to fall," explained the First Consul, indicating a custom-made release mechanism, and an attached string leading off into a hole in the ceiling, "eet will fall eento zer exact place zat will complete zer Vitrooveean Creestal, and everyzing witheen *la Malmaison* weel be alignéd with zer cosmeec background. We weel enter zer fifth realm of zer ordinaire, time will cease, and my déstiny will be fulfeelléd."

"What destiny?" asked Sean.

"Can you not guess?"

"Yes," admitted Sean. "I cannot guess."

With a reincarnated Shrodie purring in long-awaited welcome around his legs, Sean led the pro-cession of Napoleon, Laplace, the four men of letters, and a stream of clanking Invertabrakes, up the staircase and into the enormous ballroom. It looked the same as the last time Sean had been there, except the pedestal in the dead centre, which had held the watch in 1500, had been replaced by the same pink stone slab Sean had seen there in 2010 - the altar which had emailed Nonno as an attachment to another world.

Now Sean knew the hieroglyphs on it meant it was the true Rosetta Stone, carved by the hand of John the Measurer himself as a copy of the palimpsest of Archimedes - effectively an all-indemnity instruction manual for his digital watch. Any sign of its having been broken into pieces and reassembled by Napoleon had completely vanished, such was the power of the OneStone.

And in front of the altar was the same short flight of stairs, rostrum and throne, on which Sean had last seen Nonno. And above it all hung the same enormous crystal chandelier on its heavy chain, adding to the whole scene some superfluous ponderous authenticity.

By now, the large room was looking much smaller, as it was getting crowded with people and almost-so's. Sean didn't have time to count them, but he would have hazarded a non-committal guess there would be twenty-two in total - in supernatural compliance with Cespuglio's 'Mystic Age of Twos'.

Napoleon took the natural centre of attention position directly at the base of the steps leading up to the rostrum, where Nonno had been tied to the sacrificial throne. This piece of furniture now stood empty and beckoning Sean didn't hesitate to imagine who.

"Can zer star of zer show please take up 'is position?" commanded Napoleon, like any good stage manager. By a process of guess-limination, Sean figured he meant him.

"What is going to happen?" he asked inanely

enough, while an Invertabrake tied him by the ankles and wrists to the throne, as Nonno had been secured.

"Oh come now, Scharn, you 'ave more experience of zis zan any of us - except one, of course," and Sean noticed that Napoleon unconsciously touched his temple when he said this.

Behind them, some of the Invertabrakes were busy setting up the recommended ceremonial kit, which included a pot boiling on a brazier, and a grotesquely ornate casket. This latter they placed on the table - the very same table where Sean, Leo and his friends had had their memorable dinner discussing the newly fangled home entertainment industry of printed books, exactly three hundred years before.

"Breeng out zer crown!" ordered Napoleon.

One of the Invertabrakes, who Sean recognised as the Centurion he had seen take charge in Syracuse and play a chief Beefeater in London, opened the casket. He reached in to take out the Iron Crown of Lombardy, which Sean had first seen on the head of Cesare Borgia just outside in the courtyard of the Haunted House, and had not seen since the Centurion had shown it to him in 1699 on London Bridge, shortly before they had taken Geni into it.

At the sight of the crown, Laplace cried out in fear, recoiled and tried to make a run for the stairs. He was seized almost immediately by the Invertabrake ceremonial guards.

"Time to join your friends, …Pau," said Napoleon with arguably no detectable waver in his default cruelty level.

"No!" cried Pau unoriginally. "Sean… help!"

Sean made a token struggle against the bonds on

his wrists and ankles on the chair, then gave up, it could be said, slightly too quickly for form's sake.

Laplace, who was obviously now operated by Pau, struggled vainly as he was dragged to the table. Two held him down, while the Centurion played quoits with the crown on Pau's dodging head. Once on, the same mystic adult-audience only greenie glow Sean had seen take Stinto in Syracuse, and Elf in Pisa, did its special effects trick in and around Pau's face. When it was over, Laplace rose in his place.

"Thank you, your Excellency," he said. "I am so glad to be rid of that ignoramus. It was like walking around with a blob of information dark in my head."

"Good to 'ave you back, ex-Marquis," said Napoleon. He lifted his arms and announced to the room of the faithful: "Let zer sacréd mimbilly-jimbilly commence!"

"You have forgotten something," said Sean quietly and too assuredly for the others' comfort.

Napoleon turned slowly to him. "And jooste what ees zat?"

"You intend to complete the Vitruvian Crystal now - two hundred and ten years ahead of schedule, correct? But how do you think you can break the TPF - the time paradox failsafe? Anything that is out of its proper time proves that you cannot complete the VC now. I am here because of what happens in the future - you cannot change that."

"Oh, but I can. By sending all zee elements zat are out of zeir rightful place een time eento zer cosmeec background, what you call zer spenmatt, zer timeline, and zer world zat ees créatéd by eet, will be reset - reset to zee terms *I* détermine."

"But you do not have all the elements. Where is

the watch? If that continues to exist out of time in the world, you cannot reset anything."

"You zink I don't know zat?" Napoleon bunched up the green, felt-plush sleeve of his dress uniform, and there, on his wrist, was the digital watch. He took it off. "I shall mees you, ticky-tocky. You have been most inspiring…" He suddenly turned to Laplace, holding the watch possessively. "Can't I keep juste zis? Ma leetel precious?"

"I am afraid not, your 'highness'. It, along with the Shrouds, and Sean of course, must be returned to the eternity soup from whence they came."

Napoleon placed it reverently on the centre of the altar. "Adieu, petite souris, mon ami."

It is ironic that the world's only remaining officially recognised time traveller should be in such a position - playing for time - but, in the dying echo of his key stratagem blowing, that is what Sean did now. "So, you tricked me into revealing Leonardo's secrets?"

Napoleon looked up at Sean, now far above him on the rostrum. "Eet was really too easy. Your friend Pau thought 'ee could control zer great mind of ex-Marquis Pierre-Simon de Laplace?! Not a chance! All along, Laplace led him to believe so, and 'ee and I 'ad arrangéd to allow zee ingenuousness of Pau to dupe you, Scharn, into not suspecting anyzing. And you fell for eet. You took us to zer egg sauce, following zer clues of Léonard only you could solve. I followéd you up zer mountain with my faithful squad of do-and-dies, and when you enteréd zer underground Grotta we closéd een. We deed not anticipate your daring escape attempt on zer bird of cloth, but no matter - zee Invertabrakes are very good shots."

"So they weren't trying to kill me?"

"Of course not. I needed you alive."

"But why? What is it that you want?"

"To be zer Eternal Emperor."

Sean went silent for a while at this.

"But … but he is dead," he stammered.

"Not so. Merely my preesoner. I weel show you. Guards… 'old me."

To Sean's great surprise, three Invertabrakes seized Napoleon, who began to struggle and cry out in anger and frustration.

Laplace approached with the crown, and placed it on Napoleon's squirming head. The same green special effects light that had danced around Laplace moments before, now did its thing around Napoleon's face. Then he relaxed.

"Ah, zat's better. Out you come Cespuglio." The emperor-in-training squawked up at the guards: "You can release me now."

"So," nodded Sean from his platform. "Cespuglio lives. How is that possible? I saw him killed."

Napoleon readjusted his dress and hair pedantically. "You saw 'is host get zer chop and a 'alf. Cespuglio livéd on. Much weakenéd. Zat ees 'ow I found 'im een Monza…"

"Monza?" Sean realised that a century is a long time to be absent from the timeline. All sorts of people can get up to all sorts of things.

"I invadéd Italy een 1796 to free 'er from zer 'orreurs of zer Austrian foreign occupation…"

"To impose the glories of the French foreign occupation, I suppose?" finished Sean.

"Exactement! Now hask me what I deed on one of zer 'oliday weekends een Milan. What does anyone do on a weekend een summer een Milan?"

"Get the heck out of it?"

"Exactement! And where do you suppose I went?"

"South? To the beach?" Sean answered, remembering with a pang of homesickness his own family holidays.

"No. All zer roads were controlléd by zee Austrians. Like every summer, all zer good seaside camping sites were taken by German-speakers. No, I went north … to Monza."

"For the carriage racing?"

"Beh… not only. I went also to zer câthêdrâl."

"I thought Napoleon thought - thinks, sorry - that Mr Biggy is a political ally only?"

"Ah, yes. Eet ees Laplace 'ere, zer only leeveeng speaker of *spiki celestii*, 'oo deenks Mr Biggy can be deletéd from all equations zat describe reality - but 'ee ees not a politician. 'ee forgets zat zee 'ooman needs 'ave precious leetel to do with zer greater reality."

"So, what were you doing in Monza Cathedral?"

Napoleon shrugged almost sheepishly. "Zat ees where zey keep zer crown." He looked down at his shoes and scuffed them around a little. "I wanted to try eet on. To check zat eet feets." He moved over to the table, took the crown and admired its jewels.

"Zer legendary *corona ferrea*, zer Iron Crown of Theolinda, Queen of Lombardy. A t'ousand years ago, she 'ad eet made from a nail from zer cross Emperor Constantine says 'ee 'found' on one of 'is pillage-romps east. Zis crown ees magique. Why? Because eet contains zer power of imagination. All zee kings and queens of northern Italy, emperors of zer unHoly non-Roman quasi-Empire, Cesare Borgia, Cardinals Burn and Plunder, and even a leetel known English criminal called William Chaloner, 'ave worn zis crown at one time - or more precisely two times - een zeir lives. Exactement deux fois!"

Sean felt a prickle as the hairs on his neck leapt as far as they could into the midst of air.

He had to acknowledge the ingenuity of it. "And in so doing every king and demagogue of history has downloaded Cespuglio, and uploaded him back into the crown at their expiry date. But just a minute – the others I understand, but how did Chaloner, a mere king of thieves, get to wear the crown?"

" 'ee won eet as zer booby prize een a church revival pub quiz. A stop-over on one of zose 'faded glory' package tours of Northern Italy tyranny spots."

"But Cespuglio was executed with Chaloner in 1699!"

"Ah, Scharn, Scharn. You cannot keel someone 'oo ees not alive as you and I understand. Not leeving een any particular time. Zat person cannot be keeléd. Zee Invertabrakes found zer 'ead of zeir emperor's host, Chaloner, on London Bridge, and placéd zer crown on eet, extracting what was left of Cespuglio's conscious-ness. And there eet was kept, weak and ineffective unteel… I put zer crown on zat day een Monza - and een so doing I took 'im eento my own mind. 'ee thought to contrôl me - me! Napoléon I-keel-you-first Buonaparte! He could not contrôl me - non, non, I contrôlléd 'im! I made 'im compliant to my weel, forcéd 'im to reveal all 'is secrets, and to grant me zer power to command zer Invertabrakes, as you see." He indicated the honour guard around them in the room.

"And he told you about me, the watch, the house, Leonardo, … everything?"

Napoleon nodded.

"So that is why you went to Egypt? Cespuglio told you you needed to get the Rosetta Stone - to make the altar for the Vitruvian Crystal?"

"No, mon ami. Zat was you."

"Me?!"

"Mais, oui. Eet was you, Sean Seulpierre, 'oo told us everyzing. You 'ave only yourself to blame. By 'elping 'im write zer Codex, you 'elped Leonardo list for us, quite conveniently, zank you, all zee elements zat were out of zeir proper time."

There was a pause while Sean took this onboard. "And these other gentlemen? I gather they would be the Rosicrucians?"

"Secret Alphabetic Order of the Brothers of the Crucible, at your disservice," said Mr D in the cook's apron, and he curtsied comically.

"We are fully licensed and registered with the Underground Chamber of Verity Traders," stated Mr B, unrolling a blood-signed and spattered certificate.

"Who would give up an invitation to eternal life?" said Mr C, and the four bowed to Napoleon in perfect sycophancy.

"We are the keepers of the Sacred Rosy Crucible," announced Mr A, holding up an authenticised replica of the hallowed pink vessel. He placed it upside-down on the table next to the largish pot now coming to the boil on the brazier.

"Only the keepers of the Rosicrucible are entitled

to the sacred knowledge of how to prepare the eggs," confirmed Mr C with a chef's pride, and all four now produced a ceremonial spoon. On these they breathed, and wiped them on their aprons. Then they stood in a line, and positioned the handles of the spoons between their teeth. At a signal from Mr A, they then each took a stone egg from a sacred pouchy whatsit behind their sporran red rose, and placed it ever so carefully on the spoon's projecting bowl.

"L'eh de w'ssin' b'ge'," ordered Mr A, almost causing his egg to fall in the process.

The line of egg-holders moved forward, pretending not to be racing, until they reached the table. In disputed order of arrival, they waited while an Invertabrake, in clumsy ceremony, took the pot and poured a steaming stream of pinkish liquid over the upturned Crucible.

"What is that?" asked Sean.

"Wax lyrical," whispered Laplace.

Then the first egg-holder bent over carefully, and, without using his hands for some mystic reason, probably derived from ancient pre-sanitation age rituals, tipped his head so that the egg dropped from the spoon onto the top of the hot wax. It sank a little into the wax mound, so that it would be held in place when the substance congealed.

While he waited for his mixture to cool, Mr A removed his spoon from his mouth and explained: "Our sacred texts recount that the Egyptians had attempted to create Vitruvian Crystals by arrangements of porphyry inside pyramids, orientating them on the North Star, and using prismic geometry. It is said they had the power to transport to 'another world' the souls of dead kings, queens, and…" He paused and looked at Shrodie, who was happily giving herself a nether-region bath on the steps of the rostrum, "… cats."

"Reincarnation?!!" laughed Sean.

Mr C admonished him: "Tush! Someone who jumps time with the ease of making an omelette should not be so sceptical."

By now each of the Rosicrucibles had made a wax mound to hold their egg, which they removed from the crucible mould and placed over their heads, no doubt in strictest adherence to vague references in the ancient scriptures regarding the wearing of the red funny hats. In fact, Sean realised suddenly, they did resemble the hats the priests were wearing in Syracuse.

The Rosicrucibles now made another two headpieces, with eggs, for Laplace and Napoleon, who also, if somewhat less enthusiastically, placed them on their own heads. Then the six men gingerly moved into their positions in a wide circle around the altar, the eggs held aloft on their heads by their improvised wax mounts.

Thus the inner circle of Archimedes was formed inside the rhombicuboctahedron. As ordained by Luca Pacioli, the geometry of the Vitruvian three-dimensional projection was now almost complete. Sean realised that the strange sensation of power that he had sensed on entering the Haunted House had not been his imagination, and had now grown to something far more tangible, and was emanating, without a doubt, from the altar behind him.

Positions now adopted, Napoleon signalled the Centurion, who picked up the crown and took it to the altar, where he placed it at its exact centre, and over the SANG Re.al watch. Immediately all six of the red rubies around its rim began to shine and shimmery images projected from it.

"The hex-a-go-go has been re-established," explain-announced Laplace from his place on the inner circle. "The crystal is ready to receive the final egg – and then we will be able to connect across the Gappe."

"Minde the Gappe!" chanted the Invertabrakes.

Only now did Sean notice a standing lever, much like a railway points switch, in the place of honour in front of the rostrum. To this lever was attached a string, which passed down though a hole in the floor, presumably to the mechanism which would release the egg two floors below. In this way, Napoleon, while remaining in his rightful position as one of the six figures of the hex-a-go-go, would still be able to release the egg at the precise moment necessary, and complete the Vitruvian Crystal.

Although it was behind and below him, Sean could just see that the crown was now a brilliant golden bubble of glow, several times its original size, as it lifted off to hover above the altar, in the dead centre of the house, and the VC it made, illuminating the watch below it.

Six figures were forming in its projections – the same dark, hooded figures Sean had seen in 2010 when Nonno had disappeared. The figures grew larger and moved further from the altar until they occupied the exact same places as they had in 2010, forming a circle within the circle made by Napoleon and his henchshrouds. Then, gradually, the dark cloaks dissolved to reveal the features of the Shrouds.

The first he recognised was a glorious sight to Sean:

Geni. Even though every time he had seen her, she had been occupying a different person, her trademark beauty clearly identified her. She gazed ahead, but not at him. She could not see him. The next was just as unmistakingly Pau, looking as handsome and bewildered as usual, as he gazed into the middle distance. The others were Stinto, Amur and Elf. And the sixth and final figure, in front of Napoleon, in the place of honour, was that of Cespuglio the Younger, looking resplendently ugly, in his original Roman uniform, and quite put out.

The six new egg-holders, Napoleon, Laplace, and the four Rosicrucians, stepped forward into the places where the images were hovering. To Sean's horror the images of the Shrouds began to flicker and dim.

"Stop!" cried Sean. "What are you doing to them? You're causing them to disappear! Geni! Pau!"

"You see, Scharn, when I complete zer crystal, zeir raison d'être, literally, disappears. How can zey be present een zer VC at zer time of eets completion een 2010 eef eet no longer completes zen, but now? Eh?"

"What will happen to them?"

"Zey, like all zer future from zis moment on, weel 'ave to Minde zer Gappe."

"Prisoners of another world? Like my Nonno?"

"Yes."

"But… its not fair!"

"It is not unfair to someone who does not exist. As far as my new world is concernéd, zey never did, or should I say weel, exist. Zey exist only een *your* memory."

"And me?" demanded Sean. "I have to pass across the Gappe now because if the VC completes in 1800, 2010 will never happen?"

"Exactement. Eternity, Scharn. Just deenk, you weel

be surroundéd by people," he waved his hands to indicate the Shrouds and the Invertabrakes, "but only *you* weel 'ave a soul - because only *you* weel 'ave a memory."

"All of this, this suffering, just so you can play war games through history like Cespuglio?!"

"No, not like Cespuglio. Better. Infinitely better. Whereas Cespuglio brought war and 'avoc - commendable in 'is own, quaint way - I instead weel breeng peace to all zer world and eets 'istory forever."

"But don't you see?" appealed Sean. "Somehow the creation of the VC causes the timeline to collapse. There is no future. *There will be no time*, just as my Nonno warned!"

"But I don't need a future. I can play een zer past. I 'ave always wanted to be Julius Caesar. Weethout zer stabbing een zer back part zees time." Napoleon indicated the Rosicrucibles and Laplace in the hex-a-go-go. "Zat is why I 'ave invitéd dees gentlemen to accompany me. Juste dink, Scharn, a troop of five TimeRiders fanatically loyal to me, and me alone, occupying zer minds of all zer key scienteefeec and poleeteecal figures of every age of 'istory - zen I weel be zer true Empereur éternal."

"What are they chanting?" asked Sean, only noticing now the metallic voices of the Invertabrakes calling "Om...Om...Om..."

"When his Extreme Excellency the Eternal Emperor releases the last egg downstairs," explained Laplace, indicating the lever by Napoleon's hand. "It will be the last egg, the 24th egg. The 24th letter in Archimedes' Greek alphabet is 'Omega'. That is why we are wearing these wax eggholders - they are the shape of omega symbols. They symbolise the last egg needed to complete the Vitruvian Crystal as described by Luca

Pacioli: the Omega Egg."

"Om-ega, om-ega, om-ega…" the crustaceans in the audience were chanting. "Om-egg, Om-egg."

After a while the chant reduced to just "Om.. Om.. Om.."

All this time, the Rosicrucibles had themselves been reciting something mystical and self-impressionable. It ended with their own chant: "Let it fall. Let the last egg fall." After a while, sensing the competition of 'Om, Om, Om' they insisted on the 'Let, let, let'.

From Sean's central position all he heard was 'Om-let, Om-let, Om-let'…

While the others were distracted by their cholesterol choir competition, Sean appealed to the Centurion who was still standing next to the rostrum. "Sir… please. My grandfather was transported somewhere by the Altar. Do you know where he is?"

"Yes."

"Where?"

"He is the Extreme Being," responded the creature in its metallic, synthesised voice.

"The Supreme Being?"

"No… Extreme. He is out on a limb."

"And what is this 'Extreme Being'?"

"The soul of the Invertabrakes. Across the Gappe, where we come from."

"Is that where you intend to send me now?" asked Sean.

"Yes."

"Centurion…" demanded Sean. "Can there be two of these 'Extreme Beings'?"

"No."

"Then if I am sent across the Gappe - what will

happen to my Nonno?"

The Centurion did not answer.

"What will happen to Nonno?!" shouted Sean. "What if he is lost by my taking his place?! Don't do this... please!"

The Centurion adopted the good soldier's selectively deaf posture.

"Please..." stammered Sean, then rallied. "I command it! The Extreme Being does not wish it."

The Centurion hesitated, obviously trying to determine the legitimacy of advance orders.

"Please..." begged Sean. "I don't know what you are... what the Invertabrakes are... obviously not human..."

"We *are* human," replied the Centurion slightly miffed. "What is left of humans in 2,222 years after the completion of the Vitruvian Crystal."

"After...?! So... you are robots?"

"Cyborgs. We have lost all organic parts."

"How is that possible and yet still be human?"

"Our soul is run by the One and the six."

"The Extreme Being? ... And the Shrouds? They are *all* your souls?"

"Collectivised to a single, time-shared anima. One Soul, Happy Army. It is more efficient."

"Efficient? For what? Survival?"

"For the War."

"What war?" Like you and me, this discussion had lost Sean entirely, but he knew he needed to learn what he could while he still had time.

"The Eternal War," replied the Centurion tonelessly.

"Is that why you need an Eternal Emperor?"

"Yes."

"But why is Cespuglio, the Eternal Emperor, here in *my* world?"

"He escaped when the Vitruvian Crystal was completed."

"Escaped? He was a prisoner?"

"We are all prisoners across the Gappe."

"Then why are you here?" asked Sean.

"To brake the inversion of time."

"Ah... *That's* how you get your name. And how do you propose to prevent this... 'inversion of time'?"

"By eliminating all rogue elements."

"But, don't you see? It is Cespuglio. *He* is the rogue element. And Napoleon will be as well if he takes his place." Sean looked at the figures projected from the Crown, still barely visible over the new usurpers. "The Shrouds, I think, belong to my world, not yours."

"I obey the Emperor," said the Centurion as matter-of-obediently as a cyborg can aspire to.

"I see. So you're in a Catch-22, aren't you? *That* is what Cespuglio the Younger meant when he asked the Oracle if this was the era of the two-by-two. He was laughing at you. You will never solve the problem because while the rogue elements are still on the loose, you are programmed to obey the Eternal Emperor."

"We must obey the Extreme Being across the Gappe, and the Eternal Emperor here in this world."

"But the Eternal Emperor has no intention of resolving anything. Don't you see? That is why he always found a way to secretly let me escape - in Syracuse, from this house in 1500, from the Leaning Tower - that's why Cespuglio allowed Galileo to do 'one last experiment' with the watch! Of course! With me and the watch still free, you were forced to continue to obey him."

Sean nodded at the savage face of Cespuglio, now almost entirely absorbed by that of the First Consul taking his place. "He loves this situation - able to wage non-stop war through history like this. With your help he is invincible, and even if he does lose, he can upload himself into the crown, knowing he will be downloaded by the next power-hungry megalomaniac that comes along. That's why, when he was finished playing Emperor Constantine, he arranged for his helmet to be made into a crown – to ensure he would always occupy a king."

The Centurion's eyes flickered a little as he processed this data that had made his existence an eternal do-and-die loop.

"Listen to me, Centurion," Sean went on. "Like this you will never save your people, your world, from the destruction of the timeline. I don't know what this 'inversion' is you wish to brake, or what the solution is, but I think I know where to find it. Tell me, is there any other way of getting across the Gappe without dislodging the Extreme Being?"

"Yes." answered the Centurion.

"Zat ees enough!" ordered Napoleon. The chanting stopped abruptly. "Eet was geeveeng me a naughty 'ead." He placed his hands on the lever. "I deenk Scharn Seulpierre eet ees time to say our 'eternal' goodbyes."

"Marquis?" pleaded Sean.

"Good-bye, Sean Seulpierre," replied Laplace, his voice a little croaked with emotion. "In a way I envy you this opportunity you have to vision the entirety of time - but I am sorry it had to be like this. Remember me kindly."

"That I will," replied Sean, recalling similar farewells to other great scientists, his troop of unlikely consultants through the ages.

On a signal from Napoleon, the Centurion, still at his post beneath the rostrum, turned and reached up to grab the leg of the throne, ready to push the chair and Sean back onto the altar at the same moment in which Napoleon pulled the lever to release the egg two storeys below.

Then he did a kind of double-take as he sensed something. He suddenly clank-ran around to the front of the rostrum and up the stairs. Once at Sean, he carried out a short search, and found in Sean's pocket a stone egg. This was the egg Sean had caught falling from the pouch on the glider before it could hit and break on the ground when it had crashed. Sean had had just enough time to secret it into his pocket before the Invertabrake had put his lights out.

The Centurion held the egg up for Napoleon to see.

Napoleon looked surprised and said: "Zis ees strange. You 'ad zer means to escape all along, Scharn, yet you chose to remain. Why?"

"I am tired of running," said Sean sadly, his last hope crushed. "I wanted to put an end to all of this, one way or another. I thought if there was a chance of seeing my Nonno again, helping Geni and the others, I should take it. They are counting on me. I had to at least try."

"Very noble, young Scharn," nodded Napoleon. "Worthy of respect."

"Thank you."

"I said worthy… I did not say you would get eet. Throw 'im een!"

The chair began to move backwards.

"I, thus, pull zee streeng on 'istory!" And Napoleon pulled the lever.

Sean closed his eyes.

After a long while, he opened them. He was looking up at the chandelier above him. He was hovering, and everybody in the room was completely still.

After quite a while he realised that assessment was not correct, and in fact he was moving, downwards, and the Centurion above him was also moving - only very, very slowly. And ever more slowly. The golden light of the crown was now all around him, only it seemed to have taken a bluer tinge.

This blue light deepened, and gradually darkened more and more, until everything went piecemeal black, and Sean found himself wondering about Laplace's blob of dark.

"Hello, reality," he thought.
"Hello victim," he fancied he heard it answer.

* * * *

Chapter Sixteen

Heavy Front Coming

SEAN caught the tail end of a few moments of darkness, which were trashed by a bright white light that flooded and sputtered quite rudely over everything. It exposed a lunatic landscape - white regolith pocked with deep black craters drawing in everything about them as the flare descended. In one such hole, Sean was lying in mud-splattered snow while something insistently heavy was pushing down on his head. He shifted to sit up.

A harsh whisper bellowed at him. "Stay down you fool. You want to lose your thinker!?"

As if in illustration, a passing whizz informed him that there was indeed danger to be had. He threw himself back down in the mud, and tried, from a perspective akin to that of a very small ant on a fat boy's dream sugar-iced chocolate cake, to take in his situation, and to latch on aurally to his latest saviour.

The heavy thing weighing down his head was of course a helmet. On digital examination it had a single large spike on top. And this probably wasn't for keeping receipts on. He and the human forms around him were wearing military great coats, and each had a rifle. And all around them were festive decorations celebrating war: barbed wire, shell holes, bodies, and, on closer inspection, bits thereof. The flare was still coming down dangerously slowly, and murderous fire was progressively reducing the reconnaissance party he was in to just him and an officer.

This officer was writing some figures into a small notebook. He finished a column, snapped an elastic band around both it and his pencil, and said: "Right. That's enough field theory for one night. Back to the trench, men... er... man."

Sean copied the man's manner of movement, slithering like an apprentice eel through the slush and earthy goo, from blast crater to crater. All around them bullets were popping into the snow and mud, and the occasional rat-a-tat-tat of machine guns broke any ascendant complacency if any had been tempted.

Then one last good long slither brought them into the welcome depth of a trench, and wading through icy water that came up over the knees.

"Come to my office," said the man he had followed.

"Office?! Here?!"

"Well, I am an officer. What's the difference between other ranks and an officer? An office, of course! Got to keep up appearances. Foreign visitors might drop in on us any moment. Aggressive takeovers are likely, they say."

His office was a digression of the trench, up-market by virtue of a jumbled covering of timber throw-overs, with an ensuite latrine and no jokes aside running water.

It was freezing, and Sean was wet everywhere imaginable. He stood there shivering while the man lit a lantern, which only served to give the shadows a sense of victory. When the officer took his helmet off, Sean could see he was balding and was attempting to compensate for it by an enormous bushy moustache. Otherwise he was a gentle-looking, soft spoken man in his early forties. The only thing aggressive about him were his penetrating intelligent eyes.

The officer took out his notebook again and made ready to take notes by holding his writing hand against the tiny lantern, trying to get some life into his frozen fingers.

"So, tell me… what is your name?"

"S..S..Sean, s..s..sir," stuttered Sean through jittering teeth. He'd never regretted his name before. "S..S..Sean S..S..Seulpierre."

Now the officer gave him a second reason to regret his name. "Jean Seulpierre? That's a foreign name. French, isn't it? If it's not a personal question - aren't you the enemy?"

"No… no I am not."

"Sure?"

"Yes, s..s..sir. S..s..sure."

"I seem to remember there is a procedure for this. I have a feeling I'm supposed to have you shot, or dock your wages, or something…"

"I'm not the enemy! I am S..S..Swiss. I'm neutral."

"Then what are you doing here, in a German uniform, holding a rifle?"

"Er… delivering chocolate?" suggested Sean lamely, then quickly threw out a back-up invention: "I mean observing."

"Or spying?"

"What is the difference?" asked Sean.

"A firing squad." Before Sean could panic fully, the officer brightened. "Oh, all right, then. Sometimes you have to take a person's word for it. Put me down for a Nuts 'n Raisins. My name is Karl Schwarzschild, by the way. Artillery. That's why they call me 'Artie Charlie'." They shook hands. "Actually, my real job is astrophysicist - artillery officer is just a temping job between peaces."

Karl Schwarzschild picked up his pencil and wrote 'Debrief Report, 0720 hours, about January, 1916' in his battered, stained and hipbone-bowed notebook.

"What did you see?" he asked.

"What?" surprised Sean back. "Out there? Just now?"

"Yes."

"S..s..snow. Mud..."

"Yes... but anything unusual?"

"Flares, dead bodies..."

"Yes...yes...yes... anything *unusual*?"

"Well, no."

"*Hündepiddel!*" swore the man, and put down his notebook to rub his exhausted eyes. "We'll have to go out again, tomorrow night."

"But... sir, what is it you are looking for?" asked Sean.

"Data. Proof. To verify Einstein's field theory."

"Sorry? What did you say?"

"I am trying to solve Einstein's General Relativity field equations."

"Out there?!" gasped Sean.

"Well... where else?"

"It is a lot safer in here."

"Yes, but this is a deep, dark hole. Here I can verify deep, dark hole theory. But I obviously need to be out there, IN .. THE .. FIELD .., to test *field* theory."

"You're completely barmy, aren't you?" said Sean.

"I certainly hope so. Being sane out here would be… well, mad! Wouldn't it corporal?"

"Totally inconsistent, sir." said the corporal, who had come in on his regular louse-collection round for the morning's cappuccinos.

"Excuse me, sir, but what is this 'field theory' you're trying to prove?"

"Out here we know all about field theory," replied the artillery officer. "The equation goes like this: take a night, any night, then add one soldier, enclosed by barbed wire brackets, over an open field, multiply by a factor of a lit cigarette, and this all equals one dead duck."

"What is that supposed to mean?"

"The secret is in the translation. You see, in German 'duck' is 'Ente'. And the result of any hunt is a trophy - in this case an ente-trophy. To be a true equation, things have to be equal on both sides. And it would normally, except under the conditions of this particular field. What we observe here is that as time goes on you always need more fresh ducks - so from this we deduce that the ente-trophy (entropy to save ink) count must be constantly increasing. Unless you have a good watch, the only way to measure the passage of time is by the increase in entropy."

"A watch…?" asked Sean, his interest suddenly finding a raison d'être.

"Yes. Now, this is the interesting bit." Lieutenant

Schwarzschild pulled out a sheaf of papers, on which were scribbled thousands of mathematical calculations. "See... here... no... here" he eventually found and pointed out one set of equations, which, judging by the mud, water-stains and erratic scrawl, had surely been written while face down in a bomb crater, by the light of passing flares. "The sum of dead ducks is expressed by the equation let n be the number of numbskulls in a given field at time zero, and 'x' be the number of shells per minute x-ploding in same field, the rate of increase in ente-trophies per unit time decreases by the inverse square of n. Follow me?"

"An inverse square! That's what Sacky, I mean Isaac Newton, was trying to work out a rule for, except he said he couldn't for the life of him think what an inverted square might look like."

"Well, I have found an application for it here," said the Prussian officer proudly. "While on leave in Switzerland, I bought a Bernoulli Bros. pirated copy of Newton's calculus. Although unlicensed, I managed to crack it, and use it to stretch classical maths to the limit."

"And did it work?"

"Not really. It only approximated the dead duck count well at large numbers. As you can imagine, the classical prediction curve assures us that, at a certain point, there are fewer than one left to kill, and the exponentiality of the equation specifies that to fulfil the conditions of perfect symmetry, this last soldier is neither fully dead nor fully alive when in non-vectored flight from the epicentre, weighted of course by the parameters of leg length and hearing acuteness. Which I call the 'get the eff out of the field you dumb effer' factor. Or better, the general field eff-fect.

"Plotting this effect using a broad sample range, I have discovered that death is quantised - whole numbers: you don't have fractions of dead, only fractions of bodies."

"I see," lied Sean, but thinking of Shrodie the cat of indeterminate living status.

"It doesn't make any sense at all in a classical way," went on Karl Schwarzschild. "But it reassures the men. Infinite extrapolation using Laplace's probability functions provides just enough uncertainty to keep the supply of volunteers flowing to ensure we maintain a constant increase in ente-trophies. In the end, it is all relative."

"And you use the increase in entropy to measure time in the absence of a good watch," humoured Sean, not having found a handgrip on even one of the preceding ten minutes. "And do you have such a watch?" he threw out on a hunch.

Karl shrugged, folded and tucked his treatise into his inside jacket pocket. "I have two."

"Two?!"

"Yes. Every day. eight hours a time. A real pain in the butt."

With Sean thus suitably brain-whacked, they left the dugout office to make the morning's inspection. The sun was just coming up, but most of the soldiers in the trench seemed to be wondering why it bothered at all any more.

In the growing light, Sean began the unrewarding task of assembling a workable hypothesis to explain this brash new world he had woken in.

"Sorry, sir," Sean asked of the officer's back. "This may sound strange to you – but I have no idea where and when I am, or why I am here."

The artillery lieutenant turned and gave him a look which said eloquently: 'And this would be *strange* because…?'

As the dawn dawdled in, Karl Schwarzschild began to confide in Sean. Long nights gazing through telescopes had given the astronomer a slight permanent squint in one eye, that gave you the impression he was wearing a monocle. "My teachers were furious when I chose astronomy – they wanted me to do something useful with my life."

"Like drop artillery shells on people?"

"If nothing else, it gives me a sense of direction. Maybe they are right – I have spent too long thinking about reality – maybe it is time I returned to the human world. Where everything is preconceived. That's the way forward they said." He looked through a periscope towards the enemy lines, then handed it to Sean. "And look where that got us." Through the homemade box of mirrors, Sean could see that the Russians were hanging out their washing on the barbed wire in brazen breach of the Ziegfried Line copyright.

"By force of argument?"

The officer listened to the dawn chorus of artillery exchanges on both horizons. "More like by force *as* argument. You see our politicians know everything they need to know already, it seems. They hold that new knowledge risks compromising the old assumptions. 'Destabilising influences' I think they call it. They tell us conservatism means conserving us from the other 'ism's out there – like socialism. But, I ask, what if a war is just a bunch of mindlessly stubborn conservatives standing still while change rolls over them - the last angry, bewildered spasm of an old regime resisting the inevitable." He indicated the mass of men on death row all around them. "It is sad that those who would benefit from the change pay the price for those who would benefit from no change."

"So why fight?" asked Sean. "If it is clearly a con-trick by the rich and powerful?"

"That's what the field theory is all about," enthused Karl, patting the package of papers in his inside pocket. "Trying to find the point where it all collapses." He continued down the line, head bowed habitually from the weight of his helmet.

"What collapses?" asked Sean, glancing at the mayhem on the day's agenda.

There was a distinct glint in Karl's eye when he turned to say: "Everything."

"Ah… good old Life, the Universe, and Sundrae Phenomena…" Sean quoted Newton as he struggled through the trenchsoup to keep up with the suddenly agile officer as he march-waded along the line for the morning's inspection.

A sergeant was doing a roll-call. Each man answered his name with variations on the theme of: "One leg accounted for", or "All limbs up to two present or nearby, sir", or "Can't see to count, sir", or "Run out of fingers to count with, sarge", to which the sergeant answered "Then use your toes, laddie". There was a pause and the voice said "Ah… a little problem there…".

"These are the veterans," said Karl, proudly. "They've been here nearly a month. And… here, we have the new recruits," announced Schwarzschild. "Gentlemen, welcome to the Great War."

"What's so great about it?" asked one of the men.

"I heard it was the *first* great war," said a very young man.

"No," corrected the sergeant. "This is the *last* great war. The war to end all dispute about whose war is the greatest."

"What do you think, Private Seulpierre?" asked Karl.

"I think you'll find it is just the *latest* great war." They all went silent. "Many happy returns," said Sean.

As they moved further along the line, Karl enquired of Sean: "But haven't you heard? Apparently this is *it* - This is *the* war that will end all wars."

"This is my third of those. Anything else that makes it great?"

"Oh, lots of things. Fresh air, poetry, songs, camaraderie. Peace and quiet."

"Peace and quiet?!"

"At least that is what they told me when I joined up. Here." Karl pointed out a heavily-graffitied and shrapnel-pixellated enlistment poster entitled: 'All's Quiet on the Eastern Front.'

"I think they advertise the western front under that slogan."

"It's syndicated. I was there too. Just as noisy. That's why I decided to get away from it all. Holiday on the other front. West to East. Lots of us have done it. There's a song:

'New War, New War,
If you can win it here you can win it anywhere.

I want to wake up on the front that never sleeps,
New War, New War' …"

Some of the men picked up the tune, and began to tap wade in the water and mud, singing

'…those little town ruins, … just blow them away…'

"What do you do when you're not organising trenchfoot musicals?" asked Sean, beginning to hum unconsciously too.

"This week I'm on the alarm wake up call roster. My first job of the day is to get the clients up ready for a good day's fighting."

"Clients?"

"The ones who have engaged the German army. We are, after all, a 24-hour service. Always ready to please. Never late in response. Very professional we are."

"I see. And the other artillery batteries? What are they doing?"

"Oh, they'll be preparing the daily bulletins for the clients: delivered in 155mm HE shells. I think the HE stands for 'highly entertaining'. They say they've heard all the best ones before, but it still has them jumping and falling off the edge of their latrines."

They had worked their way back a distance from the front line, and were now in an artillery compound, where a bunch of artillery pieces were being cleaned and readied for an honest day's work. "What we need here is more shell and less shock," said Karl.

"It's relative," said a lonely gunner with a chronic digestive tract digression.

"Ah… relative," went on Karl. "I love that word. It means everything might be possible, or equally impossible, under certain conditions - provided specific elements, like an observer, are present. That is why I have invited you along, Sean. As a professional observer. You know the sort of thing… Tree falling in forest, did you hear that? said a gnat to his mum. Don't you start on that metaphysics thing again with me, replies his mum, and chew your bile ten thousand times before swallowing. And don't regurgitate on an empty stomach - you know I like to have my stomach turned."

"You're nuts, aren't you?" stated Sean.

"Totally loopy. The only way to get any work done in the trenches. Rational thoughts tend to blur focus out here." They entered the observation post. Karl gave Sean a pair of binoculars and indicated the enemy lines just two hundred metres distant from their own front lines. "The frontlines of two great powers are now so close together they are inside what I call the Schwarzschild Radius. You see, within the event horizon, everything is inverted. At a certain distance the real enemy shifts from being in front of us to being behind us." He jerked his thumb over his shoulder. "We have more in common with those poor Russian peasants we are bombarding than the idiot politicians who goaded us here in the first place. I am Jewish - I would have preferred a passover on this one. Oh well… This war is an implosion of mankind. The trenches mark out the event horizon, the point where everything inverts. I have described the effect in my mathematical treatise." He took out his package briefly and patted it in such a way that Sean had the impression it must contain his soul.

An orderly arrived and handed Karl a clipboard, on which he filled in and signed the chit for the morning's bombardment.

"How would you like it this morning, sir?" enquired the orderly deferentially.

"I think today 'short, back and sides'," replied Karl, and wrote as much in the 'target coordinates' square.

Soon the howitzers were in action. Between explosions, Sean and Karl had a strange conversation.

"And then I ask myself," roared Karl, his fingers in his ears. "Is it a single event horizon or a series of horizontal events? After throwing myself flat on my face every ten seconds for over a year, I have developed a horizontal event theory. It always ends with a big bang."

"And starts with just as big a bang!" cried Sean, commensurately inspired.

"That's good. … That's *very* good… hmm.."

"Sir, what is a genius like you doing in a place like this?" shouted Sean back through the booms of the guns.

"Riemann's space."

"Sorry?"

"I confused it with *Niemandsland*, no-man's land, on the enlistment preferences form when I joined up."

"Eh…?" screamed Sean, his head pounding, as he followed the officer out of the observation post. "What's a Riemann's space, and what has it got to do with this place?"

"Non-Euclidean geometry, of course. That's a geometry you get when you try to draw straight lines with your paper wrapped around a cannon barrel." He squinted towards the sun trying tokenly to claw its way through the winter haze and wafts of cordite smoke. "For example, if you squished up the sun, like a snowball," he grabbed two hand-fulls of snow to illustrate, "... and had really... and I do mean *really*... big hands... you could compact its usual radius of 700,000 km to just 3 kilometres across, but no smaller." His snowball was crushed to the hardest ice-ball possible.

"What for?" puzzled Sean, confirming the conjecture with his own snowball. "It wouldn't be much use as a sun if it were only the size of the distance to the nearest newspaper kiosk?"

"Exactly my point! That's exactly it! At that size it wouldn't emit enough light to read the newspaper by, anyway, you see - because it would be so dense and heavy, even light, the fastest thing in the universe, if you don't count conservatives jumping to conclusions, would not have enough 'oomph' to get away."

"Ah... I understand. You're describing the exact point where the sun would become a Black Hole?" shouted Sean, remembering with agonising nostalgia such a conversation while drinking hot chocolate in the Grand Café in Lugano with Pierre-Simon de Laplace, the serially ex-Marquis of Location, Location, Location.

"I know it as a Blob of Dark," said-screamed Karl. "Dumb name, I agree. I like 'Black Hole' - catchy - but if I am not wrong, Calcutta has a prior claim to the 'black hole' trademark? They've already got one, you see?"

"Ah..." said Sean for the n to a major power time that morning.

"And instead of giving it out, this miniature sun would draw light, and everything else within reach for that matter, back into it." Karl rubbed mud onto his iceball till it was completely dark. "That special point, where reality is inverted, is the Schwarzschild Radius." He callipered the ball's width with his index and small finger in illustration.

"I see," said Sean. "The point of all return. Tell me, sir, if the Earth were all squished up to the size of a Schwarzschild Radius, how big would it be?"

"About 9mm across - the size of my little fingernail." He stared at a hand with his monocle-like squint. "If I still had one, that is."

"That's incredible!"

"Yes. We are talking theoretically, you understand. I mean… where would you put it? Mind you, when I was on the Western Front there was this corporal in charge of repapering the dug-outs. And he said he would be very interested, because he wouldn't mind having a 9-mm world to put in his pocket. He liked the calibre."

"Is that his ambition? To have the world in his pocket?"

"That's what he said: today Trench 34b, swap sides every second Tuesday, tomorrow zer vorld!"

"Ah…" said Sean yet again, as something occurred to him. "This corporal - was he short and did he have a funny moustache?"

Karl stopped and wiggled his enormous schnautzer. "You find moustaches funny?"

"No… I just wanted to know if this corporal was a certain megalomaniac I know, by the name of Cespuglio."

"Are you seriously asking me if there is a megalomaniac out there? Just one?!"

"So, what happened then?"

"I asked him for a quote for redecorating my dugout. He took one look at me, my name, and the fact that I refused to attack on the Sabbath, and he said he'd give me a final answer soon. Now there is a candidate for your Cespuglio. Did a lousy job on the dugout, too."

"Bad was it?"

"No… just lousy. I'm still itchy now. Got any ointment?"

"Sorry." Sean patted his pockets and grey sludge oozed out.

"That's when I decided to swap sides."

"Betray your country?"

"No, that would involve getting a whole new wardrobe of clothes, and I hate shopping. I mean just swap sides. West to East. France to Russia. You see I prefer sunrises to sunsets, anyway. And the night sky out here is not ruined by so many flares as on the western front. Bloody advertising! Always reminding us the enemy are there - as if we had forgotten. For stargazing, I take all the night shifts - it makes me very popular with the men. Trouble is my reading light attracts a lot of client interest. Still, one has to take risks and annoy people if one wants to get on in life."

Sean looked at his ice ball, and something occurred to him. "Tell me, sir, what happens if you get carried away, and *do* squash the snowball smaller than the Schwarzschild radius?"

"Ah… There, something *really* weird happens. Space gets too small for its boots, and starts to behave like time, and time, in tit-for-tat retaliation, starts to behave like space. A bit petty, I agree, but they have that sort of relationship."

"Ah…ha!" Sean would have snapped his fingers if he had been confident they wouldn't have snapped right off, so numb they were. "Do you think it is possible the space inside would become… like a capsule - a vehicle to access all time, simultaneously." He thought of the

Shrouds, ever-present and unseeing, inside the Haunted House. "Anyone in it would experience space moving while time stands still…?"

"If you want to know how the *Vitruvian Crystal* works," Karl smiled at Sean's surprise. "There is someone infinitely more able to answer your questions. From first-hand experience."

"Who?"

"All in good time."

After a while, Sean burst out with: "But I don't understand - the Vitruvian Crystal is not massive like the sun, it can't distort all space and time."

"Stop thinking like a cow."

"Don't you mean like a sheep?" replied Sean, too confused to be properly offended.

"No, a cow. Remember Leonardo and Luca Pacioli's cow? How it can't look up, so exists only in two dimensions, oblivious of the yoghurt fanciers staring down on it from the upper floor window - the third dimension? In the same way, you have to be in a fourth dimension to view the first three dimensions, and, of course, in a fifth dimension to view the fourth dimension for what it truly is."

"Is that what the VC is? A cattleyard viewing platform?"

"Well, as I understand it, the Vitruvian Crystal doesn't exist at any specific moment – but specific moments do exist just outside it."

"One of your event horizons?" asked Sean, almosting it with matching facials.

"More strictly a *non*-event horizon. At its core there is what I call a Singularity. In other words, it acts as though it had the whole of its mass, all of the matter it is composed of, throughout all time, accumulated into its volume momentaneously – every formulation and reformulation of every atom in any moment past and future superimposed – it is in effect the most massive object ever – in this region of the cosmos at any rate."

"Massive enough to punch a hole in the spenmatt?"

"More like *down to* the spenmatt – not literally down - down in the sense of losing our elevation with regards the origin of the timeline. A bit like a solar flare shorting out and crashing suddenly onto the sun's surface."

Karl smiled ruefully as he remembered a more practical metaphor. "When I first met my wife, I made a mistake. I took her to my laboratory in Göttingen, and gave her a little demonstration. I charged up two rods and between them created a beautiful red arc of electricity. I then brought an earthed conductor close to its middle. Naturally, it immediately broke into two beautifully symmetrical arcs. The interesting thing is that, in order to do this, the arc 'upstream', so to speak, had to reverse its direction of flow. So the two sides looked like two arches of a bridge supported by a single central pylon. But since the polarity had been reversed on one side, it caused the far ends of the two arcs to attract each other and snap together at the heels. The result was a perfect heart shape."

"What happened then?"

"She mistook it for a proposal of marriage, drat it. … Oh, you mean the arc? Well, the experiment served to reveal how very transient anything like that is. Romance included. The whole thing collapsed almost immediately, draining down the electrical plughole so to speak, back into the earth - the great, big origin of all electrical polarity and flow, where all electrons are evenly spaced and have no particular reason to move, never mind go to all the effort of arcing."

This reminded Sean of one of Nonno's hilarious party tricks - one in which he had singed his beard in two separate places. "Do you think the spenmatt is like that? That space, energy, and matter form a cosmic background, which is time neutral. A place where time energy is by default unmotivated to arc out and create a timeline? Could the VC be causing a timeline short-out?"

"Short-out? Good metaphor. Nice and nibbly as sound-bites go. Where did you get that?"

"Oh, it's just a bit of Nonno-technology."

They had finally moved away from the guns, along another series of trenches and tunnels, to continue the inspection. Sean's ears were ringing as ding dong merrily on high as the painting of Adam on the Sistine Chapel ceiling.

A sergeant was ordering the men to remove their gasmasks, drill over.

"What are they doing?" asked Sean.

"You've not heard about our experiments? In airborne condiments? I was all in favour of the lighter ingredients: Parsley, Sage, Rosemary, and Thyme - that kind of thing. But no, High Command went for the heavy spices - mustard for one. Set back first-strike cuisine a whole season. The whole gas programme gets on my nerves."

"Good morning, general." said one of the men.

"Why did he call you 'general'?" Sean asked Karl. "Your rank is lieutenant."

"Ever since I told the men I was working on solutions for the 'General Relativity theory', they have treated me with a kind of diffident awe - I think they think I am planning to become a general through relative connections."

"General Relativity, sah!" bellowed another sergeant with a cheeky grin beneath his I-do-you-die face.

"Relatively speaking," said another.

"Oh, absolutely," said the first.

"Anything to report, sergeant?" asked Karl wading stoically through the mud and sarcasm.

"The artillery battery needs recharging, general sah!"

"I keep telling them my name is not General Relativity," explained Karl tiredly to Sean. "And that I am only doing equations, but they keep telling me it is all the same to them as well. I think we lack a basis of communication here. That is because the mass of cerebral goo is inversely proportional to the volume of the 'sah' they bellow."

"But they all shout 'sah'," observed Sean.

"Yes," said Karl sadly. "What the army really doesn't like about equations is that they are the same for both sides."

"And what *do* you use these equations for?" asked Sean.

"I calculate the flight of artillery shells."

"But they don't *fly*, sah" interjected the sergeant. "They goes up and then they comes down. Niemandsland is curved space, sah. And we knows where they lands - on the enemy."

"Ah, yes, sergeant, but can you *prove* it is the enemy? That is merely a transient state. Incoherent when you actually take a look - make an observation. We never see the live ones, and when they are dead they are not the enemy any more, just a pile of decomposite matter. Neutral at worst. So are we for that matter."

"I'd say it was an example of 'field effect transformation', sah."

"So," replied Karl with infinite patience. "You're saying to get the field equation to balance everybody has to be dead?"

"I gather, sah, that is the general gist of the 'piece plan'."

"Yessir," contributed a corporal. "They complain afterwards with their own shells. And then when we goes over the top we observe the body bits. And mix a few of ours with 'em. If the numbers balance out we has a field equation. Seems fair to me, sir." A few of the men nodded agreement and murmured 'here, here'.

"So, professor general sah," continued the sergeant. "Got us another proof today?"

"Yeah, like the distribution of gravy in a pseudo-isotropic liquid?" asked another man, holding up his mess tins hopefully.

"Gaseous homogeneity is the tricky bit, isn't it general?" said another. "In a crowded trench, naked flames. Eh?! How you're gonna do that on a two-dimensional back of envelope hopelessly rigid with regards Cartesian abscissas - that's what I would like to see. That's what keeps me awake on sentry duty."

"Doesn't it us all?" murmured the rest of the men.

Schwarzschild whispered to Sean. "When the men get bored, they start postulating all over the place. I usually send them off on suicide missions just to get a bit of peace around here."

"You want peace on a battleground?"

"Well, beats trying to get any work done at home, with the kids screaming and the wife nagging about this and that. Give me Russian mortar shells any day. Far more predictable - and here you can fight back. Haven't you always wanted to bombard your noisy neighbours with 155mm artillery rounds?"

"Oh, sure. I see your point. But what are you fighting for?"

The sergeant overheard this and announced: "We're fighting this war for freedom from the fear of condiments, and the right to be wrong."

"In other words," interjected Sean. "You forgot a long time ago what this war is all about?"

The men murmured amongst themselves, and seemed to take a vote. A spokesman came forward. "80% go for the condiments, 2% for rights, wrongs, whatever, and the remaining 15% abstained."

"You mean 18%. Get your maths right," tut-tutted Karl.

"No, begging your pardon, sir. 3% have just been killed by a mortar. It was 15% who stained themselves. Oops, sorry. Make that 16%."

"Are you sure?"

"Prima facie evidence."

As they continued down the line, Karl explained to Sean: "I treat their problem with the inner Schwarzschild solution - a mathematically based formula my grandmother swears will cure any prima facie obstacle. It is applicable to solids, incompressible fluids, and indeed any homogeneous and isotropic distributed gas." He made a face and waved his hand in front of him. "See what I mean?"

At the end of the line, in both senses, they entered a transport compound, from which passenger vehicles arrived and departed with their doomed and deathly cargoes.

Karl Schwarzschild turned to Sean thoughtfully, and asked: "Jean, what are you *really* doing here?"

Sean thought it was time to be honest. "I am drawn to a watch."

Karl looked at him closely, then said. "Let me tell you something, Jean. Before Galileo Galilei, the father of all we astronomers, gazed through his telescope, the cosmos was divided into two parts: below the moon and above the moon. This was because it was generally thought that the atmosphere reached as far as the moon. But, Galileo told us that the sub-lunar world and the extra-lunar heavens are reflections of each other, and cannot be separated. The physics was the same in both spheres - the point being that we were entitled to use the *same* language for both. It was thanks to Galileo, that Newton and Leibniz saw the need for calculus, and it was Laplace who put down on paper a concise description of the cosmos for us all to see, and finally *truly* marvel at all creation.

"And so it is for me. Mathematics, physics and astronomy, and their primary product, philosophy, are dialects of the one and the same language. Their common grammar is derived from the rotation of the elements we see in the sky at night. I sometimes wonder: what if we had lived instead on a permanently clouded planet, and had never seen the night sky - how different would our culture have been?

"In such a world we would have been doomed to orbit forever around our own petty ideas, and arrogance would have felt justified in imposing a limited vision. And sometimes nationalism, prejudice and dogma rise to cloud our horizons artificially in just such a way, and we lose our hard-earned common language.

"This is what this war is all about. Like Dante, sometimes we have to negotiate our way through a madhouse to see sanely once more."

He took out his treasured packet of notes and tapped it with extended finger-tips. "And this we have compiled into a wonderful language with which to talk to the gods who built the cosmos. And, you know what? I think they are just about to respond to us... Pity I won't be here to hear it. I know my time has run out."

Honesty forbade Sean from using empty words. He instead hugged the master astronomer. "I am so glad to have met you."

"And I you, Jean. Remember me kindly."

A staff sergeant came up, saluted Karl, then tapped a clipboard with a pencil. "Name and rank?" he barked at Sean.

"Sean Seulpierre. Private," replied Sean.

"Private..." the man scribbled. "Class?"

"Err... economy?"

The staff sergeant stopped in mid-line. "No, no, no. This just won't do. Won't do at all! Seulpierre? If you are French, then you're on the wrong front. Wrong front, my lad! You shouldn't be here. We're your right enemy - Germans and all that... but you're our *wrong* enemy. We have demarcation rules to comply with. The unions are not going to like this. Go and be killed where you belong - on the Western Front. This is the Eastern Front. If you were meant to be here your name would be Sharnski Seulstoneska or something. You'd better catch a long march back over to the west before you're missed."

He filled in a sickly-yellow E-46b form entitled "Back to Front" pointless-movement-for-the-sake-of-it transfer permit, a form still used by the trucking industry in Europe today. He tore it off impatiently and pushed both it and Sean onto a longcar about to leave.

Karl jumped up on to the running board of the vehicle to say his farewell. "Would you do me a favour? Drop by Berlin would you and give this to a certain Mr OneStone?" He handed Sean his bundle of papers wrapped up in sanguineous rations paper. "You'll find him at Big Willy's Institute of Theatrical Physics. If he's performing, he'll be wearing his mad professor costume. You know, the fuzzy hair and big nose get-up. Kids love it. And, oh, give him this as well, and say thanks, he was right, it was *very* useful."

He pulled up his sleeve, took off his wristwatch, and gave it to Sean. It was Sean's digital watch - the SANG Re.al!

* * * *

CHAPTER SEVENTEEN

WHO'S RELATIVE NOW?

THE capital of the belligerent world, Berlin, was as yet undivided on any red-flag issue, although its foreign policy statements were firmly entrenched in some corner of a foreign field negotiations, with all the noisy assertions and counter-assertions one normally associates with them. Sean found the address Karl Schwarzschild had given him, proudly wearing his watch again after so many centuries, and carrying the bundle of mathematical despatches from the front. Sometimes he changed grip and carried them from the back, but mostly he carried them from the front.

The first sign he encountered, a little down the road, read 'Kaiser Wilhelm's Institute of Theoretical Physics, dis vay', but when he was actually at the campus, he saw another sign whose distinctive Germanic typeface had been clumsily painted over in colours which had nothing sensible to say to each other, to read:

𝕭𝖎𝖌 𝕾𝖜𝖎𝖑𝖑𝖞'𝖘 𝕴𝖓𝖘𝖙𝖎𝖙𝖚𝖙𝖊 𝖔𝖋 𝕿𝖍𝖊𝖆𝖙𝖗𝖎𝖈𝖆𝖑 𝕻𝖍𝖞𝖘𝖎𝖈𝖘

with a typewritten note underneath advising: 'Two

performances a day. New theories on 'Life, the Uni's Purse and Every udder Ding' received by Royal Disappointment only - kick three times on rear door (postman twice).'

Just past the elephant excrement souvenir stand, Sean found the caravan office of 'Mr OneStone, the most famous relativiser in the known Teutonic world'. There was a note on the door reminding visitors: 'Strictly no butts: cigarette, rifle, of jokes, or otherwise.'

Sean knocked and heard a caricature German accent call out: "Na-ja, can't a theorist be haffing a moment to postulate on his own between of zer performances?!"

"Mr OneStone? My name is Sean Seulpierre. I have a message from a man called Karl Schwarzschild from the front."

"Und tso vat do you call him vrom zer back, zenn, eh?" And the caravan door opened to reveal a clown.

When I say clown, I obviously mean more of a world-famous theoretical physicist, but the braces holding ill-fitting pants, no socks, flayed cigar moustache and no-holds-barred hair, not to forget the fake-looking nose, also had me confused for a moment. He examined Sean through large, sad, droopy eyes, which somehow managed to look as though they were always laughing.

"But... you're Professor Albert Einstein!" cried Sean.

The man swung the violin he had been using to fuzz out his hair onto his back by its carrying strap, and said: "Komm, komm, John Seulpierre, I have been waiting for you such much a long time, ja?"

"Oh.. ya?" replied Sean, and followed the professor across the campus to the big top canopy strung between two unrelated buildings.

"So, you run a circus?" asked Sean, looking at the billing for a troop of acrobats called the Quantum Leapers.

"Best vay for zer crowds to zer lectures to be inbringing, ja? All zer students are being blown to bitz doing field research, tso vee at zer Institute haff opened to zer public. It's ok, but zer elephants keep stealing my peanut-Kräuter sandwiches."

"And what is this 'Relativity Show'?" asked Sean, admiring a badly weathered poster for a solar eclipse spectacle.

"It started out as a family feature called 'Zer Relative Show', but vee adapted it into a type of international reality show. It vas big flop, na-ja. To test mein theory of zer curving of space in zer presence of large masses, I zended vaan of zer contestants, a German astronomer, to Russia to vatch zer total eclipse of zer sun. But, you know, it vas August, 1914! As luck vudd haff it, zer Great Var had just been launched. Predictable script, but mit ein cast of tens von millions und a special effects bonanza... Now, all zer best theatres are out-booked for zee 'Bring zer Boyz Back to zer Heimat' revivals."

"And what happened to your astronomer?" asked Sean.

"His name vas Erwin Freundlich... you know - 'Mr Friendly'. I mean, honestly! Venn he told zer Russians zat, zey arrested him as being spy. Zey just couldn't believe his name vasn't a cover. Tso, I missed zer chance to verify mein theory against zer dying of zer light. Now, vee haff to vait for zer next eclipse.

"I haff an English agent, Eddington, who promises to redirect zom starlight in mein direction after zer Var.

Zat'll make me vorld famous, he say. But I don't vant to avay carried being. Zey say I can move zer universe, expand it mit mein Theory - but I am all time saying, zer universe ist big enough already, ja? I can't paint a clear image of zomzing zat ist moving all zer time, na-ja? In zer meantime I do matinees of our classical repertoire und I shovel out zer elephants' cage twice a day, three times on pay days. Zose peanuts…"

"But, why a circus?" asked Sean, enthralled as he watched the vastly colourful and anarchic collection of acts as they prepared for the next show.

"It vas all Big Villy's idea."

"Big Willy?"

"Kaiser Wilhelm. He ist zer money. He vanted zomzing for zee childrens to be him remembering, ja? Good idea. Kidz, zey never remember atomic structure lessons, but zey remember vell a clown who ist his foot in elephant poop stepping, ja?"

"So, how did you get into the physics show business?"

"I couldn't get a normal yob. No-vaan vudd take me on as researcher. Zey kept telling me zere vas no vacancy for zomvaan who didn't know it all already."

"But, I thought research was all about exploring the unknown?"

"Ja. But you haff to tell zem in advance exactly vat you are going to discover in order for to be getting zer fundings, ja? So, I took my big hit, zer easy-two-measy singalong equation, und turned it into a long-running musical."

"Easy two measy?"

"On graffiti text messages, teenagers zey vrite $E=mc^2$ for short. Zer full formula goes on for several pages, but I ran out of zer ink und sent in vat I had to zer publisher. Vich is just as vell, because it vas eventually an immediate hit. It ist being zer number vaan on zer Top Ten Equations list since every year."

"But, why a circus?" insisted Sean.

"As a child, I fancied I could see light as funny little guys shooting out vrom a circus cannon vaving at me as zey came. It vas not until I vas five und tventy zat I realised I had been right all along. Can you see zem too?"

"You mean you think light is not a continuous wave but little bundles of waves?"

"Vat I am saying ist zat I like circuses. Und vat better circus zann zer vorld of theatrical physics! Ah… I alvays knew I vudd make a great clown."

"Yes, with hair like that…"

"Vat's vrong mit mein hair?"

"Nothing … it's … um … distinctive."

"Vithout zer hair, enormous moustache und big nose, I vudd revert to mild-mannered Swiss patents clerk. In dis get-up I am superstar of zer equations hit parade. Und vaan day I vill get around to patenting mein invention: Mr OneStone's miracle hair exploder. All mein hairs are electrostatically charged und vill stay up like dis all zer day. No more combing, no more zer need of zer oil or zer creams. I am saving half of hour every morning by zer feigning of eccentricity. Ja ja."

"Is that why you wear no socks?"

"You can vear socks but you can't, strictly speaking, vear no socks."

"And the braces instead of a belt?"

"I may be a viz at zer kosmological calculations, but zose new-fangled, fiddly little belt buckles haff got me beat - und getting it through all zose little loops on zer trousers…!!"

"So, are you still working on the light quanta theory?" asked Sean, admiring a group of glitzily-dressed performers preparing a demonstration of research findings into the nature of light, involving various animals and loops of fire.

"Sure. Vee do both light-quanta und heavy-quanta - vhich is Italian for 'how much does it veigh zer pocket?'"

"Sorry…?!"

"Venn vee on zer touring, zee Italians zey alvay me to ask: 'Quanta?' I am saying: 'How much you vanna pay?' Zey are saying: 'Light… light… not heavy.' I am back at zem alvay saying: 'Ok, light-quanta ist zer vay into zer vunderbar vorld of zer new theatrical physics.' Zomhow zer press ist getting dis vrong und now zey are vaiting zom big statement vrom zom guy zey call 'General… zomzing'."

"Relativity?" suggested Sean.

"Zat's zer fellow. I say vat ist General Relativity vithout a lot of Private Fundings, heh?! Mit zer fundings vee can go independent, as my mother ist alvay telling at me."

"Your mother?"

"Sure: she alvay ist telling: you don't need a Big Villy if you haff a good funding."

"Something I have always wanted to know, professor, is: what is the difference between Special Relativity and General Relativity?"

"In 1905, venn I vrote Special Relativity, I vas going for zer vorld record: four vorld shattering papers in zer vaan year. I vas zerefore in a hurry: I left gravity out of zer equations."

"How could you forget gravity?"

"I know… I know…"

Sean raised his on-loan eyebrows. "As I understand it, it was the search for an explanation of gravity which gave birth to the modern science of physics. Both Galileo and Newton came down with gravity fever. But you don't fall for that?"

"Oh, but I do. How do you zink my nose is getting to be dis shape?"

"And Laplace's probability? That everything happens by chance measured against the probability of its not bothering? Isn't that what drives the universe?"

"I don't approve of zer gambling. Zat's how I lost my socks und belt. So I don't see vhy Mr Biggy should be playing at zer dice - particularly at his age."

Einstein was gradually working his way around the tent exterior, examining the suspension ropes which looped over its domed roof. He tested their tension by strumming them with his violin bow. "Dis important. During zer reality show, zer tent ist zer universe. See how zese lines look parallel down here at zer ground, but in reality zey eventually converge und meet at zer centre of zer roof - just vhere zee pigeons do zeir zingies. It ist zer presence of zer heavy tent canvas vich bends zer space inside into a curve."

"Yes," said Sean. "These ropes look like the lines of longitude on the Earth's surface. If I remember right, my Nonno called them 'geodesics'."

"Gee-I-sea-sicks? He may be right zere. If zese ropes are not tight being, venn der vind ist strong blowing, all zee trapeze artists hanging von zer roof inside are thrown about like in a ship on zer high sea. Really messy down below, believe me. Tso I alvay must to tighten zese ropes. Zey are at right-angle to zer ground, but only look to be parallel. Euclid - remember Freddie Euclid?"

"*Freddie* Euclid?!"

"Vell… Zee textbooks, zey alvay zay just 'Euclid' - but I zay he must to be haffing a first name, too, ja? Vat verr his family called, eh? Papi Euclid, Mamma Euclid und Little Euclids vaan, two, t'ree?! He needed to invent a new mathematics just to vurk out whose turn it vas to use zer bathroom… Tso I call him Freddie till zomvaan ist me bringing a birth certificate to zer contrary.

"Anyvay, Freddie vas darn certain zese perpendicular lines vudd alvay be parallel. His idea looked good on zer flat parchment. Und for two t'ousands of years everyvaan ist him believing. But he vas not a showman like me! In mein new circus time-space, all parallel lines intersect zomvhere… maybe over zer rainbow, but definitely zomvhere."

He indicated a complex array of pegs and stays holding the ends of the ropes, each numbered in a seemingly random pattern. "Vee need zese tensors or our circus space-time ist collapse," he explained.

Einstein took some of the numbers from the nearest tensors and began juggling them absentmindedly. "Mein Special Relativity ist tso special because I left gravity out. I haff spent eleven of years trying to get it inside of zer equations vithout of anyvaan to notice. But to be doing zat, I need a means to hold up zer numbers, or zey be falling, plop, tso, to zer floor - really embarrassing during juggling lectures." He picked up the fallen items in question and replaced them randomly on the tensors, then stood back to see if that helped the situation.

He suddenly changed the subject. "Archimedes, he ist saying: 'You be giving me of a place for to be standing, ja?, und I am moving of zer vorld, tso'." The professor jumped on a seesaw and sent a large model Earth on its far end flying into a vat of porridge. "Now zat's leverage!"

"What lever do *you* want to use to move the world?" asked Sean, thinking of the last time he had heard that quote, and missing Napoleon's warning of his dangerous ambition in the process.

"It's a little trick vee physicists play. Vennever vee end up mit ein difference between reality und our mathematics, vee don't are getting of zer depressed - no! Vee are pulling out zer fudge!" Einstein offered Sean some of the confectionary in question from a seriously scrunched paper bag, but Sean shook his head scoldingly.

"You mean you cheat?"

"Vee are all it to do. If nobody ist calling it zer cheating, zer public ist never it to notice. I just multiplied vatt I got mit ein number zat made it equal vatt everybody says I should haff got. Mein vurking title for it ist zer 'cosmological constant'. But I need a better name to convince zer marketing fellows. I put it on zer tensors, like zis," he applied a fudge wad to one of the rope stays, "und zer universe stays put. Neat, ja?"

"But physics is full of constants…" muttered Sean, trying the smallest piece of the fudge.

"Ah, you zee, vee do like our sveets. Bad for our teeth, zo'. Na-ja. How is?"

"It tastes… unconvincing."

"But strong enough to make my version of zer laws of physics stick."

"But, that would mean rewriting Newton's laws of motion. Why do you want to do that?" asked Sean through glued teeth.

"Because I rubbish at boxing - look at my nose!"

Sean looked instead at the unnecessarily complex and unstable array of tensors holding the tent in place. "And does your theory really prove Newton was wrong?" he asked, feeling he needed to defend his old friend.

"It is not so much a question of vether Newton vas vrong or right, but zat his description of zer universe is a little short on zer details."

"You mean his theory of gravity only applies to a limited case?"

"Exact tso. His great book, 'Principia', has just been re-released here as a popular kiddies' edition entitled 'Chippy zer Prince takes on zer New Kosmos'. Tso, I am publishing an answering sequel dis year called 'General Relativity und his Ideas on Var in Practice'."

Sean remembered Karl Schwarzshild's notes he was carrying. "Could I suggest calling it 'General Relativity and the Field Theory'?"

"Good. Catchy. How does it end?"

"Like all generals' theories - in a big bang."

"Nein, nein. No big bang. I vant grand epic version of zer kosmos. It might start mit ein big bang promotional trailer, but I prefer a slow, agonising ending to zer universe. Due to consumption. Much more zer melodrammatic."

"That plot has been flogged a bit in opera, hasn't

it?"

"You zink vee need zomzing new?"

"How about 'onwards forever'?"

"A bit socialistic. Not really in vogue. Or do you mean capitalism's infinite expansion?"

"With the possibility of sudden, unexpected contraction one day?"

Einstein looked up at the big top straining against the wind. "Sure, mit all dees vormholes I haff been finding, it ist surprising zer universe stays inflated at all."

A knot was coming undone on one of the tensor stays. Einstein took out a large wad of fudge he had been chewing and used it to hold it down. "But vithout zer sticky fudge to hold it togezzer, zer universe vudd be slipping apart..."

Sean took an old monocycle inner tube he found and used that to connect another loose tensor to its stay. The rope length expanded and contracted gently in the breeze, and the big top seemed perceptively relieved about it. "You think the universe can't be expanding?" Sean asked the clown-professor.

"You don't zink an infinite universe ist big enough already? You want more zan infinite? You greedy."

"And if you are wrong, and the universe *is* expanding?" Sean tweaked the rubber stay in demonstration.

Einstein was impressed by the rubber tube device. "Ja, in perfectly curved space-time zere shudd be no corners to cut." He looked down at the gooey mess he had made on his own tensor, already coming apart. "Zen zis vill go down in history as my biggest boo-boo." Einstein stopped suddenly and schnapped his fingers.

"Eureka!"

"I know - but I have been in the trenches…"

"Zatz true, but…"

"You mean you've discovered something about the true nature of time and space?" asked Sean, happy to be witness to yet another great Eureka moment.

"Nein again. I've just zought of a great name for mein fudge: boo-boo gum! I could market it under zat name, ja? 'Keep *your* kosmos togezzer mit Mr OneStone's Big Boo-Boo Gum'…!"

"But a model of the cosmos shouldn't need sweeteners…" insisted Sean.

Einstein twanged the rubbery rope Sean had made like a big kid. "Tso, maybe I have been vrong all along! Zis ist fun, ja? Zer trick ist to realise zat space-time ist not vat we dink it ist: it ist not fixed und immovable, but flopping about like … ein big floppy ding."

"A rubber mattress?"

"If zat ist your idea of a good time, ja."

"The inclusion of gravity in your Relativity Theory will bend space-time in such a way that every circus act fits," encouraged Sean, noting the tent lift as an elephant entered through a tight flapway.

"I prefer zer straight lines. Zey help me valk home. But after a couple of schnapps who has more zer straight lines, eh?"

"Yes, but like this you don't need any more fudge." Sean took the bag off him, and Einstein only occasionally looked longingly at it.

They had circumvented the tent and returned to the main entrance. A group of children ran out from the long queue waiting to buy tickets from the box office, which was actually only a tent flap manned by a chimpanzee. They crowded around the famous scientist and demanded he paint $E=mc^2$s on their shirtfronts.

Entertaining the waiting audience was a group of hefty pom-pom* Fräulein, dancing and chanting:

$E = m$
$E = m$
$E = mc^2$!!
E's the man
The man who can
'E showed 'em 'e's not scared!

$E = m$
$E = m$
$E = mc^2$!!
OneStone! OneStone!
All's now known
He's the one who dared!

"Komm into zer big top," Sean's guide invited. It was a standard circus ring decked out tackily to look like a university lecture hall. "Dis ist model of der kosmos." Einstein shone a spotgaslamp upwards. "Zer lights on zer ceiling are zer stars, ja? According to my relative theory, light-quanta are my unvanted extended family, vich I shoot out of zee cannons here to see how zey bend around zer stars und behave in free fall."

"Can you plot them accurately?"

"Screams make clear markers. Impact gives us a good splatter data pattern as vell. Von zee fingernail

---

* pom-pom, from Medieval German for 'those who have eaten too many pomme-frites'

scratches on zer ceiling vee can plot zeir entire flight path."

"What makes it a model of gravity?" asked Sean, impressed by the scale and daring of modern experimental physics.

"Ven zey hit vaan of zer ground energy levels…" Einstein indicated the different levels of the raked seating around the ring, "it really hurt - zat's serious. Zer more energy, zer more serious. Zer more serious, zer more gravity, ja?"

"Wow… A sort of landed gentry theory?"

"Und zen vee haff zer spontaneous emissions – zat not so nice."

"You must be running out of relatives…?"

"Ja-ja… Big problem! But, vee can't solve problems by using zer same kind of zinking vee used venn vee created zem. Zat's how I got my genial idea for zer next season."

"I am going to regret asking what that is, aren't I?"

"I dink tso. Zer best circus acts involve defying gravity, ja? Under zese stringent testing conditions, vaan figure out of place in zer balancing act, und zer whole theoretical edifice endz up in a pile of broken bones on zer floor, ja? Tso, I am zinking, vatt if zer whole big top verr being pulled zrough zee air und it ist zer audience zat does zer falling?"

Sean bulged his eyes. "Are you sure that will work?"

"Of course not! Vee don't vant to be certain. Certainty is zer mother of convention."

"Ah… I see. A principle of uncertainty, perhaps?"

"We mustn't be sure about that. At zer turn of zer

century, physicists knew just about everyzing about vat made zer universe tick. 'Just a couple of puzzles remained,' zey said. 'Sort zem out und vee are all out of business.' But zose little anomalies, zat refused to comply to zer vee-knows-it-all-already models, nagged und nagged, und finally attempts to resolve zem destroyed zer whole fabric of physics. Like pulling a single thread out of a jacket. Like tso. Darn... I shouldn't use zat example so much, nja?"

Sean remembered the mathematical despatches from Karl Schwarzschild he was still carrying. "I think you can now find an answer to the true nature of time and space - and without any cheating." He jiggled the bag of fudge reprovingly, before tossing it to a passing mongoose.

The show had started to a packed, expectant audience. Waiting in the wings for his entrance cue, Einstein pointed at the cannons. "In dis kosmic reality show, space and time tell stuff how to move..." He then waved at the vast, heavy dome of the tent above them. "But it ist stuff vich ist telling space-time how to curve." He spread his arms and imitated an aeroplane swooping around.

"And if the universe is expanding?" asked Sean.

"Vee should test zat theory, ja? To expand zer tent vee need something really explosive und gaseous... I know! I vill increase zer peanut percentage in zer elephant feed. A little dangerous to be around but shudd do zer trick. I vill call it zer 'air bag'."

"Yes," nodded Sean. "A good model should always take inflation into account. Tell me, what is that elevator equipment for?" he asked, indicating two large boxes being winched up to a high platform.

"Vee play a kind of reality game. Zere are two closed elevators. Zat man you saw being dragged screaming into vaan of zem ist zer volunteer, ja? Now he ist inside und cannot see out. Zer only equipment he haff ist a small rubber ball. Vaan of zer elevators ist accelerated upvards by a rocket, vile zer udder ist allowed to plummet freely. Zer audience can see vich is vich, but zer contestant inside cannot see out – zer game ist for zer contestant to vurk out, by only bouncing zer ball, vether he ist accelerating up, still, or in free fall. If he gets zer answer right in relatively good time, he can release a parachute. If he gets it vrong, … like now… ei-ja! He ist, let's say, relatively badly off. From zer scatter pattern on zer ground vee derive zer curve of classical inertia of thought."

"But that's not fair!" said Sean, trying not to laugh at the antics of the comic ambulance team, which had arrived to clean up in time for the next act.

"Fair ist for Var. Dis ist der show business."

"So does this 'crash course' help the public understand your complex theory?"

"In all probability, no. But it ist greatly funny."

"You think there is still a place for comedy in mathematics?"

"Oh, ja. But it vas not alvay so easy. Venn I vas just four year in zer age-ing, zomvaan is me giving a book about Euclid's geometry. 'For a joke' zey said. I also had heard zat Newton ist said to haff laughed only vaan time in his life – und zat vas venn zomvaan asked him if Euclid vas necessary. I read zer book ten times und didn't even chuckle. I knew zenn zat I vas going to haff difficulties mit zer mathematics. So I vent in for relative humour instead - you know, stand-up routines telling gags about my family missing trains und trams... I got poor reviews initially, but since zenn I have built up quite a following."

"And that apparatus over there?" asked Sean, indicating a large collapsible telescopic pole to one side of the circus ring. It was made up tackily to look like the Leaning Tower of Pisa, complete with a launch platform on top.

"I first person to be vinning zer cannonball olympics since Galileo revrote zer rules. Vee drop zer cannonball vhile zer reference tower is accelerated downwards. Zer result ist relative. Vee vin und vee vin big, believe me."

"But... just a minute... I thought your relativity theory states that the acceleration would be the same no matter what the acceleration of the reference frame?"

"Ja. But venn I say zer result ist relative, I mean zer judges are family." Einstein winked one of his enormous fun-loving eyes, then danced into the ring to do his popular equations medley routine, which has since become a standard in universities around the world, to thunderous appreciation.

After he came off, and was scraping the elephant poop from his enormous shoes, Sean asked him:

"So, what did you win in the cannonball competition?"

Einstein jiggled the coins in his pocket. "Mit today's theory, only my lunch. But mit mein electro-mojo effect theory, I zink I can sving zer hip, younger judges to avard me zer Nobel prize after zer Var."

"Wow..."

"Do you are knowing vhy it ist called zer Nobel

prize? It ist because it ist vorth such much a lot of money, zer vinner falls victim to zer udder 'Relative Effect' - resulting in huge numbers of previously unknown relatives spontaneously appearing to zer doorstep. Tso vee vinners must to take avay zer door bell. Hence zer nickname: 'No-Bell Prize', for cleverness over und beyond all recommended social decency."

"And what will you do with the money?"

"Give it to my vife tso she will accept my proposal to become my ex-vife."

"That's sad. Tell me, professor, why did you leave your wife?"

"It vas all my mother's idea."

"Really? Why was that?"

"Vee lived such much a long time in Italy, Mamma began to speak-a like zee Italians. She say to me: 'Einie' - zat means number 1, because I vas zer first - 'Einie, she say, marriage is-a all-a 'bout-a loyalty. So you be-a faith-a-ful to your-a wife, or else-a.' Tso, given zer choice, I chose Elsa. It vas Mamma's idea. Alvay listen at your mamma, Johnny."

Sean let a reluctant tear escape. "I don't even know where my mother is… I miss her so."

Einstein placed a reassuring hand on Sean's shoulder. "You know zomzing, Johnny? It zeem to me zat your mother has not vanished entirely."

"Really? Do you know where she is?"

"I zink she ist maybe just stepped outside zer Lorentz limits."

"The Lorentz limits?"

"You play zer ball for foot, ja? Vell, zee Lorentz limits are like zer sidelines in footyball games - zey describe zer area of permitted play in zer time und zer space of zer past und zer future. Even if you run like me to zer pub after vurk, you are not ever getting outsideways of zer Lorentz limits."

"Are you saying my mother is off-side in some sort of cosmic football match?"

"Zomvaan ist her to give zer red card, ja? My guess ist your mother took maybe a stroll outside zese limits. She shuddn't be able zat to do. But mammas… do zey ever listen to zeir sons, eh? If she had studied physics she vudd haff known it vas impossible, but it zeems she hasn't und zerefore felt free to give it a whirl. All you haff to do ist look in zer right place - outside zer light cone zat defines vat ist possible und vat ist ein imprecise possibility."

"You're saying it is my own decision not to see through what is hiding her from me?"

"I zink tso. It ist time for us - or more precisely you - to zink outside zer box."

By now the show had come to its end, and the happy, if slightly mass-depleted, crowd were returning to the more classical reality outside.

His personalised equation autograph duties finally over, Einstein returned to Sean. "Now, Johnny Seulpierre, vat ist it you have brought to me vrom Schwarzy boy at zer front?"

Sean handed his bundle of papers to the professor. "First of all, here are his Field Equations applying General Relativity to a large mass compressed to the critical Schwarzschild Radius, the point at which gravity is so gooey, light can no longer escape."

"The *spiki celestii* vich describes zer Blob von Dark has been found? Incredible!" Einstein opened the treatise and devoured the lines of maths like you or I might a plate of squiggly spaghetti. "Fantastish! Now I can finish my predictions for zer curvature of space … und get zem right zis time!"

"And he also gave me this. He said 'Thank you. You were right, it was very useful'." Sean pulled up his sleeve and, with a Frodoian look of regret, took off his digital watch and handed it to the star professor.

Einstein took the watch and held it for a few moments with great affection, but then handed it back to Sean. "Vy don't you keep it, ja? If I am not vrong, it is, after all, yours?"

"But, professor, how did you know…?"

"Archimedes - he be telling me."

"He what?! How?"

"Von dis…" Einstein started pulling things out of one of his deep, patchwork clown pockets. After the yo-yos, sherbert wrappers, party balloons, a live mouse, and what appeared to be parts of a relativity demonstration model train set, he found what he was looking for - an old notebook. Sean took it and began to read. His eyes nearly popped right out of his head.

"But, professor… these are by John the Measurer! This is what is written in the long lost Swansong Palimpsest of Archimedes, last seen by Isaac Barrow in Constantinople in 1659."

"He vas not zer last European to it be seeing. Zer original ist still in zer library in Constantinople, but it has been found und read by a great Dane, Johan Heiberg. Und he made zis copy."

"Wow… So you know all about Archimedes and what happened to his notebook after the fall of Syracuse?"

"Ja-ja… But it ist not complete – zer palimpsest ist in vat for ein terrible condition – it has been scraped over und zum lousy pop songs of zer time written over zer top by a bored monk. But Heiberg managed to read enough to tell us zat zer famous votchbearer ist Sviss, und vill vaan day return to zer mortal vorld to reclaim zer holy relic, zer SANG Re.al, vich der Measurer spirited out of Egypt to India und China to keep it von zer Romans."

"So, you have been expecting me… Karl Schwarz-schild knew I was coming all along?"

"Ja-ja."

"But how did you get this notebook?"

"Heiberg ist giving to me his notes because I vas been living so long in Chocoland, I feel now Sviss - as Sviss as a roll in zer hay, playing Heidi und seek…"

He swung his violin around and plucked a quick yodel doodle dandy:

"Singing heidi-heidi-ho, she's my girl you know…"

"But, how did you get the watch? The last time I saw it, it was on the altar in the Haunted House in 1800. I have been assuming that, since Napoleon evidently failed to complete the Vitruvian Crystal that day, he took the watch away with him."

"I don't know vat he did. But I found zer votch zere in 1905."

"But… how did you find the Haunted House?!"

"Venn I vas young, my family lived in Milan und Svitzzyland. It vas not hard to find zer House vrom zer trail of freaked-out door-to-slam salesmens. Und I also deduced vrom Laplace's vritings zat he knew zer Vitruvian Crystal vudd not complete zat day you disappeared.."

"He knew?! But why didn't it complete? Not that I am sorry, of course."

"Laplace vas genius. He knew he could not calculate zer geometry necessary to complete zer Vitruvian Crystal. To do zat you need not only four-dimensional geometry but five-dimensional."

"I see. *Spiki celestii* was still not complete."

"Ja. In terms of zer third, fourth, und fifth dimensions, Newton's Classical Mechanics are zer truth, zer hole in truth, und anyzing but zer truth."

"So," cried Sean happily. "Laplace was just playing along with Napoleon in order to free me and give us, you, future scientists, time to find a solution to the chronoclysm – the timeline collapse! He knew all along!"

"Exact tso. A true scientist vudd never abandon his search for truth in exchange for power und vealth, or even fame, like Napoleon assumed he could seduce him vith. Laplace vanted zer truth like I vant sherbert liquorice drops on Sunday afternoons. Zat ist vhy Napoleon must to lose in zer end - despite his brilliance, he vas satisfied mit relative truth - it vas enough just to know more zan zer ozzers. Big boo-boo. No-vaan can escape vrom zer underlying reality forever. Und zis fundamental reality determines everyzing und, most important of all, ist independent of us, zer observer. On zis point many of people are not agree mit me. Und never vill I zink." He sighed, and squeezed a bulb to make his face stream with water.

It was Sean's turn to console his new friend. "I always knew the ex-Marquis was my friend."

This cheered Einstein up. "Because I knew dis, I

knew a new t'eory of time und space vibbly-vobblies had yet to be discovered … oddervise it vudd never haff occurred to me. I had alvays zought zat vibbly-vobbly time theories verr a case for Doctor 'Oo."

"You know about Doctor Who?!"

"Ja. I meet him. Many time."

"Wow," said Sean. "Then it's all true!"

"Ja-ja. Doctor Hu - he a Chinese psychiatrist friend of mine."

"I see," said Sean, swallowing his sudden dose of regret riens. "Tell me, professor, how is it possible for me to travel through time? How can I find my family and release my friends the TimeRiders? Do you have any idea what is going on inside the VC? What is causing the disruption to the timeline?"

"Do you haff any harder questions, mebbe?"

"Sorry. It's just… I don't know… I go from place to place, time to time, genius to genius… all the time I find out that *spiki celestii* is the key, that somehow time is not what we think it is… and yet I come no closer to understanding anything that has happened to me."

Einstein thought about this for a while, before answering. "I tell you zis: for me, light is fastest thing - universe champion. Gold medal over all distances. Zer Ralph Craig of natural phenomena."

"Ah… I think I see what you mean. The speed of anything is measured by time…"

"Exact tso. Vee need to know more about zer nature of light to understand time. Und it ist zis very same light zat vee vish to cast on zer mysteries of zer universe, nja?"

Sean shuffled through these facts in a desperate

bid to find some holding pattern. "Karl said that inside his Schwarzschild Radius time behaves like space, and space like time. How does *that* work?"

"It ist all explained by zer *spiki celestii* equations: ask any accountant - if zer bottom line goes to zero, you haff infinite problems other end, ja?"

"So what goes to zero?"

"Time. If a ding, you know, like a star, get really heavy, obese even, zenn time must to slow down tso it still can to do vat it ist stars like to do. Ozzervise it no longer can to fit into reality. Und zer heavier it gets, zer more zer time it drags. You never notice? Zer fatter zer singers zer longer zer operas? Und now I ask you, vatt vudd happen if you haff infinite mass?"

"Time would stop entirely! The event horizon on a black hole…" said Sean.

"Und it ist zer same for energy und space. Und vice-versa. Zat mebbe explain vhy as time get longer my bank account get shorter, ja?"

"So, if any part of the spenmatt gets too big for its equations, time walks out on it?"

"Union rules."

"Ok… That might explain slowing or acceleration of time, but what allows me to time *travel*?"

"Vell, actually, you don't 'travel'. You are novhere tso you are everyvenn. It all depend vhere your mind is focused."

"But if it is a question of mind focus, that would mean anybody could do it?"

"Nein. Normal peoples are trapped to four dimensions. Like an ant on a leaf vee must to flow mit zer river. But you - you und your timeriding friends are be able to access zer dimension zat looks down on zer time dimension, like ein fisherman look down on zis river, und see all zee little ants on zeir little leaves, oblivious of zer ozzer little ants on zeir own little leaves. It ist only venn you are outside zer river can you to put your hook in vhere you vant."

Sean remembered only now the Shrouds' explanation, about how the fastest way between two points on a rotating Earth was to stand still and let the Earth rotate under you. "But why me? Why can I access this fifth dimension?"

"Look, zis no good - if I give you vaan answer you shooting back two more questions, ja? Stop clowning about - zatz my yob."

"So I guess what you are saying is that somehow the Vitruvian Crystal has opened for us a fifth dimension from which we can see the fourth dimension, which is time!"

"Except zat it ist no longer 'time' as vee 'four-dee-bies' zink of it."

"I see. Once you can observe something its nature changes... That is what my Nonno meant when he said time does not exist."

Einstein nodded, pleased with his exceptional student. "He cudd haff added: 'unless you vant it to'."

"Neat," concluded Sean.

"Zatz vatt everybody alvay ist saying about my formulas: neat. Totally incomprehensible but neat und tidy. Zer kids like zem because zey fit on shirt-fronts."

"Ok," said Sean, manhandling the conversation back on track. "Now what?"

"I had rather been hoping you vudd haff supplied zer answer to zat question."

In the event, the answer came in the form of a group of soldiers in classic bad-guy German uniforms, who now stormed into the tent.

"You vill be mit us komming," one of them ordered in a slightly metallic voice.

"Vhere to?"

"Zer palace. Der Kaiser demands to zee you…"

"I vonder vat Big Villy vant vrom me now? Mebbe annudder moustache competition…" Einstein prepared to leave.

"Nein," the soldier looked past Einstein at Sean. "Zer both of you."

* * * *

Chapter Eighteen

Big Willy's Revenge

THE palace was on the same side of Berlin, but further west and hogging the best bend of river view for itself. The soldiers commandeered a passing tram, and forced the driver at bayonet point to change routes to the palace, which left a trail of arterial constriction in the city's circulatory system. After a quick scrum huddle, they reached a decision and allowed other passengers waiting at stops to board, and then shared the takings from the fares amongst themselves.

Eventually, however, they reached the palace, Schloss Charlottenburg, a 17th Century monument to glorious disproportion in every possible sense. Einstein and Sean were marched across the square Court of Honour, enclosed on three sides by the two-storey building, under the watchful eye of an equestrian statue, which made Sean think with a pang of regret of Leonardo's desecrated horse model.

"Zer palace vas named after Queen Sophie Charlotte," Einstein informed his friend who was striking awe. "Zer building ist said to be designed along her own lines."

"So, this is the original…?"

"Sophie's choice. Ja-ja."

"That dome's impressive."

"It's zer Cupola."

"Couple of… what? I see only one."

"Ja-but-ja. Old Sophie vas reputed to be a bit vaan-sided."

They had to pass through an as yet GPS-unsupported maze of rooms and halls. Most were testimonials to familial self-appointment, part of a long-term genetic recycling plan. The last one, however, extended entirely from the ego of the current incumbent, who obviously carried on the family tradition and penchant for cowardly long-distance murder, expressed in hundreds of severed horns of stags and also-rans. Boar tusks offered to hold the dress-, trench-, and skinned-animal coats of guests, although they were warned that blood drippings would be cleaned at the cost of the causant.

While the dignitaries and indignants various were lined up in servility-asserting order, a page came into the room and challenged the flooring to a maintain integrity match with his conchstick, or whatever it is they smash into the ground to establish hearing rights. He announced in a strained bellow:

"Majestics, sub-majestics, lords, ladies, gentlemen, damsels-in-excess, and lower trophic levels, I give you the one and only, His Royal Majesty, by the special thumbs-up of Mr Biggy, the most Imperial of all Germans, the biggest buckstop this side of the tax divide, the King of our very own Prussia, Frederick William Victor Albert, Wilhelm the Second, otherwise known by what is left of his people as "Big Willy", the uncontested and uncontestable reigning heavyweight moustache champion of the world …"

The page took a deep breath, while his eyes entered a peculiar middle-distance focus, before he plunged into his master's secondary address list: "… and in the category of Duke: Grand Duke of the Lower Rhine and Posen, Duke of Silesia, Saxony, Angria, Westphalia, Pomerania, Junenburg, Schleswig *and* Holstein while we are at it, Crossen, Magdeburg, Bremen, Guelderland, Jülich, Cleves, Berg, Wends, Kashubians, Lauenburg, Mecklenburg, Landgrave, Hesse and Thuringia. *In* the category of Margrave: the ever-popular Margrave of Upper Lusatia, Brandenburg, and the whatever-that-is Burgrave of Nuremberg…"

One of the more pretentiously dressed and bemedalled of the courtiers stepped forward: "Your majesty…" he tried to begin with appropriate court gestures, which were akin to someone polishing his shoes while doing callisthenics.

The page went on regardless in his sonorous tone: "*In* the category of Prince: Prince of Orange, Rugen, East Friesland, Paderborn, Pyrmont, Halberstadt, Münster, Minden, Osnabrück, Hildesheim, Verden, Kammin, Fulda, Nassau, Moers…"

"Your majesty…" tried the court gesture again, to no avail.

"*In* the category of Count: Princely Count of Henneberg, Count of the Mark, Hohenstein, Ravensberg, Tecklenburg, Lingen, Mansfield, Sigmaringen, Veringen…"

"Your most gracious maj…"

"…*and* last, but not in any particular way least, the Lord of Frankfurt," and the page finished with a special flourish of his own invention.

The courtier looked menacingly at the page. "Finished?"

"Yes, my lord."

"No, he has not, if he knows what's good for him!" The Kaiser had come in by now, congruously resplendent in his white Prussian officer's uniform, with plumed helmet, ridiculous epaulettes, and black knee-high boots that would have made great waders, fully loaded with fresh pomp and trailing all sorts of circumstance in reserve. "He has left one out!" he growled.

"Sire?" mumbled the page as he quickly ran through his mental notes in acquired servile panic.

"I am Margrave of Upper *and* Lower Lusatia, if my memory serves me right. Start again…" He left to repeat his entrance.

And so, while the hallful of people stood and groaned in silence, the page went through the list again, and again, and not only that but once more, until, two hours and several fainting ladies later, the Kaiser was satisfied.

"Rightey-ho, rightey-ho," he fussed, shooing the page away. "Don't bore everybody, go away… go away."

The page bowed stiffly from cramp, and backed out of the room, rueing that his lord and master had more than five of these official ceremonies per day.

"Your Imperial and Royal Majesty," began the courtier yet again.

"Oh do hurry up, I haven't got all day," complained the Kaiser, stamping impatiently to the waiting line of guests in the 'Meet the Kaiser' ceremony.

While the group of mightey-highs made its whimmish way down the line of involuntary admirers, Einstein seemed used to the tedium, and had brought the

Field Equations to read. He marvelled at the intricacies of Karl's results.

"You know," he enthused to Sean. "Zese calculations help show us zat zere ist a set of conditions, Schwarzie's singularity, vhere vee no longer can to distinguish between of time und space or energy or matter. Zat means zat if zer spenmatt ist a vave, zenn time ist also a vave, ja? Vee are all surfers - riding a time vave through zer spenmatt." He did a beachboy hang-ten and accidently knocked a plump lady's hat off.

Sean thought of the strange underground entrance to the Haunted House, his mother and even Shrodie the half-dead cat. "If this is the case, do you think it is possible to step between the wave fronts and be lost to the timeline? Be in a frame of film out of sync with the projector shutter?"

"Ja! Exact tso! To step outside time you vudd need to in between jump zer arriving timewave fronts – to do zis you vudd need to be pretty fast. Faster even zann me to zer pub after school's out. Und believe of me, zat ist saying zomzing. Tso, I zink in our case, to beat zis vorld record it ist best to cheat."

"But nature never cheats!"

"You zink tso? Vich animal has landspeed record all time?"

"Er… the cheetah…"

"I rest my case."

Further up the line in attendance, the Kaiser was regaling some neo-vegetarians loudly with tales of his favourite bloodsports.

"And the time eggs?" Sean asked Einstein. "Do you have any theories about what is causing them?"

"You know, for my magic tricks, venn I make a hollow egg, to remove zer albumen - no yolking matter - I am need to make of two holes, und I blow in vaan, ja? Tso, if vee zink of zer Vitruvian Crystal as being not a single hole but in actual a pair of holes, vaan black und vaan vhite, shortcircuiting zer two sides of zer timeline..."

"A wormhole?"

"Vell... more like a leak in zer plumbing, ja? Und if zis plumbing is being anyzing like zer my plumbing, zer pressure vudd be enormous. Under it, time vudd surely to be compressed - perhaps even to ein liquid, vich bubbles up on our side as it ist forced out by zer pressure vrom zer udder side."

"And do you think this is disturbing the delicate balance between the spenmatt and time?"

"Nein. Time ist not being ein fundamental element of zer universe - it only can to exist relative to an observer trying to explain vatt he dinks he ist experiencing. Zomvaan trying to remember if he left his umbrella on zer tram yesterday, or vill do it tomorrow. Zer universe, it no care. Zat because it no ever rain up zere in zer kosmos, ja?"

"I see..." lied Sean. "You're saying time and the reality it creates exist..."

"... only in zer eye of zer beholder."

"Schwarzie explained the timeline as being an imbalance in the background spenmatt - like an arc of electricity between two charged points."

"Ja-ja. Und it lazy! Lazy, lazy, lazy! Zer little shirker quickly resets itself to neutral given half zer opportunity."

Sean thought to himself: 'And would that

'opportunity' be a young idiot who falls down a shaft under a house with the final time egg in his pocket?'

Einstein continued: "Time-space is like zer inner tube of a tyre, it ok till zomvaan put a pin into it - und ours has got a flat."

Sean remembered Laplace's metaphor of the pin prick in the chronoclasmic bubble. "So the VC is such a pin - puncturing a hole in space-time, causing the past and the future to flood back to the time-neutral cosmic background through a single point of collapse. Pau has been right all along. It *is* me. I am the one who has shorted out the arc of time?"

"Zat crazy!"

"Yes. Sorry."

"Tso ist probably correct."

They stood in silence for a while, contemplating the end of all time, a mere century away.

"Vithout a doubt," sighed the clown. "Zer kosmic eiderdown occasionally loses a feather."

He read on again in silence till he suddenly burst out with: "Do you know vat zese equations mean?" he asked Sean in an excited whisper.

"No."

"Till today I vas stuck on zer surface of zer Earth. Mit zese equations I can start applying my theory to zer entire kosmos. Today zer vorld, tomorrow zer universe!"

A little corporal behind them heard this and said to himself: I like that, I might use it. In his notebook, he found a section where he had scratched out 'Trench 34b', and replaced it, so the phrase read: 'Today zer groundfloor... tomorrow zer Vorld!' He added a note

Vitruvian Boy

in the margin: 'und zer day after, zer universe!' " It was a preliminary draft of a book he was planning with the working title of 'My Bitch mit zer Vorld, und vat others are going to haff to do about it.'

Big Willy had finally reached them. It was then that Sean noticed the Kaiser had a slightly withered left arm. He always carried his gloves in his left or rested it on his sword hilt, in an attempt to make the arm look longer and stronger – the very embodiment of politics, thought Sean.

"How's my circus going?" Big Willy asked Einstein, after the professor had whipped up a quick sausage balloon effigy for him.

"Vee're doing very vell," and Einstein jiggled the box of tentflap takings he had wrestled off the chimpanzee before leaving. The Kaiser took it and said: "Good. Keep up the good work, or whatever it is you chaps do down there."

"Excuse me, your imperialism, but vhy do you haff zer President of zer Prussian Academy of Sciences on a leash?" asked Einstein, indicating the bald, greedily moustached man being tugged along behind the Kaiser's sycophancy party.

"I'm walking the Planck."

He passed on to Sean. "Ah… and this puerile pile of patheticness would be?"

"Sean Seulpierre," said Sean, bowing awkwardly. "Your mostly majestic thingybob, your lordly mighty-high…"

"Sean Seulpierre… ah… interesting," said Big Willy in a faraway kind of voice, stroking his enormous moustache, by decree the largest in the kingdom,

Big Willy's Revenge

and if he has his way, soon to be hailed as the largest schnautzer in all the world. "You know what my family name is? Hohenzollern."

Sean sifted through his mental German lexicon. "That means 'high taxes' doesn't it?" he annotated too loudly.

"It's a family trademark." A servant lifted Big Willy's moustache up with a special golden rake, so he could take another puff on his cigar, carried by another servant on the prongs of what looked like a barbecue fork, and then raked it back into place. Never short of irrelevant small talk, the Kaiser went on: "Do you know why, young Seulpierre, I grow this fantastic moustache?"

"To hide your lip wobbling?" suggested Sean, guilty of honesty beyond all reasonable tact.

"Besides that. You see, it is to remind my people that Big Willy and Mr Biggy have a thing going on - *apparently*, all I have to say is that I carry out the Earthly bits of His plan which have been, *apparently*, revealed to me only, and they march off to do extraordinarily stupid things. Wonderful, isn't it?"

"Yes. Fantastic. Does his highliness, by any chance, add a little footnote of his own to this divine revelation which involves Germany becoming the ruler of the whole world?"

"I wouldn't put it in precisely those terms, but something like that," smiled the grey-heading king.

"Mind if *I* put it in exactly those terms?" asked the scruffy corporal behind them, taking notes like crazy in his scruffy notebook.

"You there! The wretched rodent rascal there!" It seemed Big Willy specialised in alliterated insults. "Yes you! The one with the total failure for a moustache," called the Kaiser at the corporal. "Show me your book and I'll give you a medal. I've got one left over. Don't want to go to all the trouble of putting it back in the bribes box."

"Dunno…" the corporal clasped the notebook to his chest defensively. "It's kind of private - for now. What sort of medal is it?"

"First tell me why you are not at the front?!" demanded an enormously fat field marshal next to the Kaiser. This was Hindenburg - whose name was mispronounced intentionally by the other staff officers to sound in German like 'mountainous backside'.

The little corporal faked a sore leg. "My cramp…" he said in a wimpy sort of voice.

"Mein Kampf?" The Kaiser snatched the notebook from the man. "Good title. But why '*My* Struggle' - surely it should be '*Our* Struggle'."

"It's a personalisation of world woes - what I call the Weltschmeltz theory. It involves a meditation technique to develop highly-focused paranoia. I use it to wile away the long sentry duties. I am thinking of turning one of its applications into a board game called 'World Conquest'."

"No doubt you will find lots of bored players to join you." The Kaiser tossed the book back to him. "Still, a deal is a deal. Take this medal off my hands, would you?"

"But… it is the Iron Cross," stammered the corporal.

"Ah yes… so it is. Any problem with that? Prefer a silver one, or maybe gold?" Big Willy showed his own metallurgical collection as proudly as any Tom Sawyer may have his junk hoard collection.

"But… I have already got one of them," retro-argumented the corporal.

"You've *already* got one?!" the Kaiser flabbered all over his gast.

"Jawohl. Some fat guy in a general's uniform stuck it into my chest in 1914. Hurt like life. I missed a whole six weeks of carnage and mayhem afterwards thanks to him. And that was only a second class one. I suppose that's because I am Austrian, not a real German. I can't possibly accept a second cross to bear - nowhere to hang it, you see." He indicated his skinny, unimpressive chest. "Unless they were made into a pair of earrings…" His face brightened at the thought.

"Corporal!" bellowed the field marshal.

"Jawohl?" His right hand snapped up by some strange reflex into a position akin to a policeman stopping traffic.

"You take this medal now, like a good boy, and let's not hear any complaints, alright?"

The little man sighed. All he had ever wanted was to be an artist.

The Kaiser hung the medal by its ribbon around the corporal's neck. Sean could swear he saw the faintest of green, eery-glowy light pass from the Kaiser to the soldier when he did so, reminiscent of past regrets, and the little corporal-artist-earring fetishist stopped his whingeing.

"Oh, and while you're here, give us a quote to repaper the palace would you?" Big Willy indicated the fading wallpaper that was starting to come off in places. "I can tell you're a paperhanger by your distinctive handslap action."

After the Kaiser and his roadies had moved out of

Vitruvian Boy

the carnage trophy room, the little corporal turned to Einstein and Sean, and said in an entirely different and sneering voice: "Well, well, this *is* going to be fun. We meet again, Sean Seulpierre."

Sean felt the presence of a dozen heavily armed soldiers sneak-clanking up behind him.

"Cespuglio!"

"At your disservice. I may as well have a little gloat at your expense, mayn't I?"

"Mayn't you?"

"Isn't that a word any more? Or yet, or whatever – getting a bit confused these days... No matter. What's a word compared to this..." The corporal indicated the concave of soldiers in spiked helmets, armed with rifles and bayonets, and looking every inch the indispensable background decoration sinister.

"The Invertabrakes?" demanded Sean, unafraid.

"And a licensed firing squad." Cespuglio pointed out the boy scout-like badges they all wore, showing a comically stylised death squad. He then flicked a lapel of Sean's uniform. "You are a deserter from the front. Penalty..." Cespuglio cherished the suspense, before saying: "My entertainment."

"But you still need me! Without me you have no more need of the Invertabrakes and they will abandon you!" Sean addressed this more to the soldiers, looking for the Centurion among their death-is-glory faces.

"I'll take that chance, just to have the pleasure," said Cespuglio. "Escort! Take the watchbearer to the Palace execution ground. I think I'll use the thirty-metre range today. You may as well come too, Herr Professor Einstein. I am sure you would like to witness the end of the hope all you mathematicians were counting on, to combat the evil that infests men's souls - i.e. me."

"Zank you for being tso considerate," replied the physicist.

As they all marched out in block formation, Cespuglio was in a chatty mood: "As the Kaiser, I had an execution range set up in the palace grounds for after-dinner entertainment, and to add spice to diplomatic negotiations. We hold execution competitions for the guests at different calibres over 30m, 50m and 100m ranges. I was also thinking of extending the range to implement a new edition of the cannonball olympics, with some major changes to the rules."

Sean checked to see if Einstein was still following them, before he asked his tormentor: "Since I am no longer a threat to you, would you mind telling me what happened after I left the Haunted House in 1800? Where did the watch go to?"

"Why should I tell you anything?" replied Cespuglio, with one of his favourite sneers.

"It would be gloating over your victim and showing off in an irritating fashion."

"Insult on fatality? Good enough reason. Yes, I may as well tell - considering you have no future left to make use of it. After you left us in 1800, the watch disappeared with you, leaving only an image. Napoleon, the little ingrate, had no option but to reabsorb me, still in my weakened condition, in order to keep the Invertabrakes on his side, while he romped around Europe trying to find you and the watch. The watch would be enough, because, as we all know, you are drawn to it. As sure as a fly to a Venus flytrap. Snap!" Cespuglio coordinated this last word with suddenly snapping shut the revolver he had been loading, and Sean immediately regretted jumping.

They had left the building now and were walking across a large open courtyard. On the other side, a beautiful garden and orangerie stretched away towards the river. "It looks like rain…" remarked Sean.

"What are you complaining about? You don't have to walk back!" replied Cespuglio.

He continued his story. "That little self-appointed emperor, Napoleon, went crazy. He thought the British had the watch, because of their famous Blackwatch Regiment. Despite the great risk of eardrum perforation from their first line of defence, bagpipes, especially to people of his low altitude, he planned an invasion to look for it. Then I whispered into his ear that it was in Berlin here, and he called off the invasion and marched east instead. But when the Austrians mistimed the Battle of Austerlitz so badly, he realised they could not have it either. Then Wellington landed in Portugal, and let out rumours that the watch was with him, in order to draw Napoleon into a war of devastating attrition in Spain.

"Finally, Napoleon's spies told him it was in Moscow. Which funnily enough was actually true. It had been drawn back to Kath the Math's porphyry egg. As soon as he had found it, he abandoned his army to the mercy of the Cossack pawnbroker packs, and raced back to Paris, intending to use it to draw you into a trap, and complete the VC finally, so that he could become the Eternal Emperor in my place – he knew, despite having found his precious watch again, that he was, after all, just mortal like any of the rest of you lesser beings, and was running out of time."

"He was always a little short in that respect,"

remembered Sean.

"But, before he could do that, somebody…" and Cespuglio smiled broadly, "betrayed him. He was captured and sent into exile on the Isle of Elba. But after less than a year, he escaped to have one last go at creating himself as the world's master. But his staff misheard his instructions to take him to the VC - and took him instead to the Battle of Wassertoeletten."

"Never heard of it," said Sean, impressed by the story despite himself.

"That's the local Belgian name for 'Waterloo'. When the incontinent English had finished with the Wassertoeletten, they sent Napoleon, with me still helpless and trapped in him, and the watch, to the Island of Saint Helena, way down in the south of the Atlantic, where it rains nearly all the time. Sometimes for the peculiar climatic conditions created by the incidence of the Gulfstream and the deepsea Atlantic conveyor belt, but usually just for the sheer heck of it."

"So Josie was right all along," nodded Sean. "He lived out his final days as a wet Nappy after all. But, how could he lose, if he had the Invertabrakes helping him?"

"Good question."

"And the good answer?"

"I was rather hoping you could supply me that."

"Me?!" cried Sean in surprise. "What do I know? I am a century behind in current affairs!"

"What did you say to the Centurion just before you time-jumped, when you fell on the altar?"

"Nothing. I mean… nothing important…"

Cespuglio stopped the procession well short of the execution range. A crowd was gathering around the official's table, and the superior classes were looking down from the more expensive viewing balconies of the palace. Sean fancied he recognised something about a figure in a sergeant's uniform, putting out little white flags to mark the execution range distances. He was sure it was the Centurion.

Cespuglio lowered his voice on sight of him, pulled Sean out of hearing range of the Invertabrake guards, and demanded. "Tell me! Tell me now! What did you say to the Centurion?!"

Sean realised just in time that he had a last card to play. He thought quickly. "First, tell me what happened to the watch after St. Helena."

"Oh very well. Much good it will do you. Twenty years after Napoleon died on Saint Helena, his body vas exhumoured."

"Exhumoured?"

"No laughing matter."

"Yes, I remember the story," said Sean. "The body was said to be in an inexplicably perfect condition."

"Exactly so. It was brought back to Paris where it was entombed in Les Invalides Military Retirement Village, where it still is today."

"And you… and the watch?"

"We were entombed with him."

"What?! But…" Sean glanced down involuntarily towards the watch on his wrist, and resisted the temptation to wipe it on his trousers.

If Cespuglio had noticed anything, all he said was: "And have a guess who it was that brought the body back and gave it an honour guard at the burial?"

"The … Old Imperial Guard! You mean…?!"

"Precisely so," gleamed Cespuglio. "The

Invertabrakes had arranged for the sarcophagus. It is a very strange one. Five nested containers. A lead casket inside mahogany inside ... I forget the flavours of the others..."

"Like Kath the Math's eggnest!"

"Oh yes. The French, they always exaggerate. But when they finally got around to the last shell, it was made of..."

"Let me guess... pink porphyry?" replied Sean.

"Chocky-block full of the time eggs. It booted up and transmitted both me and the watch to the Haunted House, where the Invertabrakes were waiting with the Iron Crown ... and an infant boy."

"Who?"

"The next crown prince-in-waiting-room of Austria-Hungary and Quiche-Lorraine, son of the Holy-Mackerel Emperor. Through the Crown, they loaded me into him. The shock overpowered the little brat's senses, and I, Cespuglio the Not-At-All-Nice, was trapped inside an imbecile for sixty years."

"Wow... Didn't anybody notice?"

"Not in a royal family."

"And the watch?"

"They left it in the House. They could not destroy it, since it exists in all time simultaneously, just like the Shrouds. But it was safe in the House, because no-one apart from the Invertabrakes knew of the secret entrance."

"Until Einstein calculated its location," applauded Sean, and the clown-professor took a theatrical bow. "Just as Galileo had, and Laplace."

Einstein acknowledged the plaudits. "Ja-ja. I vas

going to zer Haus und founded zer votch. I lent it to Schwarzie to help vurk out zer final bit of *spiki celestii*. Und I knew it vudd to draw you, Sean, to it eventually. Und here you are."

"Which saved me the effort of looking for him myself," counter-smiled Cespuglio.

"I know who you are being, Cespuglio," challenged the physicist. "You just call yourself zer Eternal Emperor, but your true place ist as zer Extreme Being, trapped alone out in zom future timeline. A timeline zat has been fractured und inverted, nja?"

This seemed to make Cespuglio a little uncomfortable. Einstein went on: "You took zer vaan opportunity to escape - at zer moment of zer completion of zer VC in 2010, by svapping places mit Sean's Nonno. It vas a perfect plan – except zomzing has gone wrong, nja?" He pointed at the soldiers. "Zer Invertabrakes are not obeying you tso blindly any zer more, ja? In zer factuals, zey are trying to neutralize you. Vhy ist zat, I vunder? It ist because zey haff realised you haff no intention of ending zer time crisis. You are tricking zem. Tso, tell us, how did you to escape vrom zer royal imbecile? Alzough I am sure you felt perfectly at home zere."

"You're barking up the wrong photoautotrophic eukaryote, Herr Professor," answered Cespuglio. "When the imbecile died, the Invertabrakes *had* to retrieve me. You see, despite what you say, they cannot disobey me truly. They thought they had the perfect plan. They thought all they had to do was load me back into the Crown when the idiot prince was dying – and then return the Crown to Italy, to Monza Cathedral. But this was only half their plan. Because sooner or later there had to be another incoronation of an Italian king. So what did they do?"

Einstein's eyes opened wide.

"What is it, Professor?" asked Sean.

"In 1900," replied Einstein sadly, "zer King von Italy vas assassinated – not far vrom zer Cathedral von Monza."

"Wow!" contributed Sean.

"They thought in this way to end me - me! Cespuglio, the one who lays time to waste…"

"Or simply zer 'TimeVaster'?" suggested Einstein.

"And so why didn't it work?" asked Sean, deciding to use his last minutes on Earth to be intrigued.

"Because I was too smart for them," smugged back the self-styled TimeWaster, sneering at the Invertabrakes standing in a defeated, servile group. "After the fall of Napoleon in 1814, the crown was taken to Vienna. The Austrians, not too up there in the originality department, imitated Napoleon, knowing the power of the myth of the Corona ferrea on the imaginations of sheep, of whom they had a seeming infinite supply. They created the Order of the Iron Crown, Austrian style. And made little souvenir medals for valour and self-sacrifice in the name of excessive wealth and prestige of the ruling elite. Now, I arranged for a piece of the Crown to be removed secretly and this was used to fashion a medal of this Order."

"Ah…" said Sean. "And this was enough to allow you to travel via the medal, rather than the Crown itself?"

"Call it a router."

"I remember now!" cried Einstein. "A pair of years ago, zer Kaiser vas given a medal of zer Order of zer

Iron Crown in recognition of his being zer very first royal to actually do zomzing for humanity."

"*This* Kaiser?!" increduled Sean.

"Ja-ja. I zink it vas for authorising zer reduction of Wagner operas vrom six days to four."

"Funny how chance always plays my way, isn't it?" smiled Cespuglio at the irony of the event.

"So you were uploaded into the Kaiser for services to humanity," concluded Sean. "And the first thing you did was start the world's bloodiest war?"

"My masterpiece."

Einstein finished the story. "Und now zat you see zer end ist coming, you haff uploaded yourself into zis Austrian corporal, who has megalomania down to a fine art."

"It is going to be delightful. Now, enough talk. Time out, Sean Seulpierre –it has been a pleasure persecuting you."

"But why, Cespuglio, why do you do it?"

Cespuglio was suddenly deadly serious and tinged with malevolent evil. "I'll tell you why. When *spiki celestii* is crushed, great fires leap - hungry fires that feed on the flesh of books and the paper of people. I fuel these flames, raise clots of smoke, to blot out the heavens, to break the sight of celestial instruction. *That* is why I do it. Guards…!"

"But I haven't told you what I said to the Centurion!" Sean punched back in desperation.

"Are you going to?"

"Well… no."

"Then it doesn't matter, does it? Guards, bring him!"

Sean was made to stand at the end of the long queue, where there was a ticket dispenser. Cespuglio tore a number off and gave it to Sean. "222. Somehow appropriate."

A board overhead showed the letters A-F, referring presumably to the six stakes at the far end of the shooting range. And the numbers constantly changing alongside were calling up the target audience.

The next batch of men were being tied to the stakes and spoon-fed some jelly and cream.

"What's going on there?" asked Sean.

"Oh, they are just shooting some desserters," replied the man in front, clutching his own number and checking anxiously that nobody was going to try to jump the queue.

A volley made Sean jump, and another. Before long, the letter F had flipped over to number 221.

"You're up next, Seulpierre," gleed Cespuglio.

"I can count," replied Sean, scanning the faces behind him in the queue, and waving his little ticket to indicate that he was willing to swap numbers with anybody in a hurry.

"You know, Seulpierre," said Cespuglio, nostalgically. "I am almost sorry. It has been delightful knowing there was always someone left for a special form of torment."

Sean appealed to him. "Cespuglio, this whole timeline thing is bigger than you. You have never really understood what is going on. I know that you act the way you do because of the horror of the future world you come from. For which I am truly deeply sorry. But we could work together, find a solution. We don't have to be enemies. This is not going to be a solution: for me, you, or the whole world."

"The difference between me and you, Seulpierre, is that all I need to know is that it works. By that I mean, of course, works for me. So why should I seek to know more? That is all anyone ever needs to know."

While Sean was thus being read his last wrongs, Einstein had slipped away to have a word with the sergeant-at-harms in charge of the firing squad.

"What did he say?" Sean asked him when he returned.

"He said he vudd be happy to talk to me, but he ist a little busy right now. To come back after zer next batch has gone zrough."

"I am in the next batch," annotated Sean verbally.

The distracted professor did not seem to register the import of Sean's words.

"Professor... I said I am in the next batch."

"Er... nein. Technically, you are in zer current batch, ja?" He pointed up at the board, just as a group of just-doing-my-duties arrived to seize Sean and pull him away.

"Professor?" Sean pulled free long enough to give Einstein a quick embrace. "I am sorry to have to leave you like this. It was just getting interesting."

"Never mind, my boy." Einstein winked encouragingly. "Johnny, alvay to remember, ja?, zat in a vorld of uncertainty everyzing ist possible. Not knowing for sure ist zer greatest of all liberations."

"I will miss you, Herr Professor."

"Und I you. But not to vorry. Haff a good trip. Say hello to your Nonno for me."

With that enigma ringing in his mind, Sean was

march-dragged over to the stakes.

"That was cruel, Einstein," commented Cespuglio approvingly. "Giving him some last futile hope!"

"Hope ist never futile, Cespuglio. It ist you zat has no hope."

"What do you mean? Even if the Vitruvian Crystal destroys the future, I don't need it. I can return to the past anytime I want. I can cycle through time forever - I am immortal!"

Einstein looked at him with disconcerting pity. "You zink zere ist ein future for you in zer past, ja? Zat because vee can't break zer Time Paradox Failsafe? Vat happens in 2010 must still to happen ozzervise Johnny vudd not here be being, ist tso you zink, ja?"

"And you know otherwise, I suppose?" snarled Cespuglio. "Against all your own precious scientific rules?"

"Zere can be no exception to zer hard method of science, no escape in human convenience philosophy. Theoreticians who cannot accept zer need for proof vill be asked outside to put 'em up mit zom pretty streetvise mathematicians. Zey mean guys – I know!" He felt his nose. "You und all your maniac armies are nozing compared to three rounds mit zer guardians of zer mathematical proofs!"

"So I disarm them. All I need to do, what I have always done, is suppress *spiki celestii*, and you, my enemies, have no means of organising resistance to my will!"

"Of course you vudd see it like zat. But vee do not wield zer *spiki celestii* just to defeat you. It means more, much zer more. Und it powerful. Zer language of zer gods can reveal all. Not even you, Cespuglio, can hide vrom zer consequences of *spiki celestii* vaance it has been unsheathed - it allows us to communicate mit nature."

"So [*insert expletive of choice*] what?!"

"Vat vee can to learn vrom nature ist zer vaan chance vee haff to avoid zer loss of our species."

Cespuglio laughed. "In the new world I am designing, I have no need of knowledge. Knowledge saps hatred and fear. I *need* them. My armies swell with them."

"Your personal kosmos ist just as likely to collapse no matter vat you zink. Your immortality is dependent on a space to use it in, nja?"

"Are you threatening me?" snarled Cespuglio.

"I am deriving a possible future for you. Zere are still zom variables you haff left – but not many. Do not be too sure about zer Time Paradox Failsafe."

"But the TPF guarantees that all of this is due to the Haunted House - the Vitruvian Crystal *is* formed in 2010 – it *has* to be! Sean *must* be there – he cannot prevent himself from being there."

"But if you are so sure being about zer TPF, vhy do you feel you need to intervene, ja? Vhy do you still fear zer bearer of zer votch?"

"Because…" Cespuglio looked around aimlessly for help. "Because…"

"Inventing certainty in zer midst of uncertainty is not an act of courage, Cespuglio. It ist zer act of a coward. You are such a coward. As are all zer generals und politicians in zis var."

"And Seulpierre? Is he any better?"

"Zat you are about to see."

"But you know as well as I that the 2010 event is a fixed point in time and space…"

"Ah ja? You should read more books zann burn zem. Remember zat later, von't you?"

"He cannot break the TPF!!" tiraded Cespuglio, and everybody turned to stare at him.

"Vell, perhaps zer answer ist zat he does not haff to. I vill tell you zis: arguments do not get resolved by zer bullets. Zey are only highlighted."

"No... I will live forever... I am Cespuglio the Eternal..."

"You are doomed mit zer rest of us, und you know it. Johnny ist our only hope. If you vant to save yourself, you must to save your own vorld too – zere can be no place for you here in a changed vorld – und changed zis vorld must to be if vee are to survive zis crisis."

"But... the TPF..."

"Vhere zere ist an impasse, you haff to let zomzing pass, ja? Johnny ist zer vaan factor zat has zer highest coincidence of zer Laplace probabilities. You are zer vaan mit zer unique position. Use it."

Cespuglio stared at Einstein for a few seconds, before he sneered from habit only, turned and walked deliberately slowly away from the problem.

* * *

The sergeant indicated the table of jellies and knödels. "Are you a desserter?" he asked.

"No, thank you," replied Sean.

"Any last requests?"

"Not just now, thank you."

"How do you like your stake? Well-done?" The sergeant pointed out a large stake full of holes and charred black by hot lead. The next was a smaller stake, a little brown on the outside. "Medium?" He pointed to the last, messy one: "or 'al sangue'?"

"I would like my stake rarer than you could possibly imagine," replied Sean.

A squad of soldiers carrying rifles was marched up and stood in a row facing him.

"Tell me," Sean said to the soldier tying him to a stake. "Why are the firing squad pouring oats into their pockets?"

"They're cereal killers."

"That's funny," said Sean, "I thought it was the English who were the experts in cuisine atrocities."

"Wollen Sie eine Augenbinde?" asked the sergeant-at-harms.

"Do you wish a blindfold?" translated the clerky man on Sean's left.

"And miss all the action?" replied Sean in perfect German. "Look, I am Swiss. I don't need a translator. We are born dictionaries."

"Hey, just doing my job, ok?" replied the man in a whisper. "Don't make me redundant or it's the Eastern Front for me."

The sergeant-at-harms now pinned a round object on Sean's jacket, just above the heart.

"What's that?" asked Sean.

"Ein Ziel," answered the sergeant gruffly.

"A target," informed the translator.

"I know what he said," said Sean.

The squad cocked and shouldered their rifles, ready for orders. The sergeant marched stiffly back to their side.

"Bereit machen!" he snap-ordered.

"Make ready," said the translator, who also stepped

well out of the line of fire.

"I know," called Sean to the translator.

"Ziel nehmen!" bellowed the sergeant.

"Take aim."

"I know."

"Feuer!"

"Fire!"

"I …"

* * * *

CHAPTER NINETEEN

This is the Way the World Ends ...

THIS was not one of the officially-approved after-life scenarios. Nothing like them, in fact.

While his mind was occupied with the bow shock of the wake, his body, and more about that in a moment, was running. Despite everything he seemed to be still in Euclidean space, which he knew was impossible, since he had just learned it didn't exist, or shouldn't ... or something ... how did that go again?... Well, if not Euclid's, then in the name of all that's curvy and internal-angley, *whose* geometry *was* this he was running through?

Then it occurred to him: if this wasn't Niemand's land, perhaps it was Riemann's land? Maybe this is hell, thought Sean, where you spend all day running in mathematical tangential extrapolations... and concluding any point you arrive at is in reality, whatever that used to be, an infinitesimal that has no absolute expression in the waterproof bedding of space and time? Stop it, yelled Sean at himself, my mind has gone hyperbolically digressive!

Stepping outside the rue-loop for a moment, he had

to admit he was doing an impressive Cartesian two-step, despite the Euclidean impossibility assurance. And what he was running on best matched the 'ravaged terrain' entry in the pull-down menubar of clichés. And that he was sandwiched in a fully convergent biplanar sense between that oft-presumed spherical planetary surface and an orange ... thing, to which the appellation 'sky' refused to adhere of its own accord. For this was such a sickly-coloured atmospheric topping, with ugly, bacon-like streaks, in such a complot of directions, that Sean's private braindrain voted overwhelmingly in favour of a general waiver of Newton's recommendations of motion.

He was running and he couldn't stop it. Motor control negated. Great! Are all establishable facts going to follow this pattern?...

A broader survey revealed he was in a red, rocky, land-unscaped desert. A large, tracked, dust-billowing vehicle was moving in front of him, others to his sides. And there were many other figures - gigantic robotic armoured suits with scorched-earth helmets around relatively tiny heads. All the figures were carrying heavy-looking blaster whatevers, blasting, yes, the cinematographically pleasing red streaks of vicious energy somethings... towards some things... on something else - all on a life-depleted Marscape ahead. He looked down and saw that he too was carrying a heavy-looking blaster whatever, and red laser light was, yes, blasting (again) from it at the same somethings as everyone (or one-things?... or in-between ones and things) else.

It was nonsense, but he couldn't stop, and nothing he saw encouraged him to.

The onethings that were the targets of all this running and blasting were firing equivalent except politely distinctive green laser blasty light back, and now he saw new figures running and doing much as his group was doing, only in their direction - with them as the targets. And they had vehicles too. From the front they looked diversely similar - boasting designs evolved liberally from the gene pool of past carnage series.

And through all of this blasting and vehicle manoeuvring, running and radio-speak in helmetphone orders flying, Sean couldn't help staring at the bizarre orange sky. Then he was suddenly on his back, still staring at it. He figured his running, robotic host had just been killed. It was probably the only way it took a breather.

'So why am I still here?' thought Sean.

"Because I am holding you here, Sean." Standing over him was a tall, princely, bronzily-armoured warrior, whose demeanour became immediately familiar yet remained elusive.

'Are you a demon?' Sean tried thinking back at him, clinging to his original hypothesis.

"No, I just wear this to battles. My other suit is at the panel-beaters."

'Am I dead?'

"But otherwise unscathed."

Sean's host's armour had been fragged, to make use of a modern diplomatic term. Whoever… or whatever else had been inside the thing, was now definitely an ex whatever.

'Fine …' lied Sean.

The heavily-armed light division that had been

pounding them and charging their position were now almost upon them. The tall princely figure spoke impatiently into his armpit mike. "Ok. That's enough over here. You boys go and play further down the hill."

Seamlessly, without dropping the rhythm of the battle for a moment, the whole mêlée moved perceptively down the hill as instructed.

"Ah, that's better. Can't hear ourselves think with all this munitions and screaming."

'Um ... You just moved a battle, didn't you? Who *are* you?' thought Sean.

"First things first," replied the creatzoid. Only now did Sean realise he couldn't tell if his interlocutor was speaking or thinking at him, but it was definitely reading his thoughts. "Aren't you going to ask me how you survived the firing squad?" it asked.

'You know about that?' thought Sean back.

"The target over your heart, dear boy. There was a time egg in it. It popped when the bullets hit it and you arrived here. As I intended."

'*You* intended?! What if they had missed?'

"Germans only miss in American films. Anyway, they weren't Germans. They were my boys." He indicated the battlefield. Bodies and bits thereof all over. Artillery was coming in. The princely figure watched the irradiation shells hit the ground in an open space short of the troops Sean had been running with. He spoke into his communicator again. "A little to the left, ... too far, ... and just a bit further up, ... ah perfect. Ta ever so." The artillery moved as instructed and the shells were now raining down murderously on the troops, who hadn't the initiative to move.

'But... why did you call down artillery on your own

side?' thought Sean.

"To be fair - so the battle finishes on time. You see, I am the commander-in-chief - of both sides. This is the last day of the series … if it is not called off for rain," he said, gazing at the green clouds building overhead.

'Rain? You're afraid of rain with all this going on?'

"Acid rain. *Very* acidic rain."

'So, where is the other commander? Did he call in sick this morning?'

"Why would you want two commanders of a battle?" replied the metallic creature. "A battle is confusing enough."

'What is the point of running a war for both sides?'

"What makes you think a war has a point?"

'I imagine you're going to say 'to win'.'

"Why two win when one win would be enough, as the saying goes. Ha ha… trench humour - nothing like it."

'Trench foot gets pretty close…' replied Sean thinkily. 'But surely there usually *is* a winner in a war?'

"Not in the perfect war. The perfect war is one that never ends. That's my job - I am a war designer. Welcome to the war that ends no war."

'How does that work?'

"By using the power of the hex-a-go-go, we can evade the TimeOut, and return to atrocitate another day - as many times as infinity will allow us. We'll be looping soon, so they're really going for it. You see, today is day eleven - Vitruvian Crystal Day."

'*Vitruvian Crystal Day*?!!' Sean think-screamed.

"Yes. A kind of anti-birthday for the world. It is the day you finish the arrangement of time eggs inside Luca

Pacioli and Leonardo's House - what we call 'the house of two-morrows'. The VC day is the day you destroy time."

'I.. *destroy.. time*?!' Sean crescendoed his emphasis evenly through the sentence.

"Yes. At least the timeline."

'But this is surely a long time in the future. All this technology and destroyed atmosphere and land and everything… if, as you say, I destroyed the timeline in the past - what time are we in now?'

"The term 'now' has lost most of its utility. Let's just say it is 2010. And has been for much of the intervening 2,222 years."

'But this can't be 2010 – I was there. It's nothing like this."

"This is the very same day you fell down the shaft in the Haunted House, only a few hours on the other side of the event. Does the number 2,222 sound at all familiar?"

Strangely enough, it did. 'That was what the oracle in Syracuse predicted. She talked about 2,222 years after minus 212 being the 'uniting of the paths' …'

"Exactly. Vitruvian Crystal Day - VC day. Understand now?"

'Ah… Sort of. The VC day is in 2010 … you mean this is the year 2010 *plus* 2222 - that makes it, er… the year 4,232. I see… No, hang on, I don't at all! I thought you said it was VC day *today*? How could that be?'

"It's quite simple. All the while you have been travelling through history from Archimedes to the 20th century, this little bit of the local universe has been trapped in a loop of perpetual war."

'Perpetual war?!' Sean tried and of course failed

- dead loss really - to sit up to see better what was happening down the hill, from which the sounds of mass extermination were continuing. 'How can that be? What happens when all the soldiers are killed?'

"Oh, they are. Regularly."

'You bring them back to life?'

"Life? Overrated. Look at this planet. There is no life here. No … but they *are* recycled every eleven days. They experience the same 11 days continuously, time and time again, in an endless loop-the-loop. They think I do it."

'Then what keeps the war going?'

"Sheer stubbornness, more than anything else, I suppose. These creatures are cyborgs. Actually not even, any more. I just call them that out of nostalgia. They are really full-blown tinker-tailored robots. Have been for centuries. You see, the future of our world is this. Look at it." He waved his hand and Sean's host's body lifted to a sitting position. "An outstanding achievement - the pure expression of a single species' nature, at the expense of every other form of life. There is no living thing left. Perfect conditions for an unending war."

'And what is with the orange sky?' asked Sean.

"The biosphere breakdown that had started in the twentieth century continued till natural life was no longer possible - at least not for yookie-yotes."

'And… what are they?'

"Cyborg word for 'eukaryotes'."

'Ditto my previous question.'

"Flora and fauna. The cyborgs developed a religion custom-designed to lubricate their loss of incarnation. Retaining the more unfortunate cultural aspects they inherited from the 2010 world, they tell a wonderful mythilised history of themselves, in which everything they represent is assumed to be superior. Hence, plant yookie-yotes were so primitive they ingested solar radiation… directly, if you can stand the thought. But that is nothing. Animal yookie-yotes would feed on their carcasses, if not each other. The stories, if told well, would turn even the strongest of energy converters to status green. Can't say I blame them."

'But…' counter-thought Sean. 'If the Cyborgs don't use solar energy, where do they get their energy from?'

"They exploit the time-entropy slipstream."

'I'll just assume for now that means something. But if there are no plants left, what cleanses the atmosphere?'

"It is no longer necessary," replied the war designer. "They have no need to breathe. Cyborgs don't like to talk about their origins as being living, breathing - although they do miss the bleeding at times, they tell me… Anyway, old-fashioned yookie-yotism goes against their 'efficiency' creed."

'How did they come to be here?'

"Humans of the late 21st century had to start to replace the parts of their bodies that were most vulnerable to the changing climatic conditions. Gradually they became more and more robotic and less and less human. You see, the bottom line was that yookie-yote life systems were less economically efficient than machinery covered by warranty. Bit by bit, parts were replaced. At first out of necessity - such as the lungs. With fewer plants left, the atmosphere contained more and more toxins and less oxygen, making lungs a liability. With twenty billion people as market potential, the economic beast which fed on the human parts conversion industry became the dominant system on the planet. The people were told that if they stopped cyborging, mass unemployment and energy starvation would follow. An old ruse but a good one."

The creatzoid gave a few more instructions into his mike, to guide a landslide victory, literally it turned out, before continuing.

"So when they had run out of essential replacements, they started with relative advantage transplants. Faster muscles, sleepless brain cortexes, that kind of thing. Then one particularly virulent economic regime began to force people to replace their blood, to boost the domestic plasma industry during a downturn in the synthetic skin export market. It was their calls for patriotic sacrifice for the greater economic good that created the conditions which eventually developed into this eternal war.

"It was then just a short step to adopting a different form of metabolism entirely - everything either replaced by artificial systems, or simply made redundant. After some intensively funding-justified R&D, they realised you don't need cell metabolism at all if there are no cells. The future was clear. The logic of economic efficiency finally won over incarnation nostalgia. Eventually they were left with just a brain on a stem. Then just the brain, then just parts of it. And then it came - the last step, when they worked out a way to scoop the last remnants of the mind out of the brain. And this opened the portal to a great compensation - and immortality beckoned."

'And you,' thought Sean. 'What are you?'

"Me?... I am many things. The most important is 'The Keeper of the Watch'."

'The what?!'

"That's right, the Watch." He pulled back a rubberised metal sleeve, and there it was - Sean's digital watch!

The creatzoid now did something which Newton would have immediately recognised as 'coalescing the aether', and through it summoned a large flat container which floated in front of Sean. Its flickering translucence revealed it to contain a seriously aged block of parchment.

"Just as well Archimedes made a copy of the watch instruction manual 2,222 years before VC day - otherwise I would never have been able to work out what all these little buttons do - and how to turn off those annoying little beep-beep alarms. Drive me batty."

'The Swansong Palimpsest! It has survived all the way to the Year 4232?!' cried Sean, as beside himself with joy as a vague sense of self inside a bunch of hexadecinary logic circuits can be. He remembered with a pang of nostalgia the day Archimedes had shown it to him, boasting its top-of-the-range clay price tag.

"Yes. At least it would have been the year 4232. Would have been if the VC had not destroyed time. Made it collapse in on itself. The Time Quake, Sean. All your fault."

'Yes… so I am gathering. Rather sorry about that. But how could this happen? It goes against all the laws of physics."

"Here, we are all lawbreakers - law of gravity," the creatzoid took a quick hover, "laws of chemistry, biology… Murphy's - we break them all."

"So… are you the Eternal Emperor?"

"Cespuglio? No. I am not him. And more importantly, he is not usually me."

'Ah… um…' responded Sean arthurdentily.

"No. I am merely deputising for him. Keeping his empire ticking over while he is away." The watch beeped. The being frowned verbally: "We will have to go soon."

'With all this magic and technology, you actually still use my digital watch!?'

"Only for appointments with destiny. That would make me a 'Time Being', wouldn't it?" Incredibly, the creatzoid giggled at his joke with a sound Sean could have sworn was a remote descendent of 'yo, ho, ho'. "In Invertabrake mythology, it is the symbol of divine right to rule. The SANG Re.al has always meant, or at least has come to mean, exactly that: Real Blood. I am the last of all humans to have blood. I am the last fully living human." It made the mechanical equivalent of a sigh - actually a sort of gas exchange that could be embarrassing at close quarters.

"You met Archimedes, didn't you?"

'Yes!' cried Sean with mental surprise and cerebral joy.

"I was almost there." The creatzoid sighed again, almost pitifully. "I would have liked that."

'Almost?'

"Yes. I am what the cyborgs call the 'Extreme Being'. Out on a limb. If you're in a hurry just say 'Mr. Being'… Your thought patterns are registering disappointed?"

'Sorry… it's just that if you're the Extreme Being … you see, I know it's silly, but I was led to believe that my grandfather was him.'

"Yes. That's right."

'Nonno!? But… but, you can't be… my Nonno …'

"Has a beard?"

'That as well, come to think of it… but I mean he can't be two thousand years in the future…'

"As you can't be?"

'Ah, yes, but that's different… somehow…' Sean went whatever is mental for silent for a moment. 'But certainly he wouldn't be running a war like some sort of scout jamboree!'

"Ah, yes. Megalomaniac was not my first option - trouble is there was no other vacancy available when I was forced to sign up."

'Please… please tell me what the…'

"Photonic splut is going on?"

'Photonic splut?'

"Yes, I know. Universal deflation has taken its toll on a once thriving expletive industry."

'Um…?'

"Just kidding," said Mr Being. "I have been waiting a long time for this moment."

'My coming?'

"No, for someone, *anyone*, who might laugh at one of my jokes. Robots are so straight-faced. Just kidding, again. Of course, it is wonderful to find you again, Sean, my dear boy."

'I can hardly believe it. Nonno, I have missed you so!'

"And I you."

A plaintive series of beeps interrupted their reunion rudely. The Nonnotech being fumbled the watch awkwardly with his enormous metal hands till he found the right button. "Unfortunately, a space-time cul-de-sac does not come with ensuite infinite time, no matter what the Invertabrake recruitment brochures promise.

You see, today we reset and then this world will have to do its 11-day routine all over again. And that gets pretty noisy, as you can imagine. So please listen carefully, I will say this far more than once."

'Nothing makes sense.'

"Well, yes, Sean, naturally it doesn't. In a way, that is what started it all. The day I discovered nothing we thought we knew made any sense. That was the subject of my theory."

'Your theory? About time and reality?'

"Yes. Living next door to the haunted house, and being somewhat lazy by nature, I decided to write a paper on the phenomenon of the haunted house - I called it 'Neighbours'. I was planning to syndicate it to TV, but I found the name was already being used."

'You were planning to turn the secret of time and reality into a soap opera?!'

"Eternity explained in an infinite number of episodes. Perfect format."

'Tell me, Nonno, what happened that day I left home?'

"I knew the Haunted House was responsible for the disappearance of your mother. Your father used this to lure me into the Haunted House on the day you completed the Vitruvian Crystal. But, of course, he wasn't really your father. He was being controlled by Cespuglio. Do you remember the Financiers' Gloat Club outing to Monza a few months before the VC day? Your father went to the cathedral and played at world conqueror for a dare. He bribed the priests to let him try on the Iron Crown."

'Ah… so Cespuglio had found a way back to the Crown?'

"Oh, yes. He has been very busy since you last saw him. His best role yet was a stint as an American president, his namesake, before slipping back into the Crown during one of his state visits to Italy, to wait for your father."

'Why did Cespuglio want to occupy Papi?'

"What better guise for Cespuglio to exercise his will and love of destruction than through the impunity of a financier? The financier is our culture's purest expression of detachment from moral sense. Who else is as oblivious and self-righteous in actions that have no regard for measure or consequence? Cespuglio leapt at this opportunity to run amok in the world, using rampant greed to wreak havoc indiscriminately everywhere through the world. Distorted and failing markets, unemployment, poverty and misery, followed in his wake, while an undeserving small minority who followed him, yelping for more like Aristotle's Dogs of Ma, sucked the world's riches into a black hole of their imaginative self-images."

'Yes,' acknowledged Sean. 'I can see Cespuglio would have revelled in that opportunity.'

"Then, when the VC moment approached, he knew his far-future self would be just a few seconds on the other side of the TimeOut. He wished to use the timequake that was forming to escape his future fate and return to joyride through history as the Eternal Emperor, to relive that sensation of omnipotence and unchecked cruelty over all people."

'But… *you* are here in this future world… not him.'

"Well, you see, he didn't 'travel' back to -212, as such. He stepped over. The timeline of the future inverted. But, and this is the clever bit, just before it did, his future self swapped places with me through the core of the newly forming reality – the altar at the centre of the Vitruvian Crystal."

'He rewrote history?'

"Not really. It has necessarily always been like that."

'But… Nonno, can *we* rewrite the past next time round? Can we stop this recurring?'

"Ah, that's where the TPF, the Time Paradox Failsafe, gets us, you see. Cespuglio has ensured that our past – what should have been the past of this future world – is now our future. And what should have been the future of our historical timeline became its past. Being both the future and the past on both sides ensures it must repeat."

'But,' objected Sean, 'if Cespuglio is really from this future world, surely this is all his making - wouldn't he prefer to be running the Eternal War?'

"He loves destruction, but what he really craves is the torment he can bring to life. Robots can destroy and be destroyed, but they can't suffer - at least not enough for his tastes."

'And what happened to the future world when the VC completed?'

"At first no-one noticed the inversion, but gradually the timeline entered an ever-contracting spiral of cycles. Each time it rebooted, it recreated the exact same conditions it had in the reigning culture at the time of the completion of the Vitruvian Crystal: this consists of a fanatical belief in a crazy economic system run for the convenience of ignorant financiers, and a residual predisposition to shift responsibility onto the shoulders of a supreme being. These two combined rather well to produce the cycles of biosphere destruction, human species deterioration, and perpetual war, which resulted in this obscenity of a planet."

'Nonno… tell me what we *can* do about all of this?'

"I can only tell you what I have been able to work out. There has been a timequake. The world on either side of the TimeOut, the moment the VC completes, is being compressed together from both sides as the time shockwave advances. Cespuglio has usurped the House technology to create the opportunity for himself to Minde the Gappe - cross over the TimeOut chasm, and become the eternal emperor in the past timeline, or what's left of it. This cross-over point allowed him to jump across the crests of the last timewave, avoiding the chasm of the trough between, what would otherwise have been the very last chronon, but is now both an eternity and no-time. Anything that falls into that last moment will never exit, because there the reality drains into the spenmatt, and has ceased to form anything that we would recognise as a timeline."

'Schwarzie's event horizon?!' cried Sean.

"Precisely! Like falling into a Black Hole. There time both reduces to zero *and* stretches to infinity. And the space, energy and matter that create it will be left a useless jumbled mess of loose ends - like sausage meat coming out of a grinder. Falling plop on the floor below – to be swept away under the spenmatt."

'How… horrid, I think. Though 'yucky' gets a look in too.'

"Not a pretty sight. Not that there is any light to see by, bouncing around inside the last chronon. Anyway, this stepping over point either side of the Time Out I have named 'the Bridge of *Psi*'s'."

'The 'Bridge of Sighs'?'

"Yes. You see, *psi* is what physicists use to describe the location and time of anything. A sort of GPS on reality. Useful for finding the odd missing sock, is the good old *psi*. Inside the Vitruvian Crystal, Cespuglio, the Shrouds and you, were able to use the Bridge of *Psi*'s to step over between the two timelines - and after the timeline had inverted, you all jumped back across again - and found yourselves in minus 212."

'Why then? A chance event?'

"No. The number 2222 is a magic number. It happens to be the first point in a mathematical sequence where all of the waves emanating from the spenmatt coincide precisely. The timeline, when it shattered, sent out a shockwave. This wave had a different harmonic in each of the elements of the spenmatt background. But at exactly 2,222 Earth orbits away either side of the TimeOut, they coincide at a perfect resonance point. Only there could time reformulate as a cohesive timeline."

'So *that's* why we all travelled to Syracuse in minus 212! It was the only possible point in the cosmic background where the cut timeline could reassemble and start again - creating a new future and past?'

"Precisely."

'And you? Why didn't you come with us?'

"This future world needs at least one consciousness to exist. That used to be Cespuglio. Somebody had to replace Cespuglio in the future timeline if he were to be free to ride the past. The cyborgs lost their individual consciousnesses centuries ago. At the break, you, the Shrouds and Cespuglio, all rode the inverted timeline back to minus 212. This is, or should have been, the year

4232."

'Should have been?'

"Yes. The mathematics of this world had a little disagreement with reality. As a result, its timeline gradually broke into fragments - cycling time loops getting always shorter, as the spenmatt reclaimed us. We're in an 11-day loop now. You see, this inversion is impossible, but it took reality a while to realise it. Even though we will experience this loop forever, reality has very little time left."

'Er ... Wow!... At least, I think 'wow!'. And on the past timeline we had no means of knowing what was happening... But how do I fit into all of this?' asked Sean. 'I am not one of the Shrouds, not part of the hex-a-go-go. Why do I time travel?'

"You are an accident. A chance event. An act of random chaos. That is why you are our only hope, and why I have guided you here."

'Through the scientists?'

"I wanted you to meet them. They are our beacon of hope through history. Only they would be able to help you find your way home, to your mother, father and me. And you were their inspiration to seek beyond the complacency of their times, to discover the only thing that can help us unravel the mystery of time before it is too late. You know what that is, don't you?"

'The language of the gods - *spiki celestii* ?'

"And the scientists left you messages. Have you been able to decipher them?"

'Some of them.'

"If their collective message is lost, it would be as if they have never been. None of us will ever have been after the chronoclysm. Without that memory, the past is no more. As you will have noticed, our memories are no longer corresponding to what we like to think of as facts. You must always remember that facts, without a cohesive context of time and space, are reduced to isolated factoids, drifting on their own, and once decoupled completely from awareness, never existed. Once our minds are no longer, that universe they created is no longer. Out of mind, out of sight."

'But I remember my friends and masters - I remember them all, and everything they taught me.'

"That makes you the only link left between the two potential worlds when the VC forms."

'And you.'

"No...," Nonno shook his robotic head, his eyes changing to a sadder shade of cyan. "Because I and the Shrouds are part of the VC structure itself. We provide the awareness that each new reality requires to become real - that creates the Minde the Gappe. Only you are important, because only you are dispensable."

'Thanks a bundle!'

Sean thought through his journey. 'So, all along you have been following my course through time?'

"Your guardian angel - every step of the way."

'And you brought me here - via the Centurion, who Einstein asked to put the egg on me in 1916 - all because of you?'

"Surmise spot on."

'So... you have a plan.'

"A logical and reasonable assumption."

'And it would be...?'

"This is where your deduction goes down the proverbial. Sorry."

'This could drift towards disappointing, if I let it, Nonno.'

"Yes. I can understand that. But, let us review the situation. Despite everything, the Time Paradox Failsafe is not on Cespuglio's side."

'Ah, good.'

"Nor ours."

'Ah, bad.'

"Yes... reality tends to be a tad fickle about its allies. You see, it means that any conscious act - such as our plotting to prevent the formation of the VC now - negates the current reality we are evidently in to do the plotting. Follow me? There is no solution. *Can be none.*"

Whatever the mechanism by which a dead robot can frown with concentration and disappointment, Sean actuated it now. 'So, are we doomed?'

"'fraid so. The Chronoclysm is an unchangeable fact in time and space with the consequence that the cosmic background, the spenmatt, will reclaim our timeline, which it sees as an accidental aberration anyway."

Mr. Being glanced at the watch. "But now we really must go."

He then did some sort of ethereal essence thing(-y) with the glimmering sphere whatsit in his hand, and Sean felt his mindset leaving the dead machine he had been occupying, and being loaded into a device which turned out to be the mega future equivalent of a field specimen jar.

'Where am I?' demanded Sean, once he had recollected his thoughts into as much of an ephemeral whole as he was likely to achieve.

"In the cerebrosphere," came Nonno's echoey thought pattern. "The device Cespuglio fashioned into the Roman helmet, then the Crown. At the end of days, the 11th day, I have to store all the world's minds in it, ready for the reboot."

'All of them?! How many more are there?'

"Five. I don't need to introduce you. You have all met before. The robots are nearly all dead, so the minds are nearly fully reformed. That is why I have to run the war 'efficiently', otherwise they would be trapped in still living robots and lost at the reboot - you see, you can't exist in two realities, even for a moment."

Then Sean could feel them. Like voices from other tents in a camping site. You can't see and feel them but they seem incredibly close.

"Sean…? Sean, is that you?"

It was Geni.

'Geni!!!'

"Shoosh, dear. It's alright. We are all together, finally. That is what is important. We have missed you so."

"Not all of us." Yes, it was Pau. In perfect form, despite his total shapelessness.

'Well, I missed you, you big lump!' replied Sean thoughtfully, which is really the only way of doing anything inside a cerebrosphere.

"The others are here, too," went on Geni.

"Hi squirt!", "Knee-knocker!", "Hello, Sweetie", came the thought-voices of Stinto, Elf and Amur, in as much a jumble as ever.

Sean was overjoyed, and they exchanged stories to fill in the gaps in their experiences.

"Ever since the Romans took me, I have been in this world," explained Stinto. "At first things were fairly normal, but gradually time started to repeat cycles - just after the 4k bug, which is when they removed the last human brain. And these cycles have been getting shorter and shorter. Now it is down to just 11 days. What does it mean?"

"It's as if we are spiralling into a single point in time," said Amur, as demurely as ever.

"That'll be the VC Day, of course," thought-said Stinto. "Each cycle finishes at the Vitruvian Crystal formation, then repeats a period up to it - only these cycles get shorter each time. It's currently 11 days. Maybe ten the next cycle."

'Then, it's all true… The Invertabrakes…?'

"Yes. They are trying to prevent it happening. They came over to our timeline to brake progress in order to prevent the creation of the VC."

"It seems they had the right idea all along," was Pau's contribution.

'I don't believe that,' replied Sean. 'It was the attempt to control what knowledge was allowed to enter the human estate that caused a distortion, that led to the VC.'

"Whatever the cause, nanobotbrain," went on Pau, thoughtfully and thoughtlessly, if you follow me. "You are the undisputed cause of the end of the timeline, as I always said you were."

"Hush, Pau. Remember our agreement. Until we know for sure we don't attribute blame."

"There isn't time for this, Geni. There never has been."

"In an infinite loop there is ample time for everything."

"Not any more. You heard the Nonnotech monster.

Botbrain here is responsible for the creation of the VC, and reality as we like to think of it is literally going down its plughole in a gurgling last spiral. Our timeline with it."

'What do you mean: our timeline with it?' demanded Sean, all his synaptic joy washed away in a flood of cerebral fear.

"Sean," said Geni gently. "It is true. We have learned from the Invertabrakes' collective consciousness that the timelines on both sides of the VC completion event are being dragged down into the spenmatt, from where the timeline sprang in the first place."

Pau concluded with a statement of predictable accusation: "When you put the last egg in place, Sean egg-on-your-face, it is literally the last thing anybody does."

'But… what has my Nonno been doing about this in the meantime? Why is he doing what Cespuglio wants? Why is he playing the Extreme Being?'

"Not 'Extreme' but Hex-stream," explained Stinto. "You see, when we are all in the VC, our minds are held in the hex-a-go-go till the world outside has rebooted the 11 days, then we are streamed back out to be the collective consciousness."

"You have to understand, Sean," went on Geni, "the Invertabrakes have lost their own human self-entities. They became cyborgs when the atmosphere went psychoderelict."

'But why do you accept being their surrogate minds? You could just refuse to do it.'

Amur answered. "Then there would be no consciousness at all in the world, and that would mean the world would cease to be."

Sean remembered his conversation with Einstein: Reality is in the eye of the beholder.

Geni went on: "We are doing this to keep the world existing till you arrived."

'Why me!?'

"Because you are the one who must, the only one who can…"

'The only one who can… what?'

"That's the problem, you little yolker," needled Pau. "Nobody knows. All we know is that since you are the one who causes the time collapse, it can only be you who prevents it."

'But I have absolutely no idea how!' Sean was getting as heated as a bundle of thought wobblies can get. He burst back at Pau with: 'So, Mr know it all still, what do you think we can do about it?'

"That's just the point. It was *always* too late to do anything."

"You see, Sean," intervened Geni, before the mate could stale, "even though we look at the VC event as being in our future, it is firmly cemented in someone else's past."

Stinto now went on: "Because it was you who did it in the first place, you can't prevent yourself always doing it, without causing the event never to have happened, which means you couldn't be here to know to go back and stop yourself, which you evidently didn't, so it couldn't, which means …" he trailed off in some confusion.

Pau actually thought he was helping when he added: "The Time Paradox Failsafe makes sure you *must* be there to complete the VC with your stupid time egg, and there is nothing you or anybody else can do to prevent it."

'I have always admired your optimism, Pau,' mumbled Sean mindfully. 'Well, one thing is for sure, we can't do anything while we're stuck inside the Crown. When do we get out of here?'

"Mr Being is taking us to the House now," answered Geni. "It is the only recognisable structure left on a wasteland planet. It serves as a resurrection centre. Our minds are kept safe and unchanging inside the VC while the world outside reboots, or rather rebots. That is when we are reloaded into the minds of the cyborgs."

'But surely there are more cyborgs than just the five of you?' queried Sean.

"We are combined into a collective consciousness and timeshared out amongst them all. We hardly perceive anything at all."

"Just enough human consciousness to give them an attitude," said Elf.

"But not enough to think for themselves," added Amur.

"The perfect army," finished Stinto.

'What happened to the cyborgs' real minds?' asked Sean.

"Lost in the Y4k bug. Humanity wiped out by a single virus. A soft micro."

'Was it called 'Windsouls 4k' from the Nanosoft company?'

"Almost. How did you know?"

'All this talk of mindless masses all following marketing orders without questioning suggested it.'

Just then Sean was drained into the body of a cyborg. Before him was an amazing sight.

"Just thought you might like to see what has happened to Lugano," said Nonno from inside the bronze warrior.

* * * *

Vitruvian Boy

CHAPTER TWENTY

Leave a Message after the Whimper

SEAN was now occupying a functioning Invertabrake robot, it seemed. The Nonno being hovered alongside, his magnificent cape of composite bronze plastic barely touching the cascade of tumbledown boulders Sean's host was balancing perilously on. And since robots don't have a giddy mode, Sean improvised one, for he saw that the tenuous terrain all around him yawned, as red and bleary as any serious hangover might, into a valley deep below. In all the terrible scene of enthusiastic desolation, there was nothing for Sean optically to get a handle on.

'Nonno – where are we?'

Mr Being indicated the chaos of jumbled rock on their left, where the remnants of what had been a mighty Invertabrake army eleven days ago were waiting for the latest edition of their doom. "This was once Monte San Giorgio." He hovered around and pointed down the talus slope to the chasm beneath them. "That ravine would have held the lake." He opened his arms to embrace the view to their front. "And that, my dear boy, is what is left of our beautiful Lugano."

Playing a bit with the telescopic vision he found he was equipped with, Sean could follow the gaze of the cybernetic Nonno, beyond where the valley floor deepened and flattened inside a triangle of mountains, then up a paradise for scree enthusiasts, to where it all relented into a raised basin.

"It has been blasted away by two millennia of erosion and chemical bombardment," continued his guide. "Somehow it never fully recovers at each timeline reboot."

Sean stared at it in horror. There was nothing but lithic wreckage, careless even by geological standards. Not a man-made thing in sight. Not, that is, until Nonno actuated a visual cortex override, and Sean saw it. A kilometre or so from the lip of the basin, what would once have been the shore of Galileo's Cherry Lake, in the midst of the well-credentialed wasteland, was the House of Two Morrows. It was exactly the same as it had always been, except for the minor discrepancy that it was hovering twenty metres above the ground. And since we are on that subject, this, at least what Sean first took to be the ground, was doing something which the word 'writhing' inadequately images.

'What is happening, Nonno? Why is the ground moving?'

"Because it is not solid," answered Mr Being.

'Liquid?'

"Not even. In fact, the exact opposite. Think of it as pure negative time energy, but of course it is nothing of the sort. It is intensifying because the TimeOut is nearly upon us. What you see is the result of a hole that has opened up to the cosmic background, exposing us to the underlying spenmatt that cradles this world. The

House is drawing everything - space, energy, matter, and the time they project - into what I would call a 'vortex', if I didn't know better. As we approach the TimeOut moment, this world's space is encroaching on the past world's, so time is being squeezed out of this side in compensation, and the timeline on the other side of the TimeOut is receiving it."

'In the time eggs?'

"Yes. Condensed time encapsulating in localised spenmatt as it surges up. Behold, Sean, the end of the world! Is it not magnificent?"

Sean nodded. For it truly was an impressive if circuitry-ruffling sight.

'What now, Nonno?'

Nonno held up the cerebrosphere. "We must all enter the House, where we will be safe, while this world reboots its time loop."

Just then Sean recognised one of the Invertabrakes.

'Centurion?!' exclaimed Sean happily. 'We meet again! How are you?'

"That question has no relevance," replied the advance model cyborg with the usual military formality, his metallic casing adding automatic irony, cheap pun intended.

'I'll take that as a 'well'. I am glad to see you.'

"Thank you," relented the Centurion with an inclination of his cranial servo-gyro. "And I you."

Sean returned to his Nonno. 'Why will we be safe inside the House?'

"Because it is not really here. It is the gateway to the

Bridge of Psi's – a perpetual no-moment that straddles the two worlds – the past and the future meet and cease to exist around it, but it survives. Ever seen two waves slap together in a bath-tub, and your rubber duck gets held up for a moment? Mine does. The House is riding the two extremes of the last moment - as the two crests of a time shockwave collide, the House becomes trapped in an inter-chronon cavity, held suspended there by the entropic pressure from the inrush of the two ends of the timeline."

Like you and me, Sean concluded, quite wisely, that it was important for his inner stability not to attempt to understand a word of that. He instead looked at the talus slope they were on, the tragic remains of his beautiful Monte San Giorgio, where Leonardo had guided him to the time egg cavern. 'Nonno, why did you bring me here?'

"This is the last stable bit of land before we reach the House. And I wanted to show you these." Nonno hovered down and psychokinetically picked up a round stone from the many that Sean only now noticed were being squeezed out of crannies all around them. Only at close range could Sean see they had a familiar shape.

'Time eggs?!' he cried electromentally, taking the egg. Like time eggs in the past world, it had the distinctive and strange characteristic of feeling both heavy and light at the same time.

"No. These are their exact counterpart. Pure deliquified untime disencapsulated in a spenmatt anti-crustation."

Ditto the aforementioned wise conclusion.

'Er… anti-time eggs?' suggested Sean, wondering

what would happen if he dropped it.

"I prefer to call them 'time void' eggs."

'Nonno,' asked Sean with a shock of sudden, guilty remembrance, 'where is Mami?'

"Inside the House. Trapped inside the Vitruvian Crystal."

'But... she disappeared long *before* the VC was completed?'

"In a world with a chronoclysm, a timeline shock-wave, there is no longer any meaning in the expressions 'before' and 'after'. Cespuglio needs consciousnesses to feed the Invertabrakes. When your mother follows him, thinking it is Papi, she is trying to find out what the devil he is up to down there in his basement of investment hell - she follows him through the tunnel and inside the Haunted House.

"There, Cespuglio uses the power of the Vitruvian Crystal to trap her mind. He does the same with me, only he waits till just before the VC moment so he can force me to take his place as the mind and soul at the core of the Vitruvian Crystal, which is linked to the psychic computer system that keeps this future world operating."

'And then he tricks me into falling down the shaft and completing the VC for him?' thought Sean. 'He made me think he was chasing me, when instead he took up his position as the last element of the hex-a-go-go?'

"Yes. He plans it all very cleverly. I am sorry, Sean. We are all just pawns in Cespuglio's evil game."

'Including the Shrouds who complete the hex-a-go-go. Nonno, who *are* the TimeRiders?'

"As the TimeOut approaches, the power of the

Vitruvian Crystal increases. Remember the bulldozer driver who tries to knock the Haunted House down? As soon as he enters the critical radius, his memory of self is drawn into the Crystal, leaving an empty shell of a body."

'The doctors said he was in a coma.'

"Which is just one of the many words people use when they want to pretend they know what is happening. Words like ghost, talent, economic indicator... The mind of the bulldozer driver is torn out of him. No mind memory - no person. A computer without an operating system - what I call 'the deramification of the mind'."

Sean sighed. There was so much to learn in Nonnotechnology. 'Um... ok... So, who is it?'

"Stinto. The bulldozer driver is the TimeRider you know as Stinto."

'Stinto! Poor, poor Stinto... And the others? Were they also captured by the House?'

"Not directly. Two of them are absorbed by the Vitruvian Crystal through the sea of time magma forming beneath it. They fall into the grotta - the cavern opening to the time volcano at the heart of Monte San Giorgio here, where you find the source of the eggs. The time magma is a channel to the House, and so they too are trapped."

'That very nearly happened to me,' agreed Sean. 'If it hadn't been for Leo leaving me the glider and an egg to escape with.'

"Yes. You see, I have been able to achieve something, even from here."

'You helped Leo?! Of course! Leo said he could sense your presence when he was in the House. Tell me, Nonno, who fell into the source?'

"Elf is a Roman soldier in the time of Caesar. Stationed at Tremonta, working for the TNT courier service."

'TNT?!'

"Sure. Transalpine Nocturnal Transmissions. Their logo is 'Who Stares, Wins'. On the mountain here is a Roman military telecom station, the last in a long chain of state-of-the-art bonfire beacons sending messages over the Alps between the northern reaches of the empire and Rome. Faster by far than the modern Italian postal system. Anyway, one day Elf falls down a crevice and is never seen again."

'Poor Elf!'

"Yes. And the woman you know as Amur is from the medieval village that disappears. She is convicted of stealing and is thrown down the chasm to appease the angry mountain tax-goblins, or whatever. It turns out that that is lucky for her, since not long after the whole village is swallowed up by a sudden eruption of chronoclysm, and ceases to exist in our world."

'How awful! That explains Stinto, Elf and Amur.' Sean was silent for a moment as he considered the corollary. 'Nonno...?'

Mr Being hovered down to look Sean straight in the optical triodes. "You must remember, Sean, that the TimeRiders are not people - not as we think of them. The closest you could get is to say they are human self-entities. You see, a person in the completed VC is drawn with it into an orientation with the cosmic background - the spenmatt. Because they are outside of it, Time becomes a visible dimension. But, a sentient mind cannot function seeing all time - we *need* the time myth

- we need a context and a sense of direction through time to create a memory which explains our existence. But memories are only a virtual reality - they exist in a flux of desires and explanatory logical conclusions. The only option the Shrouds have to escape the hex-a-go-go is to become TimeRiders, and to restrict themselves to existing in only a fraction of the timeline, and forgetting the rest."

'I see - so the TimeRiders could only ride through the timeline by inventing an explanation of themselves... Is that why they thought they had done it many times? To explain why they knew all of future history?"

"Yes."

'But... they didn't have to do that, did they? They could have discovered the truth if they had sought it?'

"They fall prey to what is surely the most unfortunate characteristic of human beings - inventing an explanation for that which they cannot understand. A great source for problems, if you're looking for one."

'But... I can't believe it. The time riders *were* there. They were so ... I don't know ... present.'

"They localise their existence in denial of all the greater cosmos. A very human trait. Their memories have to adjust accordingly."

'So they just forgot me?' Sean wanted to cry but couldn't find the right circuit.

"No, Sean. They cannot. Not entirely. Nor can they forget each other. Your father and mother are very much in love. And they love you dearly."

'But... Pau was so nasty to me!'

"He still has the banker in him. He doesn't mean it. It is just the way he has been trained. Years in investment banking have taught him that any extraneous information that challenges his firm belief in his self-created universe needs to be crushed. You threaten his cosy, self-asserted little vision of himself and his world, so he needs to belittle you. He can't prove you wrong, of course, because you are not, so he just makes you irrelevant. But it is a form of agony for him. He can see you are on a fascinating journey of discovery, while he is trapped in a deadly holding pattern. Deep down, he wants to admire you, but he just doesn't know how. It isn't his fault. Forgive him."

'Yes, of course I do. And Mami?'

"Your mother, as Geni, remembers you at some deep level I cannot even begin to understand. Love is not a memory or habit. Love is a deep frequency that a soul resonates with and cannot forget. I think it even continues after we cease to be. She feels this resonance in your presence as you do in hers, even though her existence in a specific local time demands she have no memory of any other. That is why they can never stay too long in any one time. Love transcends the constraints of reality."

Sean was silent for too long. "Sean, don't take it so hard," said Nonno gently, placing a virtual hand on a cybernetic shoulder.

"It's not that,' replied Sean. 'It's just that, speaking as an almost-teenager, it is kind of disappointing to find that after thinking I have been romping through history, on my own time, so to speak, my parents have been there all along.'

Then they both laughed - electronic, wheezy and rotary valve sorts of laughs - but laughs nevertheless.

While his gas compressor was recharging, Sean asked: 'How long do we have left, Nonno?'

Nonno shook his head. He slowly undid the strap and handed the watch to Sean. "Difficult to say... Time is not likely to behave itself as the Vitruvian Crystal forms."

Sean took the watch and looked at its display going bananas as the timewave field all around them adopted similarly fruit-inspired characteristics. He thought fondly of the day Nonno had so joyfully explained its six miracles of science. 'You know what I think, Nonno? I think that on the other side of the TimeOut, right now, I am heading home through the forest on the flanks of the time volcano.'

He looked at the Centurion, and a thought struck him suddenly. 'It was you, wasn't it, Centurion? You were in the forest when I found the egg. In fact, it must have been about here.' He tried to refigure the shape of the mountainside in his mind.

"Yes," replied the Centurion. "In our legends, this is the 'mountain of the whispers deep'."

Nonno announced a change of subject by holding up the cerebrosphere. "We must go now."

'Are you coming into the cerebrosphere too?' asked Sean, hating the idea of leaving Nonno's comforting presence.

"No. I must first load the TimeRiders at the event horizon of the House, so they may recreate the hex-a-go-go."

'But... wait a minute! There are only five TimeRiders in the cerebrosphere! How do you complete the hex-a-go-go with only five? Are you...?'

Vitruvian Boy

"No. I am in the core of the Crystal. Only so do I enter this world while you all pass to the past."

'Then I...?'

"No. You are right on the event horizon when the VC forms. No, no... it is Cespuglio himself who is the sixth Shroud. There is only one TimeOut, and it belongs to both worlds. We are destined to comply to his will, and we can do nothing to change it because it has already happened. Be certain, once we enter the House, we are lost to this and any other world."

'Till the reboot... Then it starts all over again.' Sean tremored, as the closest a robot can come to shivering. 'Nonno, I want to stay outside.'

"But that is too dangerous, Sean. Beyond here the ground has already dissolved in most places. It is converting to pure spenmatt – and contains no more time. You risk being trapped in a chronological vacuum."

'I have to take that risk. Inside the House is Schwarzie's inversion of time and space. I can surely do nothing there. I don't know how, but I *have* to try to find a way to stop this happening – before it is too late. You, Mami, Papi, everyone is relying on me.'

"But it is impossible, Sean. The Time Paradox Failsafe has us well and truly by the electro short and curlies."

'It was you, Nonno, who always told me that an imprecise possibility does not necessarily mean an impossibility.'

"Yes...," Nonno sounded guilty as charged. "I try to cling to that. But I see no solution. You are here because of what happens at the TimeOut. Ipso facto, you cannot change it *and* be here to know to change it."

'That's why I have to stay outside the House. You

see, Sacky, I mean Isaac Newton, told me that without a sense of a future, we are not able to be human. We have to try to stop it.'

Surprisingly, Nonno replied immediately, as though he had expected this: "Then I do not say goodbye, because if you fail, not only do I never see you again, but we, none of us, will ever have existed. When a people destroy their future they also erase their past. Soon, we will have only one brief moment left - the world's contracted thus. But, in truth, we never ever have more than a brief moment - that is what defines us, so, yes, even though we don't know how, we must try."

Sean went to hand the watch back.

"No," said the Nonno being. "You keep the SANG Re.al. It is yours. I have merely been its keeper."

Before Sean could reply, Nonno added unexpectedly: "The Centurion will do what is necessary." After sowing this enigmatic seed, he peered into the cerebrosphere. "The souls have all but returned now. That means the war is nearly over. It's a draw, again, of course. You must hurry, Sean. It seems we must part. I have already activated your levitator."

Sean tried this out by stagger-hover-bumping forward to embrace the figure his grandfather was speaking from. They found the courage to say their mutual eternal devotions, and then, with wrenching suddenness, Nonno was gone, flying over the dried lake bed towards the Haunted House.

Sean watched him all the way, his surrogate electronic heart heavy and fearful, but determined. He handed the time void egg to the robot next to him.

'Centurion, the Extreme Being said you would do something for me?'

The machine inclined its servo unit in compliance, shimmered and faded, then returned. Sean took the egg from the Centurion, and put it in the pouch on his belt.

He said goodbye to the machine, quickly found most of the right internal controls, and, by the means of an arguably longer than strictly necessary, and undeniably comic, gravity defiance solo, was soon describing a creative course for the Haunted House. The lake, Nostradamus's Cherry Shores, had long gone, leaving a canyon as deep as the mountains around were high. There was nothing of human origin left at all - every piece of material had been scavenged by generations past to feed the global war machine that had long ceased to require or provide any human material comforts.

Denuded of all vegetation, the hills around the town had long since collapsed, creating rivulets of rock debris, talus sculptures for him to navigate over with painful slowness to the House, the last domicile of mankind. Apart from the disintegrating robots he had left behind on the time volcano slopes, it was the only human artefact remaining on the planet. And this peculiar normality was emphasised by its location: hovering a drastically varying height above a heaving mass of time-depleted lava, which had already absorbed most of the planet below in rivulets turning to rivers of temporally-deprived goop, gradually vanishing from sight as light itself gave up even trying to register it. Sean glanced upwards. The day had turned to night and even the stars were fading to the nothing one assumes the right to expect inside a local universe warp.

Nonno was gone. The empty husk of the robot he had occupied had fallen from the House entrance, and was quickly becoming part of the erased history of the planet. Sean could only hope his family and friends had managed to reach the safety of the House in time.

But what if they hadn't?!

Oh, the *horror* of it.

But before this nightmare thesis could gain extra merit for enthusiasm, Sean's curiosity beneath the House was rewarded by a killed cat. Shrodie lay motionless on an island of temporarily resolute ground, but imminently threatened by the chaos gaining momentum all around.

He risked it, and hovered by infuriatingly amateur micro-jumps down. He felt the effects of time echoes as he approached, collective memories screaming at fates which had long lost meaning, but managed to pick up the little, inert bundle of his pet, and lift back up to the illusionary safety of the House.

And there he sheltered in the portico of the house, where he could sit and hug Shrodie as he used to do when he longed for his mother, and watch the whole of existence find an excuse not to come in for work.

Above him was Leonardo's logo over the doorway arch: AVO. Amur Vincit Omnia. Love conquers all.

'I've failed you, Leo. Despite everything you and all my masters have taught me, I could not undo my silly clumsiness - could not prevent our world ending. I am a failed ambassador for your message.'

Then grief and the enormity of the last moments

overwhelmed him, and he lamented to the ubiquitous void. 'Oh, my masters! My dear, wonderful masters! What a privileged journey this has been - because of you. I have been so lucky. But so, so unworthy.

'You, Archie. With your daft, funny hat, your bath-tub Eureka Moment, your teams of circle-ologists working round the sundial to find the limits of an unreal pi from two very real polygons - recording your *spiki celestii* through that old chiseller, John the Measurer, guiding us through all of history. Reminding us there is always something more to search for. That if it is written, it is so by the hand of man, not some priest's mumbo-jumbo found in the entrails of a cat. Sorry Shrodie - no offence.' He hugged the inert form.

'And Leo – your wisdom and guidance – the beauty that flowed from your mind through your brush and pen. And Luca Pacioli. How sadly your rediscovery of Vitruvius has ended. You never intended any of this. My masters, you have been used most cruelly.

'And Galileo – who wanted me to call him 'Lilly'.' He laughed fondly at the memory. 'Crazy, brilliant, courageous Maestro Galileo Galilei. You took the church on and beat it, smashed its dogmatic hold on the minds of men forever. All alone you faced them, and won. Such is the power of *spiki celestii.*

'And Isaac Newton. Dear old Sacky. You did achieve your dream, and became a great detective on the banks of the Thames, hunting down the worst the underworld had to offer, leading the gang warfare between the Sacks and the Socks. But you are remembered most for your laws. You were right, my dear master, nothing has moved ever since except by your say-so. You, Leibniz, and the Bernoulli Bros, drew calculus from *spiki celestii,* and the world leapt forward away from the dark age of arrogant faiths.

'But I am forgetting the exiest Marquis of them all - Laplace! Oh, my friend! It was just here, in Nonno's *doing-science* room, that we discussed so many wonderful things – and you were right – look, my master – it is exactly as you foresaw. Your blob of dark is here. You took *spiki celestii* and gave us the cosmos, and invited us to dare to dream.

'And your wonderful disciple - dear, brave Karl. Here I am – warming my back on your Schwarzschild radius. While you were giving the world your better, brighter reality, the forces of darkness were taking your life to feed the frenzy of illusion, which all my masters have fought as one against.

'And Mr OneStone. How funny, clever and good you were. How bravely you challenged Cespuglio, and all he could do was turn his back, and scurry away. You intimidated the very soul of evil in man. Bravo, Einstein, bravo! But Mr OneStone – this is the last circus call – the last show for us all. I could not follow your wonderful act. I am so sorry. There are no crowds to cheer me on. I am so alone, my dear masters, so alone. And I miss you all.'

He held Shrodie as tightly as he dared. Then he thought he felt her stir.

'Shrodie? Are you now alive? How is this possible? Here? Where there is no air to breathe or time to live. Come to think of it - how did you get here, I wonder? Of course! You fell with me into the shaft at the VC moment... Did you fall right through into this side of history? Because you, like me, were at the Schwarzschild radius – time and space are undefined there. That means we two belong to both worlds – always have done…' And for dramatic effect, just to make himself register how great an insight that was, he added: 'Wow!'

He picked up the dead cat and looked her in the face. 'I always wanted to ask you why you can never make up your mind whether to be dead or alive? I was never sure, could never be sure what the reality was, till I looked inside your box. The two worlds we live in started for you long before, didn't they? Because we cannot exist in two worlds simultaneously, you can only have one consciousness, be alive only in one place. Nonno was right – for we two the concepts of before and after no longer have any meaning, if they ever did. Two worlds Shrodie – one in which you are alive, and one dead. You split the world in two around you, Shrodie, without ever knowing it.'

Sean laughed gently. 'You split the world in two…'

He sprang-hovered up and banged his head on the portico roof. 'Eureka! … And Ouch!'

Suddenly, he had a new certainty about what to do. Yet still he hesitated. He explained to the dead cat: 'Despite the time reboot, we will only get one shot at this. If we get it wrong, Shrodie, we will get it wrong for eternity. And that would get a little wearing, to say the least.'

Despite the bulkiness of the armoured suit, he could sense the watch gaining and losing weight as it had done in the tunnel what seemed years ago, but was only a few minutes away, at least according to House rules.

He hovered around beneath the House, completely awkwardly because gravity had also taken leave of its senses. In the rapidly growing dark he moved to the end of the brick tunnel hanging exposed like some wierd, impossible proboscis. The lintel still bore Laplace's warning: 'Mind the Gap'. Most of the floor was missing, so he moved along its wall as he had done when he had first entered it, looking for his family. As he moved, flaming torches began to appear, as though his presence were changing the nature of experience.

At the steps, he stopped. If he ascended, he would pass the Schwarzschild radius, and enter the zone where time and space are inverted. Not a good idea for someone who has precious little time left as it is. So he hovered down through a gap where the floor had surrendered to some greater, innate logic, and looked under the stairs, and there he was thankful he could see the earthen outline of the shaft. He hovered over to its raggedly exposed lower end, which in effect provided an alternative entrance to the house. He tried to gaze up inside, looking for a clue, but found it was obscured by an impenetrable screen of light absence.

While he held Shrodie tightly with his right arm, he lifted his left, hoping that the watch would give him some indication. But the happy little luminous mouse just cheeped away more nonsensically than ever. He became aware that surges from the time disintegration surf beneath him were erasing parts of the robot's superstructure, starting with his feet. He hovered closer to the entrance, terrified but trying to judge the moment.

Then he decided it would be dangerous to wait any longer, but as he came to the lip of the shaft, he felt Shrodie's form stir again. On this cue, he stopped and waited.

His whole body began to shimmer as it threatened to become lava. The reality bubble was popping. It was too late, all around him the world was lost. Time was turning to matter, and matter to space, and space to energy. The spenmatt was reclaiming its own in its own secret way that no human has ever glimpsed.

'Oh, my masters, if you could see me now - what your minds' eyes saw, while your fellows were sleeping, would have been like this. I am both privileged and damned, and embrace it wholly - for your sakes.'

He felt himself drifting away, dreaming of Leonardo and Geni. Something caused him to shake himself back to grasp at the tendrils of reality he still had. 'Of course! That is what Leo has been trying to tell me! I am the figure in Leonardo's drawing of the golden ratio - the Vitruvian Man. Better dressed, I'll grant, but in a dance that unites the sphere and the cylinder, inside the square and the circle, I am the shadow between the now and the never.

'I am naked man at the point of all being and non-being, armed only with *spiki celestii*. And it instructs me there are realms of knowledge which are the realms of the gods, and we must *earn* our trespass.'

And yet still he hesitated.

'This was what it has all been about, all the time. Archie was telling me all along - if you can't measure something for certain, don't make the mistake of assuming you can, but approach it from two sides, so you can be certain of the uncertainty. Newton's infinite limits are here. That's what Leonardo meant by the Vitruvian Man - it is me, approaching the infinite point from two sides...

'I am the receptacle of your wisdom, my masters. So long as I remember you, you exist, and we have hope still. So long as we hold you clearly ahead of us, Cespuglio cannot drive us like sheep. That is why you ran from Einstein, isn't it, Cespuglio? You saw your own impotence in his eyes, heard your demise in his logic, no matter how many sheep you collected around you, or how hard you tried to exterminate his tribe.

'And Professor Einstein told me I would have to be faster than him to the pub after work to slip between the time wavefronts - but Archie showed me I don't need to be - provided I arrive from both sides, so infinity is tamed. It's you and me, Shrodie. We are both split on this issue - ha ha. Human humour - don't worry about it. Oh come on, you don't have to die laughing, it wasn't that funny...'

The cat suddenly opened her eyes and meowed her greeting.
'Oh, Shrodie! Thank you, Shrodie!' And Sean shot up inside the shaft.

'Look at me, Leo! Look at me! I am Vitruvian Boy!!'

* * * *

CHAPTER
TWENTY-ONE
HOME 'STEAD

OF course, if you have been paying attention, you will have realised that if the final words of the previous chapter are a relative truth, they cannot simultaneously also be an absolute one. And vice-versa, as Sean discovered, when to his great surprise the darkness that had engulfed him and Shrodie was broken by the light of an electric torch from above, and the worried voices of Nonno, Mami and Papi.

What greater home-coming can there be than the one extended to someone who has never been away, but feels he has been in his heart?

And that was basically it. They pulled him out, Shrodie went off in a distinctively feline style of huff, and they all returned home, with forcibly extracted promises of never again using secret tunnels to enter other people's houses and falling down other people's hidden shafts, just to give his parents a fright of their lives.

Back in his own house, old habits and routine

reasserted themselves in their usual stubborn fashion. Sean would sit on the top step of the staircase, just to have the pleasure of watching his mother arrive home and say: 'So many people in the shops today, I don't know what the world is coming to, honestly I don't.' And he would laugh and hug her, and she would be puzzled, but of course pleased.

Nobody ever mentioned her disappearing months before. It had obviously never happened.

And that was all about Mami, except for one strange incident, when, on a visit to Paris, at the Louvre, a reporter took a photo of her alongside the Mona Lisa - and the newspapers could talk of nothing else for editions - such a likeness... was this lady a clue to the true identity of the Mona Lisa?

And that saved Sean from complacency, because he remembered what Mr OneStone the clown had told him - that even if all other observations seem to point in one direction, the existence of a single fact that does not fit justifies, and will always justify in a world of free will, the complete reinvention of reality.

And Sean thought the clown would agree if he said that humans were still not playing with a full deck when it comes to facts, especially when those facts are rather a little made up, and cannot be applied any further than the object seen hanging within a mirror frame.

This was a lesson Papi was about to learn. His 'not a fruit' economic theory of perpetual accretion, which existed because it suited him to believe it so, was about to take a fall. Papi lost all his money in the inevitable global economic collapse, and as a result managed to live happily never before, with a dedicated, loving son, wife and father, who for his part seemed determined to win a tacit longevity race against anybody game to take him on.

In his room, Sean stuck up pictures of Einstein, Newton, and Galileo, and later added Napoleon and Laplace. He saluted Napoleon's frowning image every day before going to school. And any new school books were soon inaugurated with cartoons of Archimedes and Leonardo on their covers, and no number of penalties, threats, and orders to remove general, could erase his love for those essential geniuses.

And it was his watch, which, more than anything else, reassured him by its gradually losing its pristine condition, that he was now, after more than four thousand years, finally in a world able to move past 15:11:2010, the year 2010 and seven-eighths. And when, some weeks later, Sean scratched the watch playing football, no-one was more strangely pleased than he was to see that the Holy Grail was newly subject to spatial-temporal readjustments of its atomic order.

In history he failed every test from that day on. At least until he weaned himself off starting essays with 'When I met Napoleon, he was not wearing... as the textbook says, and his accent was quite funny... but I liked his horse, although its self-control left something to be desired.'

He was informed repeatedly by his teachers, that these, although they may have been true, were not the sort of facts that make history worth reading.

'Nuts to you,' thought Sean. 'These people are my friends, not yours.'

As for the Haunted House, it became normal, weathered, was lived in, renovated, lost its charm, and became just another house plunked down somewhere in Lugano's cluttered historical landscape.

Sean went to Tremonta, on Monte San Giorgio, and found the place where the time egg cavern may have opened up, but was solid earth now. And there he laid flowers to Amur and Elf, two would-have-been victims of accidents that never were. And he dreamed of the day he rode the sky above these treetops, courtesy of Leonardo da Vinci's flying machine, patent pending.

He was pleased to learn that the bulldozer driver had woken from his coma, and had achieved the prestigious rank of 'unmarketable' writer - a large and growing club of people with special insight. 'Good on you, Stinto,' said Sean.

And Shrodie? She lived and lived till she decided that was enough in a consistent, feline fussy way, and became one of the very few creatures to cross the river to the world of non-awareness more than once, giving salary to the Greek myths that perhaps had got it right all along.

But before that, the way Shrodie looked at Sean with those secret, knowing cats' eyes, left Sean in no doubt she knew what was what, and more importantly, what might have been, and therefore probably is still some otherwhen.

Now, you may be wondering what the *photonic splut* happened to cause Sean's previous world to return to normal so simply. Was there ever a Vitruvian Boy? Are we safe from a time cataclysm? Has the author been telling us fibs? Has this book been a waste of perfectly good imagination?

The answer to all of these questions is a firmly enigmatic yes and no. All the best answers are.

The Time Paradox Failsafe on a good day is still a hairy beast. It doesn't like inquisitive young children snooping about under its cloak of mystique.

You see, Sean had understood, as everybody had been telling him, that his fall down the shaft with a time egg in his pocket *had* occurred, and therefore will again occur. As Pau told him: 'And there is nothing you can do about it - so you had better do something about it.' Thank you for that, Pau.

Now, Professor Einstein had told Sean some curious things about reality which physicists today still insist on labelling 'weird', the usual flavour being 'plain', which of course they are. But if Mr OneStone liked presenting weird things in his shows, when he returned to being mild-mannered Swiss patents clerk, he didn't. He never took his work home with him. Clowns are serious artists, after all.

This means that although he showed the world that reality is not at all as we think of it in a classical sense, he didn't like the idea that reality could thumb its nose at us whenever it wanted. Some of his best friends loved to tease him, and say that although reality near

Einstein was playing along with him, chunks of reality a long way away, maybe even on the other side of the tent, were able to change the tune before they had even heard the opening note. Einstein thought this was just plain spooky, and would tap his violin and say it was an infringement of his artistic licence to create with his own free will. The rest of reality should jolly well listen first before joining in.

Sean had to contend with the fact that there had definitely been a timequake, since his existence in the future world demanded it. So, inevitably, he realised that at least one of the two worlds had to have an expiring use-by date.

Ah, but which world? Einstein's fundamental, tickets-paid-up-front reality show, or Nonno's plain weird one where time apparently did not exist?

Before you get your brains too diced up and thrown in the mixer, remember that it was Shrodie who informed Sean of how to look at this strange situation. She had no trouble whatsoever living (or not, as the case may be) with two worlds. By being a consciousness, she in effect created two worlds continuously around her, and the whole of existence had to flip from one to the other depending on which one she chose to be in.

When she came to life in his arms just before Sean as Vitruvian Boy entered the shaft, Sean knew that, since they were riding what Einstein may have called entangled time packets, on the other side of the VC moment she must have just died. And he remembered that just as he had entered the corridor where the trapdoor had been triggered open, Shrodie had fallen freshly dead under his feet, causing him to trip over her. She was the only other element besides himself that existed in both worlds almost-taneously, so helped him time the moment to enter the shaft and complete the Vitruvian Crystal.

Now, you are going to ask why he *wanted* to complete the crystal.

I thought so.

This is the way to view Time: don't think about it for too long, or it starts to assert that it exists. Try to glance at it for an infinitely short moment - and *Don't Blink*! With a bit of practice, you will notice some interesting things. For example, all the atoms of the world, when they think you are not watching, manage to dissolve into a kind of blob of nothing, then reform into the atoms you thought you knew and loved, in time for when you open your eyes again. In other words, atoms are wobbly at best.

And that is what Vitruvian Boy did to save the world - he stepped inside one of those wobbles.

You may also have been wondering what it is Sean asked the Centurion to do on the time volcano. Sean, as you know, unless you had popped out for some more popcorn during that scene, gave him the time void egg, which, as you no doubt guessed, the Centurion took to the past world and rolled in front of the Sean returning home from school. Then he brought back a real time egg, which the Virtuvian Boy carried with him into the shaft beneath the House.

Ah, you say, jumping a tad too far ahead of me, then the eggs cancelled each other out? Schoolboy Sean carried a time void egg down the shaft and met the incoming Vitruvian Boy with a real time egg, and the eggs combined at precisely the VC moment to produce an egg-nought?

And the answer, again, is an anti-charismatic yes and no.

But, I wait for you to cry in indignation, what about all this stuff about the Time Paradox Failsafe? The world *had* to undergo a chronoclysm, didn't it, otherwise Vitruvian Boy wouldn't have been there to cancel it, which means …?

This is where Shrodie comes in, you see.

As Laplace had tried to explain to his boss, and Karl Schwarzschild had worked out with frontline accuracy, as you approach a Blob of Dark, time slows down, and becomes infinitely tiresome right at the Blob's skin. The eggs didn't cancel each other out. They couldn't. To do that they would have to actually meet, and to do so they would both have to be not only on the same converging pair of timewaves, but exactly in the very same inter-moment timewave trough - but that, as we know, at the TimeOut, had had its plug pulled out, and was now a deep well drawing all of time into the bottomless spenmatt pit, as narrow and deep as eternity is long.

The two timelines are two waves. If two waves heading towards each other are perfectly synchronised, they add together and form a large slap in the middle when they meet - the timequake (in Nonnotechnology: 'flying the rubber duck' effect). But, if they are out of sync, they pass through each other as if the other were not there, except for maybe a little turbulence (see Mr OneStone's 'Gee, I seasick' effect).

By swapping the eggs over, schoolboy Sean ensured that the past timeline could not complete the Vitruvian Crystal, since he did not add the 24th egg. And more importantly, never had. So the past timeline had no gumption of what was happening, and continued on past the TimeOut moment without the slightest consideration for all the effort that had gone into its demise.

Meanwhile (although technically it was 'samewhile') the future timeline did experience the completion of the VC, since Vitruvian Boy added the real time egg to exactly the right place to make up the 24 in the Crystal's lattice. The future world's reality collapsed into the waiting spenmatt, and found to its surprise that it had suddenly never been.

Vitruvian Boy had done a Shrodie, and split the world in two. The only problem was that the future timeline it was sort of counting on had ceased to be, and so was definitely not to be.

Bereft of the disastrous future our world had been looking forward to, there was nothing for it but for our world to sprout a brand new future for itself, and go merrily about its stored memory business, unaware it was a brand new world riding along a spanking new, un-roadtested timeline.

Put another way, Shrodie had taught Sean that every moment of existence has two scenarios. Every moment contains decisions which could lead to our destroying our world, or saving it. And, the strange truth is, it must always be so - in salvation there is damnation, in the beginning there is the end, light has no meaning without dark.

Observing his father in his basement den, and Nonno in his upstairs *doing-science* room, Sean could verify another of Einstein's relative contentions that time goes faster on the upper floors than the lower. Papi and his kind were being left behind.

And, strangely enough, unlike Mami and Papi, whose memories contained nothing about the time-travelling experience which never occurred in their world, Nonno seemed to sort of remember everything, or had the uncanny knack of being able to piece it together. Primarily because he never dismissed what Sean said out of hand.

Sean loved to sit with him in the evenings on the balcony to his *doing-science* room, looking at the ex-Haunted House.

"What happened in the Vitruvian Crystal," Nonno said one day, "is the opposite of dropping a stone in water - time was not rippling out but rippling in to the VC. Archimedes told us how to see the infinite, and Newton taught us how to use it - make a tool of the unknowable, break through man's artificial ceiling of superstition and truly begin to speak to the gods.

"Truth is Archie's Pi: the Archimedean Pie - the golden ratio that unfolds the universe - never finished being calculated, never truly attained. But we can aspire towards it and in so doing learn precisely our own limits. So even though we will never find the absolute truth, we know how not to stray to the wrong side of the uncertainty limits. For within the Archimedean Pie lies certainly the uncertain truth. And although it handles like a fish in a tank of oil, the important thing is that we can see clearly there is only one."

Nonno's face became suddenly grave. "However, if you try to measure the circle directly, you are only kidding yourself if you think you have the truth, and you can never know which side of the real truth you are on. From that position, stretch and grow two infinitely misleading regions.

"It is there that Cespuglio is free to reign - two sides where people feel justified to believe whatever they find convenient, so are forever divided. And Cespuglio buys their souls by simply telling them they are right - there is where his power, all that is potentially evil, lies."

Another time, Nonno asked: "Have you worked out yet why there were six key Eureka moments?"

"Yes," admitted Sean. "Schwarzie's inversion of time and space inside the Blob of Dark. There were six Shrouds in the spatial hex-a-go-go, inside the Vitruvian Crystal. My masters composed the six time hexes."

"Yes. That is why you travelled to them."

"And why the Shrouds knew I would go there, and Cespuglio knew where to find me. And why we lost one TimeRider at every time hex - because the chronoclysm was rolling up time - with each time hex lost, a spatial one needed to disappear from the world too."

"Cespuglio was just taking the credit for what had to happen anyway," concluded Nonno. "Of course, by transferring through the medal instead of the crown in 1916, he avoided being absorbed himself back into the hex-a-go-go, until the end, when he hijacked Papi to enable him to cross the Bridge of Psi's."

One warm summer evening, when Sean had finished recounting his adventures for the umpteenth

Home'Stead 493

time squared, the old professor looked at Sean sadly, and said: "I envy you, Vitruvian Boy."

Sean laid a hand on his arm. "But we two will go together every day and visit all our dear friends, my dear masters, Archimedes, Leonardo, Galileo, Newton, Laplace, Einstein, again and again, if only in our minds. For they are the true heroes of this incredbile story. Leo was right - for us there is no time barrier."

"That exists only for those who choose to lock themselves away in a time bubble," nodded Nonno, observing Papi coming up the street, no doubt pleased with himself about some little swindle he'd officiated over.

"Nonno," asked Sean. "How can we be sure we are safe? That Cespuglio will never return?"

"By retaining the ability to choose. That means not allowing our worst inventions to run our world for us. And we can measure that by how well we learn to reverse the destruction of the biosphere. Cespuglio is, after all, a product of a possible future - a future in which we wreck this planet and make it uninhabitable. To disempower Cespuglio we must safeguard the natural world that defines us and permits us to stay human. We must, at all costs, protect nature if we hope to protect ourselves."

"Nonno... do you think we will ever know enough to time travel?"

"Perhaps we should stop asking whether knowledge will ever be sufficient for us to time travel - because I think we are learning that there is no place to go in time, we are already there in the only moment there is. That is because this is a brand new timeline - you, Vitruvian

Boy, have given us the chance to decide our own future. It is not written anywhere, except in our hearts."

"And this new timeline... is it stable?"

"We have found a way to listen in to the throb at the heart of the universe, and I for one don't like what I hear. In another universe not far away, inside the Haunted House perhaps, the music of the spheres is playing its own merry little tune - quite different to the beat and rhythm we think we respond to out here, adrift as we are on a sea of uncertainty."

"So, we could fall back over... How will we ever know which universe we are in?"

"You will know - the eleven days of the eternal war loop came from somewhere. And in one of the histories, those eleven days are missing. If you want to know which universe you are in, look for the missing eleven days."

* * * An End * * *